W9-BFM-885

Also by Boyd Morrison

The Ark

Rogue Wave

THE VAULT

BOYD MORRISON

A TOUCHSTONE BOOK
Published by Simon & Schuster
New York London Toronto Sydney

Touchstone
A Division of Simon & Schuster, Inc.
1230 Avenue of the Americas
New York, NY 10020

This Touchstone export edition July 2011

Manufactured in the United States of America

10 9 8 7 6 5 4 3 2 1

Library of Congress Cataloging-in-Publication Data
Morrison, Boyd
The vault: a novel / by Boyd Morrison.
p. cm.
"A Touchstone book."
1. Archaeologists—Fiction. 2. Antiquities—Collection and preservation—Fiction. I. Title.
PS3613.O7774V38 2011
813'.6—dc22 2011006866

ISBN 978-1-4516-2848-7
ISBN 978-1-4391-8185-0 (ebook)

For Randi. I was saving all my words for you.

PROLOGUE

Eighteen Months Ago

Jordan Orr's thumb hovered over the detonator. Two dead guards lay at his feet. He threw one final glance at his accomplices, who both nodded ready. Orr tapped the button, and a Mercedes in a car park near Piccadilly Circus exploded three miles away.

Orr didn't know and didn't care if there were casualties, but at three in the morning he didn't expect any. The important thing was that the authorities would suspect a terrorist attack. The response time from the London police for any other call would more than double, leaving Orr and his men plenty of time to empty the auction house's largest storage vault.

Orr pulled the balaclava over his face. Russo and Manzini did the same. Disabling the cameras inside the vault would take time they didn't have. The alarm would go off the moment the door was opened.

The vault door was guarded by the double lock of a card key and a pass code. The card key was now in his hand, courtesy of one of the dead guards. He inserted the card, which prompted the system to ask for the code. Orr examined the touchpad. The clever design scrambled the arrangement of the numbers on the keypad every time it was used, making it impossible to guess the code simply by watching someone's finger movements. But the manager had been careless the day before, when Orr cased the facility as a prospective client. He made no effort to shield the screen from Orr, who recorded the code with a pen-shaped video camera in his jacket pocket.

Typical complacency, Orr had thought. Security system planners always forgot about the human element.

Orr typed the code, and the door buzzed, signaling that it was unlocked. He yanked it open and heard no Klaxon, but he knew that the broken magnetic seal had set off the silent alarm at the security firm's headquarters. At this time of the morning, no one should be accessing the vault.

Unable to reach the guards, the security company would call the police, but their problem would be a low priority. A terrorist event took precedence over everything else. Orr loved it.

He led the way in. He'd seen the interior in person, but Russo and Manzini had seen only the video.

The fifteen-foot-by-fifteen-foot vault was designed to showcase the objects that were to be formally appraised the next day. Jewelry, rare books, sculptures, gold coins, and antiques—valuables hidden away in an English manor's attic for a hundred years—were illuminated for optimum effect. Together, the items were expected to fetch in excess of thirty million pounds at auction.

One item was the prize of the collection. In the center display case was a delicate hand made of pure gold. Orr marveled at the lustrous beauty of the metal.

Manzini, a short balding man with powerful arms, removed a sledgehammer from his belt.

"Let's get rich," he said, and swung the hammer toward the case. The thick glass shattered, and Manzini reached in, removed the golden hand, and wrapped it with bubble wrap before stuffing it into his bag. He moved on to the jewelry case.

Russo, so skinny that his pants could have been held up by a rubber band, used two hands to swing his own hammer. He smashed the back of the case holding a Picasso drawing and withdrew it carefully to keep it from getting cut by the shards.

While Manzini and Russo gathered the rest of the jewels and rolled up the artwork, Orr raced to the back of the vault. With a single blow, he liberated three ancient manuscripts and carefully placed them in his duffel. The collection of rare gold coins was next.

In three minutes, they had emptied the vault's entire contents into their bags.

"That's it," Orr said. He opened his cell and dialed. The call was answered on the first ring.

"Yeah?"

"We're on our way," Orr said, and hung up.

They stepped over the bullet-riddled guards and ran to the building's entrance. Outside, Orr could make out sirens in the distance, but they were going in the other direction. A stolen cab was waiting for them. The driver, Felder, wore a flat cap, glasses, and a fake mustache.

They tossed the bags into the car and got in.

"Success?" Felder asked.

"Just like the video," Russo said. "Thirty million pounds' worth."

"A third of that on the black market," Manzini said. "Orr's buyer is only paying ten million."

"Either way, it's more money than you've ever seen," Felder said.

"Drive," Orr said, impatient with their giddiness. They still weren't done.

The cab took off. Because London has the highest concentration of surveillance cameras in the world, they kept their masks on. After a theft like this, Scotland Yard would pore over every single video for the one clue that would lead back to the thieves.

Orr was confident that would never happen.

As they had practiced, the cab reached the boat slip at the Thames river dock only five minutes later. They left the cab sitting at the dock car park and made their way to the cabin cruiser Felder had hired. Orr knew the boat might be traced back to Felder, but by the time it was, it wouldn't matter.

As soon as they were on board, Felder, a native Brit who had plied these waters for ten years as tug crewman, threw the throttle forward. They wouldn't stop until they reached the Strait of Dover, where the plan was to go ashore in Kent and use a rental car to make their final escape on a SeaFrance ferry to Calais.

While Felder navigated, the rest of them emptied the contents of the bags in the blacked-out forward cabin to take stock of their haul. Russo and Manzini cackled in Italian. The only word Orr, an American, could understand was when they mentioned their hometown, "Napoli." Naples. He ignored them and carefully inspected the three manuscripts. He found the one he wanted and set it aside. The other two were worthless to him, so he put them back in the duffel.

By the time they finished sorting the goods, the boat had entered the English Channel. It was time.

Orr turned his back to Russo and Manzini and drew the silenced SIG Sauer he'd used to kill the guards.

"Hey, Orr," Russo said, "when do we meet your contact? I want my money soon, *capisce*?"

"No problem," Orr said, and whipped around. He shot Russo first, then Manzini. Manzini toppled onto Russo, the necklace he'd been fondling still in his hand.

The wind and the engine noise were so loud that Felder couldn't have heard the shots. Orr made his way up to the wheel deck.

Felder turned and smiled at him.

"Mind taking a few minutes at the wheel?" Felder said. "I'm dying to check out my share."

"Sure," Orr said. He took the wheel with one hand, and when Felder's back was turned, he shot him twice. Felder tumbled to the deck below.

Orr checked the GPS and twisted the wheel until he was heading toward Leysdown-on-Sea, a small town on the coast, where he'd parked a second car. The car Felder had hired would stay where it was until it was towed away. Orr didn't care. There would be nothing to link him with it.

When the boat was three miles from town, Orr brought it to a stop. The water here would be deep enough.

Down in the cabin, he lashed all three of the bodies to the interior, planted two small explosive charges below the waterline, and readied an inflatable raft and oars. Once he triggered the bombs, which were just big enough to tear openings in the hull, the boat would sink within minutes.

He sealed the golden hand, jewelry, coins, and the lone manuscript in a waterproof bag and put everything else into lockers that he battened down. There would be no trace of the boat once it was on the bottom of the Channel. The items like the Picasso were valuable, but they were also too recognizable to sell. He couldn't take the chance that they would lead back to him. The jewelry and the gold could be broken apart and sold for the gems and metal with little risk. He expected to net two million pounds from them, enough to pay off his debts and fund his ultimate plan.

But the golden hand and the manuscript he would keep. Although Orr's accomplices hadn't known it, the document was the most valuable item they had taken from the vault. In fact, it was arguably the single most valuable object on the face of the earth. The owner must not have realized what it contained, or he would never have tried to auction it.

Orr *did* know what it contained. He had checked it himself while Russo and Manzini had been fawning over the gold and the jewels. To the layman, the most important line, heading a section at the end of the document, looked like a string of random Greek letters, but it confirmed the document's importance.

ΟΣΤΙΣΚΡΑΤΕΙΤΟΥΤΟΥΤΟΥΤΟΥΓΡΑΜΜΑΤΟΣΚΡΑΤΕΙΤΟΥ ΠΛΟΥΤΟΥΤΟΥΜΙΔΑ.

The manuscript was a medieval codex transcribed from a scroll written two hundred years before the birth of Christ. It contained an ancient treatise by antiquity's greatest scientist and engineer, the man who kept the Romans at bay for two years through his ingenuity alone, a Greek native of Syracuse named Archimedes.

The codex was written without spaces or lowercase letters, making it tedious to translate, so the manuscript's complete contents were unknown. But that one line convinced Orr that the manuscript at his feet held the secret to the location of a treasure worth untold billions.

Orr climbed into the raft and, for the second time that night, pressed the button of a detonator. The explosive charges blasted open two breaches in the boat's hull. He rowed away but kept close to confirm that the boat was gone before he made his way to land. As Orr watched the boat sink beneath the placid sea, the translation of Archimedes' text flashed in front of his eyes as clearly as if it were written on the water's surface.

He who controls this map controls the riches of Midas.

WEDNESDAY

THE DEATH PUZZLE

ONE

Present Day

"Excuse me," Carol Benedict said as she raced to the Starbucks counter. "You've got my drink."

The man who was holding her latte already had the lid off, ready to put sugar into her pristine cup of coffee. After her daily six-mile run, no one—but no one—got between her and her caffeine.

The man, a young guy wearing a Redskins cap and a dopey expression, looked down at the coffee and back at her.

"You sure?"

She smiled at him. "Did you order a tall double-shot latte?"

He shook his head and gave her a sheepish grin. "Sorry, 7 A.M. is early for me," he said. He put the lid back and handed it to her.

"No problem," Carol said, and opened the door to a blast of heat.

By the end of her ten-minute walk back to her apartment, Carol was drenched with sweat. Washington was known for its summer humidity, but Carol had never experienced it until now, her first year taking graduate-level summer classes at Georgetown. She was astounded that it could be so muggy this early in the morning in the middle of June, but her moisture-wicking jogging top and shorts did an admirable job of keeping her from being miserable.

Carol wasn't a breakfast person, one of her strategies for staying thin. When she entered her one-bedroom apartment, she cranked up the AC, turned on the news, and drained the last of her latte in between her stretching exercises. In the shower, she turned the water as cold as it would go. The cooling spray made her shiver with goose bumps and even get a little light-headed.

She picked a tank top and shorts and put her hair in a ponytail, but she'd have to put a sweater in her bag for class. The classrooms at school were always overly air-conditioned.

A knock came at her door just as she was putting on her shoes. She stood up too fast at the surprising sound, and the headrush nearly made her keel over. She steadied herself against the bureau. The feeling didn't go away, but it subsided enough for her to walk.

Who could be at her door at 7:30 in the morning?

She peered through the peephole and saw a white man in a suit, stocky frame, not much taller than she was.

"What is it?" she asked without opening the door.

"Ms. Benedict, I'm Detective Wilson with the Arlington Police Department. I need to speak with you."

"Can you please show me your identification?" Living alone, Carol had learned to be cautious.

"Of course." He held up an open wallet displaying a badge and an ID with the Arlington PD logo. It looked all right to her, so she swung the door open. She suddenly felt unreasonably fatigued, so she leaned against the doorjamb, her head swimming. If she was getting sick, she'd have to power through it. Missing class could hurt her GPA.

"What's this about, Detective?" She really had no idea why the police would be here. She hadn't gotten so much as a parking ticket in her entire life.

Wilson, who had a thatchy unibrow, stared at her with an unreadable expression. "It's about your sister, Stacy."

A shot of adrenaline cleared Carol's head.

"Stacy? Oh, my God! Has something happened?" They had talked just last night, and Stacy seemed fine.

"There's a hostage situation at her hotel in Seattle. I need to take you down to the station, where we can coordinate with the Seattle police."

"Is she hurt? Is she okay?"

"She's unharmed for now, but you'll need to come with me. I'll explain the situation on the way."

"Sure. Sure. Let me get my purse." She snatched up her keys and her phone, threw them into her bag, and locked the door behind her. Her heart was thudding at the thought of her sister being held at gunpoint.

As she went down the stairs, she stumbled and Wilson caught her.

"Are you all right?" he asked. "You look pale."

"I just feel so tired all of a sudden." Her vision was getting blurrier by the minute.

Wilson held her arm the rest of the way to the parking lot, and she was glad he did, because her knees buckled twice.

Instead of an unmarked car, Wilson steered her to a white panel van. Another man jumped out of the passenger seat and slid the rear door open. Carol's stomach lurched when she saw that he was wearing a Redskins cap.

It was the man who had taken her latte at Starbucks. The dopey expression had been replaced by the dead-eyed stare of a cobra assessing its prey.

She sucked in a breath to scream, but Wilson's hand went over her mouth.

"I see you remember my partner," he said into her ear.

She tried to struggle, but her arms and legs felt like overcooked spaghetti, and her mind was getting cloudier by the second.

Wilson shoved her into the van, and the door slid closed behind her. He snapped cuffs onto her wrists and ankles as the other man started the van and drove off. She tried to scream again, but it came out as a weak mewl. Her tongue lolled in her mouth as if it were coated in syrup.

"You drugged me."

Wilson nodded. "Rohypnol is easy to get, with so many university campuses in D.C."

Rohypnol. Otherwise known as roofies. The date-rape drug. He had put it in her coffee.

"Oh, my God—"

"Don't worry. That's not what it's for. We just need you out for a few hours while we take care of some other business."

"What do you want?"

"We need your sister to do something for us," Wilson said.

"What have you done to Stacy?" Carol said, slurring out the *S* in Stacy. She couldn't keep her eyes open any longer and rested her head on the floor.

"Nothing. She's going to be more worried about what we're going to do to you if she doesn't cooperate. Or if she isn't able to . . ."

Wilson kept talking, but Carol's eyes could focus no longer, and darkness swept her to oblivion.

TWO

Answer your phone, Dr. Locke. You don't have much time left.

Tyler Locke peered at the text message and tried to decide whether it was a joke or some kind of marketing gimmick. He was ten minutes into his one-hour ferry commute to Bremerton, and three times his cell phone had rung with an unknown number. Tyler had ignored the calls, but the text message came soon after, again from an unknown number. The only people who had his cell number were in the phone's contact list. As a rule, he didn't answer calls from numbers he didn't know, figuring that if it was important the caller would leave a voice mail. So far, no new messages.

The boat was only half full, so Tyler had the bench to himself, with his long legs propped up on the facing seat. Any other morning, his best friend, Grant Westfield, would be next to him playing games on his phone, but Grant was planning to beat the afternoon rush hour for a long weekend in Vancouver, so he'd taken an earlier ferry. They'd been making the trip from Seattle to Bremerton three days a week for two months to consult on the construction of a new ammunition depot at the naval base.

The phone rang again. Same number. Tyler drank his coffee and looked out at the receding Seattle skyline. It was eight-forty in the morning, and even though it was June sixteenth the sun was nowhere to be seen. Low clouds and drizzle made it a typical "June-uary" day, as the locals called the cool, overcast weather that usually preceded a sunny July.

Couldn't be a cold call, Tyler concluded. A telemarketer wouldn't call him Dr. Locke. Tyler wasn't an MD. He had a PhD, and the only time anyone called him doctor was on one of his consulting gigs. None of his co-workers used the honorific unless they were making fun of him.

The call might be work-related, but he had fifty e-mails to plow through before he reached Bremerton, and he didn't want to be sucked into a long conversation. He again let voice mail handle it and put the phone away. Eventually, the caller would get the hint to leave a message.

A minute after he began working on his laptop again, the phone beeped with another text message. Tyler sighed and pulled the phone from his pocket.

> Dr. Locke, unless you answer my call you will be dead in twenty-eight minutes.

Tyler had to read the message three times to believe what he was seeing. He closed his laptop and sat up straight, taking his feet off the seat. He slowly scanned the passengers around him, but no one seemed at all interested in him.

The phone rang. Same number.

Tyler tapped the screen and said, "Who is this?"

"This is the person who is going to kill everyone on that ferry if you don't do what I say."

Tyler couldn't detect an accent in the gravelly voice on the other end. "Why don't I just hang up on you and call the police?" he said. "Should make your day when the FBI drops by."

"You could do that, but what would you tell them? My number? It's a prepaid phone bought with cash. Believe me, I've thought this through."

For a moment, Tyler considered doing just what he'd threatened: hanging up and calling the cops. But the man was right. He had little to tell them.

"What's this about?" Tyler said.

"It's about you, Dr. Locke. Actually, that sounds pretentious. I'll just call you Locke."

"This is ridiculous."

"It may seem like that now, but it won't in a few minutes."

Tyler paused. "Why are you calling *me*?"

"Because you're exactly who I need. Bachelor's degree from MIT in mechanical engineering. PhD from Stanford. Former Army captain in a combat-engineering battalion, which makes you an expert in demolitions and bomb disposal. Now chief of special operations at Gordian Engineering. And all of that before you're forty. You know, you sound very good on paper."

"So you know who I am. I should take all of this seriously because . . . ?"

"Because I just e-mailed you a couple of pictures that show how serious your situation is. I know the ferry has Wi-Fi. Take a look at them. I'll wait. Better hurry, though."

With the phone propped in one hand, Tyler reluctantly opened his laptop and checked his in-box.

One new message from an e-mail address he didn't recognize. The subject line read *27 minutes left.*

Tyler opened the message. The body of the e-mail had no text, just two images.

The first showed a two-axle truck with the name SILVERLAKE TRANSPORT on the side.

The second showed a refrigerator with its door open. Inside was a transparent plastic canister the size of a beer keg filled with a powdery gray substance. Cloth concealed an object on top. A digital timer was mounted on the front of the canister. The water was dead calm outside, but Tyler felt seasick.

"I'm listening," he said, his mind already racing to how he could warn the passengers to get to a life raft.

"I thought you might. You know a bomb when you see it. In case you didn't get it, the fridge is inside the truck, which is on the vehicle deck below you. And don't call the police. I'll know."

"You couldn't have gotten it on board."

"You think I'm bluffing? Tell me about binary explosives."

Tyler sucked in a breath before responding. "Binary explosives start as two separate inert compounds, but when they're mixed together they become highly volatile. They're often used for target practice by shooting clubs. The explosives can only be set off by a high-powered rifle round or a detonator. You can buy them on the Internet."

"See? You *are* good. There's a hundred pounds of binary in the fridge. Enough to blow a thirty-foot hole in that ferry and set half the cars on fire. I doubt there'd be many survivors."

"The bomb-sniffing dogs at the dock would have detected it," Tyler said.

"I took precautions to make sure the taggant odor was sealed in, and I paid some jobless college kid three hundred bucks to drive it on board. What's bad for the economy is good for me."

"If you want to blow up the ferry, why warn me?"

"Listen and find out. I want you to go to the truck. It has a padlock on the door. The key is taped inside the left wheel well. Go there now, or the ferry will never reach Bremerton."

Bremerton. Suddenly, Tyler had a horrifying thought: *the naval base.* This guy wanted Tyler to drive the truck into a U.S. Navy port using his credentials.

"So you want me to become a suicide bomber for you?" Tyler said, furiously thinking of a way to ditch the truck before he reached the entrance to the base.

The man laughed. "A suicide bomber? Not even close."

"Then what *do* you want?"

"Locke, you're going to be a hero. That bomb is set to explode in twenty-four minutes and thirty seconds. I want you to disarm it."

THREE

As Byron Gaul waited for the elevator in the lobby of the Sheraton Premiere, he checked his surroundings. He was relieved not to find unexpected security alterations for the conference being held in the hotel. He'd scouted the location thoroughly the week before in preparation for the mission, but given that the hotel was in Tysons Corner, Virginia, just outside Washington, there was always the chance security had been beefed up, especially for a Pentagon-sponsored conference called the Unconventional Weapons Summit.

Two Army majors approached, deep in conversation. When they saw Gaul, he nodded to them, and they replied in kind. Because they were inside with their hats off, his lower rank didn't require a salute. Gaul was dressed in a class-A Army service uniform with the rank of captain and a name tag that said Wilson. The uniform and all its ribbons and adornments were purchased off the Internet. The hardest part had been finding a size to fit his below-average height and above-average musculature.

He readied himself for questions, but the majors went back to their discussion, ignoring him. Gaul didn't know if he'd have to use his prepared backstory, but he was ready in case anyone asked. He would say that he was a liaison officer to a Washington think tank called Weaver Solutions, one of hundreds in the city. He was attending the summit to learn about the newest technologies and tactics that might be used against military or civilian objectives. These kinds of military conferences were held virtually every week in the nation's capital, but this was the only one his target was scheduled to address.

The elevator opened, and Gaul got on with the majors. At the first stop, the door opened to a buzz of activity. It was just after 11:30, the morning sessions over, including his target's keynote speech. The participants would be breaking for lunch. The majors got off, and two men in civilian attire entered. Gaul glanced sideways at their name tags, which said Aiden MacKenna and Miles Benson.

Both of them seemed to be enhanced by technology out of a science-fiction movie. A black disk was attached to MacKenna's skull with a wire connected to his ear, as if it were a hearing aid with a direct pipeline to his brain. MacKenna was walking, while Benson was driving a motorized wheelchair like nothing Gaul had ever seen. The chair was balanced on two wheels, apparently in defiance of the laws of physics, so that the eyes of the man in the chair were almost even with his own.

Though Benson wore a suit, Gaul could see that the man had the upper torso of someone who spent time at the gym. He had the intense gaze and close-cropped hair of a former Army officer, so Gaul guessed that he'd been injured in Iraq or Afghanistan. MacKenna looked more like Gaul's idea of a research analyst, with tortoiseshell glasses and a physique that suggested nothing more strenuous than typing in his daily routine.

"Think he'll take you up on your offer?" MacKenna said with an Irish brogue.

"I don't know," Benson said. "Depends how good my sales pitch is."

"It was a good keynote."

"That's exactly why I want him."

The elevator door opened at the mezzanine.

"Where is the Capital Club?" Benson said as he drove out of the elevator.

"To the left, I believe," MacKenna said.

"Okay, we should have a table reserved. We'll save a seat between us for the general."

Gaul trailed them around the corner. MacKenna and Benson went through the restaurant's glass doors, but Gaul didn't follow. He stopped abruptly, as if he'd gone in the wrong direction, and turned back toward the mezzanine's conference rooms.

Attendees were streaming from the conference seminars to their lunch destinations or milling about in the hall to chat after the sessions. The dress was a fifty-fifty mix of military and civilian clothes. Gaul blended right in.

Gaul wandered down the hall, pretending to study a conference program. He passed by the glass doors of the Capital Club but didn't see his target. He found a spot near the elevators and had to remind himself not to lean against the wall so that he would stay in character as a ramrod-straight military officer.

His cell phone buzzed. The text message was from Orr.

We're under way here. You?

Gaul texted back,

Everything's in place.

Have you spotted him?

Not yet. But he's here and
scheduled to attend the lunch.

Good. We'll know in 20 minutes. Be ready.

K.

With nothing more to do but wait while keeping an eye on the elevators and stairs, Gaul went back to scanning the program. He smiled when he saw the title of the keynote address by his target, the former military leader of the Defense Threat Reduction Agency. The speech was called "The Dangers of Asymmetric Threat and Response: How to Combat Improvised Weapons of Mass Destruction." Gaul thought the speaker would be surprised by how personal that danger would become.

The elevator emptied three times before Gaul saw who he had come for. The newly retired major general looked a little grayer than in the photo he'd memorized, but the intense gaze and the wrought-iron jaw were still the same. All eyes followed the general as he strode toward the restaurant.

Gaul took out his cell phone to text Orr with the confirmation that he now had Sherman Locke in his sights.

FOUR

Tyler liked the sense of duty, purpose, and camaraderie of the military, but he could do without the threat-of-death part, which was one of the reasons he'd left for civilian life. He took calculated risks, as when he raced cars or worked with explosives on a demolition project, but that was because he was in control. This situation was definitely not under his control.

"I'm back," the man on the other end of the phone said. "Had other business to attend to. You there, Locke?"

"I'm here," Tyler said as he descended the ferry's stairs to the vehicle deck. "Why do you want me to disarm a bomb *you* put on the ferry?"

"I need someone with your skills for a special job, but before we get started, I need to make sure you can handle it."

"A job?" Tyler said. "Why didn't you just hire me?"

"Consider this task your interview. The clock is ticking, so you better get moving. Before you go to the truck, put the keys in the glove box of that little red sports car of yours. Leave it unlocked."

"Why?"

"Because I said so, and I'm the one with the bomb. Just do it."

"I'm on my way," Tyler said. "So if we're going to be talking to each other on this job, what should I call you?"

"You might be getting ahead of yourself. We could be working together for just the next twenty-two minutes."

Tyler set his watch to synchronize with the time he had left. "I'm the confident type," he said, though he felt anything but. Bombs were tricky in the best of conditions. Tyler didn't know what this guy's game was, but he didn't sound stupid.

"I think you're more cocky than confident," the man said. "You'll know what to call me as soon as you get in the truck."

I already have some ideas about what to call you, Tyler thought. *Why do I attract all the crazy people?*

He reached the vehicle deck and went to his Viper, tucking the keys in the glove box as ordered. Looking forward from his position at the stern, he could make out several trucks, which were usually boarded first. He trotted in that direction.

Tyler saw the truck marked SILVERLAKE TRANSPORT and angled toward it.

"So what do I have to do?" he asked.

"The instructions are taped to the fridge. It's all written down for you. Well, not you, but you'll see what I mean. And remember, no police. I have my eyes and ears on you, and I've got a remote detonator, so get busy and behave yourself. Ferry goes boom if SWAT arrives or life rafts start popping over the side."

"Then what?"

"You'll know if you're successful. If you are, I'll give you a call back. If not, you'll go down with the ship."

The man hung up.

Tyler reached the back of the truck and ran his hand under the left wheel well. The key was there, just as the guy had said it was.

He looked around, but apart from an elderly woman walking her dog he was alone.

The key fit the padlock, and Tyler slid the door up carefully. He didn't think the guy was planning to have the bomb triggered by this, but he checked just in case. Nothing.

Tyler pushed the door just high enough to squeeze in. If there really was a bomb in here, he didn't want one of the deckhands to see it and sound the alarm.

He thought he was going to have to leave the door open for

light, but two lanterns were lashed to the sides of the interior. He switched them both on and closed the door.

Boxes were piled on a sofa, a couple of chairs, and a table. In the middle sat an icebox, one of the old models with a latch. A manila envelope was taped to the front of the door. Tyler examined it and, when he was sure it was safe, tore it away and ripped it open.

The envelope held one page. Tyler pulled it out expecting instructions on what to do next.

The sheet may have had instructions, but they weren't much help. The numbered paragraphs weren't written in English. Although Tyler couldn't read the words, he recognized the letters immediately. He had never been in a fraternity, but he'd used all the letters in equations while earning his engineering degrees.

The page was written in Greek.

Tyler scanned the text to see if there was any hidden code or some other message for him. He searched for a formula, something that would help him defuse the bomb, but he didn't know what he was looking for. Given how much the guy on the phone knew about Tyler, he would have learned that foreign languages weren't exactly Tyler's strength. He could order a beer and ask where the bathroom was in French and Spanish, but even that was pushing it.

The man had mentioned that the instructions weren't written for him. *Then who were they written for?*

He racked his brain trying to come up with someone he could call to translate the document, but he was interrupted when the truck echoed with the sound of pounding on the rear door. Tyler froze.

"Is someone inside?" he heard a woman's voice say.

"I'm okay," Tyler said, thinking that a crew member was checking on him. "I'm just repacking some items that came loose."

"Open the door."

Twenty minutes left. He didn't have time for this, but ignoring her would just bring more attention than he wanted. He'd get rid of her quickly and focus on how to get the document translated.

He pulled the door up expecting to see someone dressed in the crew's crisp blue uniform. Instead, he saw a petite woman in her thirties dressed in a black leather jacket, jeans, and stylish but functional boots. Shoulder-length blond hair framed her face, and light makeup accentuated high cheekbones and pillowy lips. It was a no-nonsense, attractive look.

Tyler recognized her immediately. Stacy Benedict, host of the television show *Chasing the Past.*

He didn't know where to begin, other than to say, "What are you doing here?"

The woman had been appraising Tyler as much as he had been studying her, and his abrupt demand made her pause. "A man told me someone would be waiting inside this truck for me."

"Did he have a gravelly voice?"

"That's him. But he didn't mention it would be you."

So she remembered Tyler from his appearance on her show. No need for introductions.

The instructions are taped to the fridge, the man on the phone had said. *It's all written down for you. Well, not you, but you'll see what I mean.*

"You don't happen to read Greek, do you?" Tyler asked.

Stacy's look told him that the question sounded as ridiculous to her as it did to him, but her answer made it clear that it seemed ridiculous for another reason.

"I have a PhD in Classics," she said. "Of course I know Greek. Why?"

He gave her the piece of paper. "That's why."

As she read it, Tyler could see the blood drain from her face. But she didn't panic. No screaming. No crying. Instead, her face contorted with barely contained fury.

She looked up from the page and said, "Where's the bomb?"

FIVE

Stacy boosted herself into the truck. As Tyler closed the door behind her, she read the first line on the sheet again. It was typewritten in modern Greek with awkward phrasing, as though it had been translated from another language by a free Web service. But she got the gist of it.

There is a bomb in the truck. Work with this man to deactivate it. If you don't accomplish your task, both you and your sister will die.

Only an hour before, she'd been packing for her morning flight back to New York when she received a call from an unidentified man claiming to have kidnapped her baby sister, Carol. Upon seeing the video of Carol bound and gagged, Stacy unleashed a tirade of obscenities so withering that the caller had to calm her down just to tell her what he wanted her to do.

His only command had been to board the 8:30 ferry to Bremerton as a walk-on and wait for further instructions. She'd allowed herself five minutes to react after he'd hung up, but all that came was a fit of shaking. She wasn't a crier. Neither was her sister. Except for her parents' funerals, the last time she could recall real tears was when their dog, Sparky, died. She was fourteen and Carol was twelve. Stacy supposed their fortitude had something to do with growing up as the only children on a working Iowa farm.

But that toughness didn't mean she was a loner. At least now she had a partner in this mess, even if it was a man she barely knew.

Stacy had met Tyler Locke only once, nine months ago, when she had interviewed him for her show that investigated ancient mysteries around the world. He was a big get after his rumored involvement in finding Noah's Ark. Before the interview, he made it clear that he wasn't happy being in the spotlight, explaining that his boss had arranged the appearance over Tyler's objections. In spite of his reluctance, Tyler was naturally engaging when he talked about the engineering of centuries-old mechanisms and could have been a regular if she had been able to persuade him to return.

He was handsome in a rugged sort of way, which made him perfect for TV. His tan face showed just a bit of weathering, as if he spent a lot of time outdoors, but he didn't have any deep lines on his forehead, so he wasn't into his forties yet. He was over six feet tall, brown hair, blue eyes, with a jagged scar down the left side of his neck. The windbreaker, khakis, and hiking boots were professional but casual.

"What does it say?" Tyler asked. "We have less than twenty minutes."

Stacy examined the paper. The first four lines were in modern Greek, but the rest was in ancient Greek. Not too dissimilar from the modern form, but the punctuation and all caps made it harder to read.

"The refrigerator door has a trap," she said. "To disable it, flip the switch on the lower part of the door."

Tyler knelt and ran his hand under the door. "Got it."

"You should be able to open the door."

He pulled the latch and inched the fridge open.

All the shelves had been removed from the interior. A clear plastic barrel filled with a grayish powder took up the bottom two-thirds of the interior. The barrel was topped by something covered in canvas, and a drawstring pouch hung on a hook next to it. An LCD timer stuck to the front of the barrel counted down. Nineteen minutes were left.

Wires from the timer snaked into the barrel. They terminated at a device nestled into the powder. Another set of wires disappeared into the covered object.

"I've never seen a bomb like this on TV," Stacy said. Her heart was hammering, but her voice was even. Going to pieces wasn't going to help her sister.

"There's a detonator in the powder," Tyler said. "The powder is a binary explosive."

"Could it be a fake?" She remembered his credentials from the interview because they were so unusual. He had been a captain in an Army combat-engineering unit, and one of their responsibilities had been to dispose of IEDs.

"Can't be sure, but I don't think so," Tyler said. "And if it's real, there's enough to blow a car-sized hole in the deck."

"So that's bad? You don't have to sugarcoat it for me."

He gave her a wan grin. "Seemed like you could handle it."

She forced a smile in return. "I'll freak out later."

"I'll join you. What's next?"

She read the third item on the sheet. "Carefully remove the canvas covering."

The canvas was tied at the bottom with twine. Tyler loosened it and pulled the cover off to reveal a gleaming bronze box one foot tall and six inches wide.

Stacy moved closer to get a better look. The box had two dials on the front, but it wasn't a clock. As far as she could see, the hands weren't moving and the dials were ringed with Greek lettering, not numbers. Each dial was divided into twelve segments and labeled with words spelling out signs of the zodiac. Two small control knobs were attached to its left side.

The object looked brand-new, although its design was definitely not modern. The box was clearly the endpoint of the wires, but she had no earthly idea why it was connected to a bomb.

"What the hell is that?" Stacy said to herself. She was surprised when Tyler answered.

"It's a replica of a device designed by Archimedes. It's called a geolabe. Like an astrolabe, but for terrestrial instead of astronomical use." She could tell that he wasn't guessing. He plainly recognized it.

She gaped at him. "How do you know that?"

He fixed her with a grim stare. "Because I'm the one who built it."

SIX

The parking spot along the beach in West Seattle provided a beautiful view of Puget Sound. Jordan Orr would be able to watch the ferry until it turned past Bainbridge Island for the final leg into Bremerton. If the ship made it that far. The bomb was set to go off long before then.

In the passenger seat of their rented SUV, Peter Crenshaw trained binoculars on the ferry, now visible as it passed the north tip of West Seattle.

"If Locke doesn't disarm the bomb in time," Orr said, "you won't need those to know."

"I'm just checking the deck for unusual activity. Making sure he hasn't sounded the alarm."

"He won't. By now he knows that I meant everything I said." A jogger approached, and Orr couldn't tell if she was watching them because she was wearing sunglasses. "Put those down before someone notices. No one's going to think we're bird-watching."

Crenshaw put the binoculars on the seat next to him and went back to monitoring the two video feeds on his laptop. The first was from the camera hidden in the visor of the truck.

The second feed was from the back of the truck. Orr watched Stacy Benedict reading the instructions he'd created while Tyler Locke removed the drawstring pouch, opened it, and poured out the contents: fourteen pieces of a puzzle created more than two thousand years ago.

"How did he sound?" Crenshaw asked in an irritating whine. "Think he can do it?"

"I have faith in Locke," Orr said. "He's the best at what he does, and he's the only one who can help us accomplish our mission."

"And if he can't?"

"Then Washington's going to need a new ferry."

Orr leaned over to check the GPS tracker and saw that it was operational. It showed the truck in the middle of Puget Sound, right where it was supposed to be.

He caught a whiff of body odor from Crenshaw and rolled down his window. Crenshaw was a skilled bomb designer, but his personal hygiene was atrocious. Given his scruffy beard and greasy hair, Orr wouldn't be surprised if the pig hadn't showered in a week. His belly protruded as if he were smuggling a beach ball under his T-shirt, and flecks of powdered doughnut dusted his chin. The man disgusted Orr, but the alliance was necessary.

Orr had trolled Internet sites for months disguised as an anti-tax radical until he met Crenshaw in an underground chat room devoted to rants about the U.S. government. Crenshaw was an electrical whiz whose penchant for building sophisticated pipe bombs got him kicked out of college. He escaped prison on a technicality, but his social inadequacies made him unemployable. Crenshaw still lived in the basement of his mother's home in Omaha, nursing his hatred of Uncle Sam.

Orr and Crenshaw had started sending private messages about what they could do to strike a blow for the common man. After he'd gained Crenshaw's trust, Orr suggested that they get together at some property Orr had rented in upstate New York. Orr even paid for Crenshaw to fly out. Together, they shot guns, and Crenshaw showed off by building bombs with materials Orr provided. Shortly after that, Orr had presented his plan to Crenshaw, who readily agreed to participate. The two million dollars Orr promised him had made the decision easy.

As Crenshaw grabbed his sixth doughnut, Orr shuddered at the man's lack of self-control. Orr couldn't understand how someone could let himself go like that. Crenshaw had never lacked for food or shelter or a comfortable lifestyle, no matter how much he bellyached about the government screwing him over. Orr had been through hardship Crenshaw couldn't imagine, but he didn't dwell on it. There was only one person he could rely on, and that was himself.

Ever since his parents died when he was ten, Orr had been on his own. Until then, his parents had lived lavishly and spoiled their only son. He'd had everything he could possibly want: a huge house, any toy he asked for, private school, vacations to Europe and Hawaii. But one night his father, an investment banker, crashed into a bridge abutment near their home in Connecticut, killing both himself and Orr's mother instantly.

The police found no skid marks and his father's foot was jammed against the accelerator, so the deaths were ruled a murder-suicide. The life-insurance company paid nothing on his father's policy, and his mother, a housewife, had none. Orr didn't believe the coroner's finding until he learned that his father had not only been fired two months before the crash but had also been blackballed by every firm on Wall Street for whistle-blowing on an embezzlement scheme. With their lavish lifestyle, the family had been living a hand-to-mouth existence, spending every dollar his father brought in and more, so the firing left them deeply in debt. Whether the car crash was accidental or intentional, the result was the same. Orr was left penniless.

He was placed in foster care, and went through a succession of low-life guardians who either were hosting him to collect the welfare checks or wanted a kid who could act as a live-in servant. He got back at the world by stealing from his neighbors. At first it was just a buck or two to buy some candy or a comic book, but the amount grew until he was bringing in serious cash. He got caught only once, when he broke into a house not realizing that the husband had come home unexpectedly with his mistress, and the time he spent in juvenile detention made him vow never to let that happen again. When he was sixteen, Orr ran away and started working construction by lying about his age.

For the next ten years, he bounced around the U.S., taking legitimate or illegitimate jobs, whatever paid. Then, during a bank renovation, one of his co-workers approached him and asked if he wanted to make some easy money. The guy planned to rob the bank, but he was too clever to attempt a daytime heist.

Instead, they sabotaged the wiring for the security equipment and made off with a hundred thousand dollars that night. But Orr had inherited his father's free-spending ways and blew through most of his share in two months. It was the end of his construction career and the beginning of the more high-risk, high-reward career as a thief.

He absorbed everything he could about the art of breaking into secure facilities, educating himself by reading and working with better burglars than he until he had mastered the profession. The jobs kept getting bigger, with Orr planning the heists down to the most minute detail and assembling crews that could be trusted to do their jobs, but the money never lasted.

For years he lived the high life two months at a time, until the tip about the Archimedes Codex presented the opportunity to find one of the most valuable treasures in history. If the trail really did lead to the lost tomb of King Midas and the fortune he was buried with, Orr could live the rest of his life in the style that had been stolen from him so long ago and at the same time exact his pound of flesh. His dream was within his grasp, and Stacy Benedict and Tyler Locke were going to find it for him or die trying.

Orr reflexively reached for his backpack and felt the codex still inside. He kept it with him at all times.

Crenshaw stuffed the rest of his doughnut into his mouth and nodded at the computer screen. "They're having a little trouble with the Stomachion."

Crenshaw's mispronunciation of the puzzle created by Archimedes grated on Orr. Despite dropping out of high school, he was a voracious reader and considered himself an educated man. It wasn't "Stuh-muh-CHEE-on," as Crenshaw pronounced the word. It was "Stoh-MAH-kee-on." Orr sighed but didn't correct him. "I have faith in them."

The video feed showed Benedict and Locke going back and forth between the instructions and the puzzle pieces. There were fourteen—eleven triangles, one four-sided piece, and two five-sided pieces—and when the pieces were fit together properly, they formed a square. According to Orr's research, the puzzle was originally created by Archimedes to demonstrate some kind of mathematical principle. The version of the puzzle drawn in Orr's codex had a different purpose: it was a code. The pieces were covered with Greek letters. The only problem was that Orr couldn't figure out how to solve the puzzle.

Somehow the letters on the Stomachion corresponded to the signs of the zodiac on the face of the bronze geolabe, the ancient device Orr had linked to the bomb. If the puzzle were solved correctly, it would tell you how to use the geolabe, and the geolabe was the key in the search for Midas's hoard of gold. But Orr had only five days left to locate the treasure, and Locke was his last hope for deciphering how to operate the geolabe.

Crenshaw pointed to his countdown timer, which was synchronized with the one on the bomb. It was down to nine minutes.

"They're not going to make it," he said.

"Maybe not," Orr said. "Archimedes was a clever guy. The puzzle doesn't have just one solution."

Crenshaw looked at him in surprise. "How many does it have?"

Orr smiled. "More than seventeen thousand."

SEVEN

Tyler stared at the pieces of Archimedes' puzzle hoping to see a pattern, but none was apparent. There were more than seventeen thousand solutions, but fewer than six hundred unique arrangements when equivalent rotations and reflections were subtracted. Archimedes had linked a single particular solution to the geolabe, and that was the one Tyler had to find.

On one side of the fourteen Stomachion pieces, each of the points was inscribed with a number written in Greek. On the other side, the pieces had Greek letters written on them. The puzzle would tell them how to use the geolabe, but unless the pieces were put together in the correct orientation, the results would be gibberish.

According to their written instructions, the bomb would be deactivated when the two dials on the front of the geolabe and the third dial on the back face were all pointing to the twelve o'clock position. Tyler couldn't just randomly turn the knobs that controlled the motion of the dials, because each twist affected the motion of all three dials simultaneously. The complicated set of forty-seven gears inside the device meant that there were millions of possible orientations. To get the one that would disarm the bomb, they had to solve the puzzle.

"Eight minutes," Stacy said, the edge in her voice palpable.

Tyler said nothing as he studied the Stomachion pieces.

"Are you thinking or frozen in terror?" she continued.

"My bomb-disposal instructor had a motto," Tyler said. " 'Don't just do something, stand there.' Doing nothing doesn't mean you're doing nothing."

"Just checking. What about dumping the whole thing over the side of the ship?"

"Can't," Tyler said. "We're being watched."

She swung around. "I don't see a camera."

"I haven't had time to search for it, but it's here. He said he had his eye on us."

"Who is this guy?" Stacy asked.

"His name's Jordan Orr."

"You know him?"

"He's the one who had me build the geolabe," Tyler said, glancing at the timer as it clicked below seven minutes. "I'll tell you all about it if we live through this."

"So you built this geolabe but you don't know how to use it?"

"Think of it like the Rubik's Cube. Just because someone can assemble it doesn't mean they can solve it. That must be Orr's problem. He knows that the dials should all point at the noon position, but he can't figure out how to get them there. But Orr does know that Archimedes encoded the Stomachion with instructions for how to get the dials aligned, so he built the bomb as a test. We need to solve the puzzle in order to operate the geolabe, and that will deactivate the bomb."

Stacy nodded. "Makes sense that Archimedes would hide the instructions in a puzzle. The Greeks did invent steganography."

Tyler had heard of steganography, the technique of hiding messages in plain sight, like the microdots hidden behind stamps on postcards during World War II, or the way terrorists cloaked messages in pictures and video posted on public forums like Facebook and YouTube. Not only do you have to know that the message exists; you have to know how to read it.

"Do you remember any specific methods of steganography that Archimedes might have used?"

"The Greeks developed the technique twenty-five hundred years ago," Stacy said. "Sometimes a message was tattooed onto the shaved head of a courier, who would grow out his hair and then travel with the secret message safely concealed. Secret communications could also be hidden in wax tablets."

"How?"

"In normal use you would write on the wax itself using a metal stylus. If you wanted to erase it, you'd warm it up and use a tool like a spatula to smooth it over. To send a secret message, you'd write on the wood underneath and then apply the wax and write an innocuous note in the wax. To read the hidden message, you'd just scrape off the wax."

"So the message wasn't encoded. You just had to know what to look for?"

"Yes."

Six minutes left.

Tyler ran his fingers through his hair as he thought through the problem. "When I was building the geolabe, the text of the manual for constructing it said, 'The puzzle will be solved only by the geolabe's builder.' I wondered about that for a long time, but I couldn't figure out what it meant. Now that we have the Stomachion, I see something that's too strange to be coincidental. It must have been in the codex all along, but Orr never shared those pages with me."

Stacy bent down to look at the pieces. "What?"

"There are forty-seven gears in the mechanism. I know, because I spent a few months with them."

"So?"

"Look at the pieces in the Stomachion. There are eleven triangles, one tetragon, and two pentagons. If you add up the number of all the points, the total comes to forty-seven."

"Son of a bitch," Stacy said. "I never would have noticed that."

"Only the builder of the geolabe would. Tell me some of

the numbers etched on the points. They've got to mean something."

"Uh, twenty-four, fifty-seven, four, thirty-two, seventeen—"

"Wait. You said twenty-four, fifty-seven, and thirty-two?"

"And four and seventeen. What do they mean?"

The puzzle will be solved only by the geolabe's builder.

"The gears!" Tyler shouted before he even realized that it had come out.

"What?"

"Quick! Is there a point with the number thirty-seven?"

Stacy scanned the pieces while Tyler held his breath. If this didn't work, they were dead.

After an agonizing few seconds, she scooped up a piece. "Got it! Thirty-seven."

"Okay, give me the piece with twenty-four on it."

She gave it to him. When he put the pieces together, the numbers aligned perfectly.

"What happened?" she said. "Did you figure it out?"

Tyler nodded. "I hope so. One of the gears had thirty-seven teeth, and one of the gears it meshed into had twenty-four teeth. None of the gears had four or seventeen teeth, so those numbers must be included to throw off anyone looking for a code. Only someone who spent time crafting each gear would think to look for that connection. Now hurry. We've only got four minutes left."

He told her the numbers he needed. He remembered some of them because they were such odd numbers to use in the gearing. He'd have to hope he recalled enough of them so that the others wouldn't be necessary.

Within a minute, they had assembled the Stomachion into a square. They flipped it over so they could read the letters on the other side.

"It still looks like gibberish," Tyler said.

"No!" Stacy yelled. "It makes perfect sense now. Notice that some of letters seem to run in a crude spiral?"

"What does it say?" Tyler's eyes flicked to the timer on the bomb. Three minutes left.

"Alpha Leo. Beta Libra. Alpha Pisces. Beta Scorpio . . . There's twelve in all. They must refer to the signs of the zodiac written on the dials of the geolabe. But I don't know what the alphas and betas refer to."

"I do. You couldn't see it, but the upper knob on the side is labeled alpha, and the bottom is labeled beta. I'm supposed to turn the knobs in sequence to set the dials properly. Read them from the beginning."

"Alpha Leo," Stacy said.

"Which one is Leo?" It literally was all Greek to Tyler.

Stacy pointed. "That one."

Tyler turned the top knob. The hands on both dials rotated simultaneously. Tyler didn't stop until the top hand rested on Leo.

"Now what?"

"Beta Libra." She pointed again, and Tyler followed her instruction. They got into a rhythm going through the next seven signs, but the process was still achingly slow.

The timer ticked down to less than a minute.

Stacy waved her hands, prodding him to go faster. "Beta Cancer, Hurry!"

"How many left?" Tyler said as he twirled the knob frantically.

"Two. Alpha Sagittarius."

Stacy pointed to the twelve o'clock symbol, but Tyler was already turning the dial toward it. "Got it!"

Before Stacy could even say "Beta Aquarius," his fingers were twisting the bottom knob. Aquarius had to be the zodiac sign at the noon position.

"Fifteen seconds!"

Despite Tyler's frenzied twisting, the hand on the dial seemed to move in slow motion, like a nightmare where you were running as hard as you could but moved as if you were mired in tar. He raced the timer as it counted down below ten seconds.

"Oh, God!" Stacy screamed. "Go, go, go!"

As all three dials reached the noon position, Tyler felt the knob click.

A piercing series of beeps blared from behind the geolabe. Stacy grabbed Tyler's arm, digging her fingers into his biceps, but the timer stopped. It read four seconds left.

They both collapsed to their knees, completely drained. There was nothing like the relief of surviving certain death.

Stacy had her head buried in her arms. Tyler put a hand on her shoulder.

"You okay?" he asked.

She looked up and blinked several times before answering. "Peachy."

Tyler's phone rang.

"It's him," Stacy guessed.

Tyler nodded and answered the call, putting it on speaker so that she could hear.

"Okay, we did what you wanted," Tyler said. "Are we finished here?"

"Finished?" The gravelly voice was gone, replaced by the smooth tone that he now recognized as Orr's. "Locke, we are just getting started."

EIGHT

Sherman Locke laughed so hard that everyone at the eight-person table turned to look at him. He ignored them and cut another piece of his steak, still chuckling and shaking his head at Miles Benson's offer.

The Capital Club had been reserved for senior military officers, key speakers, and sponsors of the Unconventional Weapons Summit to meet and mingle over lunch. Gordian Engineering was a major sponsor, so it made sense that Miles, the company's president, got his choice of the best table in the restaurant. Sherman had agreed to join him to discuss some business, but this proposal was too ridiculous.

Sherman took a swig of his iced tea and said, "You're kidding, right?"

"Just hear me out, General," Miles said.

"Tyler will never go for it."

"He doesn't make the hiring decisions at Gordian. I do."

"Come on, Miles. What makes you think we'd last two weeks in the same company?"

"You wouldn't even be working in the same city. We would love to have someone of your stature in D.C. as a liaison for our military contracts."

"Not everyone would love it."

With his five years of service as a two-star general in the Air Force complete, Sherman had had no choice but to retire. The total number of generals was capped, so it was either up or out, and no three-star opportunities had come his way. So for the first time in thirty-five years, Major General Locke was looking for a job.

"Has the DTRA made an offer yet?" Miles asked.

Sherman's last command was as deputy director of the Strategic Command Center for Combating Weapons of Mass Destruction. In coordination with the civilian adjunct Defense Threat Reduction Agency, his responsibility had been to develop strategies and tactics for defeating WMDs.

"Not yet," Sherman said while chewing on his final bite of sirloin.

"Whatever it is, I'll double it."

"I'm considering a lot of positions right now. How do you know you can afford me?"

"General, whatever your price is, you're worth it. You've been involved in some of the biggest weapons-development programs of the last ten years. You know everyone, and they listen to you. Gordian is the largest private engineering firm in the world. We can help with virtually any project the military contracts out to civilian defense contractors. That sounds like a buttload of synergy to me."

"Does Tyler know you're asking me?"

"He'd crap a show pony if he knew I was talking to you." Miles looked him straight in the eye when he said this. Direct. No dancing around. Sherman liked that. He wouldn't have expected any less from a former Army officer like Miles.

Sherman and his son had a testy relationship at best. Lately, they'd begun to patch things up, but working in the same company might be pushing it, especially in a company that Tyler had co-founded. No doubt he'd see Sherman's hiring as an intrusion into his space. On the other hand, spending more time together might help them mend some fences, something Sherman wanted to do even more as he got older.

"Okay," Sherman said. "Just for grins, what would the job be?"

"You would interact with the Pentagon's senior officers on appropriations that might provide business for Gordian. Part of your duties would be reviewing upcoming weapons-development programs and analyses to determine where Gordian's expertise would best fit. Of course, you would have a staff, and we would offer you full partnership after two years with the firm."

"So I'd be a salesman?"

"No. We have guys for that, but I need someone who knows how Pentagon proposals are evaluated and doled out."

Sherman leaned back and studied the ceiling. He'd commanded fighter wings, the entire First Air Force, and a department of thousands of people tasked with protecting the nation from the most hideous weapons imaginable. The thought of being some kind of glorified paper jockey didn't sit well with him.

"I don't know," he finally said.

"Just promise me you'll think about it. And I know it's not all about money for you, but the year-end partner bonuses have been spectacular the last few years."

"So that's how Tyler affords that cliff-side house."

"He's worth every penny," Miles said. "Takes on the toughest assignments and doesn't bat an eye. You know, I met him when I was still teaching at MIT. Student of mine. Tyler had a combination of brains, creativity, and guts that was rare. Unique, I'd say."

"You forgot to mention that he's also pigheaded and thinks he's always right."

"He usually is."

"And he never listens to his dad."

"How many sons do? Listen, I know he's got his faults—he's a pain in the butt whenever I want him to do some paperwork—but you should be proud of him."

"I am. He just can't get it through his thick skull sometimes."

Sherman felt a tap on his shoulder. He turned to see a waiter.

"Excuse me, sir," the waiter said. "A gentleman has asked to see you. He says that it's urgent." The waiter pointed at an Army officer standing in the doorway of the restaurant.

"Will you excuse me, Miles?"

"Of course."

Sherman stood and walked over to the officer. "Yes, Captain?" he said. The name tag said Wilson. Sherman didn't know him.

"General, I'm sorry to interrupt your lunch, but I've been asked to drive you to a briefing at the DTRA. An issue has come up, and they'd like to consult you about it."

"Now?"

"They said it was quite urgent."

"What's it about?"

"I don't know, sir. They just told me to come find you."

"They could have just called. Who's running the meeting?"

"General Horgan requested your presence."

"Wonder what Bob's up to."

The phrase was rhetorical, but Wilson shrugged anyway. "No idea, sir."

"All right. I'll be with you in a minute, Captain."

Sherman returned to the table to retrieve his briefcase. "Looks like I'm needed elsewhere," he said to Miles.

"Perhaps we could talk more about the offer over drinks later?"

"If I can make it back, sure. You have my number. Call me when you're at the bar."

They shook hands, and with his briefcase in hand, Sherman went back to the door.

"Okay, Captain, lead the way."

They got on the elevator, and a hotel waiter joined them.

"Parking level, please," the captain said, and the hotel worker pressed the button.

As they descended, something about the captain's decorations caught Sherman's eye. The ribbons on a soldier's shirt indicated the medals and commendations he had been awarded. For a moment, Sherman couldn't figure out why one ribbon looked out of place until he remembered what it signified.

The elevator dinged, opening into the underground parking structure. Captain Wilson held the door open, but Sherman didn't move.

"All right, who are you?" he said. The hotel staff member fussed with his coat as he watched them.

"What do you mean, sir?" the captain said innocently. "You need to come with me."

"I'm not going anywhere with an idiot who doesn't know that he's about forty years too young to be wearing that." He pointed to the yellow, red, and green ribbon on the alleged captain's chest. The man looked down in confusion.

"I'm not sure what you're getting at, sir."

"That's the ribbon for a Vietnam service medal, genius," Sherman said. "Did you borrow Daddy's uni?"

Wilson grinned. "Well, you got me, General. And now I've got you."

Only then did Sherman realize his mistake. He had assumed he was safe with the hotel worker as a witness. But Wilson nodded at the man, who lunged at Sherman. Before he could parry the man's arm, metal prongs jabbed into his side. Sherman dropped to the floor in agony as fifty thousand volts surged through his chest.

NINE

Grant Westfield tried not to make eye contact as he hustled onto the Bremerton ferry terminal gangway. Disembarking foot passengers were pushing past him before the vehicle ramp was lowered. Even though Tyler's car was at the stern of the ferry and would offload last, he had only a few minutes to get there before the crew would be looking for the driver.

Tyler had called Grant from the ferry and told him that he had an emergency. He needed Grant to drive his Viper off the ferry, then look for a truck that said SILVERLAKE TRANSPORT on the side. Tyler wouldn't elaborate on the reason for the strange request, but he had made it clear that his life depended on Grant's help. Grant agreed without hesitation, walking the short distance from the naval base to the ferry landing. He couldn't wait to hear the explanation.

Grant passed a crewman watching passengers go ashore. He thought the man hadn't noticed him, but he got only ten feet before he heard a yell behind him.

"Hey! Hey! We're not boarding yet."

Well, that didn't work, Grant thought as he stopped. Not that he was surprised. No matter how small he tried to make himself, he wasn't exactly inconspicuous. Difficult to ignore a six-foot-tall, 260-pound bald black guy.

Normally he liked the attention, but sometimes, like now, it didn't pay off. Time for some charm. And lying.

Grant turned and saw a skinny white guy in his thirties with long brown hair and a couple of tattoos peeking out over the collar of his shirt, tagged with the name Jervis. Grant gave Jervis a huge smile.

"Oh, I'm not going to Seattle," he said. "I just came from there. I left my bag on the seat."

"I didn't see you get off."

"That's funny. I'm usually hard to miss."

Jervis raised his eyebrows as if he agreed. "What color is your bag? I'll have somebody bring it to you."

Great. The helpful type.

"Don't bother," Grant said. "I know where it is. It'll just take me a minute."

"All right." Grant breathed a sigh of relief. "But I better see your ticket." So much for the sigh of relief.

Grant patted his pockets as if he were trying to find it. "I must have left it in my bag."

Jervis scrunched his face, deciding what to do. "It's against the rules to let anyone on without a ticket. They're pretty strict these days."

Time was running short before they'd start asking questions about why Tyler's car was still on the ferry, so Grant resorted to a tactic he loathed: pulling out the celebrity card to get something he wanted.

"Actually, the bag has some important mementos in it from my days as a pro wrestler. Don't know if you're a fan, but I used to be called the Burn."

Jervis studied Grant's face. Then his eyes widened in recognition. Grant had seen the transformation many times before. People's entire demeanor changed once they realized they were in the presence of a celebrity. Grant understood. He still talked about the time he ran into Britney Spears at a Starbucks even though he'd rather be set on fire than listen to her music.

"Right, man!" Jervis said. "I remember you. Grant Westley."

"Right." Grant didn't want to embarrass him by correcting the error. When Jervis recounted the meeting to his friends later, they'd tell him it was Westfield and give him crap for it. It was enough that the crewman had heard of him.

"You left it all behind to join the Army. Rangers or special forces. There was a great article about you in *Sports Illustrated* a few years back."

Grant didn't get stopped by fans nearly as much as he used to, but he probably would if he still had the dreadlocks he wore at the height of his fame. He'd left professional wrestling to join the military after 9/11, but a knee injury he got in combat meant that trying to resurrect his pro career after he got out wouldn't work. He sometimes missed the cheering crowds, and his notoriety occasionally came in handy.

"I swear I'll only be a minute," Grant said.

Jervis looked around and waved him in. "You're fine. Go ahead."

"Thanks." Grant waved back and jogged up the gangway. He made his way down the stairs through the now empty ferry. When he got to the vehicle deck, the last of the cars were just driving off.

The only car left was a cherry-red Dodge Viper. A crewman next to it was looking around. Grant ran up to him.

"This yours?" the man said. "I was just about to call the tow truck. Be a shame with a car as nice as this."

"Sorry I'm late," Grant said to the man as he opened the driver's door. "Bad time for a bathroom break."

He opened the glove box and found the keys Tyler had left for him. He started the car and roared out of the ferry.

Tyler was waiting for him two streets over in the SILVERLAKE TRANSPORT truck. Grant pulled up along the driver's side. Tyler leaned through the window.

"We can't get out, partner. Orders."

"We?"

A beautiful blonde peeked her head around. Grant shook his head. He definitely wanted to hear what that was about.

"Your friend can't drive a stick?" Grant asked.

"We're supposed to stay in the truck," Tyler said. "Just follow us, but not too close."

"What the hell is going on?"

With his hands out the window, Tyler quickly signed to Grant. *The truck has eyes and ears. No calls.* Tyler's deaf grandmother had taught him American Sign Language, and he in turn had taught it to Grant during their stint together in the Army.

Grant nodded, but he had no clue why the truck was bugged. He shook his head and put the Viper into gear to follow.

Tyler drove off, and Grant stayed a respectful distance behind. The rain that until now had only threatened started coming down in a patter that rippled on the Viper's cloth roof.

For thirty minutes, they drove south and west, eventually turning onto a gravel road. A rotted wooden sign read STILLAGUAMISH STONEWORKS. In less than a minute, the road ended at an abandoned quarry partially filled with water. Tyler stopped the truck at the edge of the pond.

Grant parked, flipped his rain hood up, and got out. He was halfway to the truck when Tyler and his new friend exited the cab.

"Ready to tell me what this is about?" Grant said as he approached.

Tyler waved him back. He had what looked like a canvas sack under his arm. The woman next to him didn't seem to care about the rain drenching her.

"We're leaving," he said. "Pop the trunk."

Grant hit the button and followed Tyler, who laid the item down carefully.

"What is that?"

Tyler threw the canvas aside to reveal a shiny bronze device. Grant recognized it immediately.

“Isn’t that the geolabe you built?”

“Yup.”

“Now I’m really curious.”

“I’ll explain on the way.” Tyler closed the trunk.

“You want to drive?” Grant asked. The Viper had only two seats. One of them was going to have the woman on his lap.

Tyler squinted at Grant’s bulk and shook his head. “You better.” Tyler turned to the woman. “Sorry, but it looks like it’s you and me.”

The woman brushed Tyler’s apology aside. “To get away from that bomb? Are you kidding? Get in. I’ll try not to crush you.”

No chance of that, Grant thought as he eyed her tiny frame.

They piled into the cramped cockpit, the woman perched on Tyler’s legs. Once they were seated with the doors closed, Grant turned to Tyler. “Did she just say ‘bomb’?”

“I couldn’t tell you on the phone,” Tyler said, “but there’s enough binary explosive in that truck to jump-start a volcano.”

While Grant processed that bit of news, he turned the Viper around and sped toward the exit. Tyler tapped the screen on his cell phone and put it on speaker. After one ring, a man answered.

“Are you in your car with Grant Westfield?” the man said, to Grant’s surprise. “I knew you’d get him involved at some point anyway, so I thought he should join in the fun.”

Grant shot Tyler a pointed glance, but Tyler put up a hand that said, “I’ll tell you later.”

“He followed me to the quarry just like you instructed. And we disconnected the geolabe from the bomb.”

“Drive back to the ferry. I’ll take care of the truck.”

“Why are we going back to the ferry?” Tyler asked. “Another bomb?”

“No,” the voice on the phone said. “Just that one.”

As they reached the quarry’s sign, Tyler said, “Before we go anywhere else, I want to—”

A tremendous blast shook the car. All three of them ducked instinctively. Grant mashed the pedal to the floor, throwing a plume of gravel behind him. In the rearview mirror he saw a cloud of black smoke that was already being dissipated by the pouring rain. The sound of the explosion would have been heard for miles, but no one would be able to tell where it came from. It might even be mistaken for a crack of thunder, though lightning storms were rare in the Pacific Northwest.

Grant kept driving. There was no reason to stop and go back to the truck. The only thing they'd see was tiny pieces. He wouldn't be surprised if the whole truck had been blown into the water.

"What the hell is wrong with you, you maniac!" the woman shouted.

"Good," the voice said. "You're still alive."

"Your concern is touching," Tyler said.

"Do you think that explosion would have been big enough to sink the ferry? Be honest."

"Yes. What's your point?"

"So, Locke, if that's what I was willing to do to a boat full of innocent people, imagine what I'm willing to do to your father."

TEN

Tyler looked at Grant and saw the same flash of alarm on his face that he felt in his gut.

"What does that mean?" Stacy said.

"Now to your mission—" Orr continued.

Tyler hung up. He had to warn his father, but the certainty in the caller's voice made him fear that he was already too late.

He found his dad's number and called. The phone was answered on the second ring.

"Dad, it's Tyler—"

"Nope," Orr said. "I thought you'd be calling, so I had my colleagues forward his phone to mine."

Tyler gripped the phone so hard that he nearly crushed it. "If you hurt my father in any way, my mission will be to hunt you down and drain the life out of you one drop at a time."

"Yes, you're upset, but I'm not going to harm him unless you decide not to help me. Or if you call the FBI."

"Do you have any idea who you've kidnapped?"

"Of course I do, because I'm not a grade-A moron. Major General Sherman Locke is newly retired and looking for work, so he's not going to be missed right away by anyone but you."

Tyler thought about that and knew he was right. If Sherman had still been in the Air Force, the Pentagon would have contacted the FBI within hours of his disappearance, not least because he was a military officer with access to top-secret information. But out of the military he was just another civilian who was free to do as he pleased. If he took off without telling anyone where he was going, that was his business.

"How do I know he's all right?" Tyler asked.

"He's unavailable to talk at the moment because he's being taken to a secure location, but when he's safe and sound, I'll send you verification that he's fine."

"What do you want?"

"First, put the phone back on speaker. Stacy should hear this, too."

Tyler switched it on. "Go ahead."

"I did what you asked, you bastard!" Stacy yelled. "Now you hold up your end of the bargain!"

"I'm not letting your sister go just yet," Orr said.

Tyler and Grant looked at each other in confusion, then at Stacy.

"Sister?" Tyler said.

"Good. Stacy followed her instructions and didn't tell you about Carol. For that, Stacy's sister will get to keep all her fingers."

"No! You let her go!"

"Not so fast," Orr said. "Now that you've passed your test, I have a mission for you."

"What mission?" Tyler asked.

"I want you to find the location of the Midas Touch for me."

Tyler wasn't sure what Orr meant. "Is that the code word for something?"

"No code word. No metaphor. No brand name. I mean the actual Midas Touch that can turn objects to gold."

Grant snorted in disbelief. Tyler could only gape. That was about the last thing he would have guessed Orr was going to say. Tyler thought the kidnapping was going to be about paying a ransom or maybe even using his top-secret clearance to gain access to government files.

But the Midas Touch? It was ridiculous. Everyone knew it was a myth about the corrupting power of greed. King Midas was given the wondrous ability to turn anything he touched into gold, which he initially thought was a blessing. But when his feast of celebration became inedible at his touch, Midas realized that this talent was a curse. He begged the gods to rid him of it, and they did, but not before he accidentally turned his own daughter into gold.

"Say that again," Tyler said.

"You heard me right," Orr said. "The Midas Touch. The two of you are going to find it, or your father and Stacy's sister are dead. If you find it, I'll make a trade with you."

"Are you serious?"

"Deadly. I promise you that the Midas Touch does in fact exist."

"Okay," Tyler said slowly. He was already wondering how he could give the impression of going along with this wild-goose chase while figuring out how to find his father.

"I've seen it for myself, and I can prove it to you."

"If you've seen it, why do you need us to find it?"

"That's a story better told in person. Meet me at 1 P.M. outside the southwest corner of Safeco Field and I'll tell it to you. Just you and Stacy. No police and no Westfield, or both your father and her sister are gone."

The Viper's clock read 10:10. There had to be a ferry back to Seattle before noon.

"We'll be there," Tyler said. He hung up and closed his eyes, trying to absorb the news of his father's abduction. He concentrated on breathing, because it felt as if he'd had the wind knocked out of him.

They were all quiet for a moment until Grant broke the silence.

"By the way, I'm Grant Westfield," he said. "I'll be your chauffeur back to the ferry today."

He held his hand out to Stacy, who gave it a firm shake. "Stacy Benedict."

"Yeah, you're from *Chasing the Past.* I didn't recognize you at first."

"Thanks for picking us up."

"Anything for Tyler. But would you mind telling me why some lunatic just blew up a truck you were driving?"

Tyler explained about the puzzle to deactivate the bomb, that it was some kind of test to prove to Orr that they could carry out his insane quest.

"And how did he know my name?" Grant said. "Who is this guy?"

"You met him once. His name is Jordan Orr."

"Wait a minute. The guy who hired you to build the geolabe?"

Tyler nodded. "And I'm guessing Stacy knows him, too."

"Only since this morning," she said. "I was in town for a fund-raiser, and I get a call this morning that my sister, Carol, was kid-napped. All he told me was to get on the ferry and not to tell you about her or he would hurt her."

Tyler dug his fingernails into his palms until the knuckles were white. He'd never been angrier in his life than he was at that mo-ment. If he had known about Stacy's kidnapped sister, he might have been able to warn his father in time. Tyler wanted to yell and scream and pound his fists against the dashboard. But it was Orr he wanted to throttle, not Stacy. She was as much a pawn in this as he was.

Tyler shook his head and took a deep breath until the moment passed.

"It's good we decided not to talk in the truck with Orr listening in," he said to Stacy. "We're going to have to be very careful deal-ing with him."

She turned to him, and Tyler saw her faced etched with fear. "Just promise me that my sister will be all right. I know you can't really promise that, but do it anyway."

Tyler nodded. "I promise. We'll find a way to get them both back safely."

"There's something I want to know," Stacy said. "If you built that device, the geolabe, how did Orr get hold of it?"

"I was approached by Orr last year, after Miles twisted my arm to go on your show. I mentioned on the program that I had an interest in Archimedes. Orr showed me a translation from an ancient Greek document with instructions for building an object called a geolabe and told me it was from a private collector. It sounded like an intriguing job, so I said yes."

"And you weren't suspicious of this mysterious request?"

Tyler nodded. "Mildly, but the project seemed harmless enough. I had one of my guys, Aiden MacKenna, look into the documents to see what he could find, just out of curiosity. Nothing came up. It wasn't until a month after I delivered the completed project that Scotland Yard released a long-lost photo of a manuscript page that matched my document verbatim. Only then did we realize that it had been stolen."

"Did you report it to the police?"

"Yes, but by that time Orr was tipped off and disappeared."

"How long did it take you to build this thing?"

"About three months," Tyler said. "Without Gordian's engineering resources, it would have taken a lot longer to decipher the schematics."

"That doesn't make sense, though," Stacy said.

"Why?"

"Because if he blew up the ferry, the geolabe would have been destroyed along with it. Why did he risk losing something that would take so long to build again if we couldn't solve that puzzle?"

Tyler's skin prickled at the thought of how close they had been to becoming permanent denizens of Puget Sound.

"Orr must have decided that you and I were the only people on the planet who could solve the Archimedes puzzle, so if we failed the geolabe was worthless to him. Now that he knows we can operate it, we've become indispensable to him. We're a package deal along with the geolabe."

"This is crazy," Stacy said.

Tyler shook his head at the colossal understatement. "Which part? That Orr thinks the Midas Touch exists or that he thinks Archimedes constructed a device that will lead us to it?"

ELEVEN

The van slowed, but with the blindfold on, Sherman Locke couldn't tell whether it was because they were approaching another turn or because they had reached their destination.

They'd been traveling for over an hour, mostly at highway speeds, which meant they could be in D.C., Virginia, Maryland, Pennsylvania, or West Virginia. After he was hit with the Taser, a cloth had been stuck in his mouth and his wrists and ankles were cuffed. He was thrown into the back of a panel van, with the fake hotel staffer driving and the phony Army officer in back with him. He was frisked thoroughly, and his car keys, wallet, and phone were taken.

Before the blindfold went on, Sherman saw a girl lying unconscious on the floor of the van. There were no bruises or blood, which made him think she'd been drugged. He didn't recognize her, so he couldn't fathom why the two of them had been kidnapped. Blond and in her late twenties, the girl had a runner's physique. That would be helpful when the time came to make an escape attempt.

His gag had been removed for the drive, but Sherman hadn't been able to get anything out of his stoic captor, whose sole response was to tell him to shut up or he'd put the cloth back in. But if he was trying to intimidate Sherman, he might as well piss up a flagpole.

As a former fighter pilot, Sherman had taken the Air Force's Survival, Evasion, Resistance, and Escape course, but that SERE training had been decades ago. Now he wished he'd taken a refresher. Maybe he wouldn't have been captured so easily. At this point, he was more annoyed than anything else.

How he handled the situation would depend on why the two of them had been taken hostage. Was it just a chance to earn some quick cash? Maybe the woman was also involved with the Pentagon and the kidnappers wanted to torture information out of them. The well-executed operation suggested that these men weren't a couple of hustlers who had hatched this scheme in their crack house. The fact that they had abducted Sherman in broad daylight, exposing their faces to hundreds of witnesses, meant they were either desperate or had a well-thought-out plan. Sherman guessed the latter.

The van came to a stop. Sherman heard the clank of a garage door opening. It was industrial, too large and noisy for a residential garage.

The van nudged forward and stopped, and the engine turned off. His kidnapper waited until the garage door was closed again before he removed the blindfold.

The Taser was trained on him, the threat obvious. It was a dual-operation model that could either be loaded with a single-use cartridge that would shoot the electric leads thirty feet or be used without a cartridge by making direct contact with the subject. Since he was cuffed, the single-use cartridge had been removed.

The van door opened, and the guy calling himself Wilson gestured with the Taser for Sherman to get out.

Struggling against the cuffs, Sherman climbed to his feet and hopped through the door. The sound of his shoes hitting the floor echoed through a warehouse cavernous enough to hold twenty tractor-trailers. Fluorescent lights flickered above the windowless space. With the power active, it was unlikely they were squatters. The building looked as if it was in good repair and was probably in a warehouse district. If Sherman could make it outside, he might be able to find help quickly.

The warehouse was empty of the expected shelves and boxes. Instead, a small grouping of furniture sat near the van: four cots, six large tables, four chairs, and a trash can that had been ignored. Empty pizza boxes and Chinese-food containers were piled on the tables, which held a TV, two laptops, and a wireless router. There was also some metalworking equipment: drills, soldering guns, an arc welder, and a large box of tools. Metal shavings and discarded scraps littered the floor.

Beyond the furniture was a line of twelve steel barrels. Wooden crates were stacked behind them, but Sherman couldn't see any writing that might reveal what they held.

On one side of the warehouse, a peninsula of four rooms jutted from the cinder-block wall, with two doors facing the front of the warehouse and two facing the back. The doors had six-inch-by-six-inch cutouts where windows would normally be, but otherwise the rooms were completely sealed. Sherman could make out the remains of glass squares on the floor. The panes were the size of the cutouts and were cracked but intact because they were held together by wire mesh inside the glass, indicating that the rooms had been secured for valuable items. They'd been removed and replaced with crude metal plates that could be swung back and forth.

Sherman guessed where he'd be staying for the duration.

"What now, *Captain* Wilson?" he asked.

"Call me Gaul," the man said, disregarding Sherman's sarcasm. "And before we show you to your room, we have some business to take care of." He pulled Sherman to a chair set in front of a bare concrete wall and said, "Sit."

"What am I, a dog?"

"Funny. In the chair."

"Why?"

"Because if you don't, I'll Tase you again, and then you'll sit anyway."

Sherman shuffled over to the chair and sat. "What do you want?"

"From you? Nothing. This is just a little proof for your son, to show that you're still breathing."

So this *was* about money. If Tyler would be seeing this, Sherman had to get him whatever info he could.

Gaul went to the van and removed a duffel bag. At one of the tables he took out a ski mask, newspaper, and a video camera.

"Phillips," he said. The other man, who had now changed into a black sweater, took the ski mask and the front page of the newspaper from Gaul.

Phillips moved behind Sherman and put the blindfold back on him.

"Am I going somewhere else?"

"We know you were in the Air Force," Gaul said, focusing the camera, "so we're just making sure you don't blink any messages by Morse code. You'll answer my question and nothing else. This isn't going out live, so don't bother trying to blurt out anything. Phillips, start over here so I can get a close-up of the paper." After a moment, Gaul said, "Good. Now move back so we can see the paper beside the general."

Phillips did so until he was standing behind Sherman.

"What is your name?" Gaul said.

"Are you asking me or Phillips?" Sherman said. He heard Gaul make a disgusted grunt.

"Apparently I wasn't clear," Gaul said. "Give him a ride."

Sherman jerked as a jolt of electricity shot through him. His hands clenched in agony until the shock abated, and he slumped in the chair.

"Now let's keep going. I can edit that out. Name?"

"Sherman Locke," he said through clenched teeth.

"That wasn't so hard, was it? That's all I needed."

The blindfold came off. Phillips wrenched Sherman to his feet and led him to a room facing the rear. Gaul opened the door, pushing Sherman inside without taking the cuffs off. He slammed it shut and locked it with a dead bolt that had no keyhole on the inside.

The room was the size of a prison cell. The ceiling and walls were made of cinder blocks. The only contents were a cot bolted to the floor and a bucket. One bulb jutted from the ceiling out of reach. Sherman had stayed in worse conditions, but not for long.

"Here's how this is going to work," Gaul said, peering through the hole in the door. "You're going to be staying in this room for the duration."

"Which is how long?" Sherman said.

"That's up to your son."

"And I don't even get to take the cuffs off?"

Gaul tossed the keys through the hole. Sherman had to squat to pick them up. After he uncuffed himself, Gaul demanded the keys and the cuffs back.

"When we want to bring you out," Gaul said, "you'll cuff yourself again. If you don't, you get another ride. You can scream all you want, but all you'll do is make yourself hoarse. We aren't near any occupied buildings. When we eat, you eat. Any questions? No? Good." The plate covering the hole slammed shut.

"It's Carol's turn," Gaul said, and his footsteps retreated.

Massaging his wrists, Sherman started plotting his escape.

TWELVE

Stacy agreed with Tyler that Orr's warning to come alone should be taken seriously. After dropping Grant off at the naval base so that he could tie up some loose ends on the ammunition depot project and get his car, she and Tyler headed back to the dock, where they made it in time for the 11:10 ferry to Seattle. Stacy sat in the Viper's passenger seat as Tyler idled in the rain, waiting for the ferry to empty. She found the metronomic beating of the wipers soothing, reminding her of sleepy childhood rides in her father's pickup after he'd taken his daughters to a movie on a drizzly evening.

"More comfortable now?" Tyler asked.

While she had been sitting on his lap during the drive back to the ferry, she noticed that Tyler had respectfully kept his hands to the sides, but he was so much bigger than she that his arms had still enveloped her. Whether it was intended or not, being ensconced like that had given her a sense of security.

If the crew of her TV show heard that, they wouldn't believe it. The globe-trotting adventurer who would eagerly crawl into dark, spider-infested tombs needed a hug.

"I must have sounded idiotic back there," she said.

"What sounded idiotic?"

"When I asked you to promise that Carol would be all right. It's just that the thought of losing her is something I've never faced before."

"I know how you feel," Tyler said. "I have a sister, too."

"Why did he take my sister but your father?"

"My sister is hiking in Patagonia right now. I don't even know if *I* could find her."

"So you're not going to try to reach her? Tell her that your father's been kidnapped?"

Tyler shook his head. "She'd want to get the FBI involved. Orr warned us not to."

"Do you think Orr would really kill them if we brought in the FBI?"

"He's been totally unpredictable so far. I wouldn't put it past him."

"But the FBI may be able to find them."

"They might find them dead. We can go it on our own for a while. My company, Gordian, has extensive resources, and Grant will help us. If we call the FBI, we lose control. The Feds will be running the show. If this were a simple money drop, I'd bring them in. But this situation is far more complicated. And it would be almost impossible to keep Orr from finding out that the FBI was involved. It would be a risk, and once we called them, we wouldn't be able to undo it."

"I don't like that. Losing control. And if the press gets wind of this, it'll become front-page news. One of the pitfalls of celebrity."

"Then we play along. For now. Is that okay with you? If we're going to get through this, we need to work together."

Stacy nodded. "Play along for now."

The cars started loading onto the ferry, and Tyler put the Viper into gear. They left it on the vehicle deck, and Stacy took a detour to the restroom on the passenger deck.

As she washed her hands in front of the mirror, she didn't like the defeated look of the woman staring back at her. It wasn't the wet, bedraggled hair and the lack of makeup that bothered her. She'd looked worse on many episodes of her show, and viewers seemed to like her willingness to reveal that TV hosts actually sweat and get dirty. But she prided herself on keeping a positive attitude at all times on camera, and at the moment she looked anything but positive.

She took a deep breath and stood straighter. Orr wasn't going to beat her that easily. She was taking back control. When she returned to their seats, she found Tyler putting his phone away.

"Any news?" Stacy asked.

"That was Gordian's president, Miles Benson," Tyler said "He had lunch with my father."

"Today? When was your father kidnapped?"

"Must have been right after that. I asked Miles if anything unusual happened. He said my dad was called away on urgent business by an Army officer, but he didn't get a good look at who it was. He's going to question the staff discreetly and fly back here this evening."

Stacy leaned toward him, her elbows on her knees, a pose she often took when her production crew was brainstorming ideas for upcoming episodes.

"The question is, how are we going to play along with Orr?" she said. "The Midas Touch is a Greek fable. To consider it a true story is ridiculous."

"Sometimes legends have a basis in reality," Tyler said with a faraway look.

"True. Some scholars believe Midas was a real person. There's speculation that he was a king in Phrygia—part of modern-day Turkey—although he wasn't born there."

"Where was he from?"

"Some stories say Macedonia. Some say even farther away. No one really knows. But they say that Midas arrived as the son of a peasant at the exact moment that an oracle prophesied that the next leader of Phrygia would appear on a humble wagon. They dubbed Midas's father king on the spot."

"Lucky him."

"And you'll like this: the king's name was Gordias. When Midas succeeded his father as king, he dedicated the wagon to Zeus for bringing him this good fortune and declared that whoever could untie the fiendishly complicated knot on its yoke would rule all Asia."

"You're talking about the Gordian knot. Alexander the Great was the one who solved the puzzle. Except he simply cut it instead of trying to untie it."

Stacy smiled. "I assume your company Gordian Engineering is named for the Gordian knot."

"It is. The seemingly unsolvable problem with a bold solution. But I didn't know that Midas was the one who'd tied it."

"You learn something new every day. That's why I love my job."

"What happened to Midas?"

"No one knows, but there are several theories. One is that he's buried in Turkey. Someone even claims to have found his tomb. Another theory is that he was driven out by invading Persians. The myth says that Midas offended one of the gods and was afflicted with the ears of a donkey for his crime. He fled Phrygia in shame and was never heard from again."

"All of that makes for a great story," Tyler said, "but you're right that the part about the Midas Touch is absurd. Alchemists have tried to create their own version of the Midas Touch for centuries by transmuting lead into gold. They failed every time, because it's physically impossible."

Stacy hadn't taken a science course since high school, so her grasp of chemistry was rudimentary at best.

"Why is it impossible?" she asked. "Maybe it's some hidden formula that we've never found."

Tyler laughed. "Unless the hidden formula involves a fission reaction, it won't work."

"Fission as in nuclear?"

"Lead has a higher atomic weight than gold, meaning it has more protons, so the only way lead can become gold is if it sheds protons. Removing protons from an atom's nucleus is the definition of a nuclear reaction. I suppose you could accomplish that in a nuclear reactor, but it would be so expensive it wouldn't be worth the trouble."

"So you think Orr is crazy?"

"Certifiable if he believes in magic."

"I can see why he wants *you* in on this. You built the geolabe. But why me? There are a thousand other PhD classicists out there."

"My humanities studies weren't a real priority in college," Tyler said. "What are Classics, exactly?"

"The study of classical Greece and Rome."

"Which is why you know Greek. Latin, too?"

"I got my undergraduate degree in linguistics. I'm fluent in Greek, Latin, Italian, French, and German."

Tyler whistled. "That's amazing. I wish I knew some foreign languages. Just don't have a knack for it, I guess. Unless you count ASL. My grandmother was deaf. I also taught it to Grant."

"Sign language counts," Stacy said, "but I can't sign. Just verbal languages."

"So why Classics?"

"I grew up on a farm near Des Moines. My parents didn't have a lot of money, so we never traveled except to go camping in Minnesota. I always wanted to see all those wonderful cities in Europe, so I thought getting a Classics degree would help me do that. Halfway through grad school, I realized research wasn't my calling. I forced myself to finish anyway, but I still had a hundred thousand in student loans to pay back, so when I heard about auditions for *Chasing the Past* I signed up. I'm not an actress, but they wanted someone with solid credentials rather than some bimbo reading a teleprompter, so I got the job. I paid my loans off in one year."

"Your parents must be proud. They still in Iowa?"

"They've passed away. They were both smokers. Cancer got them."

"I'm sorry."

"It's just me and my sister now. She was in law school. *Is* in law school, dammit."

Tyler gave her knee a squeeze. Just a small gesture of sympathy, but she appreciated it.

His phone pinged. "Probably Grant," he said, but when he looked at the screen, his expression became grim.

"What?" she asked.

"It's Orr. He says to check my e-mail."

After a few taps, he leaned in closer and expanded a video on the screen. Stacy heard some words, but she couldn't make them out.

Tyler angled the phone so that Stacy could see it and restarted the video. The opening frame was centered on a newspaper with today's date. Then it receded until she could see a man in a black ski mask standing next to another man sitting in a chair. The seated man appeared to be in his late fifties or early sixties and was dressed in a suit. His wrists and ankles were cuffed, but he didn't look injured. In fact, he looked incredibly fit, and not just for his age. He was blindfolded, but his strong jaw and short brown hair left little doubt that she was looking at Tyler's father.

A voice in the video said, "Name." The picture changed slightly, as if it had been edited. The seated man then confirmed her suspicions.

"Sherman Locke," he said with a sonorous baritone, reminiscent of Tyler's voice but deepened with age.

The proof-of-life video abruptly ended. Stacy closed her eyes and saw in her mind a replay of a similar video she'd received this morning of Carol bound and unconscious.

She shook it off and looked up at Tyler expecting to see rage. To her amazement, he was smiling.

"That son of a bitch," he said with a chuckle. "Something tells me he's not going down without a fight."

THIRTEEN

Tyler could tell Orr was no fool by the spot he'd picked for the rendezvous. Only fifteen minutes remained until the Wednesday-afternoon baseball game started, and a crowd of fans massed outside the southwest entrance to the stadium waiting to get in to see the hometown Mariners take on the Angels. Street vendors barked "Programs!" every few seconds, and the sweet smell of kettle corn drifted over them. The worst of the rain had passed, but the roof of the steel-and-brick Safeco Field was closed to shield the fans from the occasional drizzle.

On a normal day, the trip from the ferry dock to the stadium would take just a minute, but the stop-and-go traffic extended the drive by a factor of fifteen. By the time Tyler parked the Viper in the garage, it was 12:30. He bought a couple of hot dogs and some drinks from a street vendor to eat while he and Stacy waited. Neither of them was particularly hungry, but Tyler had learned in the Army that you had to keep up your strength even more than usual in stressful situations.

"So what's Orr look like?" Stacy asked between bites.

"Dark hair," he said. "Naturally tan. Brown eyes. A little shorter than I am. Roman nose broken and not put back together right. Missing the tip of his left pinkie. Not the prettiest guy to look at."

"Can't wait to meet him."

Twenty minutes went by. They leaned against the wall next to the ticket window, Stacy looking in one direction, Tyler in the other. Twice Stacy pointed out someone that fit the description, but neither of them was Orr.

Right on time, Tyler saw Orr approach from around the corner. He looked just as Tyler remembered, wearing a bulky Mariners jacket and cap, with a backpack slung over his shoulder. His hands were in his pockets. He fit right in with the fans still streaming past.

No one was with him. He came to a stop just out of arm's reach. They appraised each other for a few moments. Tyler fought the urge to strangle the life out of his smug eyes.

"We came alone," Tyler said.

"I know," Orr said with a grin. "I've been watching. You really shouldn't wolf down your food like that." His eyes went to Stacy. "You look even hotter in person."

"Screw you," Stacy said.

"Don't I wish."

"How about we make a deal?" Tyler said. "You release my father and Stacy's sister right now, and I won't kill you."

"I'm going to have to pass on that fine offer."

"Or maybe we'll make a swap." Tyler nodded to two patrol officers working the intersection. "I bet those policemen over there would give me a hand."

Orr waggled a finger at him. "You know I wouldn't have come here without thinking of that. Remember that binary explosive? I've got about ten pounds of it under this jacket and a trigger in my other pocket. What happened to that truck could happen here if you try something stupid."

Stacy gasped and glanced at the crowds of families around her. "You wouldn't."

"Honey, you have no idea what I'd do."

"I agree with her," Tyler said. "If I put as much planning as you did into this operation, I wouldn't literally blow it like this."

Orr pursed his lips. "I don't know you very well, Locke, but I can already see what your weakness is."

"Oh yeah? What's that?"

"You think everyone has to be as sensible and logical as you are."

"And you're not?"

"The brave do what they can. The desperate do what they must. The crazy do what you least expect. Where do you think I fit in?"

Tyler mulled that over. Orr seemed to be smart, sane, and rational, but he did want them to find something as outlandish as the Midas Touch. Tyler really didn't know what was coming next, and the hand still in Orr's pocket made him nervous, so he had no choice but to continue the status quo.

"Okay," Tyler said. "We're just going to talk. You said you had proof that the Midas Touch exists?" Tyler couldn't wait to see what constituted proof in Orr's mind.

"I do," Orr said. "But first I have to tell you a story."

"A story?" Stacy said. "We know the Midas story."

"That's not the story I'm going to tell."

"My point is that you're sending us on a wild-goose chase," Stacy said. "The Midas Touch doesn't exist."

"I beg to differ," Orr said, "and I'll tell you why. Because I've seen it in action."

Tyler couldn't suppress a guffaw. "You've seen the Midas Touch? You mean, you actually met the old king himself."

"In a way, yes."

"How?"

Orr heaved the backpack off his shoulder and lowered it slowly to the ground. By the way it sagged, Tyler guessed it was carrying one item the size of a loaf of bread.

"When I was nine years old," Orr said, "my parents took me on a trip to Italy. Naples. The homeland, if you couldn't guess by looking at me. While I was there, I spent a lot of time roaming the streets with a girl named Gia. It was when we were exploring the tunnels that we found it."

"The tunnels?" Tyler asked.

"Naples is built on volcanic tuff. The Greeks, who founded the city, discovered that the tuff was very easy to carve into. They tunneled into it for building material, but they soon realized that they could dig cisterns and link them to aqueducts carrying water from nearby aquifers and lakes. There are miles of ancient tunnels snaking under Naples, many of which have never been fully explored."

"And that's where you found Midas?" Stacy asked, the contempt in her voice apparent.

Orr nodded, a fire in his eyes. "I'll never forget it as long as I live. We found a chamber made entirely of gold, including a solid-gold cube in the center that was six feet on each side. And on top of this cube rested the golden statue of a girl. She was entirely intact except that she was missing one hand."

Now Tyler had no doubt the guy was crazy. Why would he walk away from something like that? Wouldn't he have told someone?

"So what's your proof?" he asked Orr. "I don't suppose you got a couple of photos." Even if he did, what good was that in the age of Photoshop and special effects?

"Better. I've been waiting all morning to show this to you." Orr hefted the backpack and held it out to Tyler. "Be careful. And don't take the contents out of the bag."

The bag was heavier than Tyler thought it would be. He gently set the pack on the ground and unzipped it. He knelt with Stacy next to it and peered inside.

At first the interior of the bag was too dark for them to see anything, so Tyler twisted the bag to let in more light. During the move, he felt the spongy give of Styrofoam, not the hardness he was expecting from an object so dense. Then something reflected the cloudy sky with a yellow metallic glow, and Tyler understood what he was looking at.

Stacy gasped at the sight.

Set carefully into the packing material was a golden hand.

FOURTEEN

Stacy couldn't believe what she was seeing. The golden hand ended at the wrist. But what made the hand even more remarkable was that it wasn't solid.

Tyler lifted it out of the Styrofoam a few inches so that they could see it more clearly. The exposed veins, ligaments, muscles, and bones in the cutaway of the wrist were shaped with exquisite detail down to the smallest capillary. Every pore and wrinkle on the back of the hand was replicated. Even the marrow of bones was represented in its delicate latticework. It was as if they were looking at a cross-section drawing in an anatomy textbook.

"The missing hand of Midas's daughter," Orr said proudly. "I acquired it last year. It matches the sculpture I saw all those years ago."

"This can't be real," Tyler said.

Stacy shook her head slowly. "I've seen this hand before."

Tyler looked at her in shock. "You have?"

"It was all over the news last year," she said. "Someone broke into a London auction house and cleaned out one of their vaults. The most valuable item taken was a golden hand." She remembered the theft because the initial inspection of the hand baffled appraisers, who could not even speculate as to how it had been made.

"I told you this was no wild-goose chase," Orr said.

"You also killed two guards in the process."

Orr shrugged. "They were in the way."

Stacy's lip curled in disgust at his cavalier attitude toward murder.

"But this can't be a real hand," Tyler said. "It has to be a sculpture."

"If you'll look closely, you'll see that it would be impossible to sculpt that kind of detail or use a mold to cast it."

Stacy inspected the hand again and saw that Orr was right. The way the structures overlapped and disappeared into the cavities inside the hand would defy the efforts of even the most skilled craftsman.

"How much would something like this be worth?" she wondered aloud.

Orr answered. "About eighty thousand dollars at today's prices. Just for the weight of the gold, of course. I'd bet the hand itself would fetch several million at auction. If you could find a buyer, that is. Stolen property is hard to get rid of."

"Why are you showing this to us?" Tyler asked Orr.

"Because I need you to believe that what you're searching for really exists. Otherwise, I'm just a crackpot with some idiotic quest that can't possibly be achieved. You'll just go through the motions hoping you can figure out some way to find your father, which won't happen, by the way."

"You've got everything figured out, haven't you?" Tyler said.

Orr grinned again. "Not everything. That's why I need you two."

"All right," Tyler said. "We'll do it your way."

Orr held out his hand. "I'll take the bag back." Tyler zipped it back up and gave it to him.

"What now?" Stacy said.

"Suppose we believe your story," Tyler said. "The Midas Touch existed, and there's a buried treasure somewhere under Naples. You've seen it before. You know where it is. Why don't you just go get it yourself? Why go to all this trouble?"

"Just because I've seen it before doesn't mean I know how to find it."

"What does that mean?" Stacy said.

"It's a long and complicated story, but it boils down to this. There are two ways to get to the treasure. I can't go the way I've been before for reasons that you don't need to know, which means I need the second way to find it. Archimedes' way. Using the map he created."

"Archimedes lived over twenty-two hundred years ago. Do you really think that map still exists? Or that it even still applies? Naples has been built over by the Greeks, Syracusans, Romans, Italians. Not to mention Vesuvius blowing up every once in a while, covering everything with ash."

"When Gia and I were in the tunnels, we came across one cistern where we saw light coming through a well opening far above our heads. That's the entry point I'm looking for. Unfortunately, there are thousands of wells in Naples, not all of which are documented, and most of which have been plugged up."

"Why the test on the ferry?" Tyler said.

"I couldn't hire you for the job, could I?" Orr said. "You'd turn me in. Now that I know that you can solve Archimedes' puzzle, I think you can figure out where the map is. And I have a time limit."

"What's the deadline?" Stacy said, and cringed when she realized the double meaning.

"You're funny," Orr said. "I need to have the map in my hands by Sunday night. In Naples."

"Are you kidding?" Tyler said. "It's Wednesday. You want us to solve a twenty-two-hundred-year-old riddle in just four days?"

"I don't have any choice. If I haven't found Midas's tomb by then, the Fox will get it."

"Who's the Fox?" Stacy said.

"It's Gia's nickname. We're in a race to find it first. She would kill you in a second if she thought you were anywhere near finding it, so you'll want to be careful."

"But we have no idea where to start!"

"You will. The night I acquired the golden hand, I also retrieved an ancient manuscript written by Archimedes himself. Luckily, I was able to get to it before it was photographed and appraised for the auction catalog."

"That's where you got the instructions for building the geolabe," Tyler said.

"Right. I had a translation done by a retired Classics professor, but he was in his eighties and not up to the challenge of a mission like this."

"Who is he?"

"It doesn't really matter, because he is currently dead."

By the look in Orr's eyes, she doubted that the professor died of old age.

"I'll be e-mailing you a file of photographs of the Archimedes Codex as well as the translation," Orr said. "That should give you a good head start in your search, but I'm sure we missed something. Your job is to figure out what it was. I want daily updates on your progress. If you fail to deliver an update, or I think you're holding back, I will remove an ear from both Sherman and Carol. Understand?"

Stacy swallowed hard.

"We'll give you the updates," Tyler said, "but we want proof that my father and Stacy's sister are all right."

"I've already sent you proof-of-life videos."

"I want one every day, with proof that their ears are intact. You miss a day, and this is over."

Orr thought about it, then nodded. "Fair enough. Once a day." He looked around at the crowd hustling for one of the four entrances to get into the game that had just started. "It looks like it's time for me to go. I'll be in touch." Orr slung the backpack over his shoulder.

"That's it?" Stacy said.

"Understand that this is a once-in-a-lifetime opportunity for me, so I take it very seriously. You should, too. I'll be in Naples on Sunday. If you can't be there with the solution to my problem, don't bother coming."

As the skies opened up with another downpour, Orr melted into the sea of humanity. Stacy wanted to run him down and pound his head into the pavement, but that wouldn't help her sister, and she'd get blown up in the process.

"I want to kill him," she said. "I've never said that before about a person and really meant it."

Tyler, who was also staring at Orr, just nodded. They kept watching until Orr walked around the corner and disappeared.

FIFTEEN

Tyler was eager to read the documents that Orr had e-mailed to them, but Stacy insisted on stopping at her downtown hotel first to get into dry clothes. The plan was to then go back to Tyler's house, where they had more room to spread out. While she changed, Tyler went to Gordian's headquarters to print out the documents and check out a hunch he had about the geolabe. An hour later, he was back at her hotel.

Stacy came out wearing the same jacket and boots, but a fresh shirt and jeans. Tyler expected her to be carrying nothing more than her briefcase, so he was surprised to see her carry-on trailing behind as well.

"Pop the trunk," she said as she reached the back of the Viper.

Tyler swung around in his seat. "What are you doing?"

"If we're going to be working on this all night, there's no sense in bringing me back here. It'll just waste time."

"So you're just inviting yourself to stay at my place?"

"Relax. It's not like I'm planning to throw myself at you. I'm being efficient. Besides, it's not like you're married."

Tyler glanced down at his ringless hand. He had been married once and wore the ring for a long time after she died, but it now sat in his nightstand drawer. His love for Karen would never diminish, but he'd decided to treasure her memory by moving forward with his life.

He looked back up at Stacy. "How do you know I don't have a girlfriend?" Tyler didn't object to her staying at his place. He was just amused by her brazen forwardness.

"Oh," Stacy said as if she'd never even considered that. "Do you?"

Tyler had had one relationship since he became a widower. He'd really wanted the long-distance affair with Dilara to work out, but maintaining their connection through phone calls and e-mails had been difficult. Most of the time she was in Turkey excavating Noah's Ark, while he was all over the rest of the world. They kept in contact, but developing a relationship wasn't in the cards when they were separated by ten thousand miles most of the year.

"No," he said with feigned indignation, "but you don't have to seem so surprised." He clicked the trunk release.

"Sorry," Stacy said as she lifted her bag in. "I just figured you were like me. Driven. Workaholic. No time for romantic entanglements."

"It's like talking to a mirror."

She picked up the thick folder of papers from the passenger seat and got in.

"Are these the pages Orr sent?" she said.

Tyler nodded and put the car in gear. "I made two English copies for us, plus the original in Greek for you."

Within ten minutes they had entered the Magnolia neighborhood. He turned into the driveway of his two-story Mediterranean-style villa perched on a cliff overlooking Puget Sound and downtown Seattle. He pulled the Viper into the middle bay of a three-car garage, a Ducati motorcycle next to a workbench on the right, and a Porsche SUV with a flat tire on the left.

Tyler pointed at the Porsche's tire and said, "That's why we were crammed into the Viper today. I don't normally take it out in the rain."

When they got inside, Stacy walked over to the windows. "Carol would love this view."

Tyler set her bag down in the hall. "You can have the spare bedroom on the right. The sheets are reasonably clean."

Stacy shot him a *get-real* look.

"Kidding," he said. "I wash them daily."

"I'll assume it's somewhere in between."

She took a spin around the living room, then checked out the kitchen, running her hands over the granite countertop and the cherry cabinets. "This is some house. Gordian must pay pretty well."

Tyler took a seat and pulled out the three packets of paper. "You don't have much of a filter, do you?"

"I'm just saying it's not like you're hiding the fact that you make money. A mansion. Red sports car. Porsche. Motorcycle."

"As a partner in the firm, I am adequately compensated, and I enjoy the fruits of my labor."

"Good for you, Dr. Locke."

"Shall we get started, Dr. Benedict?"

"Got anything to drink?"

Tyler nodded toward the fridge. "Help yourself. I'll take a Diet Coke."

Drinks in hand, Tyler first showed Stacy the other side of the geolabe, which had been hidden from her when it was connected to the bomb. While the front had two dials with Greek writing labeling the discrete points on each dial, the opposing face had a single dial that was divided evenly into 360 individual notches and numbered every thirty notches, like the points on a compass. Tyler didn't know what they were for, and Stacy suggested that the answer might lie in the manuscript.

They spent the rest of the afternoon reading the translation of the Archimedes Codex, with Stacy referring often to the photocopy of the original Greek. Tyler had seen some of the document before while he was building the geolabe, but most of the pages were new to him.

The dense Greek writing was sprinkled with drawings and mathematical proofs. There were 247 folios in the original document, each page a treasure in itself, revealing the genius of antiquity's greatest engineer. Tyler wished he could study every one of them, but only thirty-eight of the pages referred to Midas and the geolabe, a word coined by Archimedes. At one point, Archimedes even mentioned that he'd seen the golden hand, supporting Orr's claim that the codex really had been written to lead someone to Midas's treasure. Tyler found no explanation for the purpose of the notches.

After going over the copy of the original document, Stacy told Tyler that the codex seemed to end abruptly, which could mean either that some pages were missing or that Archimedes hadn't completed the manuscript. The reading was slow going, with Tyler stopping often to ask Stacy questions, but by seven o'clock Tyler had completed a first pass-through. After Stacy made a few phone calls, it was clear what their next step had to be.

At seven on the dot, there was a hammering at the door that startled Stacy. Tyler recognized the cadence and yelled, "Come in!"

The lock jiggled as a key went through the motions, and Grant threw open the door. He was by himself.

"Where's Aiden?" Tyler asked.

"He was with Miles in D.C. They should arrive in about an hour."

"You gave my regrets to the team at Bremerton?"

"I told them you were unavoidably detained on an urgent matter."

"Good." The project wasn't at a critical point. He wouldn't be missed for five days. Stacy's show was on hiatus for the summer, so her schedule was easy to clear.

"Have you heard from your father?" Grant said.

When Tyler showed him the video, Grant smiled. "He's a tough hombre," he said.

"Which is great for the military, but try being his son." Tyler tried to smile at his own weak joke, but all he could think of was his dad blindfolded like a prisoner of war.

"He'll be okay." Grant slapped Tyler on the shoulder. "Now, what's for dinner? I'm so hungry I could eat a buttered monkey."

"We'll have to order out," Stacy said. "Except for some drinks, the fridge is empty. Not a chef?"

"I like to cook," Tyler said, "but I haven't been shopping lately."

Grant snorted. "When he says he likes to cook, he means he can throw a piece of fish on the grill. He makes it sound like brain surgery. As they say at NASA, it ain't rocket science. I'll order us some pizzas."

An hour later, they'd had their fill of pepperoni-and-green-pepper thin crust, and Grant was up to speed on what had happened at Safeco Field.

At 8:15, there was another knock at the door. This time Tyler got up to open it. Waiting outside were Miles Benson and Aiden MacKenna. Miles was in his iBOT wheelchair, but it was at normal level, on all four wheels, instead of balanced on two.

Aiden was an Irishman with glasses and bushy black eyebrows. Tyler hadn't yet seen the new addition to his appearance, a black device affixed to his skull with a lead going to a plastic object tucked behind his ear.

"How's the cochlear implant working for you?" Tyler asked him.

"Huh?" Aiden said.

Tyler raised his voice. "I said, how long until that joke gets old?"

"Never."

Tyler ushered them in. Aiden made a beeline for Stacy.

"And who is this blond beauty?" he said, taking her hand in both of his.

"Stacy Benedict," she said. "I love your accent."

"That's very kind. And I'm glad to hear yours as well. I'm still getting used to this ugly contraption on my noggin that lets me hear such beautiful sounds."

"All right, Aiden," Tyler said, feeling a pang of jealousy. "That's plenty from you. Stacy, you've already met Aiden MacKenna, our resident software expert and database guru. And I'd like you to meet Gordian's president, Miles Benson."

They shook hands and got down to business. Miles had struck out finding any more information about Sherman's abductors before flying back to Seattle that afternoon. Tyler told Miles and Aiden about Sherman, Carol, Orr, and the mission to find the Midas Touch. The two of them were incredulous at first, just as Tyler had been, but when he showed them the video of his father, the doubts ended.

"This has to be completely off the books," he said. "No police. No FBI. Not even official Gordian involvement. That's why I wanted to meet here instead of at the office. But I'll still need some Gordian resources to find my dad."

"Are you sure that's a good idea?" Miles said.

"Stacy and I have talked it over, and we think Orr will go through with his threat if he finds out the Feds are involved."

Miles eyed Stacy, who nodded her agreement.

"All right," he said. "We'll keep this to ourselves. Any and all Gordian resources are at your disposal."

"Count me in too," Aiden said. "My time is yours."

"Thanks, guys." He didn't have to ask Grant. In fact, it would be insulting. Tyler knew that his best friend would be there to watch his back as he had in their Army days.

"I don't understand why Orr would let you go off on this hunt for the Midas treasure by yourselves," Miles said. "Seems like he's taking an awful risk just handing the geolabe over to you and sending you on your way."

"I thought so too," Tyler said. "I also thought the timing of the explosion on the truck was convenient. He didn't detonate it until we were far enough away to be safe."

Grant narrowed his eyes in realization. "He knew where we were."

"That was my guess, so I took the geolabe to the RF isolation room back at Gordian."

"What's that?" Stacy asked.

"It's a room for testing electronic emissions from cell phones and other communication devices. It's completely isolated from all outside radio-frequency sources."

"You found a signal coming from the geolabe," Grant said.

Tyler nodded. "It's equipped with a GPS tracker. That's how Orr is planning to keep tabs on us."

"Did you decrypt the signal?" Miles asked.

"Not yet, but I recorded two burst transmissions from it with every detector we have."

"I'll get our comm guys to work decoding it. With any luck, we'll be able to track it back to Orr." Miles began typing a message on his phone.

"What can I do?" Aiden said.

"We need to ferret out Jordan Orr. Find out anything you can about him. If we get a lead that's actionable, then we'll call in the FBI."

"I'm on it."

"Great," Tyler said. "Now, Stacy has a theory about the Archimedes device, the geolabe. Before the codex was sent to the auction house, it was separated from a wax tablet that had been found with it. She thinks the wax tablet may have a message that will be the key to deciphering the purpose of the geolabe."

"How do you know that?" Grant asked.

"We'll explain once we get in the air."

"In the air?" Grant said. "Are we taking a trip?"

Tyler turned to Miles. "I was happy to hear you say that we could use any Gordian resource, because we need one of the company jets. We have to go to England."

SIXTEEN

Orr took another swig of coffee and stifled a yawn as he drove the van into the vacant lot near Baltimore Harbor. With Crenshaw next to him, snoring for the entire five-hour flight from Seattle to Baltimore/Washington International, he'd napped only a few minutes at a time. Now, at 2:15 in the morning, Crenshaw was alert in the passenger seat, and Orr was ready to get back to the warehouse. But this excursion was crucial to the operation, and it had to be done tonight.

A semi was already waiting for them. A beefy black man in blue overalls leaned against the back of the trailer, sweating even though there was a cool breeze coming in off the water. For three years, Greg Forcet had smuggled goods for Orr out of a local shipping warehouse, but the delicate nature of this project meant they wouldn't be working together again.

Orr put the van into park and looked around. Satisfied that they were alone, he got out, and Crenshaw did the same. As they approached, Forcet eyeballed Crenshaw.

"Who's this?" he said.

"A friend," Orr said.

"You never brought friends before."

"He's okay." Crenshaw nodded, but said nothing.

"If you say so," Forcet said.

"Is the package ready?"

Forcet wiped his brow. "Just like you asked. Real bear taking that thing apart. Took me a couple of hours. That'll cost you another two grand."

"You got it. Any problems?"

"No, but I'm glad you warned me to bring those heat-resistant gloves. Those capsules was superhot."

"That's the chemical reaction I was telling you about. These kinds of batteries can overheat if you're not careful. That's why we had you put them in the thermal-insulation container we gave you. Is it sealed?"

"Signed, sealed, and delivered."

"Then let's take a look," Orr said.

Forcet raised the trailer's door, revealing his night's efforts. Nearest to them was the black metal box that Orr had called the thermal-insulation container. He noted with satisfaction that the lid was secure. Behind the box was a cylindrical lime-green object that Forcet had taken apart to get at the capsule. The cylinder was about four feet tall, with Cyrillic characters on the base, and it was designed with projections around the exterior that acted as cooling fins. Metal fixtures, fittings, and tools littered the floor. The sides of the crate that the item came in lay against the trailer wall.

Crenshaw held up an electronic device and waved what looked like a microphone in front of the open door.

"What's that?" Forcet asked.

"A, uh, temperature gauge," Crenshaw said. "We need to make sure it's not overheating."

"And? Did I do it right?" Forcet never did like having the quality of his work questioned.

After a few more passes, the device beeped and Crenshaw nodded. "We're below safe limits."

"We'll need some help getting all this into the van," Orr said.

"Hey, I'll throw that in for free," Forcet said.

The three of them heaved the thermal-insulation container into the van first.

As he strained at the effort, Forcet said, "What's this thing made of anyway, lead?"

Orr laughed, not because it was a funny joke, but because Forcet was absolutely right. The box had walls of lead three inches thick.

The finned cylinder was next.

Once they got it secured in the van, Forcet wiped his forehead again.

"Sure is hot," he said. "What the hell is that thing? Some kind of engine?"

Forcet didn't normally ask questions, but then again this was the first time he'd seen the contents of a crate he'd delivered to Orr. It couldn't hurt to tell him now.

"It's a radioisotope thermoelectric generator," Orr said.

"That's a mouthful. What's it used for?"

"For powering remote lighthouses. Totally automated. Can run for twenty years without maintenance." Orr patted the cylindrical RTG where a yellowed and torn piece of paper was the only remnant of the radiation symbol that should have been there. "This one is from a peninsula on the Arctic Ocean. Took me months to find." Although not as long as he thought it would. The diminishing summer pack ice along Russia's northern coast made getting at these legacies of the Soviet Union much easier.

"Looks ancient."

"Probably thirty years old."

Forcet laughed. "I don't know what you'd do with the battery from a thirty-year-old generator, and I don't want to know." He put a hand on his stomach. "I'll need some Pepto-Bismol or something when I get home."

He turned to climb back into the trailer. Orr drew a pistol from his jacket and shot him twice in the back, causing Crenshaw to jump back and squawk in surprise. Forcet crumpled to the ground. He gurgled blood for a few seconds and then stopped breathing.

"Jesus!" Crenshaw yelled. "You could have warned me!"

"Don't be stupid," Orr said. "If I warned you, I'd warn him."

Orr put the gun away and took a vial of crack cocaine from his pocket and put it in Forcet's overalls. It would look like a drug-smuggling deal gone bad.

"I've just never seen anyone get shot before," Crenshaw said, backing away from the fresh corpse.

"Now you have. Congratulations."

The only heavy items left were the pieces of depleted uranium shielding Forcet had pried away from the RTG, but Orr and Crenshaw could lift them easily. In ten minutes they had the rest of the trailer's contents in the van, leaving nothing to link them to Forcet.

Before they got back into the van, Crenshaw used the Geiger counter again.

"What's it reading now?" Orr asked. He wasn't crazy about getting into a vehicle full of radioactive material.

"About two millirads per hour," Crenshaw said. "On the drive back to the warehouse, it'll be less than you'd get from an X-ray."

They got in. Orr looked at the lead container. The strontium-90 pellets inside would be cooking along at 400 degrees Fahrenheit. "What do you think the reading would be if we opened the lid?"

"In the range of two thousand rads per hour."

"Perfect."

As he put the van into gear, Orr glanced at Forcet's body lying next to the truck, but he felt no guilt. Radiation poisoning was a nasty way to go. The sweating and nausea were just the first signs. Vomiting, diarrhea, hair loss, and uncontrolled bleeding would have followed.

To his way of thinking, Orr had done his longtime smuggler a favor. After spending more than two hours in close proximity to the exposed capsules, Forcet would have been dead within a week anyway.

SEVENTEEN

When Stacy and Tyler had decided that their next step was to fly to England, she imagined heading back to Sea-Tac Airport and going through all the hassle and pain of eight hours of traveling by commercial airliner to Heathrow. Instead, barely ninety minutes after Tyler had explained to Miles why they needed a plane, she was now taking off from Seattle on her first private-jet flight, lounging in a spacious leather seat, and accompanied by only two other passengers, Tyler and Grant.

Despite the near-death experience on the ferry—or maybe because of it—Stacy reveled in the luxury. She could get used to this.

"You fly like this all the time?" she said to Tyler as the engines spooled up and the plane began its takeoff roll.

"No," he said. "I'm usually in the cockpit."

"You're a pilot, too? I don't remember that from when I prepared for my interview with you."

He shrugged as if he thought it was no big deal. "It didn't seem relevant."

"Are you kidding? A handsome engineer who's also a pilot? My viewers would love that kind of detail."

Grant leaned toward Stacy. "He may have a PhD in mechanical engineering and be able to dispose of bombs and fly jets, but don't let that fool you. He's a secret *Star Trek* nerd."

"What about you?" she said. "I suppose that in addition to being a former pro wrestler, an electrical engineer with a degree from the University of Washington, and an Army SEAL—"

"Hey, hey, hey. I won't stand for that kind of insult. SEALs are Navy. I was a combat engineer, then a Ranger."

"Pardon me. In addition to all that, I suppose you fly jets, too."

"Me? Hell, no."

"Thank God. I thought I was in a meeting of Overachievers Anonymous."

"I just got my license to fly helicopters, though."

Stacy rolled her eyes. "Maybe we should have *you* on the show next time."

The jet lifted off, heading toward cruising altitude. Tyler cleared his throat. "I'd love to add to Grant's résumé by telling you all about his addiction to trashy dating programs—"

"Hey!" Grant protested.

"—but we'd better figure out what our plan will be when we reach London and then get some shut-eye."

The three of them unbuckled and gathered around a table. They opened a laptop so they could search the file with the translation of the Archimedes Codex.

"What time do we land?" Stacy asked.

"Around 2 P.M. local time," Tyler said. "Should give us enough time to get something accomplished."

"I knew you were a workaholic."

"Just trying to be efficient. In fact, I think we should split up when we get there."

"Whoa," Grant said. "Can we just back up here? I came in late at the house. Why, exactly, are we going to England?"

"Do you want the long answer or the short answer?" Stacy said.

"We've got a few hours before I can sleep, so I'll take the long answer."

"Have you heard of the Antikythera Mechanism?" Stacy asked.

"Tyler mentioned it when he was fabricating the geolabe."

Through the plane's Web connection, she brought up a photo of three pieces of corroded bronze, the biggest about the diameter of a grapefruit. In each of the pieces, intricate gearing could be seen.

"Looks like somebody left their clock in the rain for about a thousand years," Grant said.

"About two thousand years," Tyler said. When they'd been discussing it earlier, he told Stacy that he'd researched the Antikythera Mechanism because he realized how similar it was to the geolabe he was hired to build.

"They found these bits in the shipwreck off the Greek island of Antikythera in 1900," Stacy said. "For years nobody paid much attention to them until an archaeologist realized that the gearing predated anything else as sophisticated by fifteen hundred years. Some people refer to it as the world's first analog computer. It would be like finding an IBM PC hidden in the dungeon of a medieval castle."

"What does it compute?" Grant asked.

"Debate has raged for years, but most scientists think it was used for astronomical prediction of some sort. Planetary movements, solstices and equinoxes, perhaps even solar eclipses. Ancient planting cycles and religious worship depended on knowing important calendar events, and this device might have been used to calculate them."

She brought up another photo, this time of a shiny bronze mechanism behind a protective glass. The face of the device had two circular dials like a clock, and a knob on the side. The sides were transparent, so that you could see the gearing inside. Some of the points on the dials were etched with Greek lettering.

"That's a replica at the National Archaeological Museum in Athens," Tyler said. "Built from what they could glean from X-rays of the recovered pieces."

"Looks like the geolabe you built," Grant said.

"They're very similar, but the markings on the face of mine are complete, and it has two knobs on the side instead of one."

"So this codex seems to be an instruction manual for building an Antikythera Mechanism," Stacy said.

"Or something along those lines," Tyler said. "But the most exciting part is that the codex provides evidence that Archimedes may have been the one who designed it."

Grant grinned. "You mean, the guy who yelled 'Eureka!' when he created the Archimedes Death Ray?"

Stacy could tell by his smirk that he knew very well he was conflating two well-known stories about the inventor, engineer, and mathematician. "You are so close," she said.

According to legend, Archimedes was in the bathtub pondering how to solve a problem for the king of Syracuse, his patron on the island now called Sicily. The king was given a crown that was supposedly made of gold, but he wanted to verify the claim without destroying the gift. When Archimedes realized that the material's displacement in water could be used to discern its density, he ran into the street stark naked yelling, "Eureka!" which translates to "I found it!"

The king also called on Archimedes to design weapons of war to repel a Roman siege during the Second Punic War in 214 B.C. Historians of the time recount a death ray Archimedes invented that focused the sun's light with such intensity that it made the enemy ships in the Syracuse harbor burst into flames. His feat couldn't be duplicated in spite of many attempts, including experiments by students from Tyler's alma mater, MIT, and TV's *MythBusters*, so it's assumed that the claims were exaggerated.

Nonetheless, Archimedes' reputation as an inventor and scientist was so great that even such wild assertions were given credence.

"Not only does the codex describe how to design the geolabe," Tyler said, his excitement obvious, "but it could be the only known copy of his long-lost treatise called *On Sphere-Making*. It has designs for dozens of mechanisms, not just the geolabe."

Stacy wished she could be as excited as he was, but she was more worried about how they could use the geolabe to free her sister.

"This is all very cool stuff," Grant said, "but what in the hell does it have to do with old King Midas?"

Tyler glanced at Stacy, and she shrugged for him to answer.

"We think the geolabe somehow leads to a map—a map that will show us where the treasure of King Midas is buried."

Stacy pointed at the laptop screen. "This line says, 'He who controls this map controls the riches of Midas.' "

"Ah, treasure!" Grant said, rubbing his hands together. "Now we're talking. How does it work?"

Stacy leaned back and laced her hands behind her head. "We don't know. There are two pieces of the instructions missing."

"Remember when we were building that Swedish modular home-entertainment center you bought?" Tyler said. "The one with the missing instruction page? Same problem."

"It's good we're engineers, otherwise it would've taken us more than a half hour to realize we'd put it together backward."

"In this case, the missing pieces explain how to operate the device," Stacy said. "The first step was to get all three dials pointed to the noon position, like calibrating a scale. Solving the Stomachion told us how to do that, but now we don't know how to proceed. The codex talks about how there are three keys to deciphering the geolabe, and that they form some kind of safeguard so that the owner of the codex wouldn't be able to find the map without the other two keys."

"Like a password and fingerprint scanner on the same security system," Tyler said.

"So the first key is the instruction manual for building and calibrating the geolabe, which we think may also be a version of the mysterious Antikythera Mechanism?" Grant said.

She nodded. "Now that we have the device built and we figured out how to calibrate it, we need the other two keys to operate it."

"And the other two keys are . . . ?" Grant said.

Stacy highlighted another section. "This part talks about a message that's hidden. This word is *steganos,* which means 'covered,' and this one is *graphein,* which means 'writing.' "

"Steganography."

"Literally, 'concealed writing.' Whatever the message is, it's concealed, and I think I know where."

"The wax tablet that was separated from the codex before the auction," Tyler said. "That's the second key."

"Let me guess," Grant said. "The tablet's buyer lives in England."

"Right. The tablet was bought by a holding company called VXN Industries, which also happens to lease an estate in Kent."

"Think the buyer will let you take a look at it?"

"That's what we're hoping. Stacy and I will drive out there to make our plea in person."

"While I look for clues in as many pubs as possible?"

Stacy liked these guys. Even in a situation as dire as this, they lightened the mood to keep their spirits up.

"You wish," she said, joining in. She scrolled to another part of the codex. "Here's where it mentions the third key."

"So what's that mean for me?"

"You're going to the British Museum," Tyler said.

"A museum?" Grant said, as if he'd been asked to wade through a Dumpster full of trash. "What for?"

"Orr said that the tomb of Midas is somewhere under Naples," Stacy answered. "The codex says that the third key will be revealed by 'the room of the ancestor of Neapolis.' Neapolis is the Greek name for Naples."

"Is the British Museum the best place to learn about Naples?" Grant asked.

"Not necessarily, but it does have experts on the Elgin Marbles."

"So?"

"The Elgin Marbles are marble statues and sculptured panels that were taken from the Parthenon in the early 1800s by Lord Elgin. They're currently on display at the British Museum."

"I don't follow."

"I think Archimedes was being clever," Stacy said. "Neapolis was originally called Parthenope, making Parthenope the ancestor of Neapolis. So when Archimedes said 'the room of the ancestor of Neapolis,' he could have meant 'the room of Parthenope.' *Parthenope* means 'the virgin city,' so we can further reduce it to 'the room of the virgin city' or more simply 'the room of the virgin.' "

"I think I've got it," Grant said. "The third key will be revealed by 'the virgin's room.' " He thought about it for another second and shook his head, "Nope. I still don't get it."

"The Greek word for a 'virgin's room' is *Parthenon*."

Grant laughed in disbelief. "As in the temple on top of the Acropolis in Athens?"

Stacy pointed to the manuscript. "In essence it says, 'Take the geolabe to the Parthenon. The seat of Herakles and the feet of Aphrodite will show the way.' "

"But what does that mean?"

She shrugged, both frustrated and embarrassed that she didn't know the answer, particularly with her sister's life on the line. "My specialty was classical literature, not architecture. That's why we need an expert. I don't know how or why, but the third key to finding Archimedes' map is the Parthenon."

EIGHTEEN

Sherman Locke's watch had been confiscated, so he didn't know what time it was when the opening of the garage door woke him. Given that he was still full from the take-out sandwich and water they'd given him for dinner, he suspected it was the middle of the night. He rose from his cot and went to the portal in the door. The room's single bulb had been turned off for the evening, but the crude covering over the hole left a small crack that let in a sliver of light. Sherman also discovered that it gave him a limited view of the warehouse.

He didn't know what they were trying to keep him from seeing, but it wasn't their faces. He'd gotten a good look at both of his captors, which wasn't very comforting because it implied they had no intention of letting him out of here alive.

That made escape priority number one, both for him and for the girl they'd called Carol. He'd heard her cry out a few times, but the sound was muted, which meant that she'd been placed in the room farthest from his. He'd tried tapping on the wall a few times, but she hadn't responded. Speaking to her through the cinder blocks wouldn't work because he would have had to yell so loudly that Gaul would have heard as well.

As he peered through the crack, Sherman saw that another van had just backed into the warehouse next to the one in which he'd been abducted. He watched as two white men got out, the driver trim and dark-haired, the passenger pasty and doughy. They circled to the back of the truck, where they met Gaul and Phillips, who were still rubbing their eyes from their naps on the cots. They stared at something in the back of the van.

"You sure it's safe to touch, Orr?" Gaul asked. He was speaking to the driver. Their voices were barely audible to Sherman.

"Crenshaw," Orr said to the passenger, "show them the readings."

Crenshaw had his back to Sherman, so he couldn't see what the man had in his hand. Crenshaw motioned his arm back and forth several times and then held up what looked like a voltage meter.

"See?" Crenshaw said. "No problem."

"I still don't like it."

"Do you like two million dollars?" Orr said. Because of the authoritative way Orr said it, Sherman was sure he was the leader of this gang.

"I love two million dollars," Phillips said.

Two million dollars each? Sherman thought. How much were they asking for *him*?

"Consider it hazard pay," Orr said. "Now help us get it on the floor next to that table."

The four of them lifted something from the van, and just before they disappeared from view Sherman spied a black metal box that couldn't have been more than a foot on each side. Even though the object was small, they were straining from the load. Whatever was in there was surprisingly heavy.

Once it was down, they went back to the van.

"How are our guests doing?" Orr asked.

"The general was a pain in the ass, but we handled it. The girl is still groggy from the roofies."

Orr looked directly at the hole in the door, but Sherman didn't think there was any way he could be seen.

"What about the rest of this crap?" Gaul said.

"Drive the truck to the far end of the warehouse and dump it,"

Orr said. "We don't want some kids to stumble onto it in a junkyard and alert the FBI."

Gaul and Phillips did as he ordered, stopping the van at the far wall fifty yards away. With the van facing toward him, he couldn't see what they were tossing out, but pieces of metal clanged onto the concrete every few seconds, with some of the impacts noisier than others.

Orr's and Crenshaw's voices lowered, so Sherman could hear only snippets of their conversation. ". . . truck . . . by Monday . . . enough dust . . . bank . . . thirty years . . ."

That was all he could make out before the van started up again and returned to its original parking spot.

With the van out of the way, Sherman could now see what they'd tossed out. One of his greatest assets as a fighter pilot was his vision, and although he needed reading glasses now, his distance acuity was as good as ever.

His eye was drawn to a green cylinder with fins around its core lying on its side. Something about it was familiar. At first he thought it was an unusual compressor design, but then he saw the stenciled Cyrillic letters on the base and realized where he'd seen a photo of it.

During his final three years in the Air Force, Sherman had been the deputy director of the Defense Threat Reduction Agency, whose mission was to determine ways to counter weapons of mass destruction. As the agency's highest-ranking military leader, he had been briefed on every major risk to national security posed by nuclear, chemical, and biological weapons. In fact, his keynote address the previous morning had been on unconventional tactics that could make the effects of these weapons more widespread and deadly.

Two years ago, he was part of a team that went to Moscow to discuss the security of rogue nuclear weapons and materials. The fear was that terrorists would be able to get their hands on uranium or plutonium to fashion their own crude atomic bombs, then smuggle them into American cities.

As part of the discussion, they also talked about other sources of nuclear material. One potential hazard was from radioisotope thermal generators, similar to the power sources used in American space probes like *Voyager.* Russia had hundreds of unmanned lighthouses and signal stations ringing the coasts of the country in locations so remote that maintaining them on a regular basis was costly. So, instead of conventional diesel generators that would have to be fueled and repaired routinely, the Soviets constructed RTGs to power them and provide guideposts for their Navy. Then they forgot about them.

With the collapse of the Soviet Union and the subsequent cost cuts in the military, little emphasis had been placed on safeguarding these power plants, and they were abandoned. Because they were unmanned, they made tempting targets for thieves hoping to scavenge the metal for profit. In taking the devices apart, the thieves would sometimes expose the core capsules that held the radioactive strontium-90 power source.

In the former Soviet republic of Georgia, three villagers had either stolen or come across two of these capsules containing ten pounds of the highly dangerous material. The capsules generate their power using heat, so the men thought they would make a good replacement for their campfire in the winter cold.

Within hours, they became sick with radiation poisoning and would have died without immediate care. Two of them were hospitalized for months and never fully recovered. The only reason they didn't die within days was that the capsules were still partially shielded by lead. The entire town of Pripyat, near Chernobyl, had been permanently evacuated for a radiation reading lower than the output of one of these unshielded capsules.

The green object sitting a hundred yards away looked exactly like one of the RTGs his DTRA team had been shown during the trip to Moscow. Now Sherman understood why the container they'd been carrying was so heavy. It was made entirely of lead.

For whatever reason they had taken Sherman and Carol, this was no simple kidnapping. His captors had something far grander planned. He had to get a message to Tyler, had to make him understand the deadly danger they faced.

Escape was no longer Sherman's highest priority.

THURSDAY

THE ARCHIMEDES TABLET

NINETEEN

A strong tailwind helped get the Gulfstream into Heathrow ten minutes before 2 P.M. Tyler had requisitioned a motor pool car from Gordian's London facility for him and Stacy to drive west to the estate leased by VXN. He had also called ahead to ask for a meeting with the estate's owner or resident, but the assistant he talked to said the owner of the company was very busy and had no time for them. Only after Stacy jumped in and used her celebrity credentials to explain that the request involved an ancient puzzle devised by Archimedes did the assistant tell her that the owner would agree to an audience if Stacy and Tyler could get there by four o'clock.

Grant would be heading in the other direction, straight into the heart of London during rush hour, so he opted to ride the express into Paddington Station, then take the Underground to the stop nearest the British Museum. His appointment had been easier to make. With a few carefully worded clues revealed by the codex, Grant had persuaded an archaeologist named Oswald Lumley to provide his expertise on the Parthenon.

Tyler had placed the cushioned pack containing the geolabe in the back of the Range Rover in case they needed to consult it when they were at the estate. He then wished Grant good hunting and left the airport, with Stacy riding shotgun.

On the drive, Tyler called Aiden MacKenna hoping to get an update on tracking down Jordan Orr.

Over the SUV's speaker, Aiden's answer came out sounding groggy. It was just a little past six in the morning in Seattle.

"Were you up all night?" Tyler asked as he drove on the M3 motorway toward Basingstoke.

"Caught a few winks between database searches," Aiden said. "I'll sleep later."

"Thanks, Aiden." Tyler was truly appreciative that he worked with friends who would go all out to help him like this. "Any luck?"

"Of course, the credentials he gave us when he hired you to build the geolabe turned out to be bogus. Now he seems to have disappeared off the face of the earth. Without prints, we don't have much to go on."

Before Tyler left Seattle, he had the geolabe dusted for fingerprints, but as he suspected, Orr hadn't been that sloppy.

"What about the auction-house heist?" Stacy asked.

"Scotland Yard ran into a dead end on that," Aiden said. "None of the perpetrators were ever caught, and none of the art objects resurfaced."

"You'd think he would have made enough money on the robbery to retire to Fiji in style."

"Maybe it wasn't enough for Orr. During my search, I ran some calculations based on the size of the block of gold Orr told you he found in the Midas chamber. You said the golden statue of the girl was lying on top of a solid-gold cube six feet on each side, right?"

"Along with walls made of gold," Tyler said.

"And who knows how thick those are. But just consider the pedestal itself, and remember how dense gold is. If it's twenty-four karat, it would weigh about a hundred and eighteen thousand kilograms, or around four million ounces. If it were melted down and sold on the open market, the cube alone would be worth around four billion dollars."

Stacy coughed. "Four billion? With a *b*?"

"Give or take, depending on the price of gold."

Tyler had been so busy worrying about his father and trying to interpret the clues in the Archimedes Codex that he hadn't calculated the money involved, but hearing the figures made him realize what they were up against. Criminals would kill their own families for a hundredth that amount. No wonder Orr was going to such elaborate lengths to get the treasure.

Any legitimate treasure hunter would get only a small percentage of the take, if anything, once the Italian government got involved. That's why Orr was so desperate to keep it a secret.

"What about the tracker?" Tyler said. "Has Miles decoded the signal?"

"Still working on that. I'll get back to you when we've got it."

"Okay. And let me know the minute you have anything on Orr."

"Absolutely," Aiden said, and hung up. Tyler had no doubt that if there was a way to track down Orr, Aiden would find it.

"If Orr is really after the gold in that chamber," Tyler said, "why would he make up that story about seeing the Midas Touch in action?"

"Because he's messing with us," Stacy said. "I've met guys like him before. They like to manipulate people. They get off on it."

"I'm just trying to figure out his angle. What about the hand?"

Stacy shook her head. "You've got me. Archimedes does talk about the hand in the codex. He saw it in person, which means the golden hand is at least twenty-two hundred years old."

"I know. That's what bothers me."

"Because the hand is so old or because it looks so real?"

"Both."

"Like I said before, I don't have a scientific background, but it did look pretty convincing."

"However it was made, there was nothing magical about the transformation." Tyler simply refused to believe that a magical power could perform alchemy in violation of every known chemical law.

"Would you bet our families' lives on that?" Stacy asked.

Tyler didn't answer, because it didn't matter what he believed.

His mission was to find the map left by Archimedes so that he could get his father back.

They were silent for the rest of the drive. When they reached the gates of the estate thirty minutes later, Tyler pressed the buzzer.

"What is your business?" a man said in a thick Italian accent.

"My name is Tyler Locke. We have an appointment."

"Yes. Drive to the house."

The ten-foot-tall gates slowly drew apart. Tyler wheeled the Range Rover along a winding brick driveway toward a gray stone mansion a half mile away.

As they got closer, he realized how immense the home really was. The front façade alone was at least a hundred feet long. He could picture the original owner reigning over a vast estate of feudal vassals.

Several cars were parked in front of the mansion, but only one caught his eye. It was a red Ferrari 458 Italia, with a top speed of more than two hundred miles per hour. Tyler was a connoisseur, regularly driving loaners when Gordian tested them for auto and insurance companies at its track in Phoenix, but he hadn't yet driven an Italia.

He parked the Range Rover next to it and got out to take a closer look before they knocked on the door. For just a moment, he imagined himself hearing the roar of the car's mid-engine V8 behind his head.

The clop-clop of approaching hooves made him turn around.

A chestnut horse trotted toward them. Tyler instinctively backed away.

"What's the matter?" Stacy said.

"I don't like horses," Tyler said, eyeing it warily.

Stacy looked at him as if he'd said he hated rainbows. "Who doesn't like horses?"

"Me."

"Why?"

"They're big and they're unpredictable."

"They're friendly."

"I forgot. You grew up on a farm."

"I practically lived on my horse, Chanter, when I was a teenager. Have you ever ridden one?"

"Yes," Tyler said, but he didn't elaborate.

The rider pulled on the reins and expertly guided the horse to a stop. She was a striking woman in her thirties, dressed in impeccable traditional English riding togs and helmet. A black ponytail flicked back and forth every time she moved her head.

"She's a beauty, isn't she?" the woman said to Tyler, her Italian accent softer than the security guard's. "I saw you looking at her."

Assuming that the woman was either the home's owner or related to the owner, Tyler didn't want to kick off his introduction by insulting her.

He nodded cautiously and said, "Definitely. What breed is she?"

"Breed?" She looked down at the horse and laughed with a throaty roar. "You must not be much of a rider." She patted the horse's neck. "This is Giuseppe, and he's a male. An Arabian. The beauty I meant was my Ferrari."

Tyler joined in the laughter at his gaffe.

"Prancing horses I know," he said, meaning Ferrari's logo. "Five hundred and sixty horsepower, in the case of this lovely lady. She must be a treat to drive."

The Italian looked Tyler up and down, almost as if he were a horse she was considering purchasing.

"She is. Maybe I'll take you for a spin later."

Her inflection left no doubt that the double entendre was on purpose.

The woman dismounted and led Giuseppe toward them. Tyler

willed himself to stand his ground. Stacy, on the other hand, held out her hand and stroked the horse's nose. In return, Giuseppe nuzzled her palm.

"See?" she said to Tyler. "He's a sweetheart."

Tyler wondered what it was about women and horses.

"He doesn't care for our equine friends?" the woman said.

"I'm more of a mechanical type," Tyler said. He held out his hand. "I'm Tyler Locke, and this is Stacy Benedict. We called earlier today."

The woman took his hand in a strong grip, and then shook Stacy's.

"When I heard what you wanted to talk about, I couldn't resist meeting you," she said. "Welcome to my home. I am Gia Cavano."

Stacy stifled a tiny gasp too late at hearing the name Gia. Tyler held his own amazement in check. It couldn't be a coincidence that the woman who owned the next key in Archimedes' puzzle had the same name as someone they'd heard about the day before from Orr, who had told them two things about his childhood friend Gia.

One, that Orr had discovered the Midas chamber while exploring the tunnels of Naples with her. And two, that if Gia found out that they were also searching for it after all these years, she would kill them.

TWENTY

As he exited the train at Holborn Tube Station, Grant wasn't swept along with the crush of rush-hour passengers, one of the benefits of being a big man. Instead, the mass of people flowed around him or stepped aside when he approached. He strode briskly along the station's platform trying to make up for lost time, a backpack containing the Archimedes translation slung over his shoulder.

The trip on the Underground had taken longer than he'd expected, so he had only fifteen minutes until his appointment with Dr. Lumley. Grant stopped at streets only long enough to remember to look right instead of left so that he wouldn't be run over. He hadn't been to England in years and would have loved to explore the neighborhoods and see how much things had changed since his last visit, but that would have to wait for next time.

Despite Tyler's determined optimism, Grant knew that his friend was worried about his father. Tyler and his dad had their icy patches, but Grant had perceived some thawing lately. The two had started speaking again, even if it was sporadic. But when someone threatened your own blood, it didn't matter how close the two of you were.

Grant and Tyler weren't blood, but they might as well have been, and if Grant could help his friend by solving this crazy riddle, he would do whatever he had to.

In another five minutes, he walked through the front courtyard of the British Museum and into the entryway. Though admission was free, a small display asked for a donation to enter the museum.

Grant hadn't had a chance to get any British currency, so he took out a twenty-dollar bill and tucked it into the slot before heading into the Great Court.

The soaring ceiling made the space feel airy despite being packed with tourists wandering around the beige marble floor in search of antiquities like the famed Rosetta Stone. Steel latticework supported the impressive glass skylight that wrapped around the central reading room.

Grant waited at the information desk until the confused American in front of him could be convinced that the museum did not have a display of Harry Potter's Quidditch broom.

"I'm looking for the office of an archaeologist named Oswald Lumley," he said.

After a quick call, a curatorial assistant arrived to guide Grant down to see Dr. Lumley. She led him through a maze of halls and stairs before showing him into a cramped office stacked high with books on every surface. So much for the modern paperless office.

A short balding man in his sixties circled from behind the desk as the assistant made her exit. His striped dress shirt had seen better days and was stretched by a slight paunch. Like most archaeologists, Lumley wasn't likely to be cracking any bullwhips.

"Dr. Lumley," Grant said.

"And you must be Grant Westfield," Lumley said. He didn't say it, but his arched eyebrows made it clear that a brawny ex-wrestler was not what he'd been expecting. "I'm happy that you sought me out."

"And I appreciate you seeing me on such short notice."

"Not at all. Not at all. After I saw the sample from your manuscript, I was eager to hear more."

When he had first called the museum, Grant had used his connection to Stacy, hoping her reputation would get him an audience with someone. He claimed that he was a consultant for the TV show *Chasing the Past,* which was researching an ancient manuscript owned by a private collector. After being routed to several different archaeologists, his call was taken by Lumley.

To make sure he got Lumley's attention, Grant had faxed one sheet of the original Greek codex from the section he needed the archaeologist to examine. There was no mention of Archimedes or Midas, just the allusion to Herakles and Aphrodite. Since the Archimedes Codex had been stolen before the auction house could catalog it in detail, there was no way Lumley might suspect that Grant's manuscript was the stolen one.

Lumley waved to a chair. "Please sit down."

They each took a seat, and Grant gave Lumley an abbreviated rundown of his interest in the codex, especially the reference to the seat of Herakles and the feet of Aphrodite. Then he showed Lumley the full section of the translated codex. Lumley spent ten minutes reading it, gasping in astonishment every few paragraphs.

Finally, he looked up and said, "Remarkable."

"Can you help us decipher it?"

"I think I might. Or, at least, part of it. But I'd like to review the Marbles in person before I draw any conclusions."

"Great," Grant said as he stood. "Let's take a look."

Lumley held up a finger. "Forgive me, but I must make one call before my colleague leaves for the day."

"No problem. I can go on ahead."

"Perfect. If you return by the route you took to arrive at my office, you'll see signs leading you directly to the display containing the Elgin Marbles. I shall join you momentarily."

Buoyed by the prospect of new information in their quest, Grant took the stairs back up two at a time. He was eager to see what clue the Elgin Marbles held. He just hoped the archaeologist wouldn't take long.

When Grant Westfield was safely out of earshot, Lumley took out his cell phone. He didn't want the call to go through the museum's central switchboard. He chose the contact listing that had no name, just the number he'd been given if any ancient Greek documents relating to the Parthenon came to his attention. As a senior archaeologist in the museum, he had been able to wrest Westfield's original inquiry away from a more junior staff member.

Lumley's call was answered on the second ring. He didn't need to say who it was. His voice quavered as he spoke.

"I think I've found what you've been looking for."

TWENTY-ONE

If Tyler thought he had any other choice, he and Stacy would be long gone from Gia Cavano's estate instead of sitting in the study of her mansion. The wood-paneled room at the rear of the house had a spectacular view of the stables and the hundreds of acres of pastureland beyond. Flames in the brick fireplace warded off any chill the drafty windows let in.

A tanned and muscled "assistant" with enough gel in his hair to rival a major oil spill had escorted them to their waiting spot while Gia Cavano excused herself to take her horse back to the stables and change into fresh clothes. The door to the study was closed behind them, but Tyler had no doubt that the man was standing guard. It was also quite possible someone was listening to them.

"Do you think Orr knew his old friend Gia Cavano had the tablet?" Stacy said in a whisper. She leaned so close to Tyler that her lips brushed his ear. He felt goose bumps on his arms in response to the light touch.

"No, but we should have anticipated it," he whispered in reply. "VXN Industries."

"Of course. Vixen. Orr called her the Fox. That must be her nickname." A vixen is a female fox, and Cavano had shortened it to VXN. They had simply never considered that his nemesis would be holding one of the important clues that they needed.

"Do you think she knows why we're here?" Stacy asked.

"If she doesn't, we'll get a look at the tablet and then get out of here."

"And if she does?"

Tyler raised an eyebrow. "Then we're in trouble."

Not only did he not like the coincidence of running into the one person Orr had warned them about; his first impression of Cavano reminded him of the Cheshire Cat, the smile and purr hiding mischief just beneath the surface.

The door opened behind them. They both stood while Cavano swept in, now dressed in a stylish gray pantsuit tailored for her curvaceous figure. Her raven hair draped across her shoulders, framing sculpted cheekbones and mahogany brown eyes.

As she glided to her desk, Cavano never took her gaze off Tyler.

"My apologies for keeping you waiting," she said, "but I'm feeling much refreshed." She took a seat and indicated for Tyler and Stacy to do the same.

"Thank you for taking the time to meet with us," Tyler said.

"I understand this has to do with an ancient tablet I purchased a year ago. May I ask what your interest in it is?"

Before Tyler could respond, Stacy cleared her throat. "I'm the host of a television show called *Chasing the Past,* and we're interested in featuring it in an upcoming episode." Not bad. Using her position as a TV personality just might work. Even though Tyler didn't understand the craving for fame, he knew that most people would do anything for their fifteen minutes.

"And you are the producer?" Cavano said to Tyler.

"I'm an adviser to the show," he said.

"And what is your interest in the tablet, Ms. Benedict?"

"We believe it may represent a significant highlight of Greek culture from the time during the Second Punic Wars, which would be of great interest to my viewers."

"I see. So you are an archaeologist?"

"A classicist specializing in Greek culture, with a PhD from Duke."

"Impressive. And you want to film my tablet?"

"Not today. We just want to inspect it to see if it's the piece we think it is."

"I don't think that should be a problem. In fact, it is in this very room." Cavano pulled out a drawer and pressed a button. Two panels in the wall slid apart, revealing a glass case displaying several ancient objects, including two illuminated manuscripts, a bronze short sword, and a wax tablet the size of two hardback novels.

Stacy practically jumped out of her chair and reverently approached the display, followed by Tyler. Cavano joined them, putting her hand on Tyler's arm. Subtlety wasn't her strength.

"I think it's exquisite," she said. "Can you read it?"

"Yes," Stacy said without hesitation. She concentrated on the tablet, which was hinged and separated into two halves. Exposed wood around the edges surrounded rectangles covered in beige beeswax. The Greek words were quite legible, as if they'd been written the week before instead of two thousand years ago. Despite their precarious situation, Tyler was agog at the sight. If Stacy's suspicions were correct, he was now looking at the handwriting of Archimedes himself.

"It says, 'Whosoever desires truth shall divine the greatest treasure. Do not look outside of yourself, but within. The skies, the stars, the moon, the sun, and the planets will be forever yours. The Parthenon provides the key.' "

Cavano clapped her hands. "Excellent. That is precisely how my own expert translated it, although it took him much longer than you did. Do you have any idea what it refers to?"

Stacy glanced at Tyler and shook her head. "It's quite mysterious. Just the kind of thing we like to feature on our show."

Cavano laughed and returned to her seat.

"Please, Dr. Benedict. There's no need to go on with this farce. If you'll sit down, I have something to tell you that I think you'll both find very interesting."

A flash of alarm crossed Stacy's face. Tyler shared the sentiment. This wasn't good. But they were committed now. Might as well hear what Cavano had to say. He and Stacy went back to their chairs.

"You have seen a document that was stolen before I could buy it," Cavano said. "A manuscript referring to a map that leads to the treasure of King Midas."

"What makes you think that?" Tyler said.

"Because Dr. Benedict called to ask about a puzzle created by Archimedes. That is the only reason you would ask to see my tablet."

"You're jumping to conclusions."

"Not at all." Cavano took a deep breath. "When I was nine, a boy and I were exploring the basement of a condemned apartment building in my home city of Naples when we came across a hidden room that led into a network of tunnels. We heard two men speaking around a corner and crept forward until we could see them stacking bags of white powder into crates. We immediately realized that the room was being used to hide smuggled drugs where the police would never find them."

Cavano's eyes glazed over as she recalled that night.

"The men must have heard our whispers because they stopped talking and ran after us, one waving his crowbar, the other taking shots at us with a gun. We were cut off from our entrance, so the two men chased us into the tunnels, screaming that their boss would kill them if we escaped to tell his enemies where they were. In the mad scramble, we became lost, but we couldn't elude the men. We ran for what seemed like miles until we saw a glow reflected in our flashlights. We thought it was daylight and charged ahead."

Tyler hadn't realized until this moment that he was sitting on the edge of his chair. Cavano's tale was much more detailed than Orr's.

"We skidded to a halt in a chamber made entirely of gold. You may think I'm exaggerating, but every single surface was covered in a yellow metallic sheen. In the center of the room was a golden pedestal, and lying on the pedestal was a life-size statue of a woman who was perfect in every detail except that her left hand was missing. At one end, a pool of water bubbled, drenching the chamber in a steamy fog. On a high terrace at the other end of the room was a golden coffin, the sarcophagus of King Midas."

"How could you possibly know that?" Stacy said.

"Because of what happened next," Cavano said. "We took shelter behind the pedestal, where we were sure to be found, but there was no other exit. We were trapped. However, when the men entered, they completely forgot about us."

"I can understand why," Tyler said.

"After a few moments of staring in awe, the two men began to argue about what to do with their find. Neither was planning to report it to their boss, but they couldn't decide how they were going to get the gold out without being discovered. They thought there might be bricks of gold or coins in the sarcophagus, but when the one with the gun turned toward it, the man with the crowbar bashed him over the head, killing him instantly. After putting the gun in his waistband, the second man pried the coffin open just far enough to reach inside. He pulled his hand out with a scream, as if he'd been bitten, and the lid slammed close again."

"What happened?" Stacy said.

"I don't know. He held his hand like it was on fire. He tried to wipe it on his pants, but the screaming got louder. Then his hand went to his throat. As he staggered around in agony, he slipped and fell into the pool of water."

Cavano's eyes gleamed, thrilled at recounting the tale, no fear at all.

"Then the most marvelous thing happened. When we emerged from our hiding place to look at the man in the water, we saw that his hand had begun to turn to gold. It started at his fingertips and worked slowly toward his palm. In five minutes, nearly his entire hand had been consumed. He was a victim of the Midas Touch. There is no other possible explanation."

Tyler struggled not to roll his eyes, because the yarn was too fantastic, the fevered dream of some scared kids.

"And why don't you just go back and find it?" he said.

"Believe me, I've been trying to ever since that day. We told our parents about the gold chamber, leaving out the part about the two dead men, but they were so mad about our all-night absence that they thought we were making up the story to avoid punishment. The apartments were torn down soon after, and a building for the Italian Ministry of Health was put up in its place. I ventured into the basement once after the construction was complete, but the concrete foundation had covered the entrance to the tunnels."

"That's an amazing story," Tyler said. "And I don't believe a word of it."

"I think you do," Cavano said, "otherwise you wouldn't have taken on the job to find it. How much is he paying you?"

"Who?" Stacy said a little too quickly.

"The person who stole that codex from me."

"From you?" Tyler said.

"The codex and the golden hand—the same one missing from the statue in the Midas vault—were to be auctioned, and I had a plan to obtain them before anyone else realized the secret those two treasures held. They were stolen from the auction house along with other valuables, and not a single item in the theft ever resurfaced. Until now, I thought the perpetrator of the heist was dead."

"Why do you think we know anything about that?" Tyler said.

"Because this afternoon I received a call about an inquiry into an ancient Greek document, one involving the Parthenon, and the bearer of that manuscript happened to say he was working with Stacy Benedict."

Tyler felt his stomach drop to the floor. She was talking about Grant.

"The only way you could have seen that manuscript is if you're now working with the person who stole it," Cavano said. "You see, the boy with me that night long ago in Naples grew up to be the thief who took the Archimedes Codex. He wasn't just my friend; he was also my cousin from America. His name is Jordan Orr, and I plan to kill him."

TWENTY-TWO

In the Duveen Gallery, specially built to display the Elgin Marbles, Grant wandered along the sculptures lining either side. The captions called them metopes, which were square reliefs that had decorated the exterior band running around the top of the Parthenon. Most of them were damaged in some way, whether by an explosion that blew the Parthenon apart in 1687, by weathering, or during their removal.

At either end of the long gallery were the large three-dimensional pediment sculptures that had adorned the eaves of the Parthenon's pitched roof. Like most of the sculptures Grant had seen in museums, a majority of the Elgin Marbles were missing their heads and hands.

"Magnificent, aren't they?" Dr. Lumley said behind him. The curator had followed a group of tourists into the gallery, so Grant hadn't noticed him.

"Couldn't ask for better," Grant said, even though they didn't impress him. Maybe he was missing something. "The captions said something about the Parthenon getting blown up. What happened?"

"A true tragedy. During its first two thousand years, the Parthenon had undergone damage when it was first converted into a church and then a mosque, but it was still recognizable as the temple of Athena. In 1687, the Ottoman Turks occupied Athens and were at war with Venice. For some reason, they thought the Acropolis was the best site to locate a gunpowder magazine. The Venetians lobbed mortar shells at the ammunition storehouse until one of them connected. The entire building blew apart, destroying many of the columns and sculptures."

Grant nodded knowingly. He and Tyler had been working on the modern version of an ammo dump for the Bremerton naval base. During the design phase, they had reviewed several case studies of ammo storage and transport that had resulted in calamities, such as the World War I transport ship SS *Mont-Blanc*, which had collided with another ship and exploded in Halifax Harbor. It had been carrying the equivalent of three thousand tons of TNT when the ship blew up. Almost two thousand lives were lost, and five hundred acres of the city were destroyed, either by the pressure wave or by the sixty-foot tsunami caused by the blast. It was the biggest man-made explosion in history until Little Boy leveled Hiroshima.

The devastation of the Parthenon hadn't made the case list, probably because it happened so long ago. But Grant wasn't surprised that the explosion had caused so much damage. In fact, he was more surprised that any of the building was left standing.

"That's a shame," Grant said.

"Indeed."

"So these are all the sculptures?"

Lumley chuckled. "Goodness, no. Lord Elgin only procured half of the Marbles. The rest now reside in the New Acropolis Museum in Athens. Of course, they'd like to have them all, but we'll let our governments wrestle with that."

"What do you mean?"

"Oh, the Greeks continue to argue that the Turks illegally sold the Marbles to Lord Elgin, who in turn sold them to the British Museum. The museum has maintained for years that the Marbles are safer here, but now that the New Acropolis Museum has a state-of-the-art facility for preserving the sculptures, the Greeks are keen to have the Marbles returned."

"And what do you think?"

"There is great risk in moving them at all, but I prefer to remain neutral. I am an archaeologist, not a politician."

"So do you have the sculptures that are referred to in the manuscript?"

"I think we may. You see, the manuscript refers to 'the seat of Herakles' and 'the feet of Aphrodite.' You may know Herakles better as Hercules."

Though Grant's grasp of ancient mythology was limited to what he'd seen in the Disney movies his nieces watched, he nodded. "Sure. Herakles."

Lumley pointed at a reclining male figure from the east pediment. His head was intact, but his hands were missing. "Do you see that paw there?" Grant squinted and then nodded. Just the barest form of a great cat's paw peeked out from under the robes the figure lay upon.

"We believe that is a lion's paw, which would indicate that the figure is Herakles." Lumley moved to the opposite side and indicated two female torsos, one lying against the other. "No one has been able to determine with certainty who these figures represent, but I favor the theory that it is Aphrodite relaxing upon her mother, Dione."

The seat of Herakles and the feet of Aphrodite will show the way.

Grant looked beneath the statues and saw that they were supported by a marble base.

"What should be under the statues?" he asked.

"They would rest on the pediment itself, which rests atop the pillars."

"So the seat of Herakles and the feet of Aphrodite are reference points. For what?"

"It may help if I knew what you're looking for."

Grant couldn't reveal the link of Midas, but he knew that being too evasive would only raise more questions. He hesitated while he decided what to reveal.

"We think this may be a clue to finding a map," he finally said. "Maybe something about the architecture of the Parthenon."

"A map? How interesting. Perhaps the golden rectangle is important."

"How?"

"Architects consider it the most perfect rectangle because it is so pleasing to the eye. Golden rectangles are a recurring feature in the design of the Parthenon. The symbol phi, which represents the golden ratio, is named after the Parthenon's architect, Phidias. Let me show you."

Lumley took a notebook from his pocket and drew a line and then a dot two-thirds along its length. He labeled the longer section A and the shorter one B. "In the golden ratio, A divided by B is equivalent to the sum of A plus B divided by A." He drew a rectangle whose sides were length A on the short side and length A plus B on the long. "A golden rectangle has sides proportional to the golden ratio, which makes it aesthetically pleasing."

"And the Parthenon is built in that layout?" Grant asked.

"No, but the façades of the Parthenon are in the shape of a golden rectangle, and one can see many more of them in the spaces between the columns making up the façade."

Grant would bring up Lumley's speculation with Tyler and Stacy, but he had no inkling of how it would help them find the map.

"Thanks a lot, Dr. Lumley," he said, shaking Lumley's hand. "If I have any more questions, is it all right if I call you?"

"Of course." He gave Grant his cell-phone number. "Any time of the day or night."

Grant turned to leave, but Lumley tapped his arm to stop him.

"Mr. Westfield, may I ask if your manuscript will be displayed anywhere in the near future? It will provide fascinating insight into the culture of ancient Greece."

"I don't know what the plans for the document are."

"It would be a shame if such an important piece of history were not studied by appropriate scholars. Our museum would treat it with great care."

"I'm sure it'll get a good home."

"On the other hand, if you are interested in selling it, I know a buyer eager to purchase it."

"What do you mean?"

"That is, of course, unless you'd care to lend or donate it to the museum."

Why would Lumley have a buyer lined up for the manuscript already? Unless . . .

Grant grabbed Lumley's arm. "You haven't told anyone about this, have you?" Lumley winced at the pressure, and Grant released him.

"I'm terribly sorry," Lumley said, "but my contact has been looking for this codex for quite some time. She has indicated that she would pay a handsome price to anyone who could proffer a deal for it."

"You would sell it?" Grant asked in astonishment.

Lumley cast his eyes down in embarrassment, like a chastened teenage boy who'd been caught joyriding in his father's car.

"Facilitating the sale is a better way of putting it," Lumley said. "Being a curator is not a high-paying profession, and my divorce has been messy and quite costly. I thought there would be no harm—"

"When did you tell her?"

"While you were waiting. I assure you, I have the best of intentions."

But she might not, Grant thought as he scanned the gallery for anyone who looked out of place.

"Who is she?"

Lumley bit his lip. "Her name is Gia Cavano. She simply paid me a retainer to keep watch for this kind of document. I do hope I haven't inconvenienced you."

Grant recognized the name immediately. Orr's childhood friend Gia. She was using her contact with Lumley to keep an eye out for the codex.

As Grant reached for his phone to text Tyler that Cavano was now onto them, he spotted a huge man in a gray suit studiously reading a museum map. Twice in one minute, he glanced up and looked at each person in the gallery, but his eyes stayed on Grant just a little longer. Amid the tourists in shorts and rain jackets, the dark-haired muscleman looked as out of place as a wolf at a sheep ranch.

Grant thought he was just being paranoid until a third surreptitious glance in his direction convinced him that someone really might be out to get him. And he'd bet that someone was hired by Gia Cavano.

TWENTY-THREE

For the past ten minutes, Tyler and Stacy had listened to Cavano explain her background with Orr, and Tyler didn't like what he was hearing, mainly because it showed how much bad blood there was between them.

Jordan Orr was Gia Cavano's second cousin on her mother's side. When Orr was just a boy, his family decided to take a trip back to his grandparents' home region of Campania. Cavano's parents welcomed them and hosted the three of them for two weeks while the Orrs visited Naples. It was during that time that Cavano and Orr went exploring and stumbled onto the Midas treasure.

The Orrs returned to the United States, planning to come back to Italy every year or two, but Cavano didn't hear from Orr again until many years after his parents died. She said it had never occurred to the authorities to send him back to Italy to live with his extended family. And by the time Cavano was an adult, and ready to follow up on what she'd seen in the tunnels, she couldn't track Orr down.

Five years ago, Orr took a trip to Europe and reconnected with Cavano. Only then did he learn that an Italian Ministry of Health building had been built atop the original entrance to the tunnel they'd discovered. It would take major demolition to cut through the foundation, and days more to map out the tunnels before finding the chamber again. But Orr and Cavano remembered the well opening they'd seen and realized that there might be another way in. He proposed that they search for this entrance to the vault.

For three years, they combed through every available historical document that had even a passing reference to Midas or gold, but they could find no mention of the Midas chamber.

Then the Archimedes manuscript and the golden hand were discovered in an English landholder's attic and made headlines around the world. When she and Orr saw the golden hand, which matched the statue in the Midas chamber, they knew the one line from the manuscript that had been released to the public was not just a fable.

He who controls this map controls the riches of Midas.

The codex would lead them to the treasure map. Orr and Cavano realized that they would have no chance to get the manuscript once the auction house's appraisal and cataloguing were completed and the document's full contents were known. So they came up with the plan to steal it before the appraisal was done.

The heist went off without a hitch and then . . . nothing. She had provided the muscle, including two men who had been loyal to her and reported Orr's movements back to her without his knowledge, but everyone in the crew had disappeared without a trace. Cavano assumed the escape boat had gone down at sea with all hands.

"I purchased the tablet several months later," Cavano said, finishing the story. "It had been found with the hand and the manuscript, but it wasn't part of the original auction. After the theft, the seller didn't trust the auction house, so I was able to make a generous preemptive offer. I believed that tablet might have something to do with the search for Midas, but I could not divine its purpose. I thought I never would. Until now."

"What makes you think we know anything about this search for Midas?" Stacy said.

"Because Jordan must be alive and in possession of the manuscript. He knows I'm days from returning to the Midas chamber myself, and he's trying to beat me to it. Loyalty is prized above everything else in my culture, and Jordan betrayed me. For that, I will make him pay."

She pressed a button, and her bodyguard opened the door. He came in carrying the pack Tyler had put in the Range Rover's trunk. The bodyguard laid it on the desk. Cavano reached in and pulled out the pack's only content.

The geolabe. Cavano's eyes glittered as she looked at it.

"Fascinating device. You'll have to explain what it does later."

She put it back in the pack and spoke to the man in Italian. This went back and forth for a minute, and the man finally said, "*Sì,*" and left with the pack.

"What do you want?" Tyler said.

"I want you to help me find Jordan."

"We'd like to," Stacy said, "but we don't know how to find your cousin."

"You're not a very good liar, Dr. Benedict." Cavano drummed her fingers on the desk. "So. How much for you to give up your search and tell me where he is?"

"How much?"

"I'll give you a share of the gold."

Tyler and Stacy looked at each other as if they were contemplating the offer. Tyler knew this offer would be made only once. If they turned it down, they would be forced to do what she wanted anyway. Tyler briefly considered allying with Cavano against Orr, but it was too risky. If he and Stacy weren't able to complete their task, Orr would know they had failed. Then Sherman Locke and Carol Benedict would die.

"Supposing we know anything about this," Tyler said. "How do we know you can deliver our share if we turn him in to you?"

Cavano smiled. "Remember the Ministry of Health building? I now own it. Or I will on Monday. Italian austerity measures forced its sale. Once I take possession, my demolition team will tear the foundation apart until we find the tunnel. After that, it will merely be a matter of time until I find the chamber. You can either get nothing with Jordan or you can name your price with me."

"And if we don't know him?"

"I'll soon find out the truth if you don't cooperate." Cavano obviously meant torture.

Tyler paused, then said, "Three million dollars. Each."

Stacy swung her head around so fast, her own hair hit her in the face. "What are you doing?"

Tyler put a hand on her arm. "It's okay. If she wants to triple the million Orr is paying each of us, I'm happy to go with the high bidder." He looked at Stacy, who nodded slowly.

Cavano arched her eyebrows. "Done. Three million."

She pressed the button again, and the bodyguard returned, this time holding a gun. He frisked Tyler and took his Leatherman multi-tool and cell phone. Stacy handed over her phone as well.

"What's this?" Tyler said. "What about our deal?"

"I'm sorry," Cavano said, "but I'll have to detain you until our business is complete. If you fulfill your end of the bargain, you will get your three million dollars each, but until then you will have to remain here as my guests." She spoke Italian again, leaving Tyler to guess that she was telling the bodyguard which room to lock them up in.

"I am needed elsewhere at this time, so Pietro will show you where you'll be staying. I assume you don't mind sharing a room." She grinned at her intimation and left.

Pietro motioned with his pistol for them to get up. English didn't seem to be his forte.

Tyler and Stacy stood.

"You know," Tyler said, "you could shoot your eye out with that thing."

Nothing. The bodyguard's face didn't change a bit. Not that Tyler thought his joke was funny, but if the man understood even a bit of English, he'd at least expect a roll of the eyes.

They began the walk down the hall, confident that they could talk without being understood.

"So what do we do now?" Stacy said.

"We get out of here."

"How?"

"I'm working on it."

"Work faster."

The bodyguard said something in Italian and gestured for them to start climbing a wide marble staircase that wound around and up to a second-story balcony.

At the first corner, an enormous porcelain vase was precariously perched on a wooden pedestal.

Tyler nodded at it. "Be careful."

Stacy shot him an annoyed look. "You're worried about a stupid vase—" That's when Tyler pushed her into it with his hip.

Stacy bumped the table, and the vase teetered over. Her instinct was to try to steady the delicate artwork, and that was exactly the first impulse of the bodyguard as well.

Pietro was distracted for only a moment, but it was enough. He reached out to catch the vase, and when he did, Tyler slammed him into the wall. Pietro's head knocked against the hardwood, and Tyler bashed his wrist at the same time. The pistol dropped to the marble, and so did Pietro, who cracked his head again. He tumbled down the stairs, still breathing but out cold.

Tyler picked up the gun and took back his Leatherman and his phone. He also took Pietro's phone and handed Stacy's back to her. "Fast enough for you?"

It had all happened so quickly that Stacy was still holding the vase.

"What . . . I . . ." she stammered as she pushed it back onto the stand.

"Come on." Tyler grabbed her arm, raced down the stairs, and turned toward the study.

"Aren't we getting the hell out of here?" Stacy said, looking over her shoulder.

"Not without that tablet."

They ran into the study and closed the doors. Tyler flipped the gun around and used the butt to shatter the glass around the tablet.

"Let me take it," Stacy said. "It's very fragile."

She plucked the hinged pieces of wood out of the display case and folded them together. Tyler was about to open the door for a dash to the Range Rover when shouts outside the office stopped him. Somebody had found Pietro.

"Crap! What do we do now?" Stacy said.

Tyler pointed to the field outside. "Through the window."

He took out Pietro's phone and dialed a number as quickly as he could. He was relieved when it was answered on the first ring.

"Aiden MacKenna."

"It's Tyler."

"Whose phone are you—" Aiden started before Tyler interrupted him.

"Aiden, start recording this call, and whatever you do, don't hang up."

Tyler took the phone, reached as high as he could on the bookshelf, and placed it out of sight on top of a row of books.

Stacy waved her hands at Tyler to hurry. "Let's go!"

He threw open the window. By now, alarms would be going off throughout the estate. Tyler didn't know how many other Pietro types Cavano had, but he wouldn't be surprised to see a small army materialize.

He lowered Stacy to the ground, then jumped down. She started to run around the house, but Tyler pulled her in the other direction.

"But the cars are that way," she protested.

"That's where they'll expect us to go."

"Aren't we going to get the geolabe?"

"We can't right now. This way." They ran for the stables. Tyler was hoping to find a workman's car inside because it wouldn't be long before Cavano's men realized where they had gone.

In half a minute, they'd crossed the lawn and reached the stables. Tyler motioned for her to stay behind him. With the pistol in front of him, he opened the stable door and swept the room. Clear. No stable hands visible. Except for the chuffing of horses and the clopping of hooves pawing at the hay in the stalls, the stable was silent.

There wasn't a single vehicle in sight.

"We're out of luck," Tyler said. "I thought they might have a pickup or something in here. Without a car, we're stuck."

"What are you talking about?" Stacy said, pointing at the stalls. "These are even better than cars."

Tyler blanched when he realized what Stacy was suggesting. She wanted him to ride a horse.

TWENTY-FOUR

After a few more profuse apologies, Lumley went back to his office, leaving Grant on his own. As he walked through the hall of Greek statues and vases, Grant texted Tyler to tell him that someone had picked up the scent of the codex and warn his friend to be careful. Tyler replied immediately.

Too late. We got probs of r own. Meet at Heathrow.

That didn't sound good, but at the moment Grant had to deal with his own situation. No doubt he could take the man tailing him in a fight, but an altercation might get the police involved, which would complicate things. If he had to, Grant would test his skills with Krav Maga, a style of fighting perfected by Israeli commandos, but he remembered an old joke about the merits of martial arts. When an elderly man was told that karate was the oldest form of self-defense, the man replied, "It ain't older than running."

Running wasn't something Grant did often, because speed wasn't his strength. Strength was his strength. He looped the backpack around both shoulders, leaving his arms free, and he looked at his map of the museum. He was one room over from the gallery with the Elgin Marbles. There were only two exits. He could either go back and exit through the Great Court, or he could keep going forward, which would lead him through the gift shop.

He didn't like backtracking. Forward. Once he was outside, he would head back to the Underground and lose his shadow in the maze of passageways.

The man stayed thirty feet behind him. Grant checked out his follower in the reflection of the glass cases.

With acne-scarred cheeks and bushy black eyebrows, the guy wasn't going to win an award in a Brad Pitt look-alike contest. But what he lacked in looks he more than made up for with his size. At least four inches taller than Grant, he had the bulk of a grizzly. The only place the guy would be inconspicuous was coming out of an NFL locker room.

He carried himself as though no one would ever dare give him trouble, which meant that he likely got by on intimidation and brute force rather than any skill, so Grant wasn't too worried even if the guy confronted him. He just had to make sure he lost the man before reinforcements could arrive.

After the next archway, Grant turned left and picked up his pace, walking through two galleries and past the gift shop to the front entrance. Outside, it was a clear path through the courtyard to the entrance gate. From there it was just three blocks to the tube station.

At the gate, Grant realized that he wouldn't get that far. As he walked through the gate, two men got out of a BMW and penned him in. Both looked like uglier relatives of the big man following him. One of them had a thin, perfectly shaped mustache that must have taken an hour to trim, and the other had a widow's peak sharp enough to be classified as a weapon.

Grant turned and saw that the guy behind him had made up ground and was now only ten feet away.

The man with the mustache called the big guy Sal and said something in Italian.

"*Sì,*" Sal said. "Mr. Westfield, you come with us."

Grant took a look at the three of them, who now had him surrounded. "What if I don't feel like it?"

Sal held his coat open to show a holstered pistol, warning Grant that he wouldn't get twenty feet without becoming a bull's-eye.

"You know, those are illegal in London," Grant said. "You could get in big trouble if the bobbies caught you with that."

"*You* are in trouble."

"Gia Cavano sent you, didn't she?"

Sal's eyes flickered at the mention of her name. "Get in the car."

"You really want to cause a stink out here?"

Sal narrowed his gaze in confusion. He probably didn't know what Grant meant. "Get in the car."

The three of them moved closer.

Grant remained still, his muscles tensed. "So you want me to get in the car?"

"Now."

They were within five feet of him.

"I'm going to have to say, screw you," Grant said.

That got exactly the response he was hoping for. Sal nodded to the other two, who reached for Grant's arms.

Whoever they were, they were street brawlers, not trained in hand-to-hand combat as he was. If they had been, they wouldn't have left themselves so open to attack.

Grant swung his arm around and smashed mustache man in the back of the neck with brutal force. Before the guy with the widow's peak could react, Grant threw his elbow back and slammed it into the side of his head. Both men went down in a heap.

During the time it took for Grant to put the two men out of action, Sal drew his pistol, but he'd made the mistake of standing too close. Grant chopped his wrist, sending the gun to the sidewalk. Then he smashed his knee into Sal's groin. Simple, but effective. Sal fell to his knees and toppled over, cradling his crotch and screaming in pain.

Like most real fights Grant had been in, this one had lasted less than five seconds. Shaking his head at how easy it had been to disable the three men, Grant reached into their jackets and removed their guns. He ejected the magazines and removed the slides from each of the pistols before dumping them on the ground. There was no reason to make it easy for them to give chase, so he ran around to the driver's side of the still-running car, shrugged off the backpack, and got in. He'd drive the BMW three blocks to the Underground station and dump it there.

Putting the car in gear, Grant smiled at the men still lying on the ground. Through the open window, he called out, "Piece of advice, Sal. Next time, bring more men."

Then he stepped on the gas and left Sal still on his knees, shouting curses at him. Grant didn't know what he said, but the Italian sure made it sound classy.

TWENTY-FIVE

I'm not getting on one of those death traps," Tyler said.

He kept watch at the stable door while Stacy hurried to cinch up the straps on the saddle of a second horse. Out of the corner of her eye, she caught him nervously changing his grip on the pistol and realized that he was more scared than she was. She had marveled at how he had calmly disarmed a massive explosive, faced down Orr, and dispatched a gunman without breaking a sweat. Now she was the one trying to quiet his nerves.

"Come on, you big baby," she said. "It's just a horse. How else are we going to get away?" Cavano and her men would discover their hiding place any minute.

"You go. I'll try for the car."

"Don't be stupid. You'll get yourself killed. Don't tell me you've never ridden."

"I have. About twenty-five years ago. That's why I'd rather take my chances with Cavano." He wouldn't look at Stacy.

They'd already gone over their options, and there weren't any. The cars at the front of the house would be impossible to reach without getting captured. Calling the police wouldn't help. At best, Cavano would say they assaulted her bodyguard and destroyed her property. Tyler and Stacy would be hauled off to jail, endangering any chance of meeting Orr in Naples on Sunday.

Some of Stacy's fondest memories were of riding her horse, Chanter. Dressage and jumping occupied a big part of her childhood, not to mention chasing rabbits around the fields after the harvest. She hadn't had the opportunity lately, but saddling the horses had brought it all back. Technology marches on, but riding equipment hadn't changed significantly in hundreds of years, so she finished outfitting the horses in record time.

"We're ready," she said. "Are you coming or not?"

"Not."

"You'll ride a motorcycle and not a horse?"

"A motorcycle goes where I tell it to."

Now she got it. He was a product of the mechanical age, and he didn't like it that a horse had a mind of its own. Something must have sparked this irrational fear, but she didn't have time to dig into that now.

She marched up to him and grabbed him by the arms. "You are going to get on that damned horse, and we're going to get the hell out of here, do you understand me?"

Bullets ricocheted off the door, and both of them dove to the ground. Through the crack in the door, she could see four men running toward them, snapping off shots with their pistols.

"All right," Tyler growled as he rolled to his feet. "We'll do it your way."

Stacy leaped up and handed the reins of the nearer horse to Tyler, who acted as if she'd given him a used tissue. He eyed the horse, but another crack of gunfire goaded him into action. He put his foot in the stirrup and, in the most ungainly display of horsemanship she'd ever seen, clambered into the saddle. He pawed at the leather.

"Where is the horn thing?" He was talking about the grip on the front of Western saddles.

She mounted her own horse. "It's an English saddle, so it doesn't have one. Just keep your feet in the stirrups and don't let go of the reins. Follow me. Your horse will do the rest."

Stacy trotted to the large door that was open at the opposite end of the stable. With a jab from her heels, the horse launched into a gallop.

Over her shoulder she saw Tyler's horse go into a trot, with Tyler bouncing up and down like one of those rubber balls on a paddle board.

"Say 'canter'!" she yelled.

Tyler cried, "Canter, dammit!" and his horse took off, with him barely holding on. He looked like an idiot, but he was moving.

They'd gotten fifty yards when Cavano's men burst out of the stable. One of them lifted his weapon to fire, but Cavano raced out and pushed him aside, sending his shot awry.

"They're worth more than you are," she screamed in Italian loud enough to be heard even at that distance. Stacy couldn't tell if Cavano meant them or the horses.

Two Range Rovers raced around the drive and skidded to a stop to let Cavano and her men pile in. They weren't giving up. Cavano just wanted to get closer so that they wouldn't injure one of her precious horses. The Range Rovers took off after them, spraying gravel from all four wheels.

Stacy angled her horse toward a stand of trees to the right. If she and Tyler could get through, it would give them some breathing room while Cavano and her men went around the long way.

Tyler's eyes kept darting up to her and down to the horse. He didn't look terrified, but he sure didn't look happy, either.

She slowed to a trot to get through the dense thicket of oaks and shrubs. They wove through, Tyler cursing as branches swatted him.

"You okay?"

"I'm fine." He sounded anything but.

In seconds they were through to another pasture. Stacy kicked into a canter, and they raced across the field. To Stacy, it felt perfectly natural. Tyler, on the other hand, crashed into the saddle instead of using a half-seat, a method of supporting yourself in the stirrups during a gallop. She could only imagine the amount of pain he must be experiencing to his privates. From his grimace, she'd say extreme.

They'd put a few hundred yards between themselves and Cavano, but the Range Rovers were catching up fast. Any moment they'd decide to take another shot, no matter what happened to the horses.

Up ahead, Stacy saw a potential lifesaver. A river, forty feet across, knifed through the field. The only visible crossing was a wooden footbridge just large enough for the sheep grazing on the other side. It would be tricky, but the horses could make it if they stepped carefully.

"Head for the bridge!" she yelled.

"Are you crazy?" he yelled back.

"I don't want to die!"

"Neither do I!"

Despite his protests, she didn't stop, but slowed to a trot, allowing time for Tyler's horse to get nose to tail with hers.

She pointed her horse straight across the bridge. They'd get only one try at this.

Her horse stepped onto the bridge. She nudged it forward, and the horse bolted ahead. The wood groaned under the load, but the bridge held. She was almost to the other side when she heard a tremendous splash behind her.

When she reached the pasture on the other side, Stacy wheeled around to see that Tyler had plunged into the water. The horse must have lost its footing and jumped into the river. She didn't think the horse had fallen, because Tyler was still on top of it, although he was now soaking wet.

His horse charged out of the river, trailing a torrent of water behind it. They rode through the herd of sheep to the top of the next hill and stopped when they saw a hedgerow blocking the way forward.

"Did you see that?" Tyler yelled. "This is why I hate riding!"

"You're no John Wayne, that's for sure."

"And this horse isn't Seabiscuit."

The roar of the approaching engines put a stop to their argument. Safely out of pistol range, they watched as one of the Range Rovers went into a four-wheel drift to avoid the river, barely skidding to a stop before it hit the edge.

The other Range Rover decided to go for it, but the bridge was too narrow. It plowed into the river with a great splash, burying its nose in the mud, and came to a stop. Men scrambled out of the open windows and waded back to the opposite shore.

The passenger door of the dry Range Rover opened, and Cavano stood with her hands on her hips staring up at Stacy and Tyler. There was no smile this time, just a look of pure hatred.

Stacy squeezed her legs to get the horse moving, and they rode along the hedgerow until they found an opening and left Cavano behind.

"Where to now?" she asked. She was completely lost.

Tyler pointed to his left. "On the way to Cavano's mansion, we passed a town about a mile that way, I think. We can try to get a car there."

They rode fast, worried that Cavano would find some way to cut them off or intercept them at the town.

When they arrived at the quaint village, the pedestrians didn't give them a second glance, as if it weren't unusual at all to see riders on horseback on the main street.

The sound of a train horn indicated something even better than a car to hire. They rode two more blocks and found the station. After handing their horses over to two astonished teenagers, Stacy and Tyler hopped aboard the train as it pulled away.

Stacy asked one of the passengers where they were headed. With a disdainful glare at Tyler's sopping form, he told her they'd be at London's Victoria Station in a little more than an hour. By the time Cavano found her horses and figured out their destination, they'd be long gone.

Stacy felt much better now that they were out of danger. She smiled at Tyler and took his hand to pull him forward, as if they were a loving couple on a holiday trip gone wrong. As they made their way down the aisle, she said, "That ride wasn't so bad, was it?"

Tyler gave her a dirty look and said nothing. He waddled to a seat and eased himself down. For the rest of the trip, the only time he talked was to ask the ticket collector where he could get a bag of ice to sit on.

TWENTY-SIX

The midday sun poured through the windshield of Clarence Gibson's semi cab, overpowering the truck's balky air conditioner. He slammed his hand on the dashboard and swore a streak that the Lord wouldn't be proud of. With a full load in the trailer behind him, the engine strained as he climbed the twisty back road over the Virginia Appalachians.

In his thirty years with Dwight's Farm Services, Gibson had never complained about his job, but he was tired of truck maintenance at the company being a low priority. Just last week he'd been hauling a load of fertilizer to a farm down in Blacksburg when the bearings on the drive axle seized, leaving him stranded for three hours out in the middle of nowhere until a tow truck made it up from Roanoke.

He rolled down the window, but the wind didn't help. Not with this humidity. The sweat continued to pour down the back of his neck, and his shirt was completely soaked. At least the radio worked, although there was only one country station.

It had been ten minutes since he'd turned off the state highway headed for a farm west of Deerfield. In that time he'd been passed twice by cars that didn't want to wait behind his groaning rig. One of them even jumped the gun and didn't bother to wait for a passing lane. Probably some doped-up college kids who were going to get themselves killed someday.

And now behind him was lucky vehicle number three, this time a white van. It was accelerating fast behind him on the first flat section Gibson had seen since the highway. There wasn't another car in sight, so he waved the van around and pulled over onto the shoulder to let him by.

The van shot past and roared ahead. Gibson pulled back onto the road and tried to coax a little more speed, hoping to get a bigger dose of the natural breeze. He poked his head to the side to get closer to the airflow, then snapped it back when he saw the van weave back and forth three times and then stop dead across the road, blocking the way.

What in the world?

Gibson stuck his foot on the brake. The truck shuddered to a stop less than twenty feet from the van. Though they were sopping wet, the hairs on the back of his neck pricked up. If the van had a flat tire, why didn't the driver just pull over to the shoulder? Something wasn't right.

The van door slid open, and two men clad in black from head to toe jumped out holding M4 assault rifles. They wore balaclavas, so Gibson could see nothing but eyes. He lunged for the Smith & Wesson .38 revolver he kept in the glove compartment for emergencies, but the passenger door was thrown open before he could get to it. He stared into the black depths of the barrel that could introduce him to his maker.

An accented voice yelled, "Get out now!"

Gibson put his hands up.

"Now!"

He unlatched his seat belt and opened the driver's door. A hand snaked in and yanked him out, tossing him to the ground.

The passenger door slammed, and the one who had pulled him out said something Gibson didn't understand, but he'd certainly heard the language before on TV. Arabic, or at least something along those lines.

Terrorists? What would they want with him? He was a middle-aged, overweight nobody.

"I don't have—" he started.

"Shut up!" the man yelled, and punched him in the back with the butt of the rifle. Gibson went down on his stomach, sucking for air. The knee in his back made breathing even harder.

The taller of the two walked over to the plain silver trailer, reached under the metal chassis, pulled out a white box the size of a pack of cigarettes, and pocketed it. That's why they'd shown up in the middle of nowhere. They'd used some kind of tracking device.

The other one grabbed Gibson's hands and twisted them behind his back. He felt cool plastic zipcuffs locking his wrists together. The two of them hauled him to his feet, hustled him to the van, and pushed him inside. He fell to the floor. Another set of zipcuffs went around his ankles.

The first gunman raised his rifle above his head and shouted, "*Allahu Akbar!*"

"*Allahu Akbar!*" the other cried in response. Then he ran back to Gibson's truck. The van door slammed shut.

This was a hijacking? It seemed crazy, but the sound of his truck revving told him that it had to be true.

Although the past few moments had seemed like a lifetime to Gibson, they couldn't have been more than thirty seconds. Whoever they were, his kidnappers had planned this well.

The van took off, rolling Gibson against the back doors. His phone was still sitting on the passenger seat of his cab, so calling for help wasn't an option. He struggled to sit up, but the winding roads tossed him down every time he made any progress. In twenty minutes he was exhausted. He asked where he was being taken, but he was met with stony silence.

Twenty minutes later, the van slowed and turned onto another road. Instead of the smooth hum of asphalt, Gibson could feel the tires crunching over dirt. He thought it must be some kind of driveway, but it kept climbing uphill, and the ride got rougher, bouncing up and down over deep ruts and potholes. They didn't stop for another half hour.

When the van came to a halt, the driver, still in his balaclava, wrenched open the door and held a Beretta 9 mm on Gibson. He then unsheathed a wicked-looking blade, but he did nothing more with it than cut the ankle ties.

"Out," he said.

Gibson draped his legs over the side of the van and stood briefly before falling to his knees. His feet had lost all feeling. It didn't matter, though. He could see where he was now. They were surrounded on all sides by the thick woods of the George Washington National Forest. The weed-covered track they'd crawled along was a barely used fire road.

He had been brought here to be executed.

"Up!" the man shouted.

Gibson's heart pounded with fear, but he wasn't going to make it that easy for this terrorist. He got to his knees.

"Why don't you make me?" he said, sounding much braver than he felt.

The terrorist kicked Gibson. He fell over hard and rolled into a ditch. Before he could get up, he heard the crack of the pistol and a searing pain at his right ear. He fell back to the ground, his eyes away from the terrorist. The headshot hadn't killed him. Should he get up and keep fighting or play dead? He held his breath.

The door slammed shut, and after making a three-point turn the van accelerated back down the road.

Gibson remained motionless for another minute until he realized that he must be the luckiest son of a bitch in the world. He sat up and felt blood coursing down his temple, but he was alive. The angle into the ditch must have thrown off the terrorist's aim. With all the blood, the shooter had just assumed it was a kill shot.

Gibson thanked the Lord for His mercy and then found the

sharp edge of a rock to cut the tie on his wrists. With his hands free, he ripped off the bottom of his shirt and pushed it against the side of his head. It would stanch the blood, although it wouldn't do anything for his headache.

As he trudged down the road back to civilization to report the hijacking, he pondered why they had targeted his truck. Sure, he could see Arab radicals taking a load of ammonium-nitrate fertilizer, the explosive compound used to make bombs like the one that blew up in Oklahoma City.

But he had no earthly idea what two terrorists would want with one hundred cubic yards of sawdust.

TWENTY-SEVEN

Tyler wasn't happy about having to wait for a shower when he and Stacy rendezvoused as planned with Grant at the Heathrow Airport Marriott. For convenience, they'd reserved a suite with a living area between a king room for Stacy and another one with double beds for the guys. Grant was already in the bathroom, so Tyler had to endure the smell of horse and river muck for a little longer. Tyler had their luggage sent over from the plane, and the clean clothes beckoned from his suitcase. After Grant finished, Tyler took his turn, feeling grateful for the invention of indoor plumbing.

After they ordered dinner from room service, Grant regaled them with his findings at the museum and his fight with Sal. Gia Cavano must have sent her men in London to abduct Grant as soon as she heard from the curator.

In turn, Tyler and Stacy recounted their visit to Cavano's estate. When Stacy came to their escape from the mansion, she began to tease Tyler with wicked glee.

"And when we got to the stable," she said, "it was obvious the only way we were going to get out of there was on horseback, but Doctor Fraidy Pants here almost blew it because he's scared of horses."

"I am not scared of horses," Tyler protested. "Not anymore. Now I just hate them."

"You looked scared to me."

"Wait a minute," Grant said, pointing at Tyler. "You got him to ride a horse today?"

"Why is that so hard to believe?" Stacy asked.

"Weren't you almost killed by one when you were a kid?" Grant asked Tyler. "I thought you said you'd never get on one again."

"I didn't have much choice," Tyler said.

"Hold on. What's this about almost getting killed?"

Tyler sighed. He didn't enjoy telling the story. "When I was ten, my father took me and my sister to a ranch for a weekend. I was big into go-karts and motocross, not horses. I hadn't been to a farm in my entire life until that morning."

"I can't even imagine that," Stacy said. "I've been riding since I was four."

"Well, I'd never seen a horse up close until I got to that ranch. I was a little hesitant at first. Those things are even bigger when you're a kid. We got lessons for a couple of hours—walking, trotting, cantering—and I was feeling okay. Not loving it like my sister was, but okay. As I was dismounting, I put my foot in the stirrup by accident and for no good reason the horse spooked."

"That can happen."

"Not with a car, it can't. My Viper has never decided to hit the gas after I opened the door to get out. Anyway, the stupid horse took off running with me dragging alongside, bouncing around like a can tied behind a honeymooner's car. After a couple of spins around the corral, my boot finally came off, but not before I bashed my head on a fencepost. I spent three days in the hospital with a concussion and a torn ACL. Needless to say, I hadn't been on a horse again until today."

"And now you're cured?" Grant said.

"Very funny. Next time I hope we get stuck with a couple of ATVs instead."

"Still, we couldn't have gotten away without them," Stacy said.

"My horse didn't have to jump off the bridge to do it."

Tyler told Grant about their ride through the fields and the river incident.

"Sounds like more fun than my day," Grant said.

"Why didn't you tell me that story this afternoon?" Stacy asked Tyler.

"We didn't have time," he replied. "Besides, would it have made any difference?"

A knock at the door stopped her from answering. Tyler checked to make sure it really was their dinner and let two busboys in. The feast spread out across three serving carts.

As they ate, they tried to figure out their next move.

"The most important priority is to get the geolabe back," Tyler said. "Without it, we're still missing one of the three keys of Archimedes' puzzle to find the map."

"Can't you just make another geolabe?" Stacy said.

"It would take weeks to forge all those gears," Grant explained. "They require delicate machining. Tyler had to find a bronze specialist to make it the first time."

"And we only have another four days. We need that one back, so we'll have to figure out a way to get back into Cavano's estate and liberate it."

"We can't. She's leaving tonight."

"How do you know that?"

"Cavano either assumed I didn't understand Italian or she didn't care. When she gave the geolabe back to her bodyguard, she said, 'Put it in the trunk. We'll take it to Munich with us.' "

"Crap," Tyler said. With Cavano on the move, it would be exponentially more difficult to get the geolabe back. "Okay. I had Aiden send me an audio recording of the call from Pietro's phone in Cavano's office. I was hoping we'd get some intel about when they'd be out of the house, but maybe it'll tell us about her travel plans instead. Intercepting them en route is our only option. We'll have you listen to it and see if there's anything useful."

Tyler's own phone had been drenched and was ruined. Before they reached the hotel, they had stopped at a cellular-phone store and gotten a replacement, transferring his number and his backed-up contact list to it.

"What about the text on the tablet?" Stacy said.

"And all the stuff about the Parthenon?" Grant said.

"None of that matters if we can't get the geolabe back. I'll talk to Aiden and see if they've been able to decode the tracker signal from the geolabe."

Stacy's head snapped up. "Oh, my God! If Orr figures out that we lost it, he might hurt Carol and your father."

"Then we need to make sure he doesn't find out." He looked at his watch. "Speaking of which, it's time for our daily check-in. Ready?"

He dialed and put the call on speaker. Orr answered immediately. "Right on time. How is the search going?"

Tyler ignored the question. "Are Carol and my father all right?"

"You go first. Then I send the proof-of-life."

Tyler told him about the tablet and its link to the Parthenon, but he left out the details. All Orr had to know was that they were making progress.

"Where are you off to next?" Orr asked, as if he were talking to a friend about his vacation plans.

"Munich," Tyler said. "We've tracked down a document there that we think might be helpful."

"Good. Then carry on. We'll talk again tomorrow."

"What about your end of the deal?"

"Check your e-mail." Orr hung up.

Tyler opened the laptop and pulled up his e-mail app. In addition to the recording Aiden had sent, he had another message from Orr. Two videos were attached.

Stacy put her hand to her mouth when she saw the first video, which showed Carol sitting in a chair, her wrists and ankles cuffed, the man with the ski mask and newspaper standing next to her.

Carol was alert and wore no blindfold. She looked terrified but unharmed.

Tyler squeezed Stacy's arm. "Are you okay?"

Stacy nodded but said nothing.

Tyler dreaded seeing his own video, but Sherman Locke sat in the same chair in seemingly good shape, though he was blindfolded and grizzled stubble dusted his face. Tyler checked the *USA Today* Web site just to make sure of the date on the front-page story.

Then Tyler saw Sherman's hands, and he ran the video again, freezing it when his father's fingers were contorted in a particular orientation for just a second. He showed it to Grant and Stacy.

"Another message?" Grant asked.

"I think so."

Stacy frowned. "What do you mean, *another* message?"

Tyler hadn't told her about the first message when he received it because he didn't want to raise false hopes that his father might be able to free Carol.

"You were surprised yesterday when I said he wasn't going down without a fight," he said to Stacy.

"No, I thought you were nuts."

Tyler brought up the previous day's video. "Look at his hands. He sent me a message."

Stacy peered at the video, and then her eyes went wide. "Sign language."

"If you weren't looking for it, you'd think he was just straining against the cuffs."

"What did he say yesterday?"

"He couldn't do full signs because they require motion, so he just formed letters. Two sets. The first two letters were *M* and *K*. I think he was saying 'I'm okay.' "

"And the second set?"

"*F* and *M*."

Stacy thought about it for a moment and then laughed. "Eff 'em?"

"Right. His way of saying that he was planning to fight back."

"What did he say today?"

Tyler played the second video again. "Today's message is a little harder to figure out. Again two sets of letters. Actually, the first are letters and the second are numbers."

"Maybe he's trying to tell you how many kidnappers there are," Stacy said.

"I doubt it. The numbers are nine and zero. Ninety."

"And the letters?"

"*S* and *R*."

"SR 90?" Stacy clapped her hands together in triumph. "State Road 90! He's telling you where he is!"

Tyler didn't share her enthusiasm. "Possibly. But that wouldn't help us narrow down the search very much. There must be hundreds of miles of State Road 90s in the U.S. It's got to be something else."

"I'll see what Google comes up with," Grant said as he tapped on his own laptop. His face fell when he saw the results. "This is not good."

"Why?" Tyler said.

"Because the first result that comes up for SR 90 is an entry for strontium-90."

Tyler shuddered as a chill ran up his spine. Given that his father used to head up the agency responsible for rooting out weapons of mass destruction, it wasn't a huge leap to guess that strontium-90 was what he meant. Grant rubbed his forehead as if he were massaging a headache.

"What's strontium-90?" Stacy asked.

"It's a highly radioactive isotope," Tyler said. "My father could be saying that Orr has gotten hold of some Sr-90."

"How radioactive is it?"

"Sr-90 is one of the key constituents of the radioactive dust from the Chernobyl disaster."

"Where could Orr get his hands on something like that?"

"Radioactive materials are available on the black market," Grant said. "It says here that Sr-90 is found in spent nuclear fuel. It's also used as a power source in old Soviet thermal generators."

"And if Orr has some," Tyler said, "he could be planning to make a dirty bomb."

"Which is what?" Stacy asked.

"It's also called a radiological weapon. A poor man's nuclear bomb. You set off a conventional bomb along with some radioactive material and it coats everything around it with fallout dust. The radiation could be dangerous enough to render a major city uninhabitable for decades. For some reason, Orr may be in possession of a weapon of mass destruction."

"And both my sister and your father were kidnapped in—" A gasp caught in Stacy's throat. "Oh, God."

Tyler slowly nodded. The last time anyone had seen Sherman and Carol was in Washington, D.C.

TWENTY-EIGHT

Tyler wished he hadn't eaten so much for dinner. The idea that Orr was building a WMD was turning his stomach.

"I hate to bring this up," Stacy said, "but maybe we should reconsider calling the FBI now."

"And tell them what?" Tyler said.

"That Jordan Orr has his hands on strontium-90."

"Does he?"

"You just said he did."

"That's what *I* say. You said it could be a state highway, which it also could be."

"Or an address," Grant said. "Or someone's initials. Or any one of a hundred other things."

"Then there's the question of why Orr would want a dirty bomb. If he's planning to blackmail the U.S. government, he wouldn't need us for that."

"Maybe he wants to nuke the Midas chamber once he finds it," Grant said. "It almost worked for Goldfinger." When Stacy gave him a confused look, he continued, "You know, the James Bond movie where the villain Goldfinger is going to set off an atomic bomb inside Fort Knox."

"But Goldfinger already had a stockpile of gold that would rise in value once the nuke went off," Tyler said. "I don't think Orr has a stack of gold lying around that he wants to increase in value."

"But what if talking to the FBI could lead to finding Carol and your dad?" Stacy said.

"Let's think about what would happen if we got the FBI involved right now. I'm not saying it's the wrong thing to do, but we have to be smarter than Orr about this. Grant, you play the FBI."

"Okay, but I'm not putting on a suit."

Tyler got up and paced. "I call you up and tell you that my father and Stacy's sister have been kidnapped."

"When were they kidnapped?"

"Yesterday morning."

"And you're just calling now? From London?"

"We were worried about Orr killing them."

"And you're coming forward now because . . . ?" Grant asked.

"Because I have new information that the kidnappers may have an unknown quantity of strontium-90."

"What's your evidence?"

"My father sent us a message via sign language. I have the video."

"Maybe he's sending you his location. Why jump to the conclusion that it's strontium-90?"

"My father is a retired general who specialized in tracking threats from radioactive materials."

Grant shook Tyler's hand. "Thank you, Dr. Locke. We'll start our manhunt for this Jordan Orr and alert every agency in the country that there is the possible threat of a nuke. By the way, we'll need to tap your phones and have you come back to the U.S."

Tyler stopped and pointed at Grant. "And now Orr finds out he's being investigated and kills Carol and my father."

"Or maybe he sets off his radiological weapon prematurely," Grant said. "Or he doesn't set it off, because we can't be sure he has one. Right now it's just a hunch."

Stacy threw up her hands in defeat. "Okay, okay, okay. You've made your point. We don't call the FBI. So what's the alternative? We're just going to go along with Orr's demands?"

"No," Tyler said. "If he really has a WMD and my father has seen it, Orr will never let him live whether or not we can lead him to the treasure."

"And Carol?"

When Tyler didn't say anything, Stacy folded her arms and crossed to the window.

"I know it looks hopeless," he said, "but the good news is that if we can get the geolabe back, we can stop playing defense and go on offense."

"Offense?" she said.

"The next time we see Orr, we won't let him get away."

"What about your dad and Stacy's sister?" Grant said.

Tyler took a deep breath. "We trade with Orr. His life for theirs. Then we bring in the FBI."

"Let's just tell him we've solved Archimedes' puzzle and meet him in Naples," Stacy said. "Why are we going through all this?"

"Because I'm sure Orr has some way of knowing if we're lying about where the entry to the tunnel system is. He wouldn't go to all this trouble without that kind of safeguard. We have to show up holding some aces because I'm sure he'd call our bluff."

"So what's the plan?"

"The plan is to figure out a way to get the geolabe back from Cavano. Let's listen to the audio file from Cavano's office."

Tyler played it back. The voices on the phone were muffled, and they faded in and out as people walked around the room. He just hoped Stacy could catch enough of it to do them some good.

She peered intently at the computer as she jotted down notes. Tyler admired how she was handling all of this, never complaining, focusing completely on the job at hand. But he could see that the strain was beginning to wear on her. He'd seen it before with soldiers in his command who were suddenly thrust into battle. They wanted to stay strong for their buddies, but the haunted stares and creased brows betrayed their fears.

That's why he and Grant had joked around when things got too grim on their tour of combat duty. Some of their subordinates appreciated it, but a few found it off-putting. Those were the guys Tyler had to worry about the most. So far, Stacy didn't worry him.

After a couple of playbacks, Stacy stopped the audio. "Here's what I could understand. After Cavano finished swearing about the mess you made of her office, a man said, 'Do you still want to leave on the six-twenty tomorrow?' Cavano said, 'No, move my reservation to the eight-thirty. Just make sure the Ferrari is ready to go in Brussels by the time I get there. I'll call Rödel in the morning and tell him I may not reach Boerst until four. The meeting shouldn't take more than twenty minutes.' " Stacy looked up from her notes. "Any idea what all that means?"

"Apparently she's flying to Brussels," Tyler said. "But you said earlier she was going to Munich."

"Maybe she's stopping in Brussels on the way."

"I'll see if I can find the flight," Grant said as he tapped on the keyboard. After a few minutes he said, "Not a flight. Eurostar. The high-speed Chunnel train. Leaves from St. Pancras."

"So she must be taking the train to Brussels, then driving to Munich from there," Tyler said. "That's why the geolabe is in the trunk. The car is being shipped ahead to meet her in Brussels. What about Boerst and Rödel?"

Grant checked again. "I can't find Rödel, but Boerst is a German commercial real-estate brokerage headquartered in Munich. Rödel might work there."

"We'll find out tomorrow. Anything else about the brokerage?"

"Says they specialize in international transactions." Grant scrolled down the page. "Boring . . . boring . . . boring . . . Wait a second. This is cool. Their new headquarters building in the heart of Munich features a state-of-the-art robotic parking garage."

"A what?" Stacy said.

Tyler got a distant look in his eye. "You drive into a bay and park your car on a movable platform. You get out, take your ticket, and the platform automatically slides out of sight to an empty spot inside the structure. No valet ever touches the car. The purpose is to maximize space in crowded areas like city centers."

"You thinking what I'm thinking?" Grant said.

Tyler nodded. "If she leaves the geolabe in the car during her meeting, Munich might be the best opportunity to get it."

"Do we leave tonight or tomorrow?" Grant asked.

"It's been a long day," Tyler said. "Let's get some sleep and clear our heads." He looked at Stacy. "You, too. You can try to interpret the tablet in the morning."

Tyler and Grant stood, but Stacy didn't turn for her room.

"Can I talk to you for a minute?" she said.

Grant yawned. "I'll call our pilot and tell him to be ready at seven. Should get us into Munich before nine. Night." He closed the bedroom door behind him.

Stacy and Tyler sat down. He locked his eyes on hers. Every time she started to speak, the words caught in her throat. Tyler finally interrupted the silence.

"We're going to catch Orr," he said. "I promise."

She gave him a thin smile. "You don't have to promise. You can't, really."

"I know."

She paused again before speaking. "I was going to say I've never been through anything like this before, but I realized how stupid that would sound."

"That's okay. I haven't been through anything like this, either."

"Yeah, but you've been in the Army. You've faced death before."

"So have you."

"My parents, yeah. But this is different."

"Yes, it is."

She held his gaze. "I just wanted you to know that Carol was going to law school because she wanted to become a prosecutor."

"If she's anything like you, she'll make a damn fine one."

"What I mean is, she wanted to catch the bad guys. She would never forgive me if we let Orr use a nuclear weapon. Even if she . . ." Her voice trailed off with the scenario she couldn't utter.

"My father would feel the same way. But it won't come to that."

"I won't ask how you know that. But thanks for saying it."

She stood to leave, and Tyler did the same. Before she went into her room, she surprised Tyler and gave him a hug, her hands tight against his back. She barely came up to his shoulder, and he held her head gently to his chest. He soaked in the comforting warmth of her body against his. Until that moment, he hadn't realized how much he needed it. Before Tyler realized it, he was tenderly caressing her hair.

They stayed like that for a minute, neither wanting to let go, before Stacy silently pulled away and went into her room. Tyler was acutely aware that he was now alone.

He was also exhausted, but before he could go to bed he had one call to make.

"Hey, Tyler," Aiden said. "Was Stacy able to translate the audio I sent?"

"She was. We now have an idea where the geolabe will be, but we need the tracker location to make sure it's where we think it is. Did our guys have any luck deciphering the signals that the geolabe was emitting?"

"I'm able to help you there. The recordings you made in the lab ended up being comprehensive enough for them to decode the tracking signal. It's broadcasting GPS coordinates every thirty seconds. Off-the-shelf technology. I'll send you the URL where you can get the updates."

"Will it alert Orr that we're tapping his feed?"

"You know me better than that. I've cloned the Web page where he gets the tracker feed. He'll never know."

"Outstanding work."

"Even better, I've got some info on your new lady friend, Gia Cavano."

Tyler had texted her name to Aiden in the hope that he could track down some information on her. Tyler wanted to know what kind of woman he was dealing with. He was already convinced that she was as dangerous as Orr had warned them.

"What about her?"

"You're not going to like it."

"Why?"

"Because I found her name using some creative and not technically legal searching of the Interpol database. Apparently, they think she's an up-and-comer in the Camorra. I found pictures of what she supposedly did to some of her enemies. The worst involved a meat grinder. The authorities haven't been able to pin anything on her, though."

Aiden was right. Tyler didn't like it.

"What's the Camorra?" he asked, though he thought he knew the answer.

"The Camorra is to the Naples area what the Cosa Nostra is to Sicily, but more vicious. You're being chased by the Italian Mafia."

FRIDAY

LA CAMORRISTA

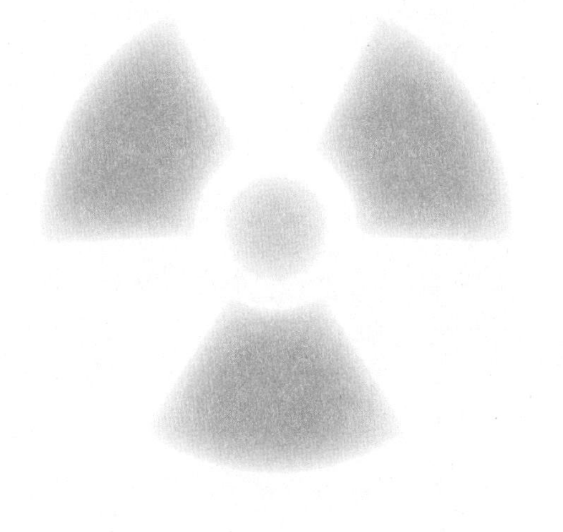

TWENTY-NINE

Seated in the Business Premier car of the Eurostar high-speed train, Gia Cavano ate a light breakfast while her three bodyguards kept watch on the other passengers around her. As the French countryside flashed past the window at 186 miles per hour, she occasionally twirled the knobs on the device Tyler Locke had stowed in his vehicle. The dials spun in a seemingly random fashion; she could divine no purpose for their movement.

It was a beautiful piece of engineering, both in design and in construction. Perhaps it was something Locke had built. Once she had the Midas treasure, she would track him down and ask him before she killed him.

Cavano had considered flying to Munich directly from London, but her new toy was too tempting to ignore. Ever since she had acquired the Ferrari 458 Italia from a German buyer who'd been higher on the waiting list, she had been itching to unleash it on the autobahn, the only freeway system in the world that had no speed limits. The specifications listed the Ferrari's top end at 202 miles per hour, and she had every intention of reaching it.

As punishment for letting Tyler Locke and Stacy Benedict escape, Pietro had been relegated to cargo duty and sent ahead with the truck carrying the Ferrari and a BMW M5 sedan on an overnight trip to Brussels. He would join the other three in the BMW and try to keep up with her on the drive to Munich, which normally took seven hours. If it took them more than four hours, it would be because of traffic.

She caught an older businessman looking at her, perhaps longing to spice up his Thursday morning by striking up a conversation about the unique object on the table in front of her, but he wouldn't dare approach with her cousins all around her. One of the benefits of having an intimidating family. They kept paunchy executives like him from making pathetic advances.

Tyler Locke, on the other hand, was just the kind of man who excited her. Tough, handsome, intelligent, resourceful. Ungraceful on a horse, but that could be corrected. Not many men stood up to her the way he did, and that was a quality hard to come by for a woman in her position.

For six years she'd been the head of the Cavano family, growing it from a small player in the Naples Camorra. Few women, especially one in her thirties, headed families in the Camorra. The macho society of the Mafia rarely tolerated it, but she'd maintained her position through cunning, using brutality when it was necessary to make a point. Her late husband, Antonio, had been murdered by the capo of the rival Mezzotta family for infringing on their concrete-supply business. In response, Gia Cavano ordered the deaths of every member of the Mezzotta clan, and as a result of her careful planning, most of them were now stinking up a landfill outside San Marco. The rest of the corpses had been dumped in strategic locations to show that she was now in charge.

Unable to have children because of a series of miscarriages, she encouraged her cousins to build families themselves, promising to bring them wealth as long as they remained loyal to her. They stayed by her side because she delivered on her promises, and some of them had married into families from Albania, Libya, and England, expanding her reach into the arms, drug, and financial sectors. She had pushed into legitimate businesses that allowed her and her extended family to maintain a lifestyle far better than that of her rivals, who had to hide in the Naples fortress neighborhoods of the Secondigliano. Plummeting profits had recently begun to jeopardize her position, though.

Now she was facing new assaults on the expansion of her businesses. Chinese and Russian gangs were supplying other families with arms and men. Without a radical change in the situation soon, she would become a bit player in the Camorra.

But she had something none of the other families had: the secret to finding the Midas vault, a treasure so vast that she would be able to elevate her stature in Naples and become the new "boss of bosses."

And that's what this trip to Munich would allow her to accomplish.

Hans Rödel, the vice president of Boerst Properties and Investments, was negotiating her purchase of the building along Piazza Cavour that had been out of her grasp for so long. She was going through a German firm so the Italian authorities wouldn't know that the new owner was going to be a Camorrista. She had been trying to buy the Ministry of Health building for the past six years and only now was about to close the deal, allowing her to tear apart its foundation and probe into the tunnel that she and Orr had found as children.

Rödel would help her sell the gold on the market once she began recovering it. It had to be done quietly, or the Italian government would seize her property, claiming it as a national treasure. She would die before she let that happen.

Cavano placed the bronze device back into its case and considered what to do about Locke and Benedict as well as Grant Westfield, whose identity had been revealed to her by Oswald Lumley. Orr had chosen his search team well, but he obviously hadn't told Locke about their connection. The engineer seemed too smart to deliberately deliver himself to her home so conveniently. Locke, Benedict, and Westfield were a mortal threat. If they helped Orr find the Midas treasure before she did, it could ruin her.

That meant she had to find them and persuade them to divulge how she could find Orr. Failing that, she would simply kill the three of them, setting back Orr's efforts to take what was rightfully hers.

Cavano's network of informants in European police departments meant that she had eyes and ears everywhere looking for any sign that Locke had surfaced. All she had to do was hold Orr off until next week. The demolition would commence on Monday, with an estimated two days needed to break through to the tunnel. Once she had the gold in her possession, the race would be over, and it wouldn't matter where Orr and his friends tried to hide. She would have unlimited funds to spend on the vendetta and would spit on each of their graves.

The blood of her dead enemies proved that no one got away with betraying Gia Cavano.

THIRTY

In the Audi rental sedan provided courtesy of Gordian Engineering, Tyler sat in the passenger seat while Grant drove out of Franz Josef Strauss Airport and onto the A92 autobahn toward Munich. Stacy sat in the back reading her printouts of the writing on the tablet. The flight had taken less than two hours, giving them plenty of time to get to the Boerst building and scout the location before Cavano arrived. He was just glad that his company had the resources to fund this venture, something Orr surely must have known when he picked Tyler for his blackmail scheme.

Stacy had spent the flight poring over Archimedes' tablet, scraping the beeswax from it as best she could under the circumstances. More than once she'd winced at the process, which destroyed the writing on top, but the only other method would be painstaking analysis using a CT or MRI machine. Tyler had convinced her that they didn't have that kind of time, and she reluctantly agreed.

Even after millennia, the writing on the bare wood had been preserved remarkably well by the tablet's layer of beeswax. They took photos of the writing and sent copies to Aiden and several other e-mail addresses for safekeeping.

They had debated whether to bring the tablet with them in the car. Taking the geolabe with them hadn't gone so well, so they left the tablet behind with the pilots, who would remain on standby with the plane. On any other occasion, Miles would object to the extravagance of that expense, but with Sherman Locke's life at stake and now a suspicion that strontium-90 was involved, he hadn't uttered one word of objection.

"Are you ready to tell us what the tablet says?" Tyler asked.

Stacy scribbled a few more lines on her notepad and said, "Just a minute, bunny."

Grant belched out a laugh. When the rental-car agent had seen Tyler's last name, she'd snickered. When Tyler asked her why, she told him that the German pronunciation of Locke was a name you'd give to a pet. Grant and Stacy had ribbed him for the past twenty minutes about it.

"Okay," she said. "I'm ready."

"Let me guess," Grant said. "We have to find some other old document somewhere."

"You're not even close," Stacy said, and her eyes sparkled with wonder as she handed the translation to Tyler, who read the text aloud:

The spy of King Hieron has brought us a gift that may yet win our war. While seeking an underground path to enter the Roman fortress, the spy came upon the treasure of King Midas, a vault of gold the likes of which has never before been seen. As proof of his find, the spy produced a golden hand of such excellent design, it could not have been fabricated.

Three keys—this tablet, a manuscript, and the Parthenon—provide the map for finding the treasure, which cannot fall into Roman hands or they will rule the earth and all who dwell within it.

Grant gaped at Tyler. "So it's real?"

"Apparently," Tyler said. "And Archimedes created this puzzle so that someone other than the Romans would find the treasure. But why didn't they go after the gold themselves?"

"Because for two years," Stacy said, "the city of Syracuse, which was a Greek city-state on what is now the island of Sicily, was under siege by the Roman Navy. If the city fell—which it eventually did, resulting in the death of Archimedes—the Romans could have found the map and claimed the treasure, funding their military campaigns for a hundred years. That's why Archimedes used the Parthenon as the third key. It was the most famous building in the world at the time, but the Romans wouldn't have access to it."

"And we know the Romans never found the gold," Tyler said, "because Orr and Cavano saw it. Now we have to follow Archimedes' instructions to find it again."

"Keep reading," Stacy said. "I've tried to translate his writing as plainly as possible."

As the seat of Herakles is to the island of Megaride, the feet of Aphrodite are to the Parthenope acropolis.

All dials must start by pointing to the top position. When you are facing the Parthenon, the geolabe must lie on its side with its knobs up so that it blocks all but the pediment. As the shadow moves on the sundial, rotate the left-hand knob so that its dial points at the seat of Herakles. The opposing dial will now reveal the direction from Megaride.

With the geolabe in the same position, rotate the right-hand knob so that its dial points to the feet of Aphrodite. The opposing dial will now reveal the direction from the Acropolis.

Thus, the combination of directions will reveal the well from which you will begin your journey. From that point, marked by the sign of Scorpio, the geolabe will show the way.

Tyler read it a second time to make sure he got what Archimedes was suggesting.

"Incredible," he said. "He's telling us to use triangulation to home in on how we get into the tunnels."

"How does triangulation work?" Stacy asked.

"You use triangulation to pinpoint a location using two other points. You don't need the distance to the location from those two points, just the angles. Once you have those, you can draw a line from each point, and where they cross is the location you're looking for. So the directions from the island of Megaride and the

Parthenope acropolis will point to the tunnel entrance. It'll be a crude approximation because the angles provided by the geolabe won't be exact, but it will give us a small region to search."

"And we get those angles from the Parthenon?"

"In a way. Let's take it one step at a time." Tyler read the first paragraph out loud:

As the seat of Herakles is to the island of Megaride, the feet of Aphrodite are to the Parthenope acropolis.

Tyler turned to Grant. "You said that Lumley showed you statues of Herakles and Aphrodite on the Parthenon's pediments, right?"

"Yeah. But they're both in the British Museum now."

"Doesn't matter. We can look up where they used to be on the building itself. I'll text Aiden to find some detailed schematics of the Parthenon."

"Why?" Stacy said as he typed the message.

"Because I think Archimedes had visited the Parthenon at some point and constructed the geolabe based on its dimensions."

"What is Megaride?" Grant asked. "Sounds like a roller coaster at Disney World."

"Tyler pronounced it wrong," Stacy said. "It's May-gah-REE-day. I know I've heard it before. Let me look it up."

She used Tyler's laptop.

"Aha!" she said. "Megaride used to be an island off the coast of Neapolis, but they've built a stone pier to it now, creating a peninsula. It's now a famous attraction in Naples called Castel dell'Ovo, a fortress first built in the twelfth century."

"But it says the second point is the Acropolis," Grant said. "You're telling me the triangle is formed with two of its points in Naples and Athens?"

"It says the *Parthenope* acropolis," Stacy corrected. "*Acropolis* is a generic Greek term for the high point of the city. In Parthenope—

Naples today—the acropolis would have been what's now another castle called Castel Sant'Elmo, on a bluff that has a commanding view of the city. Megaride and the acropolis would have been the two most prominent locations in Neapolis in Archimedes' time."

"Which makes them perfect for two triangulation anchors," Tyler said. He looked at the map of Naples that Stacy had brought up on the laptop. "Once we have the angles from those two points, we'll know where to start our search for the tunnel."

"So how do we get those angles?" Stacy asked.

Tyler read the next two paragraphs to them:

All dials must start by pointing to the top position. When you are facing the Parthenon, the geolabe must lie on its side with its knobs up so that it blocks all but the pediment. As the shadow moves on the sundial, rotate the left-hand knob so that its dial points to the seat of Herakles. The opposing dial will now reveal the direction from Megaride.

With the geolabe in the same position, rotate the right-hand knob so that its dial points to the feet of Aphrodite. The opposing dial will now reveal the direction from the Acropolis.

"The shadow on a sundial moves in the clockwise direction, of course," Stacy said.

"And all dials pointing to the top refers to the calibration we did," Tyler said. "That's why we needed the Stomachion puzzle. Orr's original translator realized it related to the geolabe, but he didn't know how. The dials had to be zeroed out to the twelve o'clock position before we could use the geolabe. Archimedes says that the geolabe must lie on its side to reveal only the pediment, which is the triangular part at the top."

"Makes sense," Grant said. "Lumley said the façade of the Parthenon was build in the shape of a golden rectangle."

"And if the geolabe is also in the shape of a golden rectangle, it would be a perfect match."

"But we need to be at the Parthenon to use it," Stacy said. "I get it now. Only a Greek would be able to go to Athens and see the Parthenon in person. Even if you had the other two keys, they would be useless if you couldn't get to the Parthenon."

"Right. We have to actually be standing there, knowing where the seat of Herakles and the feet of Aphrodite would be, and then twist the knobs until the dials point to those locations. That's what the three hundred and sixty notches on the third dial of the geolabe are for. They'll give us the correct triangulation angles. Then we transpose those to the island of Megaride and the Parthenope acropolis."

Tyler read the last paragraph:

Thus, the combination of directions will reveal the well from which you will begin your journey. From that point, marked by the sign of Scorpio, the geolabe will show the way.

"So the triangulation will lead us to a well?" Grant asked.

"Many of the points of entry into the Naples underground are wells leading to the cisterns and aqueducts that carry water into the city," Stacy said. "The spy must have come out of the Midas treasure chamber and wended his way through the tunnels until he found an exit. Droughts were not uncommon, which would make it possible for him to walk through the tunnels that served as aqueducts and were normally filled with water. The spy marked his exit well with the sign of Scorpio so that he could find it again. Maybe the mark on the well will still be there."

"So all we have to do to find this well," Tyler said, "is go to the Parthenon with the geolabe, turn it on its side, twist the knobs to get the angles of triangulation, and transfer them to a map of Naples."

"Sounds easy when you put it that way," Stacy said. "But we need the geolabe to do it. Then the triangulation will lead us to the map."

"Wait a minute," Grant said, snapping his fingers. "There is no map."

No map? Tyler thought. There had to be a map. How else would they find the treasure?

From that point, marked by the sign of Scorpio, the geolabe will show the way.

Up until now, Tyler had just assumed that a map was hidden somewhere, possibly in this well. But Grant was right. The map wouldn't be hidden in the tunnels. The spy would have brought his drawn map back with him to Syracuse, and Archimedes would have destroyed it to keep it from falling into Roman hands.

Tyler sucked in a breath at Archimedes' boundless ingenuity.

The geolabe will show the way.

The geolabe wasn't leading to a map that would show them how to find the Midas treasure. The geolabe *was* the map.

THIRTY-ONE

After two days cooped up in his cell, Sherman Locke was spending most of his time trying not to go stir-crazy. He'd persuaded his captors to let him read the newspaper they used in the proof-of-life video, but the copy of *USA Today* could have been purchased anywhere, so it didn't tell him anything about his location. With a diet of Subway sandwiches and McDonald's hamburgers, he could be anywhere. He spent the majority of his time doing calisthenics. When his chance at escape came, he would need to be ready.

The only time they let him out of the cell was to record the daily proof-of-life video. His two choices were to escape when he was brought out for the video or to break out of the cell. With just the one crude window in the heavy steel door, the cell was virtually impregnable. That left overpowering two or more guards while he was shackled at his wrists and ankles, then breaking Carol out before escaping the building.

The odds were slim, but he had a plan. The only question was when to try it.

On his first day, only two men had been there to make the video. Sherman would have tried his plan on the second day, but three of them had been present. There was no way he could take out three men. It had to be when there were only two recording him.

He had the means to get out of the handcuffs, but the problem was the short time he had to put them on after they handed him the cuffs through the hole in the door. If they weren't paying attention, he just might be able to make his plan work, but it would require split-second timing, and he'd get only one chance.

The garage door opened, letting in reflected rays of the dawning sun through the crack in the portal.

Sherman rose and went to the door. Through the sliver of space, he saw the second van return and pull in next to the semi they'd brought in the day before. The trailer of the semi was the same steel gray it had been when they brought it in, but Gaul had pasted a new logo saying WILBIX CONSTRUCTION onto the blue cab's door over the old logo saying DWIGHT'S FARM SERVICES. Sherman hadn't seen any clue to what the trailer might contain.

Crenshaw had been working around the clock on some kind of project out of Sherman's view. Sherman would occasionally hear the grind of metal or see the bright spark of a welder, but otherwise he couldn't tell what Crenshaw was doing. The man would emerge wearing headphones and nodding his head to music, and he kept his interactions with the other men to a minimum.

The van door opened, and Gaul, Orr, and Phillips got out dressed entirely in black. Gaul stuffed a balaclava in his pocket and slid the side door open. He and Phillips pulled two handcuffed men out. They were both wearing hoods, which Gaul removed, revealing two skinny dark-skinned men in their twenties, one in a short-sleeved white shirt and slacks, the other dressed in a T-shirt and gray sweatpants. Both were of Middle Eastern descent.

"Who are you?" the one in the T-shirt said in a thick Arabic accent. "Why have you kidnapped us?"

"I have done nothing wrong," the other one said, sobbing. "I am in this country legally."

"I know," Orr said. "Why do you think we chose you?"

"Chose us for what?" the T-shirt man said.

"That was rhetorical. Put them away."

"But I don't understand! Are we under arrest?"

"That's right. You're under arrest. And you'll be tried soon enough."

As they continued to protest, Gaul and Phillips dragged them to the other cells next to Sherman and locked them in. He watched in silence. There was nothing he could do for them.

Orr walked toward Sherman's door, and Sherman crept back to his cot. Orr opened the covering on the portal and stared at Sherman, who returned his gaze without blinking. Then Orr smiled.

"Hello, General Locke."

Sherman didn't respond.

"You're the stoic type. I like that."

"Who cares?" Sherman said.

Orr laughed. "Your son must have had a great time growing up with you."

"My son doesn't give a rat's ass about me."

"You two might have your disagreements, maybe a lot of them. But blood is thicker than water. If he didn't care about you, you'd be dead already."

"Maybe the FBI is on their way here right now."

"I don't think so."

"What makes you so sure?"

"Well, I think I just said I *wasn't* sure, but I've been evading the authorities for a very long time, and they haven't caught me yet."

"There's always a first time," Sherman said, "which would be the last time for you."

"You can't get high rewards without high risks. As a former fighter pilot, you should know that."

"And you should know that Tyler will never let you get away with whatever you're planning."

"So you've been observing our preparations on your little excursions out of the cell. Have you put all the pieces of the puzzle together?"

"You're either a traitor to your country plotting some low-rent terrorist action or you're a greedy bastard with some plan to get rich quick with money you don't deserve." Sherman remembered when Gaul had talked about his payment. That was the only time he'd seen Orr get a gleam in his eye about anything. "My bet is on the greed. You don't look like someone who gives a shit about politics."

Orr smiled. "This has certainly been a fun pissing match. Now, let's do your video."

He threw the wrist and ankle cuffs into Sherman's room. Gaul and Phillips were standing outside, one with a pistol, the other with the Taser.

Sherman put the cuffs on. With three of them out there, this wasn't the opportunity for his escape, but it would have to be soon.

According to the newspaper, it was now Friday. He'd heard Orr say something about getting the truck out by Monday. Whatever they were planning would be done by then, and if Sherman didn't make a break in the next three days, he never would.

THIRTY-TWO

Grant watched Boerst Properties and Investments from inside the café across the street. Designed to blend in with the eigteenth-century construction of the other stone buildings north of Marienplatz, the structure had been built by Boerst only two years before as a showpiece headquarters. From his position, Grant could see the ground-level entrance into the seven-story underground parking garage as well as the door leading from the garage into the glass-encased lobby.

Boerst abutted another new building, whose first floor was taken up by an exotic car dealership showing off its merchandise to tourists who gawked through its windows. A truck pulled up, and Grant was worried that it would block his view, but it stopped in front of the dealer and began unloading a bright yellow Lamborghini Gallardo.

Grant looked at his watch. Nearly four in the afternoon. On his laptop, he checked the GPS readout for the tracker inside the geolabe. Cavano was only a few minutes away. Right on time.

Stacy sat across from him nursing a cup of coffee.

"You think Tyler's okay?" she said.

Grant waved his hand. "Ah, he'll be all right. He's probably taking a nap."

"And you think this will work?" she said.

"If Cavano leaves the geolabe in the car like we think she will, it should go off without a hitch. Tyler will be in and out in five minutes."

"What if she takes it in with her?"

"There's no reason for her to, but if she does we'll know from the tracker. You ready?"

"I can handle my end of the plan as long as Cavano doesn't see me."

"You'll be fine," Grant said. "You won't go in until Cavano is in her meeting."

Guided by Grant's expertise with electronic surveillance and security systems, Stacy had called Boerst claiming to be with the firm's security company. They'd found out that the garage was observed by security cameras, but the building had only a minimal guard presence. The guard at the front desk of the Boerst lobby was tasked with monitoring the garage's cameras along with the other cameras at the back of the building.

The cameras posed the only problem with their plan, which was why they'd pressed Stacy into service, not only because she spoke German but also because she was sufficiently distracting.

Grant appraised her blouse, which Stacy had buttoned up to the top.

"You sure you don't think my idea would work better?" he said.

She rolled her eyes. "Showing him my boobs? Really?"

"It would work on me."

"That's because you're as mature as a fourteen-year-old. Besides, he could be gay for all you know."

Grant smiled. "All true."

"Just leave it to me. Keeping someone's attention is my job. How are you going to let me know to wrap it up?"

"I'll text you when Tyler's got the geolabe."

Stacy drained the last of her coffee. "Is this the craziest situation you've ever been in?"

Grant thought about it. "It definitely ranks up there."

Stacy laughed. "It ranks up there? See, that's where you and Tyler are different from me. Everything that's happened in the last two days would make up the top ten craziest events in my life."

"That's because you've never been in the Army."

"You and Tyler both were together?"

"He was a captain and I was his first sergeant."

"The first he ever had?"

"No, that was my rank. It meant I was the top NCO—non-commissioned officer—in his company. We were in some hairy combat situations."

"Is that how he got the scar on his neck?"

Grant nodded. "Along with a Silver Star and a Purple Heart."

"What happened?"

Grant took a deep breath. "Ambush. We were traveling from our outpost to Baghdad when a roadside bomb went off next to our convoy. Destroyed the Humvee in front of us and damaged the lead one. We were pinned down on all sides, and we didn't know if there were more bombs on the road."

"Sounds horrible."

"Two guys in the unit died instantly. Another three were injured. Tyler and I and two other soldiers took cover in a ditch. Help wasn't coming anytime soon, so that meant we had to get out of there, but the guys in the front Humvee couldn't move. While we provided cover fire, Tyler ran back and forth between us and the damaged Humvee. He dragged all three injured men to safety."

"And the scar?"

"Grenade. With all those bullets whizzing around, he hadn't gotten a scratch until then. I thought for sure someone was looking out for him. Then, while he was pulling the third soldier back, a grenade landed near him. He kicked it away, but not far enough. He shielded the soldier's body with his own before the grenade went off. Shrapnel got him in the neck. You've never seen so much blood."

Stacy leaned forward in her seat with a horrified look. "My God."

"Once we got Tyler back to the combat medical hospital, they got him some blood and patched him up. I wasn't even sure he'd make it to the hospital alive, but he was back with our unit two weeks later."

"Sounds like a brave guy. I'm glad I got paired up with him."

Grant thought he heard more than admiration there, but he didn't want to ask. "I've trusted him with my life many times. You should, too."

Stacy gave him a wry grin. "I already have."

Grant checked the tracker again and saw that the geolabe was just around the corner.

"Here they come," he said.

Right on cue, the Ferrari zipped into view followed by a BMW sedan. They both turned into the garage. In two minutes, Grant could see Cavano enter the Boerst building with three men. The guard didn't make them sign in but instead waved them on to the elevators.

Grant looked at the tracker. The signal was gone. That meant the concrete floor of the garage was blocking it. If Cavano had taken the geolabe with her, he'd still be getting the signal.

"All right," Grant said. "You're up. Just keep your phone handy."

Stacy stood and threw him a jaunty salute. She may be little, Grant thought, but she's feisty.

She left the café and walked across the street. Once she was inside and speaking to the guard, Grant called Tyler, whose stronger cell signal could penetrate the garage floor while the tracker couldn't.

"You awake?" Grant said.

"It's actually more comfortable than I thought it would be," Tyler said.

"Cavano's in, the geolabe's in the garage, and Stacy's chatting up the guard. You're clear."

"What's the car look like?"

"BMW M5." He gave Tyler the license number. "The geolabe's probably in the trunk."

"All right. Time to stretch my legs. I'll call you when I've got it. Just one request."

"What's that?"

"Next time I do this," Tyler said, "remind me to bring a bottle of water."

"I'll have one for you when we're done."

"You're a prince among men. Call you back in a few." Tyler hung up.

Grant caught the waitress and asked for the water. With that easy task done, all he could do was wait and hope that Tyler wouldn't have any trouble finding the BMW once he got out of the rental car's trunk.

THIRTY-THREE

Using the spare key fob for the rented Audi, Tyler popped open the trunk. The rear of the car was so close to the back wall that he had only a foot of space to get out and stretch his legs. He closed the lid and looked around to get his bearings as he adjusted his Seattle Mariners cap.

He'd brought a flashlight in case the garage was cloaked in darkness, but the seven-story structure was well lit, probably to give the security cameras a clear view. Tyler took the heavy flashlight with him anyway. It would be the easiest way into the locked BMW.

The robotic system for parking cars was simple for the driver. On the ground floor, there were two bays enclosed with glass doors, one for cars entering the garage and the other for cars exiting. Once the driver parked the car in the bay and got a ticket, the car sank into the underground structure on a tray.

The garage itself was designed to maximize space. The cars were stacked in cubbyholes on either side of a center atrium, and the tray moved on a track system to place each new car in an empty slot with its rear to the wall. The tray with the car would slide into the slot, and the empty tray already there would slide out at the same time.

The garage was supported by girders, so there were no walls between the vehicles. Since people weren't parking the cars, there was no chance of getting a door ding. Another advantage of the automated garage was that thieves couldn't break into or vandalize the cars. Unless, that is, they hid in the trunk of a car as Tyler had done.

That's what the cameras at either end of the atrium were for, in case anyone tried this kind of trick. Tyler just hoped Stacy could keep the guard's eye away from the monitor while he prowled around the garage.

Tyler went to the front of the Audi and stopped at the edge of the center atrium to note that he had ended up on the sixth level up from the bottom. It had been difficult to gauge how fast the system moved from inside the trunk.

In answer to his unspoken question, a bare tray whooshed by and stopped in front of a VW two levels below him. In a few seconds of whining motors, the bare tray was exchanged for the tray holding the car. It zipped along the tracks until it was at the end of the garage, where it rose until it disappeared into the ceiling. The VW's entire retrieval took no more than a minute.

He searched the garage and saw the BMW with the license number Grant had given him. It was one level below him on the opposite side. Cavano's Ferrari was on the lowest level, its bright red paint job shining like a beacon.

Cavano had mentioned putting the geolabe in the trunk when she was in her office, which had to mean the BMW. Since the Ferrari was a rear-engined V8 with no room for a trunk, it had only a small storage space under the hood. Still, it might have enough room, so he'd check there if he didn't find the geolabe in the BMW.

To get to the BMW, he'd have to cross the center atrium, but at twenty feet wide the span was too far to jump. Mounted on either end of the garage were access ladders and narrow walkways for maintenance crews to work on the equipment.

Tyler was in the middle of the row of cars, so he squeezed past their trunks to make his way to the catwalk on his level, trying to stay out of view of the cameras as much as possible in case the guard glanced at his screen. He pulled his cap lower to shadow his face, making him unrecognizable even if the camera did catch sight of him.

In two minutes, he had crossed the catwalk, climbed down the ladder to the fifth level, and trekked past the back ends of the cars to the slot with the BMW, approaching from the passenger side. The heavily tinted windows and the darkness of the parking spot made it impossible to see the interior, but the most likely place for the geolabe was the trunk. The rear of the car, however, was so close to the wall that it would be difficult to stand behind the car and thoroughly search the trunk. He decided he'd push the car out from the wall to give himself some space to look through the luggage.

With no key fob to disable the security system, he'd have to do this the old-fashioned way. No one would be able to hear an alarm down here.

Tyler put on the leather gloves he'd brought with him and raised the flashlight to shatter the window but stopped before he swung it down. Would they really set the alarm? he thought. Maybe they wouldn't even bother to lock it.

He lowered the flashlight and tugged on the passenger-door handle. The latch released.

With nowhere else to put it, Tyler stood the flashlight on the roof. He pulled the door open and put a knee on the passenger seat of the left-hand-drive car. He flicked the manual transmission to neutral and released the parking brake so that he'd be able to push the car away from the wall. The trunk release was by the driver's foot just inside the door. He leaned over and punched the button. The trunk popped open.

Tyler rose and was about to get back out of the car when he felt the cold metal of a pistol barrel press against his left temple.

He froze, and heard Pietro say, "*Buon giorno, Signor Locke.*"

THIRTY-FOUR

Pietro couldn't believe his good fortune. He'd been forced to remain with the BMW because he had let Locke escape just the day before. Now he had a chance to make up for his failure.

He was supposed to keep an eye on both cars, but when he saw the interior of the garage, he couldn't imagine there would be any kind of security threat. So he had stayed in the backseat to stretch out and listen to his iPod.

The music had been so loud that he hadn't heard Locke approach. It wasn't until the door opened that he realized someone was there. When Pietro saw who it was, he knew it was the perfect opportunity to redeem himself. He silently drew his SIG Sauer pistol and when Locke was upright again, he made his move.

He didn't know much English, but the gun at Locke's head made any additional communication unnecessary. His captive didn't move.

With his free hand, he took out his phone and dialed Salvatore.

"Sì?" Salvatore answered.

"Sal, I have a surprise for Gia," Pietro said in Italian. "Come and get me."

"She's busy."

"Then you and Tino. I have something she's been looking for."

"Okay. But this had better be good."

"Just get me," Pietro said, and hung up.

He tilted his head toward the door so Locke would close it. Locke pointed at it questioningly, and Pietro nodded.

But instead of closing it Locke slowly got out of the car with his hands up.

Pietro said, "No, no, no!" But the imbecile kept going until he was leaning with his hands against the roof, as if Pietro were a police officer making an arrest. *Stupido.*

Pietro didn't really care about killing Locke, but Cavano would want him alive. Wounding him was always an option, but that would get blood all over the car. Pietro didn't know how to say, "Get back in the car, you idiot!" He'd have to work on his English.

With his gun trained on Locke, Pietro opened his own door. Locke remained standing by the side of the car with his hands still up high.

Pietro got out to put Locke back in the passenger seat. As he stood and brought the pistol up, Locke whipped around in a lightning move and the heavy flashlight smacked into Pietro's arm, sending the SIG flying.

Pietro cried out in pain at his shattered wrist. He stumbled back and lashed out with a kick as Locke came at him with the flashlight raised for the knockout blow.

His foot caught Locke in the midsection, sending Locke reeling back against the Mercedes parked in the slot next to the BMW. Pietro reached into his jacket pocket, drew his switchblade, and clicked open the wicked five-inch blade.

He crouched and warily moved toward Locke, his limp right hand cradled against his body. Pietro wasn't going to bother trying to keep him alive anymore. Even with one hand useless, he was a master with a knife. If he could just get in close enough, nothing would stop him from cutting Locke's throat.

In the narrow space between the two cars, Locke feinted with the flashlight. Pietro dove forward hoping for a killing thrust, but Locke shoved him backward, knocking Pietro against the BMW's back door, which slammed shut. Pietro swung around. The only thing between him and Locke was the open front door.

Locke rushed forward, the flashlight low, going for the upper cut. Pietro was ready to slash him across the neck as he went by, but before he reached Pietro, Locke struck the window of the open door, sending chunks of safety glass hurtling at Pietro.

Pietro instinctively shielded himself from the flying glass and only realized too late that it was a diversion. While Pietro had his hands up, Locke rushed in and brought the flashlight down like a lumberjack.

Pietro's world went black.

Tyler kicked Pietro a couple of times to prove that the Italian wasn't feigning unconsciousness. Convinced that his hammer blow had worked, Tyler knelt and caught his breath.

In a few seconds his heart rate was below hummingbird speed. He picked up the switchblade and put it in his pocket. The gun was nowhere to be seen, and he had no time to look for it.

Tyler searched Pietro's pockets, but there were no more guns, just a passport, a wallet, and a key chain with keys to both the BMW and the Ferrari. He was surprised that Cavano shared the keys with anyone. Either she wanted someone else to carry her spare or someone was being a naughty boy and taking the Ferrari out for joyrides when he wasn't supposed to.

Tyler pocketed the keys and took out his phone to call Grant.

"You got it?"

"Not yet," Tyler said. "I've had a run-in with one of Cavano's men."

"She left one down there?" Tyler knew Grant was kicking himself for not warning him, but with the heavily tinted windows there was no way Grant could have known that someone was in the car.

"Doesn't matter. He's down for the count, but I think he made a call to her. We may need an alternate exit strategy. And tell Stacy to get out of there before they see her."

"Crap! It's too late. They're in the lobby."

"I'll call you back," Tyler said, and hung up.

He pushed the car forward far enough to get behind it and opened the trunk. He didn't have time to go through the bags and search for the geolabe. There were five pieces of carry-on luggage inside. The geolabe must be in one of them. He put the flashlight down and swiftly removed the luggage, sliding the cases between the BMW and the Mercedes.

He had just taken out the last case when he saw movement inside the car and heard the glove box open.

Pietro. The blow hadn't left him incapacitated long enough. Tyler picked up the flashlight, ready to finish the job, when bullets started blasting through the backseat.

He dove under the bumper. In his haste, he hadn't checked the interior for more pistols, and with the switchblade in his pocket he was the proverbial guy who had brought a knife to a gunfight.

The shots were wild. Pietro was probably woozy from a concussion, but one of the shots would eventually connect. Tyler had only one chance.

With his feet against the wall, he put his back against the bumper. The BMW rolled forward. A bullet creased his shoulder, but Tyler ignored it and heaved with everything he had.

His legs were fully extended when the front wheels fell over the edge. The BMW tilted forward and plunged into the abyss as Pietro screamed from inside. An earsplitting crash echoed through the garage when the car slammed into the concrete floor.

Tyler got up and went to the edge. Five floors below, the BMW had landed on its roof. The air bags hadn't saved Pietro. His lifeless body poked out of the wreckage, blood pooling around his head.

The empty tray began to lower from its spot at the exit bay. Pietro's friends were coming for the BMW.

Tyler had to hurry. He unzipped the first bag and rifled through its contents. Nothing but clothes. He did the same with the second, third, and fourth, but came up empty. He tossed each of them into the atrium as he finished with them.

That left the fifth bag. The tray from the exit bay came and lined up to switch itself with the tray the BMW had been on. Tyler picked up the last bag and jumped onto the hood of the Mercedes so that he wouldn't be crushed as the trays were exchanged. With luck, the empty tray would buy him more time as they tried to figure out why the car was missing.

With the new tray in place, Tyler got down and opened the final bag. He was aghast when he realized it was just another bag of clothes.

The geolabe wasn't here. He'd gotten enough of a view of the BMW's interior to know that the geolabe wasn't inside. But if it wasn't in the smashed car below, that left . . .

The retrieval tray came down a second time, but it didn't stop at the sixth level. It kept heading to the bottom.

Puzzled by the empty tray and the noise from the crash, Cavano's men must have inserted the ticket for the other car.

If Tyler didn't move fast, he'd lose his best chance to get the geolabe, which had to be inside the Ferrari.

THIRTY-FIVE

The TV screens at the guard station in the Boerst lobby were at the front of the desk, so Stacy had positioned herself to the side with her back to the elevators. Her strategy to use the map from the rental-car agency to ask for directions worked to perfection. The guard, a thin blond kid who looked straight out of high school, seemed to be the helpful type, and she was right. In her experience, men liked having a problem to solve, so she had made her predicament as complicated as possible, intentionally flubbing her German for good measure. The guard hadn't once glanced at the security-camera feeds.

Then the crash had reverberated through the building. The guard had been looking at her map and Stacy had been looking at the video feed when the BMW fell to the bottom of the garage. She feared the worst for Tyler until she saw his familiar form peer over the edge of the chasm. Something had gone dreadfully wrong, and all she could do was delay the guard's figuring out what had happened long enough for Tyler to get out of there.

The guard's head snapped up when he heard the noise. Stacy grabbed his arm and pointed outside.

"Did you see that?" she said, and frantically pulled the guard with her to the front door, not giving him a chance to check his screens.

"What happened?" he said.

"I think I saw a car just crash into the building next door."

As they looked outside for evidence of the accident, her phone buzzed.

The text message from Grant said,

> Two of Cavano's men just passed you. Don't turn around.

Stacy stiffened. She hadn't been expecting them down so soon.

"I don't see it," the guard said.

"It was a blue car," Stacy said, her heart pounding at the danger they were all in. "I saw it speed by way too fast. It must have hit a car around the corner. We should go look."

The guard turned back toward the reception desk. "But I'm not supposed to leave the building—"

"Did you see the car?"

She was debating whether to leave or stay when the elevator dinged. Out of the corner of her eye, she caught sight of Cavano, her long raven hair distinctive. She was with her other bodyguard. If they realized it was Stacy with the guard, they'd be on her in a second.

Cavano and her hulking escort went out the door to the garage.

Stacy held on to the guard's arm and continued to pepper him with questions, trying to keep him engaged as long as possible. The second he got back to his station, all hell would break loose.

The empty vehicle tray had already been swapped for the tray with the Ferrari on it, and Tyler was watching his chance of recovering the geolabe being whisked toward the exit. His plan to climb down and get it before leaving through one of the maintenance exits had vanished.

Tyler had to get to the Ferrari before it rose into the exit bay. He ran along the front of the cars, not caring if the camera could see him at this point. If the guard even glanced at the camera, he'd sound the alarm when he saw the crushed remains of the BMW.

The Ferrari stopped at the bottom as the system transitioned to lifting the tray. Tyler was still three cars from the end. He pushed the unlock button on the Ferrari's key fob that he'd taken from Pietro.

The tray rose. With a couple of leaps over the hoods of the last two cars, Tyler banged into the wall. As the Ferrari reached the level below him, he jumped.

His feet barely caught on the edge of the tray, and he thumped into the Ferrari's rear. He had no time to get into the front boot, the only other possible storage place for the geolabe. He opened the driver's door and squeezed inside, slamming it behind him. He crouched down across the passenger seat as the Ferrari stopped and waited for the exit bay's floor to slide aside for the tray to rise up.

He redialed Grant's number.

"Yeah," he said.

"Is Stacy with you?" Tyler said.

"No, she's still in the lobby. If Cavano goes back in, she'll see Stacy for sure."

"Tell her to leave through the front door in fifteen seconds."

"Okay." He and Grant had known each other long enough for Grant not to waste time asking why.

"And, no matter what you see, stay where you are."

"But Cavano—" Grant wouldn't like that request, but Tyler hung up before he could hear more.

The Ferrari began rising again and stopped in the exit bay. As the doors opened, Tyler sat up and started the engine.

Right in front of him were the three bodyguards and Cavano, who stared at Tyler in disbelief.

When Sal had left to find out what the surprise was, Cavano suspected Pietro was attempting to get one of the other bodyguards to switch places with him.

But a few minutes after he'd gone, Sal called to say that the

BMW was missing and that they couldn't get hold of Pietro. Cavano wondered if Pietro had left his post and taken the BMW for a drive, but she realized that he couldn't have exited the garage on his own. Retrieving the car could be done only from outside the garage. Perhaps the computer system had directed the tray to the wrong spot in the garage, but a nagging feeling told her that something was wrong, so she instructed Sal to retrieve the Ferrari to make sure it was still there.

As Cavano hurried from the elevator to the garage exit, she had barely registered the sight of the guard speaking to a woman at the front door, their backs to her.

She was standing in front of the bay with Sal and the other two bodyguards when the Ferrari arrived, seemingly intact. But as the doors opened, she was stunned to see Tyler Locke sit up in the seat of her car and start it up.

Before any of them could react, Locke gunned the engine and smoked tires out of the bay, sending the four of them diving to avoid being run over.

Cavano had thought the whole business with Locke was a sideshow until this moment. Now she realized how important that device must be to him if he was willing to take this kind of risk to get it back.

As she pushed herself to her feet, Cavano vowed again that Orr and Locke would not beat her to the Midas treasure. She ran out into the street and saw her new Ferrari screech to a halt. The woman the guard had been talking to burst through the doors and ran to the Ferrari.

"Get in," Locke yelled through the open passenger window.

At the Ferrari's door, Stacy Benedict turned and locked eyes with Cavano, who was momentarily frozen with rage.

Benedict jumped in, and the Ferrari took off.

An alarm went off in the Boerst building, but Cavano ignored it. She had to get her car back, and the BMW was nowhere to be found.

Cavano could hijack a car driving by, but it would never be able to keep up with the Ferrari. Then she remembered the exotic car dealership, the same one that had brokered her purchase of the Ferrari.

She whirled around and saw the truck delivering cars for the dealership. Two were already parked on the street, a yellow Lamborghini Gallardo and a black Pagani Zonda. Both of them were supercars at least the equal of her 458 Italia.

Cavano waved to her men and pointed at the cars.

"Let's go!" she yelled.

A salesman from the car dealership was inspecting the cars. Cavano ran to the driver's door of the Zonda and opened it.

The salesman started yelling in German.

"What are you doing?"

Sal jumped into the passenger seat of the Zonda, while the other two took the Lamborghini. The keys were still in both cars.

The Lamborghini took off after Locke, leaving the salesman screaming at them.

Cavano started the Zonda and revved the twelve cylinders to the redline.

"Tell your boss Gia Cavano just bought these cars," she said to the salesman through the open window in her passable German.

The salesman sputtered in amazement, but Cavano didn't wait to hear his response. She threw the Zonda into gear and laid down a patch of rubber twenty yards long.

THIRTY-SIX

With a yellow Lamborghini in the rearview mirror, Tyler knew his escape wasn't over. It had to be the one he'd seen as he exited the garage, which meant that Cavano wasn't giving up on her Ferrari that easily.

He had hoped to find a good place to ditch the car and make their escape on foot into Munich's U-Bahn subway, but the rush-hour traffic had slowed them enough to allow their pursuers to catch up. Because he and Stacy were unarmed, a footrace would be suicidal. And going to the police wasn't an option after trashing the garage, killing a man, and stealing a car.

"Oh, my God!" Stacy shouted above the roar of the engine. "You're bleeding!" She took off her sweater and pressed it against his arm.

Tyler winced. In the escape he'd forgotten about the gunshot wound, but now the pain in his shoulder howled.

"I'll be fine," he said through gritted teeth.

"It looks like you got shot! Are you hit anywhere else?"

"I don't think so."

"I saw a wrecked car in the garage. What the hell happened? Why are we in Cavano's car?"

"Had a little trouble getting into the BMW. Pietro surprised me."

The traffic slowed ahead, so Tyler cranked the wheel to the right, turning onto a street called Steinsdorfstrasse that ran alongside the river. Stacy squealed as he weaved through the traffic, occasionally zooming into the oncoming lane when he saw an opening.

Now she'd get an idea of what it had been like for him on the horse. Using the paddle shifters, Tyler had complete control, as if he were part of the car. Stacy, on the other hand, looked distinctly unhappy as she struggled to keep from getting thrown back and forth.

"Put your seat belt on," Tyler said. "This could get dicey."

She snapped the belt into place. "Dicier than this?"

"Could be."

Tyler couldn't put any distance between them and the Lamborghini, which had now been joined by a black Pagani Zonda.

"Did you get the geolabe?" Stacy asked.

"It's got to be in the front boot."

"Where are we going?"

He had to get out of these narrow streets. They could corner him if he ran into a traffic jam.

A blue sign flashed by depicting a highway overpass and an arrow toward 95.

The autobahn. The sleek sports cars following them were a match for the Ferrari. Outrunning them would be next to impossible, but the open highway was better than a city traffic jam.

He gave Stacy his phone.

"Call Grant and tell him to head this way."

"But he'll never catch us."

"Just tell him that we're getting onto the Ninety-five."

As she dialed, Tyler thought about the evidence he'd left behind in the garage. Now he was glad he'd worn the gloves. If he had been successful in keeping his face out of sight of the cameras, there would be nothing leading back to him.

Of course, none of that would matter if Cavano and her men caught up with them.

He passed through an intersection just as the light turned red, but that didn't deter the Zonda and the Lamborghini. Horns honking, they blew through.

The Ferrari's gas gauge read more than half full. Cavano must have filled up before she arrived in Munich, which sparked a brainstorm for how to get out of this mess.

Tyler's plan was simple. At high speed, these cars all gulped fuel at a prodigious rate. Because the Lambo and the Zonda were being delivered to a dealer, Tyler was sure that they had only a token amount of gas in their tanks. If he could stay ahead of them long enough, they would run out before he did. Then he could leisurely plan a place to rendezvous with Grant.

On the phone, Stacy said, "No, he's busy trying to kill us. Where are you? . . . On the road? . . . Thank God." To Tyler, she said, "He got the Audi. The police got there just after he took off. He says Cavano's driving the Zonda, and she looked pissed."

Tyler wasn't surprised. He'd be pissed, too, if someone had stolen his $250,000 supercar.

Stacy told Grant they were about to get on the 95. "What then?" she said to Tyler.

"Tell him to take the autobahn south, and we'll call him back when we can."

While she did that, Tyler swung onto E54, the highway leading to the autobahn. He couldn't get above eighty miles an hour as he constantly squirted through tiny spots between cars, much to the annoyance of the Germans he passed, who were used to the rigid law of cars passing only on the left.

The honking horns behind him meant that Cavano and the other car were using the same tactics, and they were gaining ground.

A minute later, a sign said one kilometer to 95.

The traffic in the left-turn lane leading onto the autobahn was backed up and at a standstill.

"Don't stop!" Stacy yelled.

"I'm not."

When Tyler reached the intersection, he stood on the brakes, throwing him and Stacy against their straining seat belts. With a flick of the wheel, he veered left from the middle lane and charged past a turning truck, eliciting another scream from Stacy.

They now had a clear stretch of autobahn in front of them. Tyler snapped the Ferrari through its gears. In ten seconds they were doing over 120 and still accelerating.

The Lambo made it through the intersection faster than Cavano's Zonda. Tyler had to slow as he waited for a station wagon that was tooling along at 100 to pass a semi, giving the Lambo time to catch up. By the time the lane was free, the Lambo was right behind them.

Tyler floored it, and the Ferrari leaped forward. Stacy had forgotten about his wound and gripped the sides of her seat.

Within seconds they were skirting 200 miles per hour on the sweeping turns through the Bavarian Forest. Even in a car meant for the track, 200 was eye-watering. Tyler was now so focused on the road that he didn't dare glance at Stacy again.

A Porsche sedan up ahead must have noticed the two supercars headed its way and decided to see if it could match their speed. The car pulled into the passing lane and sped up, but it was still slower than the Ferrari.

Tyler caught up to the Porsche and had to tap the brake to keep from rear-ending it. That was all the Lambo needed to make up the distance, and the Zonda was nearing them as well.

The Porsche pulled aside to let Tyler pass. The Ferrari rocketed forward, but the Lambo stayed with them. The Porsche fell behind, unable to keep up.

In the rearview mirror, Tyler saw the Lambo's passenger window roll down. The man in the passenger seat stuck a gun out the window, ready to take aim at the Ferrari's tires, but he hadn't counted on the force of the 180-mph wind. The pistol was torn from his hand and skipped across the road into the grass.

If they had another gun, the Lambo's passenger wouldn't make that mistake again, and a blowout at this speed would mean the end of the Ferrari and both of the people it carried.

Tyler let up on the accelerator.

"Why are you slowing down?" Stacy said. Even she was getting used to the speed when slowing down meant going under 175.

"I want them to get closer," Tyler said.

"Closer? Are you nuts?"

The road was curving to the left, so Tyler hugged the inside of the left lane, letting the Lambo pull along Stacy's side. He'd have to do this just right, or they'd be eating metal.

The driver raised a pistol. He was gesturing for them to slow down or he'd shoot. Perfect. Only one hand on the wheel.

Tyler jerked the wheel to the right, bashing the Ferrari into the Lambo. The driver got off two shots, but they both went into the hood.

The Lambo was nudged over just far enough to catch the edge of the shoulder. The unevenness made the driver overcorrect, and the back wheels spun out. When it reached the grass embankment, the Lambo flipped, spewing body panels and engine parts all over the side of the autobahn. Tyler saw the bodies of both occupants go flying. At that speed, they would be pulped on impact.

Now Tyler was responsible for the deaths of three men today. He had killed before in self-defense, so he understood the grim necessity of it, but Stacy was aghast at the carnage.

Tyler was so fixated on the crash that he hadn't noticed the Zonda closing the gap. Cavano's car had just a little more horsepower, so she was slowly creeping up on them no matter how hard he pushed the Ferrari.

The Zonda pulled up on Tyler's side, and the man in the passenger seat had his own gun pointed at Tyler. Tyler tried the same maneuver he'd used to destroy the Lambo. He yanked the wheel over, but Cavano was too deft and avoided the impact.

When she pulled even again, she leaned over so that Tyler could see her smile and wag a finger at them.

"She's got us," he said.

"You're giving up?"

"Never. I just have to think of something else."

"Like what?"

"That's the hard part."

Cavano's passenger fired two warning shots into the air. Apparently, Cavano wanted her Ferrari back in one piece. But her passenger made it clear that the next two shots were going to end Tyler's and Stacy's lives one way or the other if they didn't pull over.

Tyler saw a sign that said AUSFAHRT. An exit. Two kilometers. If he could reach it, maybe he could figure out something. He slowed to give the impression that he was obeying her command.

The Zonda suddenly lurched as if the car were having a seizure. Tyler thought Cavano had hit the brake, but then it sped up before lurching again.

The passenger turned away to see what was happening, but Tyler already knew. She was out of gas. He mashed his own pedal down.

Cavano gestured wildly to the gunman, but by the time he turned back around, the Ferrari was already directly in front of the Zonda. Not learning from his dead comrade, he stuck the gun out to shoot them and had it snatched from his hand.

The Zonda continued to slow and finally pulled over to the shoulder.

Tyler cruised to the exit, satisfied that he and Stacy were in the clear. He blipped the throttle and soon the Zonda was out of sight.

Taking a back road that ran parallel to the autobahn, they met Grant at a rest-area parking lot where they'd dump the Ferrari. Cavano would get it back, though with about eighty thousand dollars' worth of bodywork.

"You guys okay?" Grant asked as they got out.

Tyler nodded, holding his wounded arm. "Nothing that a bandage won't take care of."

Stacy steadied herself against the Audi. "After that ride, I feel like I'm bathing in adrenaline."

"Let's make a pact," Tyler said. "I never drive you in a car at two hundred miles an hour again, and you never make me ride another horse."

She smiled. "You've got a deal. Next time we'll compromise and make it a horse and buggy."

Tyler groaned playfully, opened the front boot, and saw a case inside. He lifted its lid to make sure the whole car chase hadn't been for nothing.

There was the geolabe shining brightly at him. He breathed a sigh of relief and was about to close the case when he heard it rattle, as if a piece of metal was loose inside. Then he noticed a protrusion on the side. He turned it over, and his heart sank when he saw what it was.

"Uh, guys," he said. "We've got a new problem."

"It's not there?" Stacy said.

"No, it's here all right. At least, most of it is."

Tyler held it up to his eye and could see Stacy straight through the bullet hole.

THIRTY-SEVEN

They found a clinic that bought Tyler's story about injuring his arm with a piece of jagged metal. After the doctor put ten stitches into the arm and gave him a tetanus shot, the three of them returned to the Gordian jet. Tyler and Grant had just begun to disassemble the geolabe to assess the damage from the stray bullet when Tyler's phone rang.

"Is it Orr?" Stacy asked.

Tyler nodded and put the call on speaker.

"How are you doing, Locke?" Orr said. "Found the map yet?"

"We're working on it."

"I already know you work well under pressure. You have to meet me in Naples in two days."

Tyler remembered Cavano's explanation about beginning her excavation on Monday. There would be no wiggle room in Orr's schedule, but he had to put up at least a token resistance.

"We need more time," Tyler said. "There's no way we can finish our task by Sunday."

"Find a way, or start making funeral arrangements."

Tyler hesitated a few seconds for effect. "Fine. We'll be there. How are we making the exchange? I don't imagine you're bringing my father and Stacy's sister with you to Italy."

"Have someone ready to confirm their release at the Lincoln Memorial that day at 3 P.M. eastern time. At the same time on Sunday, 9 P.M. in Naples, there's an outdoor concert taking place on Piazza del Plebiscito before a fireworks show. Meet me there. Both you and Stacy."

"Just me," Tyler said.

"Both of you, or don't bother showing up."

"We haven't seen our proof-of-life videos today."

"I'm sending the video now. When I confirm that you've solved the puzzle, I will release Sherman and Carol."

Hearing Orr use their names as if they were friends made Tyler's bile rise. He didn't believe Orr was going to give his hostages up that easily, but they had no choice but to continue playing along.

"How will we find you at the concert?"

"I'll call you with more instructions then. Just make sure you're there at 9 P.M." Orr hung up.

Tyler checked his e-mail. Carol and Sherman looked more haggard than they did the day before, but they seemed uninjured. There wasn't any more signing to decode, however. This video was from the chest up. Sherman's hands weren't in the frame.

"Orr isn't leaving us many options," Tyler said to Stacy as he showed Grant the video.

She nodded as if she were expecting it.

"Without any more leads from Aiden," Grant said, "I think we're going to have to go through with this."

Tyler sighed. "I think you're right."

Ransom handoffs were notoriously messy for everyone involved. Double-crosses were too easy to pull off. One side would bring the money, but the kidnappers would take off with it without delivering the hostage, sometimes by killing the bagman. Or the kidnappers got nabbed by the police as soon as the hostage was recovered. A successful handoff depended on a degree of trust on both sides, but that was sorely missing in this case. Tyler sure as hell didn't think Orr was going to let any of them go free.

"So what's the plan?" Grant said.

Tyler had the start of an idea for how to approach the handoff, but he had to mull it over before he told Grant and Stacy.

"Let's work on that later. First, we need to see if the geolabe can be saved."

The bullet had gone in through the side of the geolabe and out through the top. If it had been struck through the face, the entire device would have been destroyed, but since only a minor portion was damaged Tyler was hoping it could be salvaged. As it was, though, he'd tried turning the knobs, and something inside was definitely broken.

The outer metal faces of the geolabe were fitted together using tiny screws. Tyler unscrewed them using his Leatherman tool and lifted the single-dial plate. As he'd suspected, there was the tracking device affixed to the inside of the plate with epoxy. He set down the plate so that he could inspect the interior.

He shined a flashlight into the device and saw the problem. The gears meshed together precisely. Any warping or misalignment would cause the teeth to miss each other, rendering the device nonfunctional.

"Crap," he said.

Stacy leaned forward. "Is it bad?"

The gears could be lifted out one at a time. He took out three, all of which were perfectly intact. Then he reached the main universal gear, the one that drove the entire mechanism.

The bullet had grazed just this one gear. A dozen teeth were missing, and the gear was hopelessly bent.

Stacy picked it up and turned it over in her hands.

"Can it be fixed?" she asked, giving it back to him.

Tyler gave Grant a somber look.

"How long to make that gear?" Grant asked.

"A couple of days. If I had the right equipment."

"A couple of days?" Stacy said. "Can't you just buy one?"

"This isn't an off-the-shelf gear ratio," Grant said. "It requires precision machining."

"I'll call Miles," Tyler said. "We can send out the specs. He probably knows someone in the U.S. who can whip one of these out quickly."

"It's Friday afternoon there. Even if we could get the gear fabricated, it wouldn't make it over to Europe in time for us to fix the geolabe, use it at the Parthenon, and then get to Naples."

"There's got to be some way to get a new one more quickly," Stacy said. "Too bad we can't just use Archimedes' original one."

Tyler put the damaged gear down. That was it.

"We *can* get the original," he said. "The gearing inside the Antikythera Mechanism is very similar to the geolabe's. Its main gear has exactly the same dimensions as this one."

Stacy laughed and then stopped when Tyler didn't join in.

"You mean the one in the National Archaeological Museum in Athens? I was joking. It's corroded and embedded in a rock. It'll never work."

"Not the one they found in the shipwreck. The replica. It might require a few modifications to fit it on the axle, but the diameter, thickness, and number of teeth are identical."

"Isn't that one also in the National Archaeological Museum?"

"Right next to the original."

"Wait a second," Grant said. "You think they're going to let us borrow their replica of the Antikythera Mechanism, take it apart, and use a piece of it in our own reconstruction?"

Stacy shook her head. "Museums are stingy with their display objects. Even for a respected institution, it would take months of negotiations to get a loan approved by the cultural ministry. For us, there's no chance."

"That's if we asked," Tyler said.

Grant scowled. "You're kidding."

"We're only going to borrow it. We'll give it back."

Tyler expected Stacy to protest, but she stared at the ceiling. He could see that her mind was churning with the implications of his proposal.

"Are you on board?" Tyler asked her.

Stacy's eyes focused on him. He'd never seen a more serious and determined expression.

"I just saw a video of my sister in handcuffs," she said. "The question isn't if we should steal that thing, but how."

SATURDAY

THE ANTIKYTHERA MECHANISM

THIRTY-EIGHT

Orr asked the flight attendant for another glass of champagne, and she brought it to him within seconds. He winked at her and got a dazzling smile in return. With a good six hours left on the flight to Rome, he saw no reason not to toast the culmination of years of planning. He even thought Alitalia's name for first class fit his mood: *Magnifica.*

He put the footrest up and closed his eyes, but he wasn't the least bit sleepy. After all this time, he was nearing his final retribution. He visualized Midas's vault of gold that had haunted his dreams for the past twenty years, running his hands over the gleaming metal that would make him richer than Midas himself could ever have imagined. But, more than the impending wealth, he savored the thought of vengeance for a life snatched from him. His targets would know what it was like to have comfort and prosperity ripped away and replaced by misery and poverty. They would have to scratch and claw out of the abyss the way he had.

Orr would become rich beyond belief, while the people who'd made his life hell would lose everything. He relished the poetic justice of it.

Gaul sat next to him watching a movie, while Phillips and Crenshaw were back in the U.S. completing their part of the plan. There was no sense discussing the mission with Gaul until they got to Italy, not with so many potential eavesdroppers around them.

Orr had the entire sequence in his head. With all the heists he'd pulled in the past, meticulous preparation was second nature to him. Of course, he'd had to put it all down on paper for Gaul,

Phillips, and Crenshaw, but he made sure they'd burned all the evidence once it had been committed to memory.

After they arrived in Rome, it would be only an hour and ten minutes on the Frecciarossa high-speed train to Naples. There he'd rent a car and pick up the items he'd sent by overnight service—items that would have gotten him arrested if he'd checked them on an airline flight.

Orr hadn't been to Naples in five years, but he remembered it well enough. At a population of more than four million for the Greater Naples metropolitan area, the sheer size of the city would let him do his business without alerting Gia Cavano. Cavano was well-connected in the city, but Orr had cultivated a wide range of aliases to travel under, only one of which she knew besides his real name.

That meant he could get into Naples a day early, put everything into motion, and wait for his bigger problem: Tyler Locke.

Was Locke really accomplishing his task? Orr suspected that he was at least trying. The tracker showed the geolabe first in England, then in Munich. What information Locke and Benedict were gleaning in those locations Orr couldn't guess, but it didn't really matter. He was results-oriented, and Locke was the type who delivered.

If Locke and Benedict failed, Orr had a much less lucrative but simple backup plan. He'd let Cavano know that he would reveal the existence of the gold chamber to the Carabinieri, Italy's national police force, unless, of course, she cut him in on the deal and shared the take. The Italian authorities would never let her get away with looting a national treasure if they knew about it. Sharing the spoils with Cavano would be a bitter consolation prize, but it was better than nothing. She wouldn't care much for it, either, since he was the one who'd double-crossed her originally.

Orr had every confidence in himself, but where plans often had the potential to go awry was with his partners in crime. That's why he'd chosen the participants in this job so carefully. Gaul and Phillips were solid. Not that they didn't have their faults. Gaul was a gambler, always in debt, but that made his need for money useful. Phillips's weakness was women, throwing away thousands at upscale S and M clubs. Orr shuddered at the thought of the diseases he must be afflicted with, although he didn't worry about leaving Phillips with Carol Benedict. Phillips was the masochistic type. He wouldn't be interested in a helpless woman.

On the job, Gaul and Phillips were total professionals. Orr had worked with each of them many times before, and they'd never let him down.

Crenshaw was the wild card. A brilliant bomb-maker, but squirrelly enough to be a prospective liability. Phillips would take care of him when the time came.

Orr had no doubt that Gaul and Phillips would eventually blow through their two-million-dollar shares and become threats, but by that time he would be safely ensconced in the lifestyle that a billion dollars could provide. If those two so much as implied that they would blackmail him, he would have many tools at his disposal to silence them.

When he'd first formulated his long-term plan all those years ago, he'd debated whether to go into an arrangement with Cavano. The discovery of the Archimedes Codex had made the uneasy alliance pay off. She'd needed his expertise, and she had the resources to make the theft possible. Returning the manuscript to her, however, would have made Orr another of her minions, sharing in the proceeds, but nothing more than a bit player.

That wasn't enough for him. When his parents died, he had given the authorities the name of his relatives in Naples. But Cavano's father had made it clear that they would not help him. He felt that the suicide of Orr's father was a disgrace and the murder of his mother dishonorable. Whether Cavano had been aware of her father's refusal to take him in Orr didn't know and didn't care. She had to pay for the sins of the father.

But Orr wouldn't kill her. He had discovered how close she was to losing her position as the head of a Camorra crime family and that the Midas treasure would reverse her financial slide, making her one of the most powerful leaders in Naples. So he would take the fortune they had found together and make it his own. She wouldn't see a single ounce of the gold.

Orr guzzled the last of his champagne and leaned the chair back to the full sleeping position. To help him doze off, he entertained the wonderful thought of her world crumbling around her. Cavano would lose the status she had grown accustomed to, just as Orr had all those years ago.

Then the other Camorra families would take her down and finish the job for him.

THIRTY-NINE

As soon as the National Archaeological Museum in Athens opened its doors on Saturday morning, Grant bought three tickets and went inside. While he cased the museum, Tyler and Stacy went out shopping for supplies. They'd left the tracker from the geolabe in the airplane to give Orr as little information as possible about their movements.

The flight from Munich the night before had taken only a couple of hours, so the three of them had spent the rest of the evening thinking about how to steal the replica of the Antikythera Mechanism. It was a risk they all agreed to take, but it would really be Tyler putting his neck on the line despite Grant's objections.

Using photos and a map of the museum they'd found on the Web, Tyler sketched out a plan for getting the replica out. It wasn't foolproof by any means, but it seemed solid if the layout of the museum matched their information. There was minimal possibility of anyone getting hurt, except for Tyler if he got caught.

The classically designed building was laid out with marble-floored halls wrapped around two central open-air courtyards. The only way to the Antikythera Mechanism was to wind through the maze of exhibits toward the rear of the building and then walk back through an outer hall, where the pathway ended at a tiny room on the north face of the museum. Without the map, Grant would have been totally lost. Greeks and their labyrinths, he thought.

Grant took photos as he walked, as if he were just a tourist gawking at the bronze and stone statuary on display. He made only a token gesture to point the camera at the art objects, instead focusing most of his attention on the location of the cameras and attendants in each hall. Most of the attendants looked like young, casually dressed college students, one to each room.

Sweat soaked Grant's shirt. He'd never before been in a museum that lacked air-conditioning. He thought respite from the heat outside was one of the benefits of visiting a museum in the summer, but the National Archaeological Museum was stifling. He couldn't feel much of a breeze. The visitors seemed to be moving most of the air.

Grant passed a few display cases containing ancient gold jewelry and pottery fragments. Each of the cases was attached to the ceiling by a coiled cord. That would be the electricity for the lighting and the alarm system.

It was ten minutes before Grant saw his first guard. The man in a blazer was chatting with one of the pretty young attendants. The only thing he was armed with was a walkie-talkie. A key chain dangled from his belt attached by a retractable cord. Grant made sure to get a picture of him.

Grant continued on until he reached the room that held the original Antikythera Mechanism.

His first impression was *That's it?*

The ancient bronze device was in the center of the room, mounted in a display case with glass all the way around. The device had been discovered in the remains of a two-thousand-year-old shipwreck and consisted of three separate pieces corroded by exposure to seawater. None of the pieces were larger than Grant's hand. He was amazed that a replica could be built on the basis of what was there, but next to it was another, identical display case with the glittering bronze reproduction. It was mounted on a clear base and rested on a pedestal, but it didn't appear to be attached to the base in any way.

The cases were seven feet tall, with the top foot taken up by a metal cap that contained the light. Grant walked around until he saw the hole that Stacy had told him to look for. It was for the unique key that every museum had specially made to access its displays. The proper way to reach the object inside was to switch off the motion-detector alarm, insert the key that unlocked the cap from the ballistic glass, and open the front window. If the key was turned without deactivating the alarm, the central security room would immediately be alerted that someone was making an unauthorized entry into the case.

Between the two cases was a stand that showed X-ray images of the original Antikythera Mechanism, which was how they'd seen the internal gears without damaging the artifact.

Grant pivoted around and saw that only one of the cameras was in place. The mount for the second camera was empty, which meant that part of the room couldn't be monitored remotely. He backed into each corner and snapped more photos. Some of the other display cases around the room had gaps behind them that were big enough for Tyler to use, including one that was directly under the lone camera.

The exhibit hall dead-ended in the next room, which had a fire exit that opened out to the north side of the building. An attendant sat in a chair next to the exit.

With his interior survey complete, Grant wound his way back out of the museum and walked around to the exterior of the north side so that he could see where the fire exit led.

A courtyard filled with broken pieces of marble sat between the fire exit and the street that bordered the museum property. Trees shaded a bus stop and an information kiosk, and the fence that separated the courtyard from the sidewalk was lined with parked motorcycles and scooters, which in Athens were more numerous than cars.

Grant clicked through his photos and concluded that he'd seen enough. It wasn't a perfect setup, but it was damn close.

He dialed Tyler, who picked up on the first ring.

"How's it look?" Tyler said.

"I'm sorry to tell you," Grant said, "but I think your crazy scheme might actually work."

FORTY

Tyler hung up the phone as he and Stacy exited the hotel.

"Grant says we're a go," he said. They were both dressed in shorts, with Tyler in a T-shirt and Stacy in a tank top. He noticed a tattoo of two small Chinese symbols on her shoulder. "What does that mean?"

She pulled her shoulder forward to look at it and said, "A promise I made to myself when I was a teenager itching to get off the farm. It means 'adventure.' I guess I found it."

"I like it." Tyler lifted the sleeve of his T-shirt to reveal his own tattoo: a castle with a sword through it. "That was my battalion's insignia. It was a popular tat in the unit, so I decided, what the hell? Grant has the same one on his arm."

Tyler watched as she traced the outline with her finger and nodded in appreciation. The intimate moment lingered until he lightly cleared his throat.

"You ready?" he asked her, putting his helmet on.

"Hell, yeah," she said, donning her own helmet. "I love motorcycles."

Tyler started the second of the two BMW motorcycles that he and Grant had rented. It would be much easier to zip around in the dense Athens traffic with it.

While Grant was scouting the museum, Tyler and Stacy had called various stores looking for the supplies he'd need. Since Tyler didn't speak Greek, Stacy had done all the talking. It had taken almost an hour to find a paintball store and an electronics store that sold what they required.

Armed with the addresses on his phone, Tyler would drive while Stacy navigated. He gave her the backpack to wear.

Stacy hopped on the back of the BMW and pressed herself against Tyler, wrapping one arm around his waist.

"Just tell me where to turn," he said, and roared off.

In twenty minutes, they were in the western part of the city. Even though Tyler had looked at the map before they left, he felt disoriented. He couldn't even pronounce the words on the signs.

Stacy pointed to a store on the right. This sign he didn't need to read. It had a picture of a paintball splatting against a stylized figure, so he knew they'd arrived at the first location.

He pulled to a stop, and they dismounted. Stacy removed her helmet and shook out her hair, her blond tresses bouncing back and forth. Just a hint of perspiration glistened on her neck, and her tank top and shorts revealed her toned form.

He eyed her until she said, "Undressing me with your eyes?"

Tyler felt blood rush to his face. "No, actually I was trying to dress you."

"I've never heard that one before."

"It just occurred to me that no clerk in his right mind would forget you."

"Why, thank you."

"I'm not objecting to how you look, but we don't want someone making that connection between this sale and what goes on later. So just pay in cash and get out as fast as you can."

Tyler took the backpack from her and pulled out his Mariners cap.

"Hold still," he said. He took off her sunglasses and gathered up her hair until it was piled on top of her head. She kept her eyes on him as he tried not to tug on her hair. She didn't help, amused at his struggle.

Holding her hair in place with one hand, he plopped the cap

on, then put the sunglasses back on her. "Don't take them off inside."

"That was very gentle of you," she said.

Tyler flushed again. "When you work with bombs, you have to have a light touch."

"Is that right?" She tilted her glasses down.

"You getting saucy with me?" he asked.

"Twelve near-death experiences in three days make you appreciate life."

"We'll try to minimize those from now on. You know what we need in there?"

Stacy nodded. "A flameless electric-ignition smoke grenade. It's not a phrase I learned studying ancient Greek, but I'll get the point across."

"Great. And make sure it's the half-million-cubic-foot model."

"I'll get two, just in case."

"Good. And buy other supplies with it. Doesn't matter what, but make the smoke grenades seem like an afterthought."

"No sweat. Be right back."

Tyler waited by the motorcycle. Stacy came back out five minutes later.

"Any problems?" he asked.

"Piece of cake." She opened the bag. "Is this what you wanted?"

He looked inside the bag and saw the two grenades. He couldn't read the writing, but they were the right dimensions. She'd also bought two bags of paintball ammunition and a generic black baseball cap.

"That's them," he said.

"The hat's for you, since I took your Mariners cap."

Stacy stuffed the bag into the backpack and took off the sunglasses. Her smile was gone.

"You sure you want to go through with this?" she said.

"You mean at the museum?"

"I mean, the possibility of you spending ten years in a Greek prison if you get caught."

"Believe me, I wish there was another way. I like my freedom as much as the next guy."

"But don't you think this is insane?"

"Absolutely. I also think it's insane that someone kidnapped my father and your sister to force us to find a treasure map created by Archimedes so that this criminal can find the Midas Touch. But if Orr really has nuclear material for a dirty bomb, we have to do everything we can to stop him."

Stacy considered that. "Why do you think Orr would want a dirty bomb?"

"Who knows? Maybe it's his backup plan. If I don't go along with him, he threatens to detonate the bomb. Or if he can't find the Midas vault and get rich that way, maybe he'll blackmail the U.S. with the nuke."

"Or maybe the two aren't linked at all."

Tyler shook his head. "I'm sure to Orr they are. He has some kind of plan, but I have no idea what it is."

"And you're sure Sr-90 means strontium?"

"No, but my father is an expert in WMDs. If that's what he was trying to tell me, he'd know we'd connect the dots when we looked it up."

Stacy peered at him for a few seconds, and then smiled.

"Then we better go get this remote igniter that you need," she said as she put on her helmet.

Tyler did the same. "Sounds good to me."

Stacy gave him the backpack and held out her hand.

"What?" Tyler said.

"The keys, please." She winked and flipped down the visor. "It's my turn to drive."

FORTY-ONE

Gia Cavano stormed into the entryway of her villa along the Mediterranean coast just west of Naples and picked up the first thing she could grab, a crystal Steuben vase displayed on the hall table. She hurled it into the wall, showering the floor with glass shards.

The destruction felt good, but she still burned with fury.

As a maid rushed over to sweep up the remains of the vase, Cavano stomped through the living room and onto the terrace overlooking the sea. Her cousin Salvatore followed her. He wasn't too bright, which Cavano liked, but he was efficient and provided the necessary brawn. He'd been a faithful servant since her husband died.

"Quell'idiòta, Pietro!" Cavano yelled, kicking one of the chairs over. "If he weren't already dead, I'd kill him," she continued in Italian.

"Locke will pay. I'll make sure of it."

"Do you realize what yesterday cost me? The wrecked Lamborghini and the repairs to the Ferrari will cost over three hundred thousand euros, not to mention the destroyed BMW and the Zonda I had to buy."

"And we lost three men."

"Yes, of course. Three more families to feed." The Cavanos looked after their own, especially when soldiers died. It guaranteed their loyalty to know that their families would be secure.

Rödel had sent a car to pick her up when the Zonda ran out

of gas. She left the police to investigate the death in the Boerst garage and the disintegrated Lamborghini. The Ferrari was found not long after with two bullet holes in it. Through Rödel, she reported it stolen and left the city before they could ask her any questions.

Now she had full ownership of the Ministry of Health building, but demolition work couldn't begin until Monday morning. Even with her power, she couldn't compel the Italian unions to bring in the heavy machinery she'd need on a weekend.

As long as she kept Orr at bay until she broke through into the tunnels, the gold would be all hers.

But Locke had followed her specifically for the device. The video recordings that Rödel had supplied for her showed that Locke had tried the BMW first and had fought Pietro, eventually pushing the car over the edge. The cap Locke wore had hidden his face, so the police wouldn't be able to make a positive identification, and she certainly wasn't going to report him. She wanted to take care of him herself.

She just had to figure out why he'd risked so much to get it. It was obviously critical to his search, as was the tablet he'd stolen. Eventually he would come to Naples. He and Orr would have to.

"Are we keeping watch on the airport and the train station?" she asked.

"I have men waiting at both. If Orr, Locke, Benedict, or Westfield shows up, we'll know."

She wasn't so sure about that. Orr was a master at hiding his identity, and he'd know he would be vulnerable in Naples. Locke, on the other hand, seemed determined and resourceful, but he wasn't a criminal skilled at covering his tracks.

"Put feelers out to all the hotels, too. Have them look for anything different from the typical tourist or businessman."

"What should we do if we spot any of them?"

"Protecting the gold is the first priority." Sal was the only one of her men who knew what they were searching for.

"So we should kill them when we find them?"

Cavano paused. Killing them on sight was the smart thing to do. Three shots, execution style. Naples had the highest murder rate in western Europe, and the *polizia* made few arrests.

But unease crept over her. What if Orr or Locke already knew how to find the gold? If she killed either of them, she wouldn't know what the other was planning. If they got to the chamber before she did, she might lose out on the Midas treasure altogether.

"Kill them only as a last resort. Capture them if you can. But do not let them get away, no matter who has to die to prevent it."

"Understood."

Cavano paced as she tried to think like her adversary. "Orr is looking for some other way to the gold. I'm sure the tablet and Locke's device have something to do with his search, but I don't know what."

"What about the British Museum?" Sal said. "When I was following Westfield, he talked to Lumley for a long time."

"When I called Lumley back, he told me that he couldn't decipher what the codex meant."

"Maybe the device has something to do with the codex and that's why Locke took it back from us."

That stopped Cavano. Maybe Sal wasn't as dumb as she thought.

She felt her blood pressure rising again. Lumley had withheld information from her. She retrieved her phone and dialed the archaeologist's cell.

"Hello," he said tentatively.

"It's me. Don't lie to me this time. Tell me what you told Westfield."

"I didn't lie. I really couldn't help him—"

She didn't have time for this. "If you don't tell me what you know, I will strap you to a table and make you watch as I pull out your entrails one by one."

Lumley gulped audibly. "All . . . all right. Of course. Mr. Westfield was particularly interested in two statues of the Parthenon's west pediment—Herakles and Aphrodite."

"Why?"

"The codex referenced those two figures as a key to some kind of puzzle, but I don't know what."

"Have they come back to the museum?"

"Oh, no. I don't think they would."

"You mean they solved the puzzle?"

"I don't know. The codex implied that one would have to be at the Parthenon in person to understand what it meant."

At the Parthenon. "*Grazie,* Doctor."

"Am I free now?"

"No. I may call again at any time, and if you don't answer, I will take that as a sign of disrespect. Do you understand?"

Lumley wheezed into the phone. "Absolutely."

She hung up.

With a day's head start, it was possible she was already too late to get Locke, Benedict, and Westfield, but it was the only lead she had.

"Get Adamo and Dario," she said to Sal. "Since they were at the museum, they'll recognize Grant Westfield. Send them to Athens tonight. I think Locke and his friends may be there already."

"Should I go with them?"

"No, I want you here in Naples. If they slip through, they'll come here next."

"What should Adamo and Dario do in Athens?"

"Find photos of Locke and Benedict to give them. I want them at the Parthenon from opening to closing."

"And if they find all three of them?"

Getting them all back to Italy would be difficult. The best bet would be to charter a boat.

Cavano could already feel her heartbeat ease and her muscles relax. For the first time in twenty-four hours, she felt back in control.

"We don't need all three," she said. "Capture Locke. Kill Benedict and Westfield."

FORTY-TWO

It was 2:45 in the afternoon, and with the 3:00 closing time fast approaching, the visitors at the National Archaeological Museum were beginning to wander back toward the entrance. Using the tickets Grant had bought earlier in the day, Tyler and Stacy had entered the museum separately.

Tyler had put on a collared shirt and jeans for the operation, with the backpack slung over his shoulder. His earpiece was in and connected to his cell phone's open line to Grant, who was with their motorcycles next to the emergency exit.

"You ready out there?" Tyler said.

"A little crowd at the bus stop, but otherwise we're good to go."

"Give me a shout if something wicked comes that way."

"Will do."

Tyler wore the new black cap on the off chance that his Mariners cap would be connected to the Munich garage incident. He pulled the bill down and made sure to keep it between his face and the cameras in each room as he followed Grant's directions to the room with the Antikythera Mechanism. Having studied the photos thoroughly, Tyler knew exactly what to expect, but seeing it in person for the first time he was still amazed at how much the replica sitting behind the glass looked like the geolabe he'd built. Other than the single knob on the side of the Antikythera Mechanism, as opposed to the dual knobs on the geolabe, they were virtually identical.

The attendants from this room and the one with the emergency exit were chatting, paying no attention to Tyler. No other tourists were around, giving him the chance he needed.

He positioned himself directly beneath the working camera next to a display case that had a small space between it and the wall. Tyler knelt as if to tie his shoe, plopping the backpack next to him. With a smooth motion, he removed the smoke grenade from the pack and rested it behind the display case. Unless someone was looking for it, it wouldn't be seen.

He stood back up and pretended to spend a few more minutes reading the captions on the Antikythera Mechanism. A walk around the case holding the replica showed him the keyhole that would unlock the front glass.

He strolled back out the way he'd come, just another visitor browsing relics from Greece's ancient past. He really did wish he had more time to inspect the fragments of the Antikythera Mechanism. It was incredible that he'd been looking at a device more sophisticated than any other created for fifteen hundred years.

They'd planned to set things in motion in the gallery containing tombstone sculptures, about a hundred feet from the room with the Mechanism. When he turned into the hall, he saw Stacy peering intently at the statue of a robed man carrying a bowl into which offerings would be placed.

She made a slow 180-degree turn, and Tyler nodded as her eyes passed over him. It was a go.

Grant had noted the locations of all the fire alarms, and Stacy found one near a group of elderly tourists listening to a guide speaking English. She pulled it discreetly as she walked by. A Klaxon began to blare.

The sound came from horns in the ceiling, so no one turned to where Stacy had just been standing. She looked as confused as the rest of the patrons.

Attendants began to appear from both ends of the hall. Fire was a major threat to the artwork, but the sprinklers were not set to come on automatically for fear of damaging the statues unnecessarily.

Tyler gripped the unfolded Leatherman in his pocket, waiting for his cue.

Within seconds, a guard appeared. He was speaking loudly into his walkie-talkie and headed directly for the alarm pull. He stopped in front of it and swung around, looking for any hint of a fire.

The tour group was watching the guard, not moving toward the exit as Tyler had hoped. He sidled up to one of the group members, a gentleman who looked to be in his eighties.

"Did you hear that?" Tyler said.

"Hear what?" the man said.

Tyler pointed at the guard. "I think that guy said there was a fire in the back of the museum."

That seemed to be confirmation enough for them, and the tour group began shuffling toward the front exit.

Stacy was already engaged in an animated conversation with the guard in Greek, performing her bit to perfection. She gestured at the ceiling as if the fire might be up there. She put her hand on the guard's back. Two attendants who had joined them also looked up. Whatever Stacy was saying, they were buying it.

Tyler took the Leatherman out of his pocket, the wire cutters at the ready. The guard's keys were dangling off his left hip. Tyler stood next to him as if he were also trying to see the cause of the alarm.

Stacy yelled, and that was his cue. He bent slightly, grasped the keys, and snipped the cord. The guard didn't feel a thing.

Tyler turned and headed back toward the Antikythera Mechanism.

As soon as he made the turn into the next room, he bumped

three display cases with his hip. According to Stacy, each case would have a silent alarm built in. The sudden motion would set them off, creating more distraction.

Then he flicked the button on the remote, igniting the smoke grenade. Grant had spent his lunchtime rigging the igniter. The flameless paintball grenade could be set off just by holding a nine-volt battery to the leads, but it could also be attached to a simple electric ignition switch and activated with a push-button remote.

The grenade began to spew out enough smoke to cover a football field. In three minutes, the entire hall would be full of the nontoxic gas. Tyler just needed it to fill the room that held the Mechanism replica.

He flipped through the keys until he found the odd-shaped one that opened the display cases.

The attendants in the room cried out in alarm. Tyler was only twenty feet away now and saw an orange cloud of smoke billowing through the entryway. The two attendants came out hacking and coughing, convinced that the gas was poisonous.

Tyler had expected them to go out the emergency exit. Their sudden appearance complicated things, but he decided to just go for it.

Tyler skirted around them and plunged into the room, which was now completely engulfed in smoke. Unable to see more than a foot in front of him, he moved to the display case by feel.

He was about to insert the key when he felt someone latch on to his arm. One of the attendants had gotten brave and gone back into the smoke to save Tyler. She pulled on him insistently shouting at him in Greek.

Tyler nudged the attendant forward and made as if to follow her out. But once she got two steps ahead, he stopped and went back to the case, confident that she wouldn't know where he'd gone. He ran his hand along the top until he found the keyhole.

He inserted it, and with a twist the case popped open. Orange smoke flooded into the purified air inside the case.

Tyler unzipped his backpack. He snared the Antikythera Mechanism replica and stuffed it into the bag. Then he wiped the keys down with his shirt and tossed them into the case.

"Got it," he said.

"You're clear," came Grant's reply.

Tyler walked toward the exit door, pushed it open, and tumbled through, holding his hand over his face and wheezing for the benefit of anyone who might be watching.

He stumbled to where Grant waited with the motorcycles. No one else was near the bus stop. Any looky-loos were drawn to the museum entrance.

They both got on their bikes, rocketed away, and made a circuit around the museum. When they reached the front, Stacy was running toward them.

She hopped on Tyler's ride, and they took off.

Three intersections later, they stopped at a red light. They heard some sirens, but all of them were headed toward the museum.

"Any problems?" Grant shouted above the traffic.

"Other than the attendant making a last-second grab for me, it went off without a hitch," Tyler replied. He turned to Stacy. "Nice acting job. I almost looked up at the ceiling myself."

"I have to please my public," she said. "Think the attendant will be able to identify you?"

"With all that smoke? She'll be lucky to remember it was a man."

"You mean, *you'll* be lucky."

The light turned green. "I'm highly skilled at being lucky," Tyler yelled over his shoulder as he opened the throttle, putting more distance between them and the scene of the crime.

FORTY-THREE

After they dropped Stacy off at the hotel, Grant and Tyler went to a local metalwork and fabrication shop they had rented. Tyler paid the owner a handsome fee to leave them alone for the evening with the grinding, cutting, and welding tools they would need to remove the gear from the Mechanism replica and transfer it to the geolabe.

The approach to constructing the replica was different from the one Tyler had used on the geolabe, so he had to remove the axle from the gear before he could fit it to the geolabe. The entire process took seven hours, and by midnight he had all forty-seven gears of the geolabe back together. The dials spun freely, as if the gear had been in place from the beginning. The geolabe was once again in working order.

"Now we just have to wait until morning," Grant said, as he gathered up the scattered pieces of the replica. "The Acropolis opens at 8 A.M."

"Shouldn't take us more than ten minutes once we're up there. Then we can head back to the airport. With the hour time difference, we'll be in Rome by lunchtime."

Landing in Naples was too risky. They didn't know how far Gia Cavano's influence reached, but Tyler didn't think it extended to Rome. They'd hire a car and make the one-hour drive down to Naples in time to meet with Orr.

Tyler rubbed his eyes. He needed a good night's sleep, but he didn't know if that was going to be possible with his mind racing.

Grant must have seen the worry etched on his face. "Your dad's going to be okay, you know."

"I know. He'd want me to be more worried about that nuclear material than about him."

"I still can't figure why Orr would want it. It's bizarre."

"It has something to do with the gold," Tyler said. "Why else would he have us hunt for the treasure and prepare his nuclear material simultaneously?"

"If he sets that thing off in D.C.," Grant said, "it'll turn Washington into a ghost town for the next twenty years."

"Maybe he's got a grudge against the government."

"Yeah. He might hate paying taxes even more than I do."

Tyler placed the geolabe in his backpack, then paused before speaking. "Do you think we're doing the right thing not calling the FBI into this?"

Grant shrugged. "Man, I don't know. It could go either way. They do have more resources than we do, even with Aiden's snooping powers and Miles's connections. On the other hand, I think you're right that Orr would find out. The longer he thinks we're on our own, the longer he doesn't do anything to the general or to Stacy's sister."

"I know. And I know my father's not going to sit idly by while they hold him hostage. Keeping Orr occupied could give him a chance to break out."

"You think he'll try something?"

Tyler nodded. "If we can't find him first. But Aiden said there's no way to track the videos Orr is e-mailing to us. They're routed through three different anonymizers in eastern Europe."

He didn't have to go through the rest. Grant had seen Aiden's e-mail. Gordian Engineering was one of the top forensic accident-investigation firms in the world. Miles had assembled a team of volunteers close to Tyler and gone out to the site of the ferry truck explosion to gather evidence, first calling the local sheriff to notify them that they had gotten a tip about the blast.

Under the sheriff's guidance, they had sifted through the wreckage and found nothing that would lead back to Orr. The truck had been stolen the day before, and all the bomb components could be found at any Radio Shack. The binary explosive was also impossible to track. Without any other leads and with no injuries, the sheriff was already concluding that it was the work of yahoos who got a kick out of blowing up stuff.

Aiden's efforts to sniff out Orr through the use of his electronic communications had been no more fruitful. Orr's cell phone was a disposable. The Web site for tracking the geolabe was set up with a false identity. Unless they got a lucky break, their only opportunity to free Sherman and Carol would be to nab Orr himself.

"All right," Tyler said, hoisting the backpack. "Let's get back to the hotel. We've got a long day tomorrow."

When they reached their suite, they found Stacy in the living room reading over the Archimedes Codex yet again.

"Does it work?" she asked eagerly.

Tyler smiled. "Like a Swiss watch."

"I'm going to hit the hay," Grant said. "I'll set the alarm for seven. I'll need a good breakfast."

He shut the door behind him, leaving Tyler alone with Stacy. Tyler set the backpack with the geolabe on the table and sat down next to her. Suddenly, the pace of the past few days caught up with him. He slumped against the back of the couch and closed his eyes.

"Poor guy," she said. "You look beat."

Tyler turned his head toward her and cracked his lids. "You look pretty alert."

"I took a nap while you were gone."

He twisted his neck around, the muscles sore from bending over the geolabe for four hours straight with no break.

She pushed him up. "Here. Let me work on those knots."

Before he could argue, Stacy had grabbed his shoulders. For a small woman, she had strong hands. Tyler had to admit that it felt damn good. He leaned into her thumbs, which found the most gnarled spots.

After five minutes of work, the stress wasn't completely gone, but his muscles were no longer cramped. Tyler leaned back into the cushion and looked at Stacy. Her eyes searched his.

"What?" she said.

"This situation is tough on you, isn't it?" she said.

"And it's not tough on you?"

"Of course it is, but I have faith it'll all turn out for the best."

"So do I."

She casually brushed his hair. "No, you don't. You want to *make* it turn out all right. That's why it's so hard for you. You hate not being in control. I saw you during that car chase on the autobahn. You were in your element. You were certain it would go exactly as you planned, and even if it didn't, you had confidence that you could react to whatever was thrown at you."

Tyler looked at her but said nothing.

"That story about getting injured by that horse when you were a kid," she continued. "You weren't afraid of being killed. You were afraid of being paralyzed."

Tyler was shocked at how close Stacy had gotten to the truth. But paralysis wasn't his fear. Miles was proof that life didn't end in a wheelchair. A coma was what scared him, the idea that he would be a vegetable the rest of his life, dependent on others, contributing nothing.

"Why are you telling me this?" Tyler asked her.

Stacy put both her hands on his. "Because I want you to know that you're not alone in this. One way or another, we're going to get through this. All of us."

The air seemed to be sucked out of the room, and Tyler got

tunnel vision. He was focused solely on Stacy's bright blue eyes. His breathing came to a standstill.

She leaned closer, her gaze passing from his lips to his eyes. Her grip on his hands tightened. If he moved even an inch more toward her, he wouldn't be able to stop himself.

Instead, as if they both sensed how wrong what they were contemplating would be, given that Sherman and Carol were still being held prisoner, the moment passed. Tyler turned away, one of the hardest things he'd ever done. He dropped her hands and stood.

"Well," he said, "I, uh, I should probably get some sleep."

She stood and crossed her arms, blushing in embarrassment. "Yeah, that's probably a good idea."

"So . . . good night."

"You, too. I mean, see you in the morning." She gave a half-hearted wave and retreated to her room. "Night." She closed the door.

Despite the gravity of the situation, it seemed that a tiny portion of the weight on Tyler's shoulders had lifted. He quickly brushed his teeth and stumbled into bed.

As he closed his eyes, a feeling of serenity settled over him at having Stacy and Grant by his side. No matter what the next day held, they would all be facing it together.

SUNDAY

THE MIDAS TOUCH

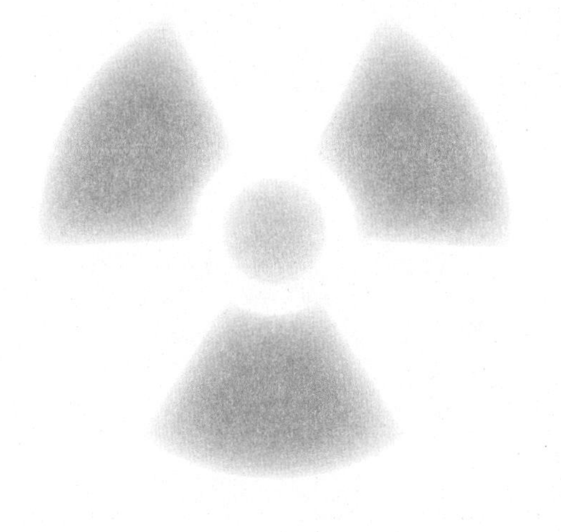

FORTY-FOUR

Adamo Cavano climbed the path to the Acropolis with Dario and two other cousins Gia Cavano had added to their ranks when she heard about the theft at the Greek National Archaeological Museum the night before. Some kind of box. Adamo didn't care. All he knew was that he'd get another shot at that black bastard who had decked him and Dario outside the British Museum.

After arriving in Athens at six in the morning, the first thing they did was buy four pistols and ammo from a local supplier the family knew. Now it was eight, and they could get up to the Acropolis. They bought four tickets and began the long walk up to the summit of the famous hill.

Many who had never been to Athens thought that the Acropolis and the Parthenon were one and the same. In reality, the Acropolis referred to the entire massive rock plateau, while the Parthenon, a temple dedicated to the goddess Athena, was one of several ancient buildings atop the Acropolis. Adamo knew that the buildings were even older than those in his hometown of Naples, but the stone walls and ruins didn't impress him. It looked like a mess. From this vantage point, the Parthenon was literally a shell of its former glory. The entire thing looked as if it would collapse at any moment.

The sun was already beating down hard, and there was little shade to be found. None of them had really thought about what to wear. Adamo had on his slacks, Ferragamos, and a loose silk dress shirt to hide the gun tucked into his belt. Every tourist they passed was in shorts, a T-shirt, and sandals or sneakers. Adamo and his crew stuck out like flies on a ball of mozzarella.

Nothing they could do about that now. Two of them would take up post at the entrance, while the other two stayed at the ready, nearby. With only one entrance to the Acropolis, Locke and his friend Westfield would have to pass them.

Adamo kept an eye out as they approached the Propylaea, the narrow staircase that led through the portico and onto the main expanse of the Acropolis.

The stairs were already crowded with a group of tourists. *How could that be?* Adamo and his group had been the first ones through the gate. Then he saw more visitors approaching from his left, and he realized that the path they'd taken wasn't the only way up to the entrance.

They had each memorized what Locke, Westfield, and Benedict looked like. The three of them were distinctive and wouldn't be hard to spot. Adamo checked out the tourist group. None of them matched the photos.

He looked around for a good place to sit down. It was going to be a long day, and he didn't want to be on his feet the whole time. But first he supposed that for the sake of thoroughness he should check the Acropolis to make sure Locke hadn't arrived first.

He pulled Dario and the other two aside.

"We don't want any trouble up here," he said in Italian. "If we spot Locke, take him as quietly as you can. The other two we take for a ride and cap them in the garbage dump. And remember, Westfield is for me and Dario."

"What if they don't come so quietly?" Dario said.

"Then Gia said we leave the Greeks some corpses next to the Parthenon, but make sure you get whatever they're carrying. Dario, you're with me. We're going to get the lay of the land."

Adamo passed the crowd and went up the steps. He squinted at the sun.

If they were going to be up here all day, he would have to get a bottle of water before he settled in.

Because they'd taken the shorter route up, Stacy thought she, Tyler, and Grant would be the first ones on the Acropolis plateau, but that notion was disabused when she saw workmen moving heavy marble blocks with the help of a gantry crane. She was surprised to see them on a Sunday morning, but then she remembered a guide they had passed saying that there was some rush to get part of the restoration completed for an event happening later in June.

She was also surprised to see an elderly man who was pushing his wife in a wheelchair, thinking he must be very spry to get up there so fast.

Stacy had been to the Acropolis a dozen times, but the sight was always breathtaking. Despite the destruction over the millennia, the Parthenon had lost none of its grandeur. Some architects thought it was the most perfectly proportioned building on earth, and she would be hard-pressed to argue with them. The columns were imperceptibly tapered like a cigar to counteract the optical illusion in which parallel straight lines appear to bow toward each other. In addition, to give the Parthenon the appearance of strength the columns leaned inward, but so slightly that they would meet only if they were extended one mile into the sky.

The brilliance of people dead for thousands of years continued to awe her.

As they took a direct route toward the opposite end of the Acropolis, Tyler and Grant couldn't help but gawk at the array of immense marble columns that supported the remnants of the temple's roof. Stacy wished she were seeing it for the first time, as they were.

She yelped as she lost her footing on one of the many slick marble slabs that were exposed in the gravel path. Tyler caught her before she could fall.

"You okay?" he said.

"I always forget about the stupid marble. One time I went down on my butt. It's like standing on inclined ice."

"Thanks for the tip."

He looked at her and smiled before walking one. She had awakened late, so she hadn't had a chance to talk to him about their brief connection last night, but there really wasn't much to say. She supposed the attraction was the result of the stressful situations they'd faced together. Under the circumstances, however, acting on it was not only inappropriate but a serious distraction they didn't need.

As they walked next to the temple, she said, "Isn't it amazing?"

Tyler just nodded.

"How long has it been here?" Grant asked.

"Since 2500 B.C. Back then, all the relief sculptures that ringed the temple would have been painted in bright colors."

"I can't imagine that."

"Most people see the pictures and think it was always white, but spectrography tells us differently now, even though weather has wiped almost all traces of the paint away."

"Where are the sculptures that England didn't get?"

"At the New Acropolis Museum built at the southern base of the Acropolis. The old museum is over there." She pointed at a tired building on the western side of the Parthenon. Wires stretching around it made it clear that the building was closed.

"Looks like it's seen better days."

"It was too small and antiquated to house the treasures properly, so they built the new museum not only as a state-of-the-art showpiece but also to counter the British Museum's insistence that the Elgin Marbles were safer in London."

"And the Greeks don't agree, apparently."

"It's been a sore point for two hundred years, but the Greeks didn't have much of a case until the new museum was built."

They passed the eastern end of the Parthenon. The east pediment was almost completely destroyed, with just the slanted edges of the roof visible on each side. The only statue on the pediment was the reclining Herakles on the left end. With the original still in the British Museum, the Greeks had constructed a reproduction to show what it would have looked like in place. Eight columns supported the roof. Counting from the left, Herakles was between the second and third columns.

Stacy took out a printout of the pediment as it would have appeared in ancient times. Aphrodite's feet would have been just to the left of the seventh column.

Tyler took another few dozen steps and removed the geolabe from his backpack. Stacy had helped him recalibrate it at the hotel using the Stomachion puzzle, so the dials all pointed to the noon position once again. He turned it on its side as Archimedes had instructed and held it up. Stacy could tell they were too close. It blotted out the entire structure, including the pediment. They would have to back up until it barely covered the columns from end to end, with the top of the geolabe lined up along the base of the pediment.

They stepped back until they were near the edge of the Acropolis, behind a small stone wall surrounding a raised circular platform. Now the geolabe lined up perfectly. While Stacy steadied it, Tyler rotated the first knob until the left-hand dial pointed to Herakles's rump. Then he flipped the geolabe over and read off the reading from the notches etched in the dial.

"Thirty-two degrees."

Grant jotted it down. "Got it."

Tyler flipped the geolabe back and repeated the steps by pointing the right-hand dial where Aphrodite's feet would be.

"Seventy-one degrees."

Grant took out a map of Naples and laid it on the stone railing. He traced the lines at those angles from the Castel Dell'Ovo and the Castel Sant'Elmo until they intersected.

"And here we are. The entrance to the tunnels leading to the Midas chamber is going to be somewhere in the vicinity of Piazza San Gaetano."

He pointed to a square in the heart of Naples. There was no Roman fortress in the vicinity, but it could have been razed thousands of years ago. Or the Syracuse spy just got lost in the tunnels.

Stacy looked up, amazed at how quickly they'd completed their task.

"Really?" she said. "Could it be that easy?"

"It's not," Tyler said. His eyes were riveted on something to the right of the Parthenon. "Don't make any sudden movements."

"Why?"

"Grant, does that look like a tourist to you?"

Stacy moved only her eyes and saw a man sauntering toward them dressed in a shiny silk shirt and dark pants. Grant slowly turned his head and got the barest glimpse before turning back.

"Nope," Grant said. "Not a tourist. He's one of the Italian meatballs I punched out at the British Museum."

FORTY-FIVE

It didn't look as if the Italian had seen them yet. Grant was sure it was the same guy. That arrowhead widow's peak was unmistakable even from this distance.

They'd all flattened behind the wall. Cavano's man may not have recognized them, but now he might be curious why they had suddenly disappeared.

"How did they find us?" Stacy said.

"I'm guessing it's my good friend Lumley," Grant said. "Cavano probably heard about the theft at the museum last night and put two and two together."

"There's too much open space to make a run for it," Tyler said. "What's the plan?"

"We need to get this guy isolated. When we capture him, Stacy can act as our interpreter so we can find out who else might be lurking around."

"Should we use the old bait and tackle?"

Tyler nodded. "And since he knows you, it looks like you'll have to be the bait this time."

"He'll have at least one friend with him," Grant said. "Probably a guy with a mustache that looks like it was drawn on with a Sharpie."

"Head around the back of the old museum. When he follows you, I'll come up behind him."

"What about me?" Stacy said.

"Stay here." Tyler handed her the backpack and put his earpiece in. "You'll be our eyes. If you see mustache man coming, let me know."

She dialed his phone, and they were connected. "Got it."

He looked at Grant. "Let's do this."

Grant slithered over the railing and dropped down through some scaffolding that had been set up to rebuild part of the wall. He was now below the eye level of Cavano's man. He scrambled over the rocks until he was next to the rear of the shuttered Old Acropolis Museum.

He looked back and saw that the guy was thirty feet from Tyler's position and getting closer. He purposefully kicked a rock, and the man's head jerked around. Grant took off behind the building. A mountain of garbage bags was piled in the corner of the Acropolis next to an unused crane lying against the citadel's southern wall.

Grant turned the corner. He glanced behind him, but it didn't look as if the man had followed him. That meant he was going to try to cut Grant off.

Grant took off, running along a narrow-gauge railroad track that had originally been built to transfer artifacts from the Parthenon to the crane so that they could be lowered to the new museum for relocation. A railroad handcart was in his path.

Before he could reach the handcart, the man appeared from around the corner and drew a pistol on Grant, who stopped and put up his hands. The Italian slowly moved forward.

"Hey, I know you," Grant said with a smile. He knew the man might not speak much English, but it didn't really matter. "How's your noggin? I bet you've still got a nasty headache."

"Zitto!" He began to creep toward Grant, the gun never wavering.

Grant understood the universal tone for "Shut up!" but he just needed a few more seconds.

"Listen, I'm really sorry about knocking you out in London, but I thought you were a Hare Krishna asking for money."

"Zitto!" the man yelled again.

Tyler, who had sneaked up behind the one-word wonder, pressed the knife of his Leatherman to the man's carotid artery.

"How about you *zitto* instead?" Tyler said.

The man froze. His lips were twisted with contempt. He wasn't happy about getting played. His gun remained aimed at Grant.

"Got him?" Grant said.

"Yeah," Tyler said, "but we've got to do this fast. Company's coming."

Stacy hadn't seen the man with the thin mustache sooner because he had gone around the opposite side of the Parthenon. She had been following Tyler fifty feet behind him, keeping an eye out for his blind side, but the gantry crane shack next to the Parthenon had obstructed her view. The only reason she had spotted him at all was because of the blinding reflection of the sun off his silk shirt. He must have seen Tyler, because he had his pistol out.

By this time, the gantry crane workers, who were almost finished setting a marble block onto a ten-foot-high stack, had stopped what they were doing. They were focused on Tyler with his knife to the gunman's throat, but none of them were making a move to help. Stacy would have to do this on her own. To her right was a four-wheel dolly for moving the marble blocks from the tracks into position for the gantry. It was empty except for two cats lazing in the sun.

In seconds, the second gunman would come around the corner and have a clear shot at Tyler. Although she was unarmed, Stacy had to do something.

She grabbed the dolly's handle and wheeled it around until it faced the corner of the shack. When she swung it around, the cats jumped off. As soon as she saw the man's shiny shirt come into view, she pushed with all her strength, the tires crunching over the gravel.

The mustache man, focused on Tyler until he heard the dolly racing toward him, turned in time to get a shot off, but it went wild. Stacy didn't stop. He was standing on a patch of the slick marble, so he couldn't get traction to jump out of the way. The dolly crashed into his legs, causing him to pitch forward onto it. Despite his obvious pain, he regained his balance, got to his knees, and brought his pistol to bear.

By this time, Stacy was at full speed. The dolly hit the outer wall of the Acropolis with a jarring thud. The man flipped backward, and before he could arrest his momentum, he tumbled over the side.

Stacy was sure she'd never forget the awful scream that ceased abruptly when he thudded into the rocks fifty feet below.

Through the earpiece, Stacy had alerted Tyler about the second gunman, but Tyler hadn't been able to make the first man give him the gun before the shooting started. When the shot went off behind him, the sound was so close that Tyler thought he was dead. No one could have missed from that distance. It was just enough of a distraction that the man in his grip was able to twist away from the knife and elbow Tyler in the stomach, driving him to his knees.

The man squeezed off a shot at Grant, who took cover behind the track cart. Then the man somersaulted to his left and aimed at Tyler, who got to his feet and dove for the cover of the stairs leading down to the Old Acropolis Museum entrance. Bullets pinged off the wall behind him.

The situation had gotten ugly quickly. Instead of getting the drop on the bad guy, Tyler and Grant were now helpless. If there were any more than these two, it would get even worse.

Tyler looked around for a weapon, maybe a missile of some kind, but there was nothing except a few stray stones. He peeked out and saw the first gunman notice Stacy and give chase. The second gunman was nowhere to be seen. With no other choice, Tyler picked up the heaviest stone he could and took off after them.

Stacy ran into the area cordoned off by the workmen, who had fled at the sound of the gunshots, leaving the gantry crane still in motion, the marble block nearing its intended position. She got as far as the crane when the Italian grabbed her by the backpack and hauled her to a stop.

Tyler had made up some ground, but not enough. The man whipped around with the gun pressed against Stacy's head. He shouted something in Italian, and it was clear that he wanted Tyler to give up.

Tyler put up his hands and dropped the rock. Grant skidded to a stop twenty feet to his right.

"What's he saying?" Tyler asked.

"He said he's waiting for his friends," Stacy said. "They'll have heard the shots."

"Think he speaks English?"

"Doubt it."

Tyler saw that they were standing just in front of the tower of blocks. The gunman wasn't paying attention to the sound of the crane, and the slab that was moving into position bumped up against another block that was already in place, straining its supporting nylon straps nearly to the breaking point. The slab had to weigh a thousand pounds. The gantry crane's control panel was in front of him, with each button labeled with one letter, but he didn't know Greek, so he couldn't tell which was up, down, left, right, forward, or backward.

"How do you spell *left* in Greek?" Tyler couldn't read Greek words, but thanks to the formulas he'd used in engineering school he could read Greek letters.

Stacy knotted her brow at the request, then said, "Alpha rho iota—"

There it was. "Got it. Grant, say something to our friend."

"Hey!" Grant shouted. "Point that gun at me!" The gunman's gaze flashed to the side just long enough for Tyler to press the "left" button unnoticed. The crane's chain began to move in that direction, the marble slab twisting around the other block. This was going to be close.

Tyler put up his hands. "When I tell you," he said to Stacy, "step on his foot and push him backward. But first tell him we're surrendering."

She nodded and spoke in Italian. The man smiled a self-satisfied grin. He took the gun away from her head and gestured with it for Tyler to get over by Grant.

The marble slab, pitched at an angle by the taut straps, slowly scraped around the tower. Any second it would be free of the other blocks of marble. Tyler saw it begin to rotate.

"Now!" he yelled.

Stacy stomped on the gunman's toe. He yelped and let go of her, and she shoved him backward as he hopped in pain. He steadied himself against the tower of marble to regain his footing. The moving slab came loose and swung around in an arc, spinning wildly toward the gunman.

Tyler had been hoping the action would simply provide a distraction, but as it spun the straps loosened and let go. The block dropped onto the Italian's head and chest with a sickening smack, crushing him to the ground. His legs twitched for a moment, then went still.

Tyler ran over to Stacy. "Are you all right?"

She was breathing hard but seemed unhurt. "I'm fine. How did you know it would do that?"

"I didn't."

Grant came over and bent down to look under the block.

"Can you reach his gun?" Tyler asked.

Grant stood up with a disgusted expression and shook his head.

"Let's get out of here," Tyler said.

"How?" Stacy said. "This guy said he had friends at the entrance."

"There's another way. Come on."

He took her hand and sprinted toward the north side of the Acropolis, with Grant at his side. He didn't have time to explain that when he'd seen the woman in the wheelchair and wondered how her husband got her up all those steps he realized there must be an elevator. He'd noticed its metal cage opening to let another wheelchair passenger out on the north side of the Acropolis when they'd walked past the Parthenon.

As they approached the opposite side of the Parthenon, Tyler spotted two more men sprinting toward where they'd heard the gunshots, both carrying pistols. He reached into the backpack and took out the unused smoke grenade from the day before, which Grant had rigged for use in case Tyler needed a backup in the museum. Tyler activated the grenade and tossed it into the open courtyard, where it began to spew orange smoke. Screams erupted from the few tourists who hadn't been frightened away by the earlier melee.

When the smoke was thick enough, Tyler nodded to Stacy and Grant, and they ran for the elevator. Shock waves from the bullets pierced the air all around them, but the smoke concealed them enough to prevent the Italians from getting a clear shot.

The next two hundred feet were the longest Tyler had ever run, but the sight of the metal cage off-loading a wheelchair passenger kept his motor going.

They reached the elevator and piled in over the operator's protests.

"Down! Down!" Tyler yelled. Two men emerged from the cloud of smoke behind them, pumping out rounds without much care for accuracy.

The bullets pinging off the metal silenced the lift operator's protests, and she slammed the cage closed. The lift lowered below the wall before the men could reach them. The operator screamed as bullets ricocheted off the roof, but the heavy steel was too thick for the rounds to penetrate.

Tyler heard one of their pursuers yell *"Polizia!"* and the shooting stopped. The police must have arrived on the Acropolis.

When the lift reached the bottom twenty seconds later, Tyler poked his head out, but no one was waiting above to take another shot. They apologized to the terrified lift operator and left her cowering in the elevator as they dodged the wheelchairs of a tour group waiting to get on. In five minutes they were back at their motorcycles. Police cars sped past them up the long drive leading to the closest point they could get to the Acropolis entrance.

As they raced back to the hotel to get the rest of their belongings before heading to the airport, Stacy clung to Tyler's back, shaken by their brush with death. Normally, Tyler would be high-fiving Grant for coming through enemy action like that unscathed, but he couldn't bring himself to celebrate. He knew that the worst was still waiting for them in Naples.

FORTY-SIX

Peter Crenshaw hummed along to Metallica's "Enter Sandman" as he inserted the detonator into the second-to-last container of binary explosive. He always listened to heavy metal while he worked. It kept his mind sharp while he built a bomb powerful enough to turn him into goulash.

Phillips had been Crenshaw's only companion since Orr and Gaul left for Europe, and all the guy wanted to talk about was baseball. Records, statistics, players, teams—it never ended. For Crenshaw, that made keeping his iPod fully charged a high priority.

Even though the warehouse had no air-conditioning, the high ceilings allowed the heat to rise, leaving his work area relatively cool. He wasn't worried about the explosives going off prematurely. They were incredibly stable. Fire, impacts, or electrical charges wouldn't set them off. Crenshaw had been working virtually nonstop except for food and sleep breaks, so stupid mistakes were the biggest threat.

He placed the lid on top of the fifty-gallon container. Phillips brought over the handcart they'd been using to move the full drums.

"Where do you want this one?" he said.

Crenshaw looked around the perimeter of the warehouse. Identical containers had been placed every fifty feet, as he'd instructed. The wiring between them was complete. That left the walls on either side of the concrete peninsula of cells.

"Put that one next to General Locke's room," Crenshaw said. "Against the outer wall."

By now an expert in handling the drums, Phillips slid the cart underneath and tilted it up. He wheeled it around, and Crenshaw got to work on the last container.

It had been Crenshaw's suggestion to rig the warehouse to blow after they'd abandoned it. Getting rid of the evidence was paramount if they were going to get away with the crime they were about to commit. And he was proud of his design. The explosives would reduce the entire building to rubble. Three drums of gasoline would char everything that wasn't blown to smithereens.

Though it was dangerous, working with the powdered explosive was a dream compared with dealing with the radioactive material. That had been more nerve-racking than any other part of the operation, and Crenshaw was glad it was over. He'd worn a heavy lead hazmat suit at all times, but the thought of getting a fatal dose of radiation kept him on his toes. The rewards, however, made the risk worthwhile. Orr thought he didn't know what this was all about, but Crenshaw wasn't as naïve as he let on.

Orr had no idea that Crenshaw had hacked into his computer and copied the translated Archimedes Codex. The treasure discussed in the ancient document was confirmed when he peeked into Orr's pack and saw the golden hand. Orr was after Midas's vast cache of gold, and Crenshaw's two-million-dollar share was starting to seem paltry.

No, Crenshaw thought as he mixed the last of the explosive powder, that figure just wouldn't do. Not for the cleverness of his designs. Not for what his efforts were going to do to make the gold quadruple in value overnight.

He looked over at the truck now labeled WILBIX CONSTRUCTION and smiled. His greatest achievement. That truck would make him go down in history as the person who obliterated America's superpower status once and for all. A pity no one would ever know it was him. But after the truck blew up, the FBI wouldn't bother looking for suspects because they would think the perpetrators were already dead.

Snatching the Muslims had been Orr's idea from the start. He picked two who had questionable ties to radical Islam. Or so it would seem, once they were blamed for carrying out an attack masterminded by Al Qaeda. All signs would point to them. Their sudden disappearance. The trucker who had been allowed to live so that he could report that he was hijacked by two Arabs, played perfectly by Orr and Gaul. The Muslims' identification found seared but recognizable in the warehouse ruins. Their bodies torn to pieces by the truck blast.

No one would suspect that it was anything other than another bold terrorist attack by America's sworn enemy.

And that would let Crenshaw and the others retire to the island country of their choice to enjoy the spoils of the operation, with no fear of retribution from the CIA, the FBI, or any other three-letter agency sifting through the wreckage.

Of course, Sherman Locke and Carol Benedict would have to be dealt with, but that was fairly simple. Once they were done with them, Phillips would put a couple of bullets in their heads and dump the bodies in the Potomac so they wouldn't be linked to the dirty bomb.

Now that Crenshaw thought about it, maybe he *would* let the world know somehow that it was he who had been responsible. Just not until *after* he was dead. He could leave some kind of testament describing exactly how he outwitted the brightest investigative minds the U.S. had to offer. Even though he wouldn't be around to savor the embarrassment and disgust aimed at the people who let him slip through their grasp, he would guarantee that his name would be immortalized in history.

The truck-bomb design was his favorite part, and he would revel in divulging the details. Five hundred pounds of binary explosive packed underneath three hundred gallons of gas, buried in sixty thousand pounds of highly flammable sawdust. The strontium shielded in a special lead case of his design that would blow up and aerosolize the nuclear material just before the larger bomb detonated. The explosion would transform the sawdust into highly radioactive ash, which would coat everything downwind for miles.

Air-handling systems would exacerbate the effect, sucking in the microscopic particles and making them an integral part of every building in the vicinity. The buildings would never be cleaned of the radiation. They would all have to be destroyed to make sure the radioactivity was gone. Even if the authorities claimed that a building was below the level of harmful radiation, who in their right mind would ever want to occupy it again?

After the warehouse was nothing but wreckage, the plan was for Crenshaw and Phillips to drive the truck and the van to their destination, and when Orr wired the payments to their accounts, they would park the semi in the pre-designated location, drive away in the van, and detonate the bomb.

By Monday evening the United States would be changed forever. The stock market would be in ruins, the economy would take a nosedive when the world's financial hub was no longer inhabitable, and trillions of dollars would vanish overnight.

Amid a crisis the likes of which the world had never before seen, only one certainty among the chaos would remain: tangible goods. Commodities. And the most important commodity in the world was gold.

When the stock and bond markets crashed, investors would flee to gold, causing its value to skyrocket. James Bond's nemesis Goldfinger had the right plan—nuke the gold reserve to make his own gold more valuable—but by targeting Fort Knox he'd chosen the wrong location.

Yes, the U.S. had a huge stockpile of gold at its disposal at Fort Knox in Kentucky, but it wasn't the largest depository of gold in the country. That claim to fame belonged to the Federal Reserve Bank, which held more than ten percent of the world's gold reserves. Depending on the daily close, its value was around $300 billion.

After tomorrow, those reserves would be worthless.

Although the bank's vault was eighty feet below street level, the building's air-handling system wouldn't be able to scrub the radiation from the dust motes circulating through the structure. Five thousand tons of gold would become radioactive.

And what amplified the impact was the fact that the Federal Reserve Bank was located in the same square mile as the New York Stock Exchange, along with all the other investment firms and brokerages that made downtown New York the single greatest concentration of wealth on earth.

At least, it would be for one more day. Then everything would change. And, merely by blowing up a single semi trailer full of sawdust, Crenshaw would eventually be remembered as the man who transformed lower Manhattan from a shining beacon of unholy greed into a desolate wasteland.

FORTY-SEVEN

Thirty thousand feet above the Mediterranean, Tyler, Grant, and Stacy were huddled around the laptop so they could see Miles Benson and Aiden MacKenna on the video chat via satellite. Their Gulfstream jet would arrive in Rome in an hour. Miles and Aiden were on their own plane, heading to Washington to confirm Sherman's and Carol's release.

Tyler had expected to have a hard time persuading his boss to go this alone without intervention by the authorities, and he was right.

"I don't like this plan," Miles said. "We should have the Feds ready to nab whoever drops off your father."

"If we do that," Tyler said, "we'll have to tip them off to everything, and I'm not ready to take that chance. If I thought there was any danger for you, I wouldn't go this route."

"That's not what I'm worried about. I want to keep you three safe. What about the Italian national police?"

"We can't call in the Carabinieri. As far as they know, Orr hasn't done anything wrong in Italy."

"Yet."

"Four specialists from Neutralizer Security should be able to handle taking down Orr on our end," Grant said, referring to the private security contractor Tyler had hired for the job. "I've worked with them before. They're pros."

"Then why didn't you hire them in Greece?" Miles said.

"My fault," Tyler said. "I didn't expect Cavano's men to show up at the Parthenon."

"None of us did," Stacy said.

"Cavano's persistent, I'll give her that," Grant said.

Aiden pushed his way in for a closer look. "For four billion dollars' worth of gold, she'd probably take on the entire Carabinieri herself." Aiden was talking about the cube of gold that supposedly sat in the middle of the chamber.

Miles shook his head. "You see what you're up against, Tyler? They'll kill all of you without hesitation to get that money."

"The strontium adds a new variable to all this," Tyler said. "If Orr really has a dirty bomb, he's going to use it. We have to stop him."

"Are you sure he has it?"

"No, which is another reason we're not going to the authorities just yet. Once we have Orr, we'll make him tell us everything."

"How?"

"We'll have plenty of bargaining chips, but they'll be useless until he's in our hands."

"So what's the plan?"

"We're going to follow his directions to meet him at the outdoor concert. Piazza del Plebiscito is a huge plaza near the Naples waterfront. It'll be packed with partyers. Orr told us to be there at nine and wait for his call. I'm sure he's chosen that location because it'll provide cover for him."

"Once we get to Rome," Grant said, "I'll meet with the Neutralizer team. We'll drive down to Naples together and set up a lookout near the plaza. We'll stay out of sight, but we'll be in constant contact with Tyler. When he gives us the signal, we'll move in and take Orr."

"What if he's got help?"

"That's where the tracker comes in," Tyler said. "I removed it from the geolabe. Grant's going to have it with him. If Orr's men try to make an early move, Grant will be ready for them."

"And if he doesn't deliver your father and Carol?"

Tyler's muscles knotted at the thought. Her threw a glance at Stacy, who looked just as upset as he was about that prospect.

"This is the only option," he said. "Once we have Orr, he'll have to bargain with us."

He didn't say any more, because he didn't know how far he'd go. But, looking at Stacy and knowing how much they both wanted Sherman and Carol safely returned, he realized that he might have to go to some dark places in order to get them back in one piece.

Miles sighed. "All right. It's your call."

"Thanks, Miles. You be safe."

"You don't think I'm showing up without my own security team, do you?"

Tyler smiled. "No, I don't suppose you would. I'll call you when we have Orr."

"Good luck."

"You, too."

The screen went blank.

"I'll call Neutralizer and coordinate with them," Grant said, and went to the back of the plane.

"So do you think it'll be that easy?" Stacy said. "Don't you think Orr has something else planned?"

"Yes, but unless we follow his rules, he'll never show up. He's got the leverage for now."

"But you've got the geolabe. We could find the gold ourselves and then meet up with Orr. Then *we'd* have the leverage."

"There's not enough time. If we don't meet his deadline, I don't want to think what would happen. Orr doesn't seem like the type to bluff."

"No, he doesn't," Stacy said.

Tyler paused. "You don't have to go through with this. I can make the exchange myself."

"The hell you will. You just said we can't change the plan. He wants me there, I'm there. I'll do worse than chop off his ear if he doesn't tell me where Carol is."

Tyler couldn't tell if she was exaggerating or being literal. Maybe she didn't even know herself how far she'd go to get Carol to safety.

"All right," he said. "Grant will have us in view the whole time. We'll be fine. It ends tonight."

"One way or the other." Stacy took a deep breath and closed her eyes. "Orr's not going to let them go, is he?"

"Not unless we make him. But we're not meeting with Orr until he shows us in the next video that they're still okay."

Tyler checked his watch. It was noon. They'd arrive in Rome and drive down to Naples in three cars, one for him and Stacy and two for Grant and the Neutralizer team, who would keep an eye out for Orr as they drove in case he planned to ambush them early. Once they were convinced that they weren't being observed, Grant would separate from Tyler and Stacy, taking the tracker and the Neutralizer team with him to a location where they could watch the piazza. At the same time, Tyler and Stacy would head to the concert with the geolabe.

It wasn't a foolproof plan, but Tyler was convinced that it was the only way to prevent a major catastrophe and save Carol and his father.

FORTY-EIGHT

Metal handcuffs rattled against Sherman's cell door.

"All right, General," Phillips said. "Time for your daily video."

The cuffs dangled through the door's portal. Sherman slowly pulled himself off the bed, ready to put his plan into motion. They'd fed him only two meals in the past two days, so he'd laid off the calisthenics and conserved his strength for this moment.

He ran a hand over his fivc days of stubble and grunted as if standing was an incredible effort. He hadn't seen a mirror in days, but he figured that he looked even worse than he felt. Good. Better that Phillips think he was completely worn down.

Sherman dragged himself over to the portal and grabbed the cuffs with a sigh. The routine he was supposed to go through was familiar by now. Ankle cuffs first, then wrists. Stand back from the door until it was opened, Phillips training the Taser on him while he turned to show that the cuffs were on and secure.

But this time he was going to shake up the routine.

The pat-down had been thorough when they brought him in, but they'd let him keep his clothes, and his dress shirt gave him something that would make his escape possible. In his palm was a thin plastic stay from his collar. He had quietly bent it at night until he could break it into a piece small and stiff enough to insert into the cuffs.

The handcuffs were the type used by most law-enforcement agencies in the U.S. When the cuffs were closed, the audible click was the pawl engaging the gear in the ratchet, which prevented the gear from opening, locking the cuffs. But if a shim were inserted between the pawl and the gear, the ratchet wouldn't engage, leaving the cuff free to open.

The stays in his collar were thin enough for the job. He just had to make sure Phillips didn't realize the cuffs weren't locked.

Sherman knelt, placed the cuffs on his ankles, and locked them. He couldn't prop them open with a stay because they'd come undone as soon as he began to walk, exposing his plan even before it got under way.

He stood and put the cuffs on his wrists as Phillips watched. He made sure to keep the stay hidden as he put the cuff on his left hand. As he closed the cuff, he jabbed the stay into the narrow opening. After a few clicks, he felt the shim slip under the pawl. Now it would slide freely if he tried to open it.

The stay was in place, but Sherman was afraid the cuffs would fall open if he raised them. He held them against his body, backed up, and rotated to show that the ankle cuffs were in place.

Phillips unlocked the door and threw it open. He had the Taser at the ready if Sherman didn't comply. It wasn't armed with the cartridge that shot the leads out to twenty feet, so the shock could be applied only at close quarters.

"Let's go," Phillips said, bored by the tedium of this daily show.

Sherman shuffled out. The chair was in the same place. Crenshaw held the camera. No one else was there.

Phillips put the balaclava on. Sherman sat and was blindfolded as usual. The rustle of the newspaper told him when they were filming. He recited his name. Nothing new.

After a few seconds, Phillips said, "All right. That's good enough."

The blindfold came off.

"Get up," Phillips said as he pulled the mask off and faced Sherman. Crenshaw was already heading back to his workbench, his iPod earbuds blasting away.

Sherman didn't move.

Phillips sneered. "Didn't you hear me?"

"I heard you," Sherman said.

"Then get your ass out of the chair and back into your cell."

"Make me."

"Oh, so you want to ride the lightning again. Doesn't bother me."

Crenshaw had his back turned to them. With a wicked smile, Phillips pulled the Taser from his belt.

"At least I get to enjoy part of my day," he said.

He walked up to Sherman and reached out to Tase him in the neck. He came at Sherman slowly, his eyes glinting in anticipation of the paralyzing reaction to the shock.

Sherman quickly worked the left cuff open. When the Taser was within a foot of him, his hand shot out, grabbing Phillips's wrist. The surprise on Phillips's face was total, giving Sherman the moment of hesitation he needed. He twisted the Taser down, forced it against Phillips's leg, and pressed the trigger.

Phillips's body seized in agony, and he collapsed. Sherman leaped on top of him, sending another jolt into Phillips's chest.

Sherman stole a look at Crenshaw, who was just turning to see what the commotion was. His opportunity to disable Crenshaw wouldn't last long, and there were guns on the table.

Phillips's pistol was in his waist holster. Sherman drew it, dropped the Taser, and rolled off Phillips's torso. As he raised the gun, Crenshaw spotted him, threw the metal table over, and dove behind it. Sherman's shots pinged off the underside.

Phillips shook off his daze faster than Sherman had expected and grabbed the Taser. He lunged toward Sherman with it, the high-voltage prongs chittering with sparks, but Sherman snapped off a shot before Phillips could reach him, and the man dropped in his tracks as the bullet blew off the back of his skull.

Sherman had to get the key. As he rifled frantically through

Phillips's pocket, he fired three more shots at the table to keep Crenshaw down. He found the key chain in Phillips's front pocket, along with a cell phone, and unlocked one of the ankle cuffs so that he'd be mobile.

As Sherman got up to find cover, a bullet slammed into his thigh. He cried out but didn't go down, knowing that he would be a sitting duck for Crenshaw. As rounds pinged off the concrete walls, he hobbled over to his cell door, leaving a thick trail of blood behind him.

The heavy steel door provided plenty of protection. He winced as he collapsed to the floor behind it. He was only now aware of the frenzied shouts coming from the other cells.

Sherman undid the remaining locks on the cuffs and threw them aside. Then he dialed 911.

After two rings, he heard, "911 emergency. How can I assist you?"

"My name is General Sherman Locke. I'm being held hostage by terrorists. I've killed one, but I'm pinned down by another."

"Can you tell me your location?"

"No. I don't know where I am. Zero in on the cell signal."

"All right, sir. I'll have the police there as soon as I can. How many assailants are there?"

"Just one more, I think."

Sherman didn't like being cornered like this, but he didn't have a fallback position. He discouraged Crenshaw from circling around by firing two more shots. He was running out of ammo.

"Are those gunshots?" the operator said.

Good God. "Yes! He's shooting at me. That's why I need the police. Now!"

"Are you hurt?"

"Yes. I've been shot in the leg. Have you got my signal?"

"We're working on it."

"Well, hurry up, dammit!"

After a pause, the operator said, "I've got you. Five two nine Business Parkway in Hagerstown."

"What state?"

The operator didn't skip a beat at the odd question. "Maryland. Near the intersection of I-70 and I-81. State and local police are on their way. They should be there in minutes."

That would put him right between Pennsylvania and Virginia. I-70 was a straight shot to D.C., and I-81 led to Philadelphia and the Northeast Corridor. Crenshaw could be in one of a half-dozen major cities within hours with his radiological bomb.

But that wasn't Sherman's biggest problem right now. He had seen the barrel next to his cell. He couldn't tell what was inside, but wires from it led to another barrel, and then another. He could see at least four of them.

Obviously the warehouse was rigged to explode, which would destroy all evidence of Crenshaw and Orr's operation.

And if Crenshaw escaped, he'd set them off before the police arrived.

Sherman pocketed the phone without turning it off. He had to see what Crenshaw was doing. He gritted his teeth and hopped up onto his one good leg.

He slid the door's portal aside, but he couldn't see Crenshaw. *Where did he go?*

At that moment, the semi's engine cranked up.

Crenshaw was making a break for it.

The external door of the warehouse was opening too slowly. Crenshaw had the truck in gear ready to go, but the door rose at a maddening rate.

He glanced out the window and saw General Locke staggering toward him, his gun pointed at the cab. Two bullets pierced the door just above his lap, smashing into the dashboard. Crenshaw returned fire.

His first two shots missed, but the third hit the general in the chest. He couldn't tell how crippling a shot it was, but the general went down in a heap, the gun flying to the side.

The garage door was almost fully open, and Crenshaw could hear the distant wail of sirens. The general must have called the police with Phillips's phone. No way Crenshaw was going to stick around with this mess.

The original plan, now literally shot to hell, had been to leave one of the Muslims they'd kidnapped in the wreckage of the burned-down warehouse and bring the other with them to leave at the scene of the explosion.

But Crenshaw couldn't corral one of the Muslims and drive the truck, not without Phillips. So instead the Feds would have to think that a third bomber had gotten away in Manhattan. Same difference. They'd still pin the attack on Al Qaeda.

Crenshaw took one last look at the general, who was still motionless on the concrete floor. He put the truck into gear and roared out of the warehouse.

No cars were around to see him exit. He turned onto Business Parkway and built up speed, keeping an eye on the rearview mirror to make sure the general didn't make a last-second escape through the open garage door, which was now closing behind him.

The aptly named road was lined with other small warehouses and industrial workshops. None of their residents had any clue that amid the distribution centers and manufacturing buildings was an operation that would change history.

Crenshaw could see two police cars approaching. As long as they didn't notice the bullet holes in the side of the door, they'd never suspect that he was coming from their destination.

They raced by him. Crenshaw was now a half mile away, with plenty of space between him and the warehouse. He flipped open the safety on the detonator and pushed the button.

A huge orange fireball erupted behind him, followed almost immediately by the noise of a tremendous blast ripping the air. Even though he was ready for it, the size of the explosion startled him. He grinned as he realized that he'd used far more of the explosive than he needed.

The police cars skidded to a stop behind him. One of the officers got out to look at the shattered building, but they never glanced back at him.

Crenshaw turned onto Greencastle Pike, which was only a block from the interstate. Ninety seconds later, he was on I-81 heading to New York. He breathed easier when he'd gone another two miles and the only emergency vehicles he saw were three fire engines speeding in the other direction.

FORTY-NINE

At an outdoor café along Via Chiaia in Naples, Orr checked the tracker signal while Gaul ate a slice of pizza. When he saw where the tracker was, he nodded with satisfaction. His plan was working out perfectly.

It was now eight o'clock, but Locke and Benedict had been in the city since 3 P.M. Orr tossed back an espresso and smiled at the thought of having the Midas Touch in his possession by the end of the night after all these years of searching.

His phone rang. It was Crenshaw.

"Where's the video?" Orr said. He was supposed to have received the last proof-of-life recording thirty minutes ago.

"The video?" Crenshaw said, his voice cracking. "Jesus, that's the last thing on my mind!" Orr heard an engine downshift in the background. Something was wrong.

"Where are you?"

"I'm in the truck heading up to New Jersey. The warehouse is toast. Had to blow it early. Phillips is dead."

Dead? That idiot Crenshaw. "What the hell happened?"

Gaul stopped chewing and looked at the phone.

"General Locke got loose somehow. He killed Phillips, but I was able to shoot the general twice. I would have stayed, but the police were on their way. Locke must have called them."

"Where is he now?"

"He's in pieces, along with the girl and those two Muslim guys."

Orr stopped himself from screaming in frustration. *This* was why he kept his team small. He had to do everything himself if he wanted it done right. Still, if Crenshaw completed his part of the mission, the situation could be salvaged.

"What about the truck?" Orr said. "Is it ready to go?"

"I've got the bomb rigged. It's buried in the trailer under the sawdust."

"Good. You know where to park it, right?"

"You think I'm doing this on my own?"

"Crenshaw, we are a couple of hours away from finishing the mission. As soon as I call you, I want the timer on that bomb set."

"No way. You think I'm dumb? I know that you're after the treasure of Midas. And I want my share."

Orr's lip curled in anger. That was not the plan, and no one changed his plan but him.

"What do you want?" Orr said.

"I know that what I'm doing is worth a lot more to you than two million dollars. I want twenty million."

Orr heard the plastic seams on the phone crack as his grip tightened. "Fine. But you'd better do your part."

Orr planned to sell off the Midas Touch in a private auction. When the price of gold shot through the roof after lower Manhattan was rendered uninhabitable, he would start the bidding at a billion dollars. Crenshaw was jeopardizing everything.

"I'm not setting off the bomb by myself," Crenshaw said. "I want you here."

"What?" Orr yelled, drawing the stares of the other patrons. "Why?"

"Because I want to see the Midas Touch in person. I want to know that it really works."

Orr snorted in disgust. Asking for more money was one thing. But this weasel was going too far by blackmailing him. He vowed silently that Crenshaw would never get to spend the twenty million.

"Okay," Orr said, "we'll be there tomorrow."

"Oh, and when we see each other, don't try to kill me. I've designed the detonator with a code. You'll never be able to set it off without me."

That little pig. Orr couldn't believe it, but he had no choice but to agree.

"All right. We'll do it your way. I'll call you when we have it."

Orr hung up. He wanted to indulge his rage somehow, upend the table or throw the phone through a plate-glass window, but he had to control himself. The Midas Touch was all that mattered right now.

"What's the problem?" Gaul asked.

"Sherman Locke and Carol Benedict are dead. Some shootout at the warehouse."

"Phillips?"

"The general killed him."

Gaul nodded slowly as he mulled over the news, his face revealing nothing more than his concentration on how it affected their scheme. "What now? Locke won't show himself without the proof-of-life video."

Orr checked the tracker again. It was headed straight down Via Don Bosco. If it kept going, as he thought it would, it would be near Piazza del Plebiscito in ten minutes.

Instead of Locke's number, he dialed Stacy Benedict's.

"Yes?" she said.

"You have the geolabe?" Orr said.

"Yes."

"Good. Let me speak to Locke."

Locke answered. "What?"

"I just wanted to hear your voice. I've missed you terribly."

"Screw you. What about the proof-of-life?"

"I'll send you the video before we meet. But I need assurance that you have the geolabe with you. Have Benedict take a picture of it right now using your phone. Put her phone next to it so I can see my number and text the photo to me."

He heard a muffled voice. Locke was covering the mic on his phone.

"It's on the way."

Orr's phone buzzed. He opened the text. There was the gleaming geolabe. His number was easily visible on the phone beside it, meaning the photo had to have been taken in real time.

"Happy?" Locke said.

"Very. I'll call you in an hour with our meeting location. You'll get the video then."

"If we don't get the video, we don't show."

"Oh, you'll get it. Ciao." Orr hung up and tapped the table absently.

"We have to accelerate our schedule," he said finally.

"You sure?" Gaul said.

"Crenshaw's stupidity crapped all over the original plan. Make the call."

Gaul nodded and pulled out his phone, dialing the number Orr had obtained through some of his local contacts.

"I need to speak to Gia Cavano," Gaul said. "A message? Okay, tell her I know how she can find Jordan Orr."

Gaul grinned. That got their attention. Orr leaned close to the phone so that he could hear Cavano.

"Who is this?" she said.

"I hear you've got eyes all over Naples looking for Orr," Gaul said.

"So? You have information?"

"Better. I can give you a man named Grant Westfield. He'll tell you where Orr is."

A pause. "Why should I believe you?"

"Then don't."

Another pause. "All right. Where is he?"

"He's heading down to Piazza del Plebiscito."

"Alone?" Cavano asked.

"No," said Gaul, who had seen Westfield and his men less than an hour ago when he intercepted the tracker signal on a city street. "He has company."

"That's a big area. How will we find him?"

Gaul gave her the Web address with the tracker location.

"How do I know this isn't some sort of trap?" Cavano said.

"You don't. Be careful." Gaul clicked END.

"Think she'll do it?" he said.

"She won't be able to resist. Once her men confirm that it really is Westfield, they'll take him."

"What if he's killed?"

"Then he's out of our hair. If not, we have provided potent bait for Gia."

Orr slapped a twenty-euro note down on the table and stood.

"Let's go. They'll be here soon."

He and Gaul gathered up their gear and headed to the car.

Orr felt the adrenaline begin to kick in. He was getting pumped for the operation, as he did before any big heist he pulled. It wasn't nervous energy. It was excitement at finally putting the plan in motion, because he had confidence that it would succeed. And it wasn't misplaced optimism at all. He had every piece of information he could possibly need, all thanks to his priceless accomplice, Stacy Benedict.

FIFTY

After dropping off their vehicles, Grant and the four men from Neutralizer made their way toward the Palazzo Reale, the royal palace of Naples built by the Bourbons in the seventeenth century. Grant wished *he* had a shot of bourbon. He didn't like the idea of holding back while Tyler went into harm's way without him.

The palazzo would be the perfect observation post for Piazza del Plebiscito. They would wait in the publicly accessible palace until Grant got the signal from Tyler that Orr had appeared. Then Grant would take two men into the crowd while another two watched them from a discreet distance, ready to wade in if trouble arose.

Grant took the team on a shortcut through the Galleria Umberto. The cavernous indoor shopping plaza was built in the shape of a cross, and the last of the afternoon sun streamed through a 184-foot-high ceiling made of glass and iron latticework with an enormous dome in the center.

Although the streets were packed, the space held few shoppers. The stores were closed for the evening, and the focus was on the concert in the square outside. Everyone on Grant's team was wearing rubber-soled shoes, so they made no sound on the marble floor.

At the far portico they got three steps outside when two light blue Alfa Romeo sedans marked POLIZIA screeched to a stop in front of them. Four cops jumped out and drew their pistols.

One of the Neutralizer men reached for his weapon, but Grant stopped him. Getting into a gun battle with the Naples police was not on the agenda. They raised their hands. A group of bystanders was already forming to watch, snapping photos of the hubbub.

"What seems to be the problem, Officers?" Grant said. One of the Neutralizer men was fluent in Italian and translated.

"Drop your weapons," came the reply.

They all looked to Grant, and he nodded. Guns clattered to the sidewalk.

Someone had set them up. Grant had picked this team specifically because they were not from the Naples area, so the chances of them being corrupted by the Camorra were nonexistent. How had the police found out exactly where they would be?

"Tell him we have permits for these weapons," Grant said. When the policeman who looked as if he was in charge heard the translation, he shook his head. He made them all put their hands on the cars, where they were frisked. Everything in Grant's pockets, including his phone and the tracker, were confiscated, along with the guns. Then they were all cuffed.

All except Grant.

The four security contractors were shoved into the backseats of the police cars. The lead cop pointed back the way Grant had come and said "Go" in English. He waited until Grant started moving, then the police cars peeled away with their sirens blasting.

Grant didn't know what was going on, but this couldn't be good. He had to find a phone and warn Tyler that their plan had already gone to hell. He trotted back through the galleria. When he got to the center, a mountainous figure emerged from an alcove to his right. It was his old friend Sal from the British Museum.

Somehow Cavano had found him. She must have pulled strings with her police contacts to have Grant's team apprehended.

Another man came in from the left. Two more from in front. Grant turned and saw another pair behind him. He was surrounded. Normally, this would be a good time to shout for the police, but Grant was pretty sure that wouldn't help.

"I see you took my advice and brought more men this time," he said.

Sal held up one meaty hand and grinned. "You come quiet, eh? We no hurt you."

"I know you won't. I can't promise the same for you, though."

That wiped the smug grin off his face.

They hadn't drawn guns yet, so maybe that meant they weren't supposed to kill him. At least it was something.

"So you want trouble, eh?" Sal said. "We can make trouble."

The most effective tactic for taking down a single man when you have overwhelming numbers is simply to rush him and get him down on the ground as quickly as possible. Once he was on his back, it was almost impossible for even the best fighter to fend off attacks from a group that had him pinned.

Instead of taking that approach, only two men approached Grant warily, the others hanging back as, what, reinforcements? Well, if they wanted to be dumb, Grant wasn't going to stop them.

As soon as they were within reach, Grant swept his leg out, sending the guy on his left to the floor, his head cracking on the marble. The one on his right swung his fist around, but only connected with air as Grant ducked under it. Using all his considerable strength, Grant hammered his fist into his assailant's solar plexus. With a grunt, the man doubled over and collapsed, gasping for breath.

Grant stood up and smiled at the ringleader. "Pretty sweet, huh?"

Sal glanced at the other three, who rushed Grant. The degree of difficulty was harder this time, but nothing he hadn't seen in the wrestling ring years before. Of course, those fights were scripted, but thanks to his Ranger training, Grant had learned a few more tricks.

He whipped around and threw an elbow into the chest of the man behind him, then kicked upward, connecting just under the chin of another guy, sending him flying backward. The third man was able to get a knee into Grant's side, but Grant slapped the man on both ears simultaneously, likely shattering both eardrums.

Grant was feeling good about his progress in beating the crap out of six men when he heard the unmistakable snap of a police baton expanding. Too late, he turned to see Sal swing the baton around, catching him in the back. His kidneys exploded in pain from the impact of the baton's steel tip, and he dropped to his knees.

Sal reared back for another blow. Grant swiped at his leg with one arm, knocking him over, but the distraction was enough to keep Grant from seeing a second baton sweep down.

A starburst blasted across his vision, and he had the vague sense to turn his head so that his teeth didn't smash into the stone as he pitched forward.

He battled to remain conscious, if not for his own sake then for Tyler's and Stacy's, but the struggle lasted only another three seconds before a feeling of nausea overcame him and his world went black.

FIFTY-ONE

For the third time, Tyler called Grant and couldn't reach him. Having separated from Grant and the security team earlier in the day, he'd agreed to stay in regular contact. The last time they'd spoken was fifteen minutes ago.

Tyler and Stacy were standing in the nave of San Francesco di Paola, the church that formed the western edge of Piazza del Plebiscito. The church was behind the music stage, and the square was already filling with concertgoers ready for a night of songs and fireworks. Tyler thought the church would be a safe haven until they needed to venture out into the square to meet Orr. Their location would keep him in close proximity to Grant's team in case Orr made a move early.

They had separated in the afternoon so that Tyler and Stacy could explore Naples, looking for the well Archimedes had identified. With Aiden's help researching Italian databases and contacting different cultural organizations in the city, they had found four possible wells that might be the one Archimedes was leading them to. They could only hope the well they needed hadn't been filled in during the intervening years since Orr and Cavano had seen it.

Tyler and Stacy had stopped to look for the sign of Scorpio in each well and found a cluster of dots on the inside of the third one that precisely matched the configuration of the Scorpio constellation. He had called Grant to tell him the location, and that was the last time they had spoken.

"What's the matter?" Stacy said as Tyler eyed his phone with concern.

"Grant's not answering."

"Do you think he can't get a signal?"

"Unlikely. And if he wasn't getting one, he'd move somewhere else."

"Then what happened?"

"I don't know, but it can't be good."

Tyler tried the Neutralizer team members and couldn't reach them, either. He didn't like using Grant as bait, but he couldn't imagine that Orr had been able to get the drop on him and the entire security team.

He put the backpack with the geolabe on the floor and checked the signal for the tracker they'd removed from the geolabe and given to Grant. Instead of broadcasting from the Palazzo Reale, it was en route away from the palace.

"The tracker's on the move," he said.

"What?"

"If it's still with Grant, he's heading north at a fast clip."

"What do we do?" Stacy said.

"We abort until we know what happened to Grant."

"But Carol—"

"Orr won't kill her yet. Not when he's this close. We'll just postpone the meet."

"Then we need to find Grant."

"I'm going on my own."

"But—"

"No buts. I can move faster by myself. I'll find the tracker and assess the situation. If I can get him myself, I'll do it. You need to hide someplace safe until I come back."

"I hate doing that."

"It's for my safety, too. As long as you have the geolabe, we still have bargaining power. I'll drop you off at an out-of-the-way pensione. Give me two hours. If I'm not back in that time, call Miles Benson and he'll help you. Do not meet with Orr on your own, no matter what he tells you."

Stacy sighed. "Fine. But I don't like this."

"Your objection is noted," Tyler said, putting the backpack on his shoulder. "Now let's go get the car."

He opened the front door to the breezeway outside. The semi-circular colonnade embraced the piazza. Their car was in a lot to the north. He looked in both directions, but no one in the crowd paid any attention. With tens of thousands of people attending the concert and dozens of ways into the square, the chance that Orr would spot them was small, but with Grant no longer backing him up Tyler had to be prepared for anything.

He waved for Stacy to come out, and they weaved through the strolling crowd.

They had reached the end of the breezeway when a man in cargo pants and a U2 T-shirt stepped out from behind the last pillar and faced them. He had a jacket draped over his folded arms so that his hands weren't visible.

He stared at Tyler. He had to be one of Orr's men.

Tyler grabbed Stacy's arm to run for it but froze when he felt the barrel of a pistol in his back.

"You're early, Tyler," Orr said behind him.

"So are you," Tyler said.

"I had to change my plans. By the way, Gaul has a gun aimed at you."

"I figured that out."

With his free hand, Orr removed Tyler's Leatherman from his pocket, tossed it to Gaul, and pocketed the Glock pistol he took from Tyler's waistband. He didn't bother to search Stacy. Her shorts and tank top couldn't have hidden anything dangerous.

"I'll take your phones," Orr said.

Stacy whirled around with her fists clenched, ready to take on

Orr, but Tyler grabbed her shoulders to stop her. Orr backed off but kept the gun trained on them from under his folded coat.

"What are you doing?" Stacy said. "They're going to kill us!"

"If they wanted to kill us, they would have done it already."

"Listen to Tyler, honey," Orr said. "Now toss your phones to me."

"Only if you never call me honey again."

"Fair enough, sweetie."

Stacy tensed again, before giving in. Tyler let her go. He took her phone and threw it to Orr along with his.

Orr dropped them both to the ground and stomped on them.

"Now we're on our own. And finally the backpack. Slowly."

Tyler didn't move. "It won't do you any good."

"I'd just feel better holding it. I can shoot you in the leg and I'd get it anyway. Your choice."

Tyler grudgingly held the backpack out for Orr, who took it and rested it on his shoulder.

"Good. Let's go." Orr motioned them forward, and he and Gaul fell into step behind them.

"Where are we going?" Tyler said.

"Where do you think?" Orr said.

"I don't know. And you're dreaming if you think we're going to tell you where the well of Archimedes is. This is an exchange, and you haven't offered us anything yet."

"I do know where we're going, thanks to Stacy. The church of San Lorenzo Maggiore near Piazza San Gaetano. You found it there."

And it suddenly made sense to Tyler. Orr didn't find them by luck. He had been waiting for them to come out of the church. He would have known where Grant was because of the tracker, but there was only one way he could have known where Tyler was. He and Grant had had a mole in their midst from the very beginning.

Tyler stopped and looked at Stacy, shocked at her betrayal.

"I trusted you," he said. "You've been telling Orr our every move."

"What?" Stacy said with a puzzled look. "No, I don't . . . You can't think I've been helping him?"

Tyler shook his head grimly. "How else could Orr have found us?"

"I don't know! I'm his hostage just like you are. So is my sister."

Which Tyler now realized could have been a setup from the very beginning. For all he knew, Carol Benedict was in on it as well.

"Oh, Stacy's been a good informant," Orr said, "giving me updates along the way, but she got greedy and demanded more than her fair share. I'd kill her right now, but I still need her."

"He's lying!" she shouted at Tyler before turning on Orr. "You bastard!"

"Am I? Then how would I know that you went to Gia's home outside London? That you rendezvoused with her in Munich? That you went to the Athens museum yesterday and the Parthenon this morning?"

Stacy sputtered, "This is crazy!"

"No, it's not," Tyler growled. "The tracker might have told him about our visit to Cavano and Munich, but he couldn't have known about the Parthenon. We left the tracker in the plane." He turned to Orr. "Where is Grant?"

Orr smiled. "Dead. Or captured. I don't really know which, and I don't care. That's up to Gia."

"You told her how to find him?"

"It got him out of the way, didn't it?"

"And my father?"

"He's all right. For now."

Orr was a great liar, but something about his expression made Tyler think he was covering up.

"I want to see him."

"When we find the treasure, I'll let him go."

"If you already know where the well is, why do you need us anymore?"

"Because I'm on a deadline, and even though we might have the correct well, I can't spend days looking for the right tunnel that leads to the chamber. Your expertise with the geolabe will take us there. I have some pages from the codex that you haven't seen."

Tyler remembered Stacy saying on Wednesday night that she thought the codex was missing some pages.

"Those pages show how to navigate the tunnels?" he said.

"Using the geolabe, yes. At least, I think they do. You'll have to figure it out."

"And if I won't?"

"I'll kill you both right here and take my chances on my own. What'll it be?"

"Don't listen to him," Stacy said.

Tyler considered the options and realized that he had none. He didn't know what was going on with his father, but to have any chance of taking Orr and finding out about the nuclear device, he had to stay alive until he had an opportunity to make his move. If he could escape once he was in the tunnels, he might be able to get back to the surface and get reinforcements. At the very least, he could keep Orr from coming back out.

Tyler nodded. "All right."

Orr smiled. "Good. Keep walking."

In three minutes, they were in a parking lot next to a Fiat sedan. Gaul opened the trunk and took out two belts.

"Put your arms up," he said.

"Why?" Tyler asked. "What are these?"

"Stun belts," Orr said. "Used in prisons to control inmates. You'll wear them so that I can keep you in line when we're in the tunnels. I don't want pistols sticking out of our belts. With the close quarters down there, you'll be too tempted to grab for one."

Orr removed two wristbands from his pocket and strapped them to his left arm. Each of them had a color that corresponded to the color of the belt—red for Tyler and blue for Stacy. The buttons were enclosed in a plastic covering. Orr tapped them lightly. "For easy access."

Tyler didn't resist. This meant Orr was planning to give them freer range in the tunnels. If Tyler could figure out a way to get his belt off, he might be able to get away before Orr could activate it.

Gaul snapped the belts on Tyler and Stacy and locked them with a key. The nylon belts were snug enough that they couldn't be slid off. A box the size of a pack of playing cards was centered over their bellies.

"Get in the backseat," Orr said. Tyler and Stacy climbed reluctantly into the Fiat. Orr and Gaul got into the front.

As Gaul threaded the car out of the lot, Orr turned in his seat. "Oh, one more thing. Those stun belts have been modified by a colleague of mine. It'll be difficult for me and Gaul to keep an eye on you at all times while we're in the tunnels, so these are our fail-safes to keep you from escaping."

"You think I'm scared of a shock collar?" Stacy said.

"Actually no," Orr said, holding up a Taser. "But I have this just in case you need some prodding."

"Then what are the belts for?" Tyler asked.

"As I mentioned before Stacy interrupted," Orr said, "they've been modified. They're not stun belts anymore. They've each been fitted with three ounces of C4 and molded into a clever shape charge. If either of you is out of my sight for more than ten seconds, I push this button. I'm told you'd be cut in half before you hit the ground."

FIFTY-TWO

Concussion. That's the word that swam into Grant's mind as he was driven across Naples. He'd experienced one before when a wrestling move went wrong and a chair hit the back of his head. With effort, he focused on recalling the symptoms. *Fuzziness:* check—squinting helped a little. *Nausea:* if he'd had a bigger dinner, the backseat would be a mess. *Lack of concentration:* had he already thought of that? *Loss of memory:* that was a tough one.

He remembered some of the fight in the galleria, but he didn't know how he ended up in the car. He tried to focus on the two men on either side of him. One was massaging his knee and the other was holding his stomach. Only the driver and Sal in the front passenger seat looked unharmed. Grant knew there were more guys, but they would be in even worse shape. As far as he could recall, he'd kicked the crap out of five of them. Not bad, but not good enough.

The car was waved through an iron gate and up the driveway to the gaudiest mansion he'd ever seen. Eggshell color, pillars dominating the front, ornate decorations curling around the windows and doors, cherubs adorning the eaves. It looked like the White House redecorated by Liberace.

Two new guys yanked Grant out of the car and hauled him up the steps into the house. He was taken through the foyer and to an outdoor patio that was situated on a cliff a hundred feet above the sea.

He'd only gotten a glimpse of Gia Cavano when she'd hopped

into the sports car outside the Boerst building in Munich, but the woman sitting in front of him was unmistakable. Her voluptuous form was squeezed into a tight black T-shirt and black jeans. Her long dark hair was wrapped on top of her head in a sexy updo. She looked sleek and curvy all at the same time. If Grant had been in a bar, he would have sidled up to her by now and offered to buy her a drink.

"Welcome to my home, Mr. Westfield," Cavano said.

The fuzziness was fading, but Grant had to hold himself steady to keep from falling over. "If you want to invite me over to tea, an engraved invitation would be appreciated next time."

"You're a tough man to bring down, I hear."

"Give me one of those batons and I'll really show you what I can do. You know, I'm kind of parched." He nodded at Sal, one of the three men hovering around them, guns at the ready. "Could you ask your girlfriend to get me an ice water? And a scotch chaser. Neat."

Sal glared at Grant. Apparently his English was good enough to get the insult.

"Get Mr. Westfield his drinks," Cavano said.

Sal left, and Grant took a seat without asking.

"You've got your tentacles into everything if you could get the police to intercept my men," he said. "Where are they?"

"Oh, they'll be fine. A night in jail and then they'll be free in the morning. Long enough for my purposes."

"Which are?"

"Jordan Orr. You know where he is?"

"Not exactly."

"What does that mean?"

"Well, I would have known precisely where he is if your meatheads hadn't interrupted the party."

Sal returned with the drinks.

"Thanks, Sallie." Grant took them, chugged the scotch, and pressed the cold glass of water to his temple.

"Can you find him?" Cavano said.

"Why should I?"

"Because if you don't, I will have my men throw you off the patio."

Grant took a sip of water and looked at the long drop to the Mediterranean below. "That is a darn good reason. I'll have to call Tyler Locke to find out."

"Tell me his number."

Grant thought about it for a second and decided it couldn't hurt to try. He gave her the number and she dialed. She listened for a few moments, then hung up.

"Straight to voice mail."

That can't be good, Grant thought. "I don't know why he wouldn't be answering."

"I have a possible reason. I received an anonymous call ten minutes ago telling me that he's with Jordan. Where are they going?"

Grant's heart sank. He was hoping that Tyler had gone to ground when he lost contact with the security team, but this must have been Orr's plan all along. Orr was the only one who could have tipped Cavano off about the tracker. He must have cornered Tyler and Stacy virtually simultaneously, although Grant didn't know how that was possible. If Tyler wasn't dead or free, that meant Orr was taking him to find the treasure.

"I have an idea where," Grant said.

"Show me."

"First, I want some guarantees."

"The only guarantee I'll make is that you'll die slowly if you don't tell me what I want to know."

"That *is* magnanimous of you, but I need something more. I know you mafia types are people of your word." Grant didn't believe that for a second. Criminals were criminals. But he couldn't just acquiesce to her demands without negotiating. They preyed on weakness, and he wasn't going to show her any. His words hit their target.

Cavano's eyes narrowed. "What do you want?" Grant knew that she hungered for the treasure and her vengeance on Orr too much to kill him if he could lead her to them.

"I want a promise on your mother's grave that you will let me, Tyler, and Stacy go once you have Orr and the treasure."

"My mother's still alive. She's upstairs right now."

"Okay, swear on your dear departed husband's soul."

"You're working with Jordan. How do I know you weren't sent here to lure me into a trap?"

"We were forced to work with Orr. We're just pawns to him."

"Can you prove it?"

Good question, Grant thought. What would be irrefutable proof?

Proof. He had just the thing.

"Do you have a computer?" Grant asked. "I need to show you an e-mail."

Sal brought a laptop, but he wouldn't let Grant touch it. He gave it to Cavano.

"Tell me what to type," she said.

He gave her the login and password for his e-mail and told her to click on one of the e-mails that Tyler had forwarded to him with the video of Sherman Locke.

She watched it twice and closed the laptop.

"Okay, I believe that Jordan is forcing you to work for him," she said. "But if we do find the treasure, and I agree to free you, how do I know you won't talk about it to anyone?"

"Who would believe us? You won't let us get away with any evidence."

Cavano thought about that. "All right. I swear on my husband's soul that I will not kill you, Tyler, or Stacy if you fulfill your part of the bargain." She made the sign of the cross.

"No, promise that we will be safe. I don't want an 'accident' to befall us on the way to the airport."

She sighed. "Yes, you will be safe. I swear it on my husband's soul."

Grant stood. "Then we have a deal." He knew the deal was a sham, but the longer he stayed alive, the longer he had to work out some kind of scheme to find Tyler and get out of this mess.

"Where are we going?" Cavano said as she stood.

"To some place called Piazza San Gaetano. We're going to church."

FIFTY-THREE

Tyler couldn't tell whether the belt Orr made him wear really was rigged with explosives, but it was definitely uncomfortable. It was tight enough that he couldn't possibly slide it down over his hips. The belt was made of heavy-duty nylon. Even if he found a cutting tool, it would take him several minutes to saw through it. The clasp and key-release mechanism were integrated into the unit housing the explosives, so if he tried to pry it apart, he might set it off.

He wasn't worried about the C4 itself. The explosive was extremely stable and couldn't be detonated by impact, even by a gunshot. Tyler always hated movies that showed someone blowing up a brick of C4 by shooting it, because the scenario was complete fiction.

Stacy looked as uncomfortable with her belt as he did, and Tyler was beginning to have second thoughts about how hastily he'd assumed that she was helping Orr. Maybe it was just his rationalization for not wanting to seem like a sucker, but he didn't want to believe Stacy was capable of betraying him.

But if she wasn't in league with Orr, Tyler couldn't figure out how Orr knew every one of their movements. Orr might have learned about the museum heist from the news, but with the tracker on the plane during their stay in Athens, there was no way he could have known that the shootout at the Parthenon involved them. It was almost as if he had access to a second GPS signal. . . .

Tyler suddenly remembered Orr smashing their cell phones. Stacy's phone had been the only piece of electronics they'd had with them the entire time. Tyler's phone had gotten ruined when it was dunked in the river. Orr could have been tracking the signal in Stacy's phone from the beginning. Tyler had been so fixated on the tracker in the geolobe that it never occurred to him that Orr had a backup, which must have been why Orr had made it so easy to find.

Tyler couldn't be sure that he was right, but he had renewed faith that Stacy was innocent. So Orr was either toying with them or he was trying to keep Tyler and Stacy from trusting each other. Divide and conquer. Tyler would play along for now.

Gaul found a rare parking spot two blocks away from the church at Piazza San Gaetano. They got out and began walking, with Gaul and Orr careful to stay behind Tyler and Stacy. The shops lining the narrow streets were all closed, and the bustle of activity Tyler had seen earlier in the day had dwindled. Scooters occasionally passed them, and the few pedestrians were making their way to tiny restaurants or the entryways of their walkup apartments.

Along the way, Tyler saw a sign for Napoli Sotterranea, the tour service that took people through the ancient passageways winding their way under the city. When he and Stacy had come this way in the afternoon, Tyler had stopped in to ask some questions.

A tour guide explained that no one knew how many tunnels and chambers actually existed underneath Naples. With subways and structural foundations constantly being excavated, new tunnels were found yearly, and some archaeologists speculated that more than thirty miles of tunnels remained undiscovered. Churches and private buildings often refused requests to map out the tunnels underneath them. Tyler had obliquely asked him about the San Lorenzo Maggiore well and whether it connected to the maze that the tourists trod. He told Tyler that he regularly traversed all the known tunnels and had never seen a connection, so the well must lead to one of the still unexplored areas.

The basilica loomed over the tiny Piazza San Gaetano. Like that of most of the other centuries-old churches in downtown Naples, the front door was set back only a few feet from the street. A sign advertised the archaeological excavation under part of the church that had exposed an ancient Greek marketplace.

Though there was no Mass that evening and the archaeological exhibit was closed, the door was wide open to allow worshippers a chance to pray and confess their sins. As the four of them walked in, Tyler mused that the priests would have to be in the confessional a long time to hear all the sins committed by this group.

They bypassed the nave, which was empty of visitors. The well stood in the center of an outdoor courtyard bordered by a cloister. The well opening was topped with a wooden frame that was designed to winch the water up in a clay amphora from a pool in the cistern below. The aqueducts had been shut off long ago, so the cistern would now be dry. The well's frame was now decorated with flowers, hardly the starting point Tyler would ever have imagined for a treasure hunt.

When they were standing at the well, Tyler tried to guess how the spy in the story from Archimedes' wax tablet wound up here. Had he swum through the tunnels that served as the aqueducts? Tyler pictured the man climbing up the rope that was tied to the winch.

"Show me the mark of Scorpio," Orr said.

Tyler walked around to the opposite side and pointed inside the well.

The light was fading quickly with the setting sun. Orr played the beam of a flashlight over stones dating from an era hundreds of years before Christ. The marks were just barely visible, fifteen dots carved out of the rock by the spy of Syracuse's king to identify the location where he intended to return but never did. Tyler had checked the constellations online. The dots matched exactly the arrangement of stars that depicted Scorpio.

"Congratulations, Tyler," Orr said, while Gaul extracted a rope and climbing gear from the duffel. "I knew this whole mission was a long shot, but you both came through with flying colors."

Tyler wanted to strangle him right there. "I'm so happy you approve."

"We're not done yet. We still need to get down there."

"We could jump. You go first."

"Funny," Orr said, looking around. They were still alone in the courtyard. Tyler didn't want to find out what Orr would do to someone who innocently stumbled onto them.

Gaul looped the rope around the wooden frame and tested it for strength. It held, so he lowered himself into the well. Three feet down, he hammered a piton into the stone and put a carabiner on it. Gaul tested the metal spike and D-ring to make sure it would hold his weight, then attached a second rope to it.

Tyler understood what he was doing. Both ends of the rope around the frame extended all the way down to the bottom of the cistern. Once the four of them reached the bottom, Gaul would pull one end down and that rope would fall free. That way, no one walking through the courtyard would see the rope attached to the frame and investigate. To climb back up, the second rope would be left attached to the piton and out of sight.

"Okay," Gaul said. "It's simple. We're going to climb down one at a time. I'll belay you on the way down. Got it?"

They all nodded, and each of them was given a three-belt harness to put on. Tyler put his legs into each of the smaller loops and then buckled the third around his waist. The brake rope was already attached, with the carabiner dangling on the end. Gaul also gave Tyler and Stacy small headband lights that they would use on the climb down.

Gaul went first, his duffel strapped to his back. It took him several minutes to reach the bottom while Tyler and Stacy waited up top with Orr, who stood away from them with his finger ready to trigger the bombs strapped to their waists if he had to. When he was down, Gaul radioed up that he was in place and ready with the Taser.

Stacy went next. Tyler helped her into the well and made sure that her harness was attached properly. She wasn't tentative about the climb at all. Tyler remembered her talk about exploring ancient ruins and caves with her cameramen in tow, so this descent was nothing new to her. He watched her skillfully climb down until she was out of sight.

For the first time, Tyler was alone with Orr. He stared at Orr, who returned his gaze with his lip curled in a half smile.

"How do you think you and Gaul are going to carry out a hundred and twenty-five tons of gold?" Tyler asked.

Orr laughed quietly. "You think I'm after the gold? I told you. I want the Midas Touch itself."

"You really are crazy," Tyler said, shaking his head.

Orr looked as if he was disappointed at Tyler's skepticism, paused, then said, "Have you ever heard of extremophiles?"

"It sounds like someone who enjoys jumping off buildings wearing a parachute."

"No. An extremophile is an organism that can exist in conditions that would kill most other life forms. They're found around volcanic vents on the ocean floor or in acidic hot springs like at Yellowstone Park. They're microbes called archaea. Some of these microbes have been known to actually digest metals in solution and excrete the solid form. That's why companies have been trying to mine the ocean floor around these black smokers."

"And you think that's what the Midas Touch is?"

"As ridiculous as it sounds, yes. I have researched this my whole life, and that's my theory. I think Midas's skin was somehow afflicted with this kind of microbe, perhaps exposed to it during a visit to a hot spring somewhere, but he was immune to its effects. I discovered that many people live with chronic skin diseases. Believe me, you don't want to see the photos."

"So how does he turn things to gold?"

"Any object he touched would become contaminated with this microbe. If the object was then submerged in a solution with dissolved gold in it, the object would be transmuted to gold by the microbe."

"So you think you'll get rich if you can recover this microbe?" Tyler said. "What makes you think it's still alive?"

"Over twenty years ago, in that chamber somewhere below us, I saw a man turn to gold in front of my eyes."

He must have meant the drug runner from Cavano's childhood tale who chased her and Orr into the chamber. Tyler recalled her saying that the man had touched something inside the golden coffin, something that had caused him excruciating pain. If that was truly the Midas Touch, the king himself may have been immune through some divine providence, but anyone else who came in contact with it would experience mind-bending agony, maybe even death.

"These archaea can remain dormant for thousands of years under the proper conditions," Orr continued. "Whatever they used to embalm Midas could have preserved the microbe."

However far-fetched Orr's theory sounded, he believed it. He almost had Tyler convinced.

"You said the Midas chamber had a pool with a hot spring in it," Tyler said. "How do you know that's not the source of this magical ability?"

"I don't, but I have a way to test it. I have two vials of water with me, one with water containing an acidic mixture of dissolved gold, and another with seawater. If the Midas Touch is real, it will work with those samples as well."

"Seawater?"

The call came up from Gaul that Stacy had reached the bottom. Orr gestured for Tyler to go next.

As Tyler climbed over the lip of the well and attached his harness, Orr said, "Seawater has minute amounts of gold dissolved in it. If the Midas Touch proves to be as effective as I think it is, you could extract huge quantities of gold from the oceans."

Tyler's mind reeled at how much gold that could be. "We're talking millions of ounces, then."

Orr shook his head. "You're thinking way too small. I'll give you a hint. There are over a billion cubic kilometers of seawater in the world, and the average solubility of gold is thirteen parts per trillion. Now get going."

Tyler began climbing down. Steadying himself wasn't too challenging, and the mindless activity allowed him to calculate the staggering sum that was driving this whole venture. Aiden had been far off when he'd guessed that Orr and Cavano were each after a block of gold worth four billion dollars. Tyler went through the math twice and came up with the same stunning figure both times.

If what Orr told him was true, even the most conservative estimate would put the value of all the gold in the world's oceans at twenty-five trillion dollars.

FIFTY-FOUR

Orr watched as Tyler and Stacy huddled over the geolabe, the copied pages of the codex he had given them, and a lantern to see by. As Tyler talked, Stacy made notes on the copy with a pencil. Tyler had refused to work with her until Gaul gave him a taste of the Taser.

Those three pages he'd held back had been Orr's ace in the hole. Without them, he knew Tyler and Stacy couldn't have found the Midas chamber on their own. Not in the maze that faced them.

The floor of the cistern, the chamber that would have held the water supplying the well, sat 150 feet below the church, and its ceiling soared three stories above them, where it was pierced by the well opening. The cistern's floor was sunk ten feet from the surrounding tunnels, so that a pool would have formed. Now that the aqueducts were shut off, the chamber was dry. Crude steps led up to each tunnel.

Orr ran his hand over the light gray tuff that made up the walls of the room. The solidified volcanic ash from Mount Vesuvius, which had erupted regularly since humans first settled in Naples, was so easy to work that the earliest Greek settlers had excavated tons of it for building material. They soon realized that the tunnels could be used as aqueducts to transport water for the city dwellers. The network of tunnels grew as the Romans, who wrested the city from the Greeks in the third century, mined the tuff to make the finest cement in Europe, creating structures that were still intact more than two thousand years later.

Inhaling the dank air and listening to the dull reverberation of their voices, Orr vividly remembered his visit to Naples, when he had played with Gia Cavano in the tunnels despite their parents' protestations. Some children were scared of dark, closed-in tunnels, but Orr could have explored them all day, marveling at the feat the ancients had accomplished in carving them out.

Those ancients had been as busy as gophers. Four tunnels led away from the cistern. If he hadn't been looking for them, he wouldn't have noticed the Greek letters carved into the tuff at the bottom right of each tunnel opening. Alpha, lambda, sigma, and mu. Somehow the geolabe would tell them which letter would lead them in the right direction.

"Which is the right one?" Orr said.

Tyler didn't look up. "We're working on it."

"Work faster. If I think you're stalling, one of you will end up with a hole in your belly the size of a dinner plate."

Stacy blanched. She wasn't planning on trying to fool him.

"We're doing the best we can," Tyler said.

"You just sprung this on us," Stacy said. "It may take time."

"We may not have much time," Orr said.

"Why not?" Tyler said.

"Because Gia Cavano could very well be on her way here right now."

"You son of a bitch!" Stacy spat out. "You told her where we are?"

"I needed your friend Grant Westfield out of the way. Either Gia killed him or, even better, she convinced him to lead her to us. If she doesn't follow, good for me. If she does follow, I'll have a surprise waiting for her."

"What kind of surprise?" Tyler said.

"The nasty kind. Now get back to work."

Tyler stared at Orr. For a moment, Orr forgot that he was in control and felt unnerved by Tyler's gaze. Then Tyler refocused his attention on the geolabe. Orr was surprised by his sense of relief. He ran his fingers over the wrist detonators and felt better.

Tyler and Stacy went back and forth between the device and the instructions in the document. As far as Orr could follow, it had something to do with mathematical principles that were beyond him. At one point, Tyler took the pencil and jotted down some calculations. Stacy looked confused by Tyler's questions as well, but she answered with translations as quickly as he asked them.

In ten minutes, Tyler suddenly stood up with the geolabe.

"You've figured it out?" Orr asked eagerly.

"Yes." If there was any doubt in Tyler's mind, Orr didn't hear it.

"How does it work?"

Tyler shook his head. "It's too complicated to explain."

"Bullshit."

"You're right. I just don't want to tell you. For obvious reasons." He pointed to the explosive belt around his waist.

Orr grinned. "You're a smart guy. But I'll be keeping tabs on which tunnel we take. If I think you're stalling by taking us in the wrong direction or I see us doubling back, there really will be no reason to have you both along. Get me?"

"I've got you."

"So which way do we go?"

Orr saw Tyler twirl the top knob on the geolabe. When the dial stopped, he turned it over, then glanced around until his eyes settled on the portal with the sigma next to it. The opening was no more than three feet wide.

"That one," he said, handing back the pen and the sheaf of papers.

"You're sure?" Orr said.

"That's what Archimedes tells me."

Orr saw no harm in letting Tyler and Stacy see where they were going, so each of them was equipped with a lantern. The lights threw eerie shadows in the otherwise total darkness. The passageway was curved and not wide enough for more than one person at a time. Gaul went first, then Stacy, then Tyler. When Tyler was far enough ahead, Orr followed him in.

Just a few feet in, Orr opened a gum wrapper and pocketed the gum. He loosely balled up the wrapper and dropped it on the ground. The tiny piece of silver foil reflected his light in a pinpoint flash. Now Cavano would find the carelessly dropped bit of trash and know which way to go.

After forty feet, Orr emerged from the narrow tunnel into another cistern as big as the first. Three more passageways led off from it. This time, no Greek letters were present.

"What happened to the markings?" Orr said.

"There won't be any more," Tyler said. "The geolabe will tell us which tunnel to take from here on out." Tyler pointed to the tunnel on their right.

Orr now understood why the geolabe was their guide. The spy for the king of Syracuse must have created his map as he walked, perhaps marking his arm with charcoal to record the direction of each turn. He wouldn't want to etch the walls with directional indicators that could lead the Romans back to his discovery. But when the spy found the exit, he knew he would need to indicate which tunnel was the starting point back to the treasure, so he'd scratched a letter next to each of the tunnels just below the old water level of the cistern.

Orr used a knife to mark the wall with a small *x* next to the opening they'd just come through to show him the correct path out once he got rid of Tyler and Stacy. Then he sent the three of them ahead into the next tunnel while he hung back.

Orr knelt and opened his backpack. He took out a smaller knapsack specially created by Crenshaw. It would look like something they might have left behind in the course of their exploration. In reality, it contained ten pounds of phosphorus grenades. The opening was partially unzipped.

No doubt Cavano would make the trip down with her men. She wouldn't give up the chance to see the Midas chamber again for herself. She'd follow the trail left by Orr's gum wrapper, and when her group came into this room, she'd be curious to see what Orr had abandoned. When one of her men opened the zipper or picked up the knapsack, the grenades would explode, showering the entire room with burning phosphorus and causing a gruesome death for everyone with her.

Orr armed the device and stood, heaving the backpack onto his shoulder. He frowned as he climbed the steps into the next tunnel. The only downside of the plan was that he wouldn't get to see Gia Cavano open her surprise.

FIFTY-FIVE

FBI special agent Ben Riegert's laugh filled the cramped interrogation room of the Hagerstown sheriff's office. The story was just getting better and better. Mohammed Qasim was laying it on thicker as he went. Riegert's partner, Jackie Immel, was questioning the other suspect, Abdul bin Kamal, in the next room. He hoped she was getting more out of her guy. This one wasn't making any sense.

Riegert took another swig of coffee. He'd raced out to Hagerstown from the D.C. office along with twenty other agents as soon as they heard that a 911 call had come in claiming that a terrorist attack was taking place and a warehouse had blown up.

They found Qasim and Kamal beside the building behind a concrete retaining wall with a young woman and a man bleeding to death from shots to the chest and leg. The ambulance had taken the injured man away, and he was identified as retired Major General Sherman Locke. Riegert hadn't gotten word about his condition, but the paramedics had said he might not survive. A chopper was flying him to the George Washington University trauma center.

The woman, Carol Benedict, was now being examined at a local hospital. Before she was taken away in the ambulance, she told the local police that she couldn't remember her abduction, which made Riegert suspect that she'd been drugged. Rohypnol and other date-rape drugs usually caused short-term-memory loss, and the hospital would test for it, but it was probably out of her system by now. Riegert would head there to question her next.

Riegert took a seat opposite the suspect. "So, Mr. Qasim, you claim two guys busted into your house as you were getting your morning coffee and abducted you?" Riegert said without even trying to hide his disbelief. Usually these terrorist types were more than happy to come right out and show pride in their acts, but this guy was different. Qasim looked terrified, not the face of defiance Riegert was expecting.

"I swear that is the truth," Qasim said.

"Where are you from?"

"I am from Saudi Arabia. I am attending the University of Maryland to get my degree in petroleum engineering."

"Uh-huh. Why do think these men kidnapped you?"

"I don't know! They blindfolded me, put me in van, and tied me up. Then they picked up Abdul."

"You know him?"

"Only in passing. We go to the same mosque in College Park."

"You weren't associated with him in any other way?"

"We studied the Koran together several times, but that is all."

"So they took you to this warehouse in Hagerstown. Then what?"

"Then they threw me into this room and locked the door. It had a bed and a bucket and nothing else in it. They gave me water and just a little food."

Qasim was definitely hungry. Riegert had given him a candy bar, and he chowed it down in two bites.

"So you were in there for more than two days," Riegert said. "Why?"

"You keep asking me why. Ask the kidnappers why!"

"The kidnappers, huh?" Riegert opened a folder and tossed a photo of a charred body over to Qasim. "The only other person we've found in connection with this is that guy right there. Was he a partner of yours?"

"No!"

"Mr. Qasim, a truck was hijacked not too far away the day you claim that you were kidnapped. The driver, a Clarence Gibson, says that two men stopped his truck, took him to a remote forest location, and left him for dead. The trucker said the men spoke Arabic. Know anything about that?"

Qasim stared at him, wide-eyed. "You think I was part of that?"

"You did disappear that day."

"This is crazy, I tell you!"

"This morning, 911 got a call from a General Sherman Locke that he was being held by terrorists. The police arrive to find a local warehouse blown to hell, and the only survivors are two foreign nationals in the company of a frightened woman and a nearly dead man, who we believe is a newly retired two-star general in the Air Force. How do you explain that?"

"I can't! I can only tell you what happened."

"Okay. Take me through this morning."

"Can I have another candy bar?"

"Sure. After we hear your story about what happened today." By "we," Riegert meant the recording apparatus and the eight men squeezed into the observation room behind the one-way mirror.

Qasim took a sip of his water and cleared his throat. "All right. I was sleeping in my prison cell when a noise woke me up. I think it was a fight. I heard a buzz and then shouting. It sounded like someone fell. And then shots. Many shots."

"How many?"

"I can't remember. There must have been more than ten."

"Then what?"

"I heard a truck start up. Yes! I remember now. I got a glimpse of a semi truck inside the warehouse before they put me in the cell."

Excellent. This guy was burying himself, and Riegert wasn't going to stop him. "Did you get a look at the truck?"

"Only for a moment. All I can say is that the cab was blue and it had a long silver trailer."

That matched the description of the one hijacked from Gibson.

"So the truck *was* there?"

"But I didn't know it was stolen."

"Okay. So the truck started. How did you get out of the cell?"

"It sounded like someone was crawling outside my door. Keys jangled, and then my door unlocked. I thought it might be the men who kidnapped me, so I stayed away. It swung open, and I saw an older man lying in a pool of blood. So much blood."

Riegert appreciated Qasim's training. He could make up a story on the fly better than most criminals he dealt with.

"And this was General Locke. Did he say anything to you?"

Qasim nodded. "He had a beard and his clothes were dirty, so I knew he was a prisoner like me. I rushed over to him, of course. He was very weak, but he said, 'The building is rigged to blow. We need to get out.'"

"And that's when you saw the explosives?"

"Yes. I've worked on oil-well blowouts in Saudi Arabia, so I could recognize what those barrels were. I took the keys from General Locke and opened Abdul's cell. We heard the woman, Ms. Benedict, screaming, so we let her out, too. I carried the general out the nearest door while Abdul helped Ms. Benedict. We ran behind the retaining wall, and that's when the building exploded. I still hear ringing in my ears."

"And that is when the police showed up. Well, Mr. Qasim, that is quite a story. And you think Mr. bin Kamal is telling the same story?"

"He must, because it's true!"

Two raps on the door, and it opened. Immel poked her head in. "Got a minute?"

"I'll get your candy bar," Riegert said, "and then we'll go over this again, Mr. Qasim."

The suspect nodded shakily and gulped the rest of his water. He was certainly nervous, and Riegert intended to find out why.

Riegert closed the door behind him. "You will never guess the fantasy this guy has cooked up."

"I know," Immel said with a chuckle. "I've got my own tall tale from bin Kamal. Some snow job about him being kidnapped right out of his house and then thrown in a locked room inside the warehouse."

Riegert frowned. "And shots fired in the warehouse before Locke opened their cells with blood all over him?"

His partner stopped smiling. "You're getting the same story?"

"Sounds like it."

"Well, it gets weirder. We were trying to contact Locke's son or daughter, but we couldn't reach either of them. We did get his son's boss, Miles Benson, president of Gordian Engineering."

"Why is that weird?"

"Because the first thing he said when we told him about the warehouse was that we should go over there with a Geiger counter."

FIFTY-SIX

Knowing that they would be descending into the well, Grant had Cavano and her men stop for ropes and other climbing gear before they headed to the church of San Lorenzo Maggiore.

When they arrived, they found the rope anchored to the inside of the well, so they knew Orr had already gone down. Cavano had brought four men with her, Sal and the three least injured of the men from the galleria. All five were armed with submachine guns equipped with mounted flashlights. Two of her men went first, and then Grant went down. Normally, he was an expert at rappelling, but he was still woozy from the concussion and slipped twice on the way to the bottom.

One of the men steadied the rope while another watched Grant wander around the chamber with a flashlight, looking for any sign that Tyler was all right.

He spotted a crumpled bit of white paper and bent to pick it up. He began to unfold it, but before he could read it, Cavano shouted, "Give me that!"

She detached herself from the rope and held out her hand. Grant put it in her palm.

Cavano frowned at it for a moment and then handed it back to him.

"What does that mean?" she demanded.

Grant shined his light on it. Two words were scrawled in Tyler's handwriting.

Louis Dethy.

It was a message left for Grant. Tyler knew that he was coming. He might even know that Cavano and her clan would be with him, so he'd coded it in case it gave Grant an advantage. But what was Tyler trying to tell him?

Grant struggled to shake off the effects of the concussion and focus his mind. Louis Dethy. He recognized the name but couldn't quite grasp where he'd seen it.

"Well?" Cavano said.

"I have no idea." The truth was always the best lie, and Grant wasn't going to volunteer that Tyler had sent him a secret message.

Cavano stared at him a moment, then let it go. She watched Sal descend from above.

Grant wondered why she'd come along on the expedition. Maybe she was desperate. She was definitely running out of trusted soldiers. With three men lost in Munich, and then another two in Athens and a couple out of action at the galleria, her forces had dwindled quickly. Sure, she could find more grunts, but she might not trust them to keep their mouths shut about what they found. And he'd seen the glint in her eye. She wanted to see the gold again herself.

A bodyguard called to her in Italian as he came out of one of the tunnels leading from the cistern. He was holding what looked like a crinkled gum wrapper.

"Another clue, perhaps," Cavano said. She took it from him, unwrapped it, and took a sniff. "It's fresh. I can still smell the mint."

She gave orders in Italian, then said to Grant, "Rodrigo goes first ahead of us. When he gets to the next room, he calls for us to enter, with you, me, and Sal going last. That way, if Jordan is waiting for us, he only takes out one of my men."

"Does he know he's cannon fodder?" Grant said, tilting his head toward Rodrigo.

"He does what I tell him to do. You walk in front of me. I want to see where you are. Sal, you bring up the rear."

Rodrigo entered the tunnel, followed by the others. Grant had a flimsy plastic flashlight, not heavy enough to do any damage.

They wended their way through the tunnel until Rodrigo reached the next chamber. They halted while he searched for signs that there was no welcoming committee. He gave the all-clear, and they started moving forward again.

As Grant walked, he turned Tyler's message over in his mind. Louis Dethy. It was obviously a name they both knew, but it was no one at Gordian or in the Army. Then he thought about the last name: Dethy. Grant wondered if he'd been a client of Gordian's. No, they hadn't met him. He'd heard about Dethy when they were researching bomb-disposal case studies.

Then it was as if a laser pierced his fog-shrouded brain.

Louis Dethy–trap.

In 2002, Louis Dethy, a seventy-nine-year-old Belgian retired engineer, was found in his own home killed by a gunshot wound to the neck. The police had assumed it was a suicide until one of the investigating detectives opened a wooden chest and barely missed being blasted by a shotgun.

The story was well known in Tyler and Grant's combat-engineering unit because the police called in military engineers to defuse or disarm nineteen ingenious explosive devices and trick-wired shotguns Dethy had designed. Dethy had killed himself when he'd set one off accidentally. It took the engineers three weeks to clear the house, and Grant's Army company had nicknamed his home the Dethy-trap.

Tyler was warning him that Orr had left behind a booby trap.

Grant instinctively looked down for any sign of trip wires or pressure plates, but he realized that they would already have been set off by the three men who'd gone before him. He was just glad he wasn't in front.

As he approached the opening into the next chamber, Grant saw two of the men huddled around some object in the middle of the room, while the third kept his gun trained on Grant. A flashlight played over a partially opened knapsack.

It was the oldest trick in the book. In Iraq and Afghanistan, insurgents would place grenades inside an apparently harmless object and hope that a soldier would be curious enough and stupid enough to pick it up without inspecting it.

Cavano's men fit that description. They'd never been through war, so it didn't occur to them not to touch something that was lying around.

Rodrigo bent over and reached for the knapsack. Grant shouted "No!" but it was too late. Rodrigo picked up the sack. Grant turned and ran back into the tunnel, but Cavano was in his way. She lifted her weapon at the threat, but a blast concussion knocked both of them down.

The two men next to the bag had to have been killed instantly, but the third man was too far away from it to be severely injured if it was just a fragmentation grenade. Yet he suddenly began to cough, and then he began to scream.

"Sono infiammato! Sono infiammato!"

White smoke roiled toward Grant, and he pulled Cavano to her feet.

"What happened?" Cavano said. "He's on fire?"

Grant knew immediately what it was. "Phosphorus! Get back! Go! Go! The smoke is poisonous! Hurry!"

Cavano cried out to Sal, who shuffled back as fast as his big frame could move. The smoke was piling toward Grant. If they got caught in it, they'd be coughing up blood for weeks, their lungs singed by the phosphorus, which burns when exposed to air.

He pushed Cavano to go faster. She cursed at him as she nearly tripped. When they tumbled into the cistern that had been their starting point, Grant didn't stop. He raced into one of the other tunnels and kept going until he was in the next room. Cavano and

Sal followed, their faces a combination of fear, anger, and confusion.

Grant came to a halt.

"We should be okay here," he said. "The smoke should be pulled up the well by the chimney effect. But if we see any headed this way, we should retreat farther."

"What happened?"

"Orr planted a booby trap in that room. Your boys took the bait and set it off."

"They're dead?"

"If they aren't yet, they'll wish they were. The burns from white phosphorus grenades are horrific. I've used them in conjunction with high explosives. Very effective and vicious. We called it a shake-and-bake op."

Cavano's jaw clenched and her brow furrowed with hatred. "What do we do?"

"Nothing we can do right now. Even with a gas mask for protection, it would burn your skin and set your clothes on fire. We'll have to wait until it dissipates."

"How long?"

"Maybe ten minutes. Maybe an hour. Depends on how drafty it is."

Cavano explained the booby trap to Sal, who spewed what sounded like every Italian curse word in existence. Grant didn't need to speak the language to know that Sal and Cavano had just made a pact to make Orr suffer in the most terrible ways imaginable.

FIFTY-SEVEN

To Tyler, it seemed as though they'd been in the tunnels for days, but his watch told him it had been little more than an hour. Halfway through, a dull peal, like thunder, had echoed off the walls. It had to be the booby trap Orr had implied when he said he was leaving a nasty surprise for Cavano. Orr even smiled with satisfaction at the sound. Tyler just had to hope Grant had gotten the warning he'd risked writing on a piece of paper torn from the codex translation.

Only a few of the passages were as narrow as the first one, so all four of them often walked through together. At one point, Tyler had caught Orr scratching a mark on the wall of a passageway they'd just come through, presumably so that he could find his way out again. Orr must have been confident that Cavano would be in no condition to trail them, but Tyler made himself believe Grant had survived the explosion and would be following the marks.

Archimedes had made the operation of the geolabe intuitive only to someone who understood his mathematical reasoning. Once Tyler had solved the formula in the codex, the usage of the geolabe was relatively simple, but he wasn't about to tell Orr that.

Most intersections had four offshoots, but some had three and some had five. To find which direction to go, the top knob would be rotated clockwise so that the top dial would move the same number of zodiac marks as the number of openings at the intersection. The bottom knob would be rotated by the same number, but counterclockwise. Then Tyler would flip the geolabe over, and the dial on the opposing side would show the correct direction to go, with the six o'clock point indicating where they'd come from. After the tenth intersection, Tyler still hadn't seen the dial point to the six o'clock position. As long as the geolabe wasn't telling them to backtrack, he was confident that he had interpreted Archimedes' instructions correctly.

Twice they came across cisterns that were still partially filled with water. Tyler guessed that the tunnels occasionally flooded with rainwater during downpours. Maybe the aqueducts had been filled with water only part of the time, which would have made the trek that much easier for Archimedes' spy.

As they walked, he kept an eye on Stacy. She had withdrawn, saying only the minimum to keep on the path. Several times she seemed on the verge of saying something to him, but then she closed her mouth and looked away. Embarrassment, anger, fear—Tyler couldn't tell the reason, but she didn't need to apologize for anything. In fact, he realized an hour ago that he should apologize to her. After playing the events of today back in his mind, Tyler remembered another event that convinced him of Stacy's innocence. Tyler would let Orr's charade continue as long as he could, but at the right time he had to go on the offensive, and when he did, he would need Stacy's help.

Around the next corner, the passageway ended at the midsection of a steeply inclined tunnel leading up to the left and down to the right. Throughout the walk, the group had gone up or down a few steps, but overall they had stayed on essentially the same level underground. The upward direction of the tunnel abruptly ended at a brick wall.

"What the hell?" Gaul said.

"How old do you think those bricks are?" Tyler asked Stacy.

"At least two thousand years."

"Maybe they didn't want anyone to find Midas's tomb," Orr said.

"Then why leave the passage we just came through unsealed?" Tyler said.

"I don't know. You're the engineer. You tell me."

"It may have had nothing to do with Midas," Stacy said. "The tablet said that the Syracuse king's spy was looking for a way into the Roman fortress. Maybe this leads into it, and the people inside were trying to keep invaders from doing exactly what he was trying to do."

"It doesn't matter," Orr said. "Looks like we go farther down the rabbit hole."

The tunnel extended downward for another two hundred feet, and they emerged into a room twenty feet long and ten feet wide. At the far end was a pool of water that ran the width of the room and was three feet across. What looked like a foot-wide stone bridge spanned the middle of the pool and ended at the wall. Tyler turned in all directions, but there were no more tunnels.

It was a dead end.

"Is this some kind of joke?" Orr asked.

Tyler looked at him in surprise. "No. This is where the geolabe said to go." Could he have interpreted the instructions incorrectly?

"If this is it, Tyler, I'm going to press my button. You better come up with something fast to make me think you haven't been screwing with me this whole time."

Tyler was acutely aware of the explosive belt digging into his stomach as he walked to the far end and inspected the wall.

A nearly invisible crack stretched across the end wall at a height of six feet. The surface was made of the same tuff that they'd seen throughout the tunnel system, but in some places the pocked gray stone revealed a white layer underneath, as if the tuff were merely a thin veneer. Tyler scratched at the white material with his fingernail, but it didn't flake away like the tuff. In fact, it abraded his nail, almost as if . . .

Tyler flipped the geolabe over. The dial was pointing to Aquarius, the water bearer. That had to be a clue.

"What is it?" Stacy said.

He dropped to his knees and held the lantern over the water, which became opaque five feet down, obscuring the bottom.

Tyler smiled at the engineering ingenuity of it.

"Eureka," he said quietly.

"What?" Stacy said.

"Feel that," he said, pointing to the white stone under the tuff.

She rubbed it with her finger.

"What's going on?" Orr said.

"It feels like what I use to smooth my feet," Stacy said. "Pumice?"

"Right," Tyler said. "Did you know that pumice is up to ninety percent air?"

"Why does that matter?" Orr asked.

"Because it's the only rock that floats. It's ejected by volcanoes like Vesuvius. It floats so well that some scientists theorize that plants and animals might have migrated throughout the Pacific on pumice rafts created by Indonesian volcanoes."

"And your point is?"

"The whole wall below this crack is made of pumice. The tuff on the front is merely to disguise it. The wall is floating."

Orr looked confused, then glanced down at the water. "Is that possible?"

"Bricks of pumice could have been cemented together. When the pool of water below was filled, the guides in the side wall kept the end wall in place as it rose with the water until it was firmly seated against the ceiling."

"And no one would ever know it was actually a door," Stacy said incredulously. "It makes sense that Midas would have made sure his tomb was protected. Grave robbers were a bane to the ancient world, especially because so many kings insisted on being buried with vast hoards of treasure."

"Like the pharaohs."

"Wait a minute," Orr said. "When Gia and I found the chamber twenty years ago, there wasn't any door."

"This pool is probably fed by a spring so that it can be refilled. If there was a drought the year you visited, the level in the pool could have lowered enough to drop the barrier."

Orr got a faraway look in his eye. "Now I remember. We came down an incline and then crossed a bridge over water. I'd forgotten that detail. This has to be it."

"Can we swim under it?" Gaul asked.

"I doubt it," Tyler said. "That would make the floating wall superfluous."

"Then how do we open it?"

"There must be a lever of some kind to release the water," Tyler said. "When it flows out, the barrier will lower and let us through."

Tyler walked around the room and saw no sign of any kind of button, switch, or handle.

Then he realized where it must be.

"It's in the water. Something like the stopper in a bathtub. Take it out, and the water will drain. Take the belt off me and I'll open it." If he dove in with the belt on, the electronics might short-circuit, setting off the bomb.

"No," Orr said. "I don't trust you. What if there's an escape route?"

"It's the only way to get through," Tyler said, looking at Orr and Gaul, "so I guess one of you has to do it, then."

"No," Orr said again. "Gaul, undo Stacy's belt and give her a flashlight."

Stacy fixed him with a hateful stare when she realized that she was the one who would dive into the liquid gloom.

FIFTY-EIGHT

Gaul unlocked the explosive belt from Stacy's waist and gave her one of the small metal flashlights. She turned to face Tyler. Several times during the walk through the tunnels, she had thought to protest Orr's accusation of treachery, but she had no explanation for how he had known their movements, and she worried that her denials would ring hollow. But before she dove into the pool, she had to say something.

"Tyler," she said, "I want you to know that I've never deceived you. Carol's safety is my only priority."

Tyler didn't say anything, but his lip curled upward ever so slightly and he winked at her.

Stacy felt a rush of relief. Somehow he knew she hadn't betrayed him. Suddenly she had a glimmer of hope that they'd get out of this mess. She had an almost overwhelming urge to embrace Tyler, but if she did, she knew that she'd lose control and cry like a girl.

Orr missed the wink. "Go," he commanded. "That flashlight isn't waterproof, so it may not last long. We'll shine our lights into the pool from up here."

"When you get down there," Tyler said, "look around but don't touch anything. Come back up and tell me what you see."

"What am I looking for?" she asked.

"Some kind of plug or lever."

She sat and put down the flashlight to take off her shoes and socks. She swung her legs around and dipped her toes in the water. A chill shot up her spine, and she shivered.

"Quit stalling," Orr said, and shoved her in.

Stacy tumbled forward, and the sudden dunking nearly made her inhale in shock. She kicked to the surface and fought the impulse to climb back out of the frigid pool.

"Bastard!"

"They say it's better to go in all at once," Orr said.

"Just give me the damn flashlight so I can get this over with."

Gaul handed it to her. He, Tyler, and Orr leaned over the pool and held the lanterns above it. The illumination penetrated to the bottom, but she couldn't tell how far down that was. It was well over five feet, because her feet couldn't touch.

Stacy wasn't an Olympic swimmer, but she had spent many days swimming in the lake near her parents' farm. She wasn't worried about a little pool.

She took a deep breath, dove under, and kicked down. She played the flashlight around the walls, but the surface looked identical to the walls of the room above.

When she reached ten feet down, she saw the bottom of the barrier suspended above the floor of the pool. Just as Tyler said, the ends were inserted into grooves at each end to guide it up and down. Six feet below the bottom of the barrier were stops where the barrier would come to a rest.

Nothing looked like a lever or a plug, so she turned around. There was a dark spot on the wall directly under where Tyler had been. She swam over to it.

It was a square cavity six feet on each side and three feet deep. She shined the flashlight inside and got a glimpse of a stone lever jutting from the wall. Next to the lever was a flat round disk the diameter of a beach ball.

A small black notch was cut into the rock above the top disk. Stacy put her hand over it and felt her palm sucked onto it. Water was flowing through. This was the control valve.

She was out of breath, so she pulled her hand away and made for the surface.

"Did you find it?" Orr said.

Stacy sputtered water. "I think so."

"What does it look like?" Tyler said.

She explained the mechanism to him.

"It seems simple enough," he said. "You'll need to pull the lever. That should swing the disk aside to allow the water to flow through the drain."

"Got it."

"Just be careful. The suction could be strong. You don't want to get stuck."

"I can handle it."

She dove back down. When she reached the cavity, she shined the light on the lever again to get her bearings, but it flickered out five seconds later, succumbing to the water leaking in. Still, it was enough time for her to put her hand on the top handle and brace herself with her back against the side wall of the cavity.

She pushed, and the lever moved an inch. The rush of water increased. She pushed again, and it moved a little farther. Now the outflow was a torrent. She heaved, swinging the disk to the side. Almost out of breath, she kicked against the bottom of the pool, but her foot was swept into the hole.

Her foot plunged in, and the water rushing past threatened to pin her there indefinitely. Terrified at the thought of drowning that way, she gathered her strength, turned over, and pushed her free foot against the wall with every bit of power she had. She extracted her trapped foot and swam out of the way of the flow.

By this time her lungs were screaming for air. In a panic, she flailed her arms to reach the surface. As she broke through, she cried out for help.

A pair of powerful hands grabbed her shoulders and lifted her out of the pool. Tyler laid her down gently, but she didn't let go. He responded by pulling her toward him in a tight embrace. The warmth of his body felt wonderful, and she buried her face in his chest so they wouldn't see her sobbing.

"You're all right now," Tyler said. "You did it. The water's draining." Then he whispered into her ear. "It's time. Be ready."

Gaul dropped the belt on top of her and backed away to join Orr at the opposite end of the room as they watched the barrier slowly drop.

"Put it on her," Gaul said, with the Taser leveled at them. "I want to hear it click shut." Tyler complied and looped it around her waist, snapping it closed.

A wave of heat washed over them, as if someone had opened the door on a broiling oven.

They all moved to the other side of the room as the cool air from the tunnels rushed in to replace the stifling damp air coming from beyond the descending barrier.

In five minutes the wall had sunk all the way to the bottom, and the air temperature had dropped enough for them to venture in.

They walked across the threshold, through a small antechamber, and emerged at a balcony overlooking a cavern far bigger than any they'd come through in their journey.

Stacy gasped. Nothing could have prepared her for the sight in front of her. This had to be the tomb of Midas, because from floor to ceiling every surface was made of gold.

FIFTY-NINE

The lustrous golden finish reflected the lanterns so that the luminous power was amplified far beyond their meager outputs. The room stretched out before Tyler as if he were standing on the doorstep of El Dorado. The floors, walls, and ceiling were all made of gold, which ended in tendrils reaching for the chamber's entryway like a creeping mold.

The entry platform to the one-hundred-foot-long by fifty-foot-wide room was a balcony with a solid railing along its length. The chamber seemed to have been excavated from a contiguous mass of volcanic tuff, and the balcony overlooked a massive ten-foot-deep pit that took up more than half the room's length. Stairs to Tyler's left led down to the pit, and in the middle of the pit was the statue of a girl lying on a cubical pedestal of gold, just as Orr had described, her left hand missing. The golden pedestal, six feet on each side, had lines of Greek lettering chiseled into it.

A spout of water poured from an opening in the wall into a bubbling pool that ran along the far end of the pit behind the pedestal. The water must have been supplied by a hot spring deep under the crust, superheated by the immense magma chamber that fed Mount Vesuvius. Clouds of steam rose from the pool. The room would have been unbearably hot with the barrier closed.

Another set of stairs led to a ten-foot-high terrace at the opposite end of the chamber, but those stairs were on the right side of the chamber, just past where the pool of water ended. The terrace didn't have a golden railing as the entrance balcony did, so Tyler could clearly see a gold sarcophagus placed on it in a regal center position atop a platform overlooking the rest of the chamber.

There were no other golden objects in the chamber, so Midas must have been confident that the golden room itself was impressive enough to secure him a heavenly afterlife with the gods.

Tyler observed all of this in just a few seconds. He'd been preparing for the last hour, thinking about how to disable Orr and Gaul without getting Tasered or blown up. Now that they had reached their objective, he and Stacy had exhausted their usefulness to Orr. If Tyler didn't act soon, the two of them would be killed for sure. It was incredibly risky, but he could either try something now and go down fighting or die with a push of Orr's detonator button.

Gaul and Orr had been so careful to keep an eye on both him and Stacy during the entire journey that he'd had no clear opportunity to strike. Either he would have been killed in the attempt or he would have been defeated and tipped his hand. Tyler knew that he would have only one chance, and he counted on this being the time when Orr and Gaul would be the most distracted, the moment they laid eyes on all that gold.

When they had walked through the entrance, Tyler had angled to position himself so that the two men were on either side of him, with Stacy behind them. As they stood at the balcony of the golden cavern, Orr and Gaul were clearly mesmerized by the bounty the chamber offered.

Tyler took his chance.

Without warning, he pushed Stacy backward out of his way. He used the geolabe to smack the Taser out of Gaul's hand, and it went flying into the pit below, where it skidded into the pool. With a kick, he sent Gaul crashing down the stairs.

Tyler whirled around, trying to smash Orr's head with the device, but it only hit him in the back. Orr bent over, his right hand caught between his body and the stone railing. Tyler grabbed his left wrist and tried to wrench the detonators off by undoing the two Velcro clasps.

He got one open, but it slipped out of his hand and fell over the side of the railing. It was the red one that matched the red belt he wore. The detonator for Stacy's blue belt remained securely fastened. Orr yanked his wrist away and swung the bag on his shoulder around. It slammed into Tyler, knocking him backward.

Before he could catch himself, Tyler tipped over the railing and tumbled through the air.

When Tyler had disabled Gaul with lightning speed and launched himself at Orr, Stacy had understood what he was going for. He needed to get those detonators. One of them had gone flying, but the one linked to her belt was still on Orr's wrist.

It had looked as if Tyler was going to win in one shot, but Orr had been too quick. She ran toward him to try and stop him, but she got there too late, and Tyler flipped over the railing and out of sight.

Orr reached for the detonator button, so Stacy did the only sensible thing. She jumped on his back and latched on to him, wrapping her legs around his midsection, the explosive charge jammed into the small of his back.

"You touch that button and we both die," she said into Orr's ear.

He tried to pummel her with his elbows, but the angle didn't allow him much leverage. Then he landed one that sent a jolt of agony through her torso so painful that she almost released him, which would have meant instant death.

With one arm laced around his neck, she reached with her other hand and raked his face with her fingernails. Orr screamed as she gouged his right eyeball.

"You bitch!"

Orr propelled himself backward until her back connected with the wall, driving the breath from her. She struggled for air but didn't ease up. She grabbed her own wrist and pulled as hard as she could, tightening the hold on Orr's neck.

The strangled wheeze escaping from his mouth told her that it was working. It was only a matter of who would give out first.

Tyler landed with a thud on the hard pit floor, and he felt something pop near his ribs. Pain shot through his chest, but at least his arm had kept his head from slamming into the stone floor. He rolled over and spied the detonator button lying next to the golden pedestal.

Gaul, who was shaking off the fall down the stairs and holding his head, saw the button at the same time and realized what it was. He lunged toward it.

Tyler tackled him, and Gaul pitched onto his face. He continued scrambling for the detonator, but Tyler pulled the cuffs of his jeans, dragging him backward.

Tyler leaped on top of him and punched Gaul in the kidney. Gaul coughed in pain, and Tyler took advantage of the pause to jab his hand into Gaul's pocket. Gaul recovered, rolled over, and slammed his foot into Tyler's side.

If the kick had hit his cracked rib, Tyler would have doubled over in too much pain to move. But the kick was to his other side, and though it sent him reeling, he kept hold of the key he'd snatched from Gaul's pocket.

Released from Tyler's grip, Gaul scrabbled toward the detonator. Tyler knew that he had only seconds before Gaul had the detonator in his hands.

Tyler frantically stabbed the key into the lock mechanism on his belt and twisted it.

Gaul seized the detonator.

Tyler ripped open the belt and threw it.

Gaul thumbed the cap open. He sat up and had already jabbed

the button down when he realized that Tyler had hurled the belt at him.

For just a fraction of a second, Tyler saw Gaul's reaction morph from triumph to horror before the belt exploded in his face.

Gaul's head was torn apart by the blast. Blood and gore splattered the immaculate golden floor behind him. It took his body a second to realize that it was no longer alive. Gaul toppled over, twitched a couple of times, and then went still.

Tyler had saved himself, but Stacy was still in danger.

With the adrenaline still masking his pain, Tyler jumped to his feet and ran up the stairs. He got to the top in time to see Stacy clinging to Orr's back as he slumped to the floor underneath her. Her arms were choking the life from him.

He ran over and forced her arms open. She resisted letting go.

"Stacy!" Tyler yelled. "We need him alive!"

She looked up at him with a wild flash of her eyes, ready to fight. When she saw who it was, she sagged. Tyler's chest protested, but he caught her.

He set her down and turned Orr over. He had four diagonal scratches across his face, and his right eye was a ruined mess. Tyler removed the detonator from his wrist and checked his pulse.

"Is he dead?" Stacy asked. "Did I . . . kill him?" Her voice quavered with hope that she'd succeeded and fear of the same.

"No," Tyler said. "He's out cold, but he's breathing."

He unlocked Stacy's belt. The adrenaline was wearing off, and Tyler winced as he threw it aside.

"Are you all right?"

"I'll be fine. Just a bruise."

"Gaul?"

She had to have heard the explosion, but she obviously hadn't seen it.

"Dead," Tyler said.

Stacy started to tremble as she recovered from her battle with Orr. Tyler held her hand, and they both caught their breath.

After a minute, Stacy said, "What do we do now?"

Tyler glanced at the bubbling cauldron of boiling water below. "As soon as he's awake, Orr either tells us where my father and your sister are or he's going for a swim."

SIXTY

Tyler dragged Orr's unconscious form down the stairs, one slow, painful step at a time. His chest injury barked at him, but he ignored the ache as best he could. Every fiber of his being wanted to stomp the life out of Orr for what the man had done to his father, but he had to keep Orr alive if he wanted to find Sherman, Carol, and the nuclear material.

"Get his bag," Tyler said to Stacy. "We may not have much time."

Orr's feet slapped against the steps until Tyler laid him out at the bottom. Stacy dropped his bag next to Gaul's. She turned and saw the motionless body.

"Oh, my God!" she cried when she saw the remains of Gaul's shattered skull.

"Just try to ignore it." Tyler had seen much worse in the Army. That didn't make the sight any more pleasant, but he didn't have time to worry about it. If Cavano had survived the explosion, she might arrive at the Midas chamber any minute, or Tyler and Stacy might run into her and her men on their way out. Neither option would end well if they didn't have anything to negotiate with. They'd be just as dead as if Orr had done it himself.

Tyler might also find himself bargaining for Grant's life if Cavano was holding him captive. The first step was to take stock of the chamber's contents so that he could develop a plan.

He bound Orr's wrists with the shoelaces from Gaul's boots, then rifled through Orr's pockets and took his Leatherman back. He tried checking Orr's cell phone to see what numbers he had called, but the phone was password-protected. Tyler would have to get Aiden to crack it. He took the canteen from Orr's belt and passed it to Stacy, who took a swig before giving it back.

As Tyler took a drink, Stacy asked, "How did you know that Orr was lying about my betraying you?"

Tyler wiped his mouth. "Two reasons. First, Orr knew how to find us at Piazza del Plebiscito. We went directly there from the well, and I was with you the whole time, so you had no chance to tell him where we were."

How Orr had known the correct well could be found at San Lorenzo Maggiore was easier. It was the last well they had visited. Orr knew they would stop searching after they'd located it.

"And the second reason?" Stacy asked.

"He had us photograph your phone with the geolabe. I thought it was odd at the time, but later I realized that he made us do it because the geolabe tracker and your phone were in two separate locations."

"My phone?" Stacy said with surprise.

"Mine was ruined when I got dunked in the river during the chase at Cavano's estate. Did you misplace your phone anytime in the last few weeks?"

Stacy looked away for a moment as she thought, then whipped her head back around. "Last week I was eating at a restaurant and I couldn't find my phone for about five minutes. A man sitting near me said he found it on the floor. At the time, I just thought it had slipped out of my purse."

Tyler nodded. "That's it. It only takes a few seconds to clone a SIM card. Orr had us duped from the very beginning, intentionally faking me out with the geolabe tracker. Then he used it to try to sow mistrust between us. I'm sorry I didn't tell you before now, but I wanted to keep him off guard."

"I understand," Stacy said with a smile. "I'm just glad you had faith in me."

She unzipped Gaul's duffel and nearly dropped it when she spied what was inside.

"Look at that," she said. Tyler saw three canisters of the binary explosive already connected to timing devices. It wasn't enough to destroy the whole cavern, but with the proper placement it could bring down a large section of the ceiling.

"Orr must have been planning to blow the entrance once he'd secured the Midas Touch so that no one else could get in."

"What a tragedy that would be." She handed Tyler a SIG Sauer pistol she found inside. "You'll probably want this."

"Thanks." He searched the rest of the bag, but with the Taser now in the water it was the only weapon available. Orr wasn't carrying a gun, having put all his trust in the explosive belts.

Tyler opened Orr's bag and saw the box with the golden hand inside. Next to it was a leather pouch. Tyler opened it to find an ancient book. The cover had no writing on it. He began to open it when Stacy stopped him.

"Don't," she said. "That's the Archimedes Codex. It's too fragile to handle. You might damage it more than Orr already has."

Tyler put it back in the pouch. He inventoried the rest of the bag's contents. Two full clear water bottles, one marked "Seawater" and the other marked "Fresh Water." Two sets of heavy rubber gloves. An empty plastic Tupperware container. And an older model digital video camera already loaded with a tape.

"What's that for?" Stacy said.

"If he was going to sell the Midas Touch, he'd want some clear evidence that he wasn't simply giving his buyer a dud. So he was probably going to film the chamber and the Midas Touch in operation."

Stacy nodded. "And when he got his sample, he'd show himself blowing up the only entrance to the chamber."

"He definitely covers all the bases."

Stacy looked at Orr's bleeding face. "Not all of them."

He handed the camera to Stacy. "Start filming."

"Why?"

"When we get back to the surface, we're going to need our own evidence to convince the Italian authorities that this really is down here."

"All right," Stacy said, "but I'm usually in front of the camera, not behind it." She took the camera to the center of the pit, opened the screen, and started filming. First, she panned around the chamber, then focused on the statue and the pedestal. She was careful to steer clear of the boiling water churning in the pool along the base of the terrace.

Tyler hoisted Orr's pack and started slapping his face.

"Wake up, sleepyhead."

With a groan, Orr began to stir, so Tyler rose and pointed the SIG at him. Orr's moan turned to a cry and his tied hands flew to his face.

"My eye! What did you do to me?"

"That's your fault. Now get up."

"I can't!"

"Quit your whining. I've seen soldiers in battle continue fighting with wounds that make your injury look like a paper cut."

Orr grimaced as he held his palm to his eye. "What do you want?"

"I want to know where my father and Carol Benedict are."

"You'll kill me if I tell you."

"I'll do worse if you don't."

Stacy was still filming the writing on the pedestal. "My God," she said.

Tyler didn't take his eyes off Orr. "What is it?"

"This tells Midas's whole story. How he got here, the curse of the golden touch, everything. Good God! This statue is his daughter."

"Midas probably wanted to spend eternity with her likeness."

"No, this isn't a statue *of* his daughter. This statue *is* his daughter. The writing says that he turned her to gold on purpose after she died to preserve her body for all time."

Tyler backed up so that he could keep an eye on Orr while he looked at the statue. She had been posed lying down, with her arms at her sides, a beautiful girl perhaps fourteen years old. Her eyes were closed, but he could see the pain in her face. She wore a robe that was just as golden as she was, and her left hand was sawed cleanly from her wrist.

"Document everything. Tell me the rest of the story later."

Tyler went back over to Orr and gave him a light kick. "I think it's time we introduced ourselves to Midas. Come with me."

Orr staggered to his feet, his hands still covering his eye. Tyler nodded toward the stairs. Orr trudged over and climbed toward Midas's coffin. Stacy followed them and continued to film.

When they got to the top of the terrace, Tyler stopped, shocked at what the sarcophagus had hidden from view up to this point. A skeleton lay on the floor, still clad in shirt, jeans, and shoes, the bones a spotless white, the clothes disintegrating. The skull was fractured.

Tyler remembered the story Cavano had told him about the fight between the men. One of them got his head bashed in. The other died after touching the body of Midas and falling into the water.

"This one of the men who chased you?" Tyler asked Orr.

He nodded.

"Here's the other one," Stacy said, pointing over the side of the terrace.

Tyler looked down and saw a body at the bottom of the roiling pool. Like the girl, this corpse had been transformed into solid gold, clothes and all.

Stacy got a shot of both the body and the skeleton. "Why did the guy in the water turn to gold but this one didn't?"

"Because he wasn't exposed to the Midas Touch and then submerged in the hot spring," Tyler said. "And in this heat the bacteria inside the skeleton guy's body had a smorgasbord once he died. He probably rotted away in a couple of months."

"Then the walls couldn't have turned to gold on their own."

"Isn't it obvious?" Orr said. "Midas did it before he died. He must have touched the walls and then sprayed them with the water from the hot spring."

Tyler thought about the golden tendrils at the entrance. That would explain why the gold petered out there.

"There's only one way to find out if you're right," Tyler said. He pointed to the corner. "Now go over there and kneel with your hands on your head." Orr hesitated. "Do it!"

Orr complied and got on his knees. His right eye was now swollen shut. He kept the good one intently focused on them. Tyler had no doubt that he was just waiting to take any opportunity to gain the upper hand, and a small part of Tyler wished he would try.

"Make one move and I'll kill you."

"No, you won't," Orr said. "You need me alive."

"Okay. I'll shoot you in the kneecaps. So stay there if you ever want to walk without a limp."

Orr said nothing, but he understood. Tyler turned back to the coffin, but he adjusted his position to make sure he kept Orr in his sight the entire time.

The sarcophagus rested on a golden support platform about three feet high near the edge of the terrace above the boiling pool. Tyler ran his hand over the intricately carved lid. Something felt odd, and he pressed into the gold. Instead of the hard metal surface he was expecting, it gave under his push.

He had been considering how to open the lid. If it had been solid gold, it would have weighed hundreds of pounds. But now he realized that the coffin wasn't pure gold. It was made of wood. The gold leaf was merely a protective covering.

Tyler unfolded his Leatherman knife and drew it across the platform supporting the wooden sarcophagus. Gold flaked off in several spots, revealing tuff underneath.

Stacy knelt to get a better look, focusing the camera on the slash. "So the pedestal, the walls—everything is just gold leaf?"

"Apparently only organic substances are completely transformed into gold, and even then they would have to be completely submerged in the hot spring for a significant length of time. That would explain why the coffin is only gold leaf. The only substantial amount of gold in this room is in the two dead bodies."

"As I told you," Orr said, still on his knees in the corner, "the real value is the Midas Touch itself."

"Yes, you told me," Tyler said. "Good for you."

"Should we see if it really works?" Stacy asked.

Tyler nodded, handing one set of the rubber gloves from Orr's pack to Stacy. "We'll need to be careful. Remember, according to Cavano the drug runner was poisoned by whatever he touched in the coffin."

They put the gloves on. The lid wasn't hinged, so they lifted it from either end and leaned it against the side.

The mummified corpse of King Midas grinned at them, the skin stretched taught over his leathery withered cheeks. He was wrapped in regal purple robes, and a gold crown adorned with rubies and sapphires capped his head. One desiccated hand lay across his chest, but the other was twisted at his side. Each finger was encircled with a magnificent gold and jeweled ring.

Orr and Cavano's pursuer must have grabbed the hand, eager to take the rings off, but when he brushed against Midas's skin, he released the hand before he could remove the rings, and the lid dropped back down.

Orr strained to see. "Is it Midas?"

"He's here, all right," Tyler said. "In the flesh, so to speak."

"He must have spent months or years preparing this chamber

and ordered his loyal servants to place him here after his death," Stacy said. "Then they closed up the chamber behind them."

Tyler rummaged through the sack and took out the two full water bottles.

He needed an object to test. He turned and saw the skeleton of the Italian drug runner, whose shoes were still intact. The nylon shoelaces would be perfect. Tyler untied one of the shoes and unlaced it.

He took both ends and rubbed them on Midas's hand.

"Open the bottles," Tyler said. Stacy started with the seawater bottle.

Tyler dipped the shoelace into the water while Stacy filmed. Within seconds, a blush of gold encrusted the tip of the lace. They repeated the steps with the gold-bearing fresh water. This time the effect was even greater, because the solution had a stronger concentration of gold than the seawater. Tyler took the golden lace out and marveled as the water dripped from it.

Stacy gaped at it. "My God! It works!"

"Incredible," Tyler said. He wouldn't have believed it if he hadn't seen it for himself, and he knew others might feel the same.

"Let's take a sample to test when we get back," he said. "Take that Tupperware container out and open it." Stacy hadn't yet touched anything, so her gloves were clean.

While she got the container, Tyler took a breath and ripped Midas's hand off, rings and all. He dropped it in the empty container, and Stacy put the lid back on. He removed his gloves as carefully as he could to avoid exposure to the microbes and set them aside. Stacy took her gloves off as well.

Tyler held up the laces for Orr to see. "This is what you were searching for," he said. "I hope it drives you nuts coming so close and not getting it."

"Nothing has changed except for who's holding the gun," Orr said. "We can still make a deal for the information you want."

"The only deal I'm going to make with you is that I will guarantee you a short, miserable life if anything happens to Sherman or Carol."

"That's too bad, because now you're too late."

"Really? Why's that?"

Orr smiled and nodded behind Tyler.

He turned to see Gia Cavano silently entering the cavern. Behind her was a man with a submachine gun pointed at Grant's head.

SIXTY-ONE

Cavano didn't care if Tyler and Stacy were helping Orr by choice or against their will. She knew Orr well enough to believe that he had taken Tyler's and Stacy's relatives hostage, but that didn't make her inclined to share the treasure with anyone. If she let them go, the Italian authorities would be on her before she could get a tenth of the gold out.

With her submachine gun, she opened fire, but Tyler and Stacy dove behind the golden coffin, bullets pinging off the wall behind them. None of the shots were aimed at Orr, who flattened himself on the floor. She wanted him alive. A bullet to the head was too good for him.

Tyler didn't return fire with the pistol Cavano had seen him holding. He obviously wouldn't want to hurt his friend. Sal stood behind Grant, using him as a shield.

The astounding golden chamber was just as she remembered it, except for the dead body in the pit below, its head a mess of gore. Cavano was already drenched from the humidity that condensed on her skin.

She noticed Orr's bloody face and called across the long chamber. "I see you've done all of the hard work for me, Dr. Locke."

"You okay, Tyler?" Grant said.

"Not bad," Tyler yelled from behind the coffin. "How about you?"

"Your warning worked for me, but three of Cavano's men used up their nine lives."

"And for killing my men," she said, "Jordan has earned the most painful death I can possibly imagine."

"Listen, Gia," Tyler said. "I think the one thing we can agree on is that we all want Orr dead. But right now I need him alive."

"Yes, Grant told us why you have been such a thorn in my side for the last few days. Good to see you again, Jordan. I hope you're in pain."

"You can't kill me, Gia," Orr said. "The gold isn't worth what you think it is."

"If it's only a few billion dollars, I think I'll be fine."

"It's not. It's a few million."

"Shut up, Orr!" Tyler yelled.

In the face of so much gold, Cavano laughed, and Sal joined in.

"I'm serious," Orr said. "Scratch the wall next to you. You'll see that the gold is only a few millimeters thick."

Cavano looked at Sal, who shrugged. *Was her whole assessment of the treasure that far off?* She dragged the nose of her gun across the wall. She stared in horror when it left a gouge of gray tuff behind.

"The statue is solid gold," she said. "I know it is."

"The statue is, but the pedestal isn't," Orr said. "The girl might weigh a few hundred pounds. You'd clear twenty million euros at best. I know your business is in much deeper debt than that."

He was right. The purchase of the Ministry of Health building had exhausted her organization's funds. Without a major influx of cash, she would be at the mercy of the other Camorra clans, who would sweep in and gobble up her budding empire.

"How about I share a billion dollars with you?"

She frowned. "What do you mean?"

"I have an auction planned for the Midas Touch."

"Thanks for the offer, but I can find my own buyer."

"Not the group I have assembled. I'm the only one they'll trust."

Cavano paused. "And why should *I* trust you?"

"You don't have to. You can come with me to the auction. We'll split the payment into two accounts. If I'm lying about the deal, you can kill me then. But if I'm not, you go your way and I go my way. Forget about this whole vendetta thing and we'll both be superrich."

Cavano walked back and whispered to Sal in Italian. "What do you think?"

"It looks like he's right about the wall," Sal whispered back.

She nodded. Later she would figure out how to get her vengeance, but for now she couldn't afford to risk killing Orr. She was about to agree to his terms when Tyler called out.

"One problem with your plan, Gia! I'm right behind the coffin. I can dump Midas's body into that pool in three seconds, and then you'll have nothing. Once it's in the water, the body will turn to gold in a matter of hours, and the microbes that are responsible for the Midas Touch will disappear forever."

"You do that and Grant is dead."

"We're dead anyway, so you better cut me in on Orr's deal, too."

Cavano thought about it. She had no desire to cut anybody else in on the deal, but she couldn't lose the Midas Touch, either.

"All right," she said. "But I want to see a working sample first."

"Do we have a deal?"

"I swear on my husband's grave."

After about thirty seconds of silence, Tyler said, "All right. You come down to the pit. I'll keep an eye on Orr, and Stacy will bring the sample down to you. You try anything and I'll kill Orr and dump Midas into the water. Then nobody gets anything. Sound good?"

Perfect, Cavano thought. "Sounds good. We're coming down. If Stacy tries anything, she dies first. Then Grant. Then you."

She whispered into Sal's ear again. "When I'm sure we've got it, kill Grant, then Tyler. I'll take care of Stacy."

Sal nodded.

Cavano had lied when she swore on her husband's grave, but she was a good Catholic. To her way of thinking, it was nothing that a few minutes in the confessional wouldn't take care of.

SIXTY-TWO

Stacy tried not to shake as she walked down the steps carrying the container with Midas's hand inside. She was more afraid of the Midas Touch than she was of Cavano.

When Stacy got to the bottom of the stairs, Cavano was waiting for her, a black automatic rifle aimed at her. Sal was behind his boss on the other side of the pedestal, with his own gun leveled at Grant.

"Put it down," Cavano said.

Stacy stopped and put the container on the floor. She turned to go back up the steps.

"Wait!" Cavano yelled. "Leave the gloves."

Stacy gulped. She carefully removed the gloves by the fingers and laid them down next to the container.

"Now back away, but don't go up the stairs."

Stacy did as she was told, her heart pounding. She didn't know what the next few seconds were going to bring, so she had to be ready for anything.

Cavano put her hand in her pocket and took out a twenty-euro note. Smart, Stacy thought. Easy to rub the microbe onto and dip into the pool to test it.

Cavano put the gun down and donned the left glove first and then the right one. She picked up the container and was about to open it when she got a puzzled look on her face. She peered at her hands with dismay. Too late, Cavano realized that it was she who'd been tricked.

Tyler had seen the opportunity when Cavano insisted on testing the Midas Touch herself. He whispered his plan to Stacy as they were shielded from Cavano by the coffin. With Stacy's uncontaminated right-hand glove turned inside out, Tyler quickly rubbed Midas's hand on the fingertips of the glove. He then gently pulled the glove right side out using his Leatherman pliers, careful not to touch the inside lining. Stacy had put the glove on delicately, making sure to ball up her fist so that her fingers wouldn't touch the microbes.

That was why she'd been so terrified. She was deathly afraid that her hand would slip and make contact with the Midas Touch.

Cavano had been unable to detect the subterfuge, and had assumed the gloves were safe because Stacy had been wearing them. Now Stacy could see the mixture of fear and pain on her face as she endured the toxic side effect of the Midas Touch.

Cavano dropped the container and inadvertently kicked it behind her past the pedestal in her desperation to tear off the gloves. She held up her hands, and Stacy could already see the blisters forming on her fingers.

"What's the matter?" Sal said.

"Kill them!" Cavano screamed as she dove for her gun. "Kill them all!"

Cavano's cry was Grant's cue. He'd been patiently waiting for something like it ever since Cavano took him captive.

Sal raised his gun to fire at Tyler, but Grant charged him. Sal got off a wild volley of shots, and Grant couldn't tell if they'd hit anything. Sal brought the gun down to smash Grant, but not fast enough. Grant aimed his head at Sal's midsection like a battering ram and knocked him backward.

Sal's mammoth frame absorbed the blow without falling. He continued to fire shots, and Grant could feel the hot barrel against his shirt. He grabbed for the gun. They wrestled for it face-to-face, each determined to shoot the other.

Tyler hit the deck when Sal's gun blazed at him. Stacy raced up the stairs to get out of the line of fire, but Cavano already had the submachine gun in her hands. Tyler covered Stacy's retreat by snapping off three quick shots with the pistol. He had only one magazine, so rounds would soon become a precious commodity.

Although Tyler missed Cavano, his shots made her duck for cover behind the pedestal in the pit. She fired off random bursts that hit nothing but wall.

Stacy ran along the terrace, but she didn't dive behind the sarcophagus as Tyler had expected. Instead she lunged for Orr's legs, missing them by inches.

While Tyler had been engaged in the firefight with Cavano, Orr had taken the opportunity to grab his pack from behind Tyler and was running for the opposite end of the terrace, trying to make an escape. Stacy popped back up and gave chase.

Tyler took aim at Orr, but he didn't shoot. He couldn't risk killing Orr until he knew where his father and Stacy's sister were.

More shots came from Cavano, and Tyler could do nothing more than turn to lay down covering fire for Stacy.

When the shooting started, Orr's first thought was that this was even better than he had been expecting. They were all fighting one another, and he saw his chance to slip out.

While Tyler returned fire, Orr scrambled over and grabbed his bag, which held the golden hand, the Archimedes Codex, and the video camera. His hands were still bound, but he was mobile. He planned to get off the terrace by jumping over the pool.

Then Stacy had seen what he was doing. She knocked him down, but he kicked her in the stomach. His depth perception was gone, or he would have hit her with a more crushing blow. Still, it was enough, and she went down clutching her belly.

Orr got back up and took a running leap from the terrace. The pool was narrowest in this part of the pit, maybe only ten feet across. He soared into space and landed just inches beyond the edge of the steaming water.

He rolled and saw his target: the container with Midas's hand. Its exterior was uncontaminated. He scooped it up and stuffed it into his pack.

Orr used the chaos of the gunfight to dig into Gaul's duffel, still lying against the wall near the water spout. A few button pushes, and he ran for the stairs to the exit tunnel.

He thought ten seconds should be plenty of time.

Cavano knew she didn't have long for this world, and she wasn't going out cowering behind some monument to death. Her right hand burned so much from the Midas Touch that she could do no more than prop the gun up with her wrist, shooting left-handed.

She felt as if her veins had been injected with molten lava. If she was going to die, she would take Stacy Benedict and Tyler Locke with her.

After awkwardly slamming another magazine into the gun and racking the bolt, she stood and fired at Tyler's position. As she stumbled for the stairs, nearly blind from the pain, she kept firing bursts, hoping to hit someone, anyone.

She took the steps two at a time, but her stomach suddenly spasmed, and her head pounded in agony, as if an animal were tearing it apart from the inside. She collapsed at the top step, her finger clenching the trigger back until the gun was empty.

Grant was pinned against the pedestal holding the statue, Sal's submachine gun choking the life out of him.

Sal was one of the few men Grant had ever met who actually had a weight advantage, and the Italian used it. He leaned his bulk into the gun, and Grant's vision began to tunnel.

They were near the corner of the pedestal. If Grant could just work his way a few more inches to his left, he could use Sal's weight against him.

He edged over with a few solid lunges. One more should do it. Grant could see almost nothing at this point, but he felt the open space to his side.

With his last bit of strength, he jostled left and fell backward. Sal couldn't keep from falling forward.

Grant thrust his legs upward and tossed Sal's body over his head. With a howl, Sal went sliding and rolling along the floor. The slick surface gave him no purchase, and before he could stop himself he splashed into the boiling water.

Despite the heat, Grant's blood chilled as Sal's primal scream echoed through the chamber before gurgling to silence.

Stacy scrambled to her feet after she saw Orr leap over the pool. She rushed to the edge of the terrace, but the lanterns had all gone askew by this point. The odd shadows cast made it difficult to see what he was doing, but she did see him grab the container with Midas's hand.

Then for a few seconds Orr knelt by the wall, where he rummaged through Gaul's duffel, his hands still tied together. When he was finished, he picked up his backpack and ran as fast as he could for the stairs exiting the chamber.

A horrible scream registered in Stacy's ears, but it was in the background with the last of the gunfire. She was too focused on the bag where Orr had knelt before escaping into the tunnel.

Then she realized what Orr had been doing. Gaul's duffel. The explosives. The timed detonators she and Tyler had found.

Oh, no.

In the center of the pit, Grant was about to emerge from behind the pedestal.

"Get back!" she yelled. "There's a bomb!"

She turned, but Tyler was right behind her. With all her strength, she shoved him down, and the world exploded.

SIXTY-THREE

For a few moments, Tyler couldn't figure out what had happened. His ears were assaulted by a roar that seemed to come from everywhere.

When he could remember his name, he pushed himself up. Two of the lanterns were still working. He looked around and saw Stacy lying facedown. She wasn't moving.

She had saved him. If he'd been standing when the explosive detonated, he would have been pulverized against the far wall.

He gently turned her over. Blood spilled from her side. A shrapnel wound. He lifted her shirt and saw a gash three inches long. He ripped his shirt tail off and pressed it against the wound. He couldn't tell how deep it was.

Her eyes fluttered open.

"My side hurts," she said, her voice more annoyed than anything else.

"I know. But you'll be all right."

"How do you know that?"

"Because you're a tough woman. Now be quiet and hold this down. I'm going to see if Grant is okay."

He got one of the lanterns and went to the edge. He shined it down and saw Grant laid out behind the pedestal on the side away from the explosion.

"Grant! Get up!"

He heard a moan in response. "Can't a guy rest for a minute?"

Tyler's hearing was coming back. He thought the rushing sound in his ears was the residual effects of the explosion, but it was getting louder. He looked down and saw a crack in the wall, and water gushing through it. The pool started to overflow, and the boiling water streamed across the floor, right at Grant.

"Grant!" Tyler yelled. "Get your ass onto the pedestal right now!"

The crack blew open, and water poured into the pit.

Grant had gotten to his feet and saw the water rushing toward him. He scrambled up onto the pedestal and didn't stop until he was sitting atop the statue. The water splashed against the side, but he was far enough above it to escape injury. However, it would be only a matter of time before he was swamped, and he would suffer the same agonizing death as Sal.

For that matter, they all would.

A shout from across the chamber got his attention. "Tyler! I thought you'd be dead."

It was Orr. He had returned, and he'd been able to remove the shoelaces binding his wrists. Tyler didn't know whether he'd come back to make sure they'd all been killed or to gloat.

"This isn't over, Orr," Tyler said.

"Looks like it is to me. Then again, you could try to swim across, but that might be a little painful." The water was already three feet deep and rising fast.

"Before I leave you to your doom and lock you in here for another two thousand years," Orr continued, "I thought you might like to know that your father's dead. So is Carol Benedict."

"You son of a bitch!"

"Yeah, they've been dead since I first saw you this evening, and now you get to think about that for the rest of your short, miserable life while I'm off to enjoy my spoils." He pointed at his eye. "And this? It's nothing that a little plastic surgery won't fix. Ciao!"

He smiled a shit-eating grin, waved a salute, and was gone, sure that Tyler would soon be a distant memory.

SIXTY-FOUR

Tyler wasn't going to give up that easily. Orr should have known that by now.

Wading or swimming through boiling acidic water was a death sentence, but Tyler wasn't going to swim. He had a boat.

He ran over to the gilded wooden sarcophagus and tipped it over to lighten the load.

"Sorry, Your Majesty," he said as Midas's corpse tumbled out over the edge of the terrace and into the water. He flipped it back over and heaved the lid onto it.

He had to push the sarcophagus down the stairs, but Cavano's body was in the way. Tyler grasped her jacket, careful not to touch the flaming-red skin that now covered her entire body like a rash, and pulled her until she was clear. He put her back down, and her eyes popped open, the bloodshot orbs nearly bursting from the sockets. Her face was contorted in agony.

"Wa . . . water," she wheezed.

Tyler hesitated, but he couldn't refuse the dying woman's last request. He retrieved the canteen and tipped it so that water dribbled into her mouth. She swallowed, then gagged, and some of it streamed down her cheek.

"Is Orr . . . dead?" she croaked.

"No," Tyler said. "But I'll catch him."

She coughed, barely able to force the words out. "You won't. You won't find Jordan Orr."

"Why not?"

"Because he's named for his grandfather." Her breath caught. "His real name . . . is Giordano . . . Orsini."

Her eyes widened as the pain overwhelmed her. She shrieked, but no sound came out. Her head lolled to the side, and her final breath rushed out. She was dead.

But she got her wish to be the golden girl. The rivulet of water on her cheek left a streak of gold. She would be immortalized in the metal when the chamber was submerged.

"Uh, Tyler?" Grant said. "You might want to hurry before I turn into a three-minute egg."

So would the rest of them if he didn't act fast. The water was already four feet deep.

Tyler pushed the coffin toward the stairs, his rib protesting the entire way. When the coffin was at the bottom step, he left it there and went back for Stacy.

"Can you walk?" he said.

Stacy nodded as tears streamed down her face. She had heard Orr's news about her sister.

He helped her to her feet, and she went ashen from the head-rush. He threw her arm over his shoulder and carried her to the sarcophagus.

They got on top of its lid, and it sank until the top bobbed only six inches above the surface of the water.

Tyler took off his T-shirt, wrapped it around Cavano's contaminated gun, and used the stock as a paddle, rowing as fast as he could.

When he got to the pedestal, there was only a foot of clearance left.

"We'll sink to the bottom if my fat ass gets on there with you," Grant said.

He was right. Tyler kept padding. "I'll push it back to you."

Tyler rowed as fast as he could until he was at the steps leading up to the exit. He helped Stacy off. She was barely able to move on her own. When she was safely out of harm's way, Tyler laid the gun on top and used his foot to shove the coffin back to Grant.

He dragged Stacy up to the top of the stairs and laid her down.

"A little help!" Grant shouted.

Tyler went back to the railing and saw that Grant was foundering. The coffin was sinking. Cavano must have put a bullet hole in it. Grant wasn't going to make it to the stairs.

Tyler searched around him and saw Stacy's explosive belt. He picked it up by the end and lowered it over the railing.

"Come this way!" he yelled. "Hurry!"

Grant rowed like an Olympic sculling champion. When the coffin was near the wall, he stood and reached for the belt. He supported himself with it using his feet to scrabble up the wall.

Tyler strained to hold on to the belt under the weight of Grant's 260 pounds. With one last heave he jerked backward, and Grant caught the top of the railing with his hand just as the top of the sarcophagus went under.

A searing pain stabbed Tyler's side as the rib finally snapped. He ground his molars trying not to cry out. Grant heaved himself over the railing.

"Thanks," Grant said. "You okay, man?"

Tyler talked through gritted teeth. "Just get Stacy." He took a breath and stood, taking one last look at the smashed geolabe lying forgotten on the stairs, being covered by the rising water.

He staggered behind Grant as they saw the pumice barrier rising. Orr thought he had penned them in, but it had risen too slowly. There were still two feet of space left.

Grant went over, and Tyler struggled to pass Stacy through. Once she was safe, he used the last of his strength to tumble over the barrier into the cool air of the exterior tunnel.

Tyler staggered to his knees and lay down on his side, not sure if he'd ever get up again.

SIXTY-FIVE

Because Tyler was sucking wind and Grant had to support Stacy as they walked, there was no chance for either of them to catch up with Orr, but at least they could find their way out using his markings.

The tunnel maze seemed to go on forever, but Tyler knew they were getting close to the entry well when they passed three bodies that were burned and mangled by the phosphorus grenades. Tyler, still shirtless, considered taking one of the men's jackets, but he thought that wearing a burned piece of clothing from a dead man would be even worse than being naked.

Orr had been so sure he'd killed Tyler that he hadn't bothered to cut the rope that still dangled at the bottom of the cistern. Grant went up first, while Tyler put Stacy in a harness. Grant pulled her up and then helped Tyler get to the top. By the time they reached the surface, it was midnight.

None of them had a phone, except for Orr's, and because of the password protection Tyler couldn't use it to call out.

While Grant went to find a working phone, Tyler held Stacy in his lap. She was barely conscious. Her face was pale, and she'd lost a lot of blood. They'd bandaged her up as best they could, but the walk had been hard on her. Tyler stroked her hair.

Her eyes fluttered open. For a second, she couldn't focus, then she recognized Tyler's face.

"Hey, I thought I was dead for a minute there," she said weakly. "Is that the moon?"

Tyler looked up and saw a full moon shining brightly through the clear sky. He instinctively inhaled a deep breath of warm night air, but he stopped when pain convulsed his chest.

"That's the moon," he said. "We made it out."

"Good. I hated that place."

Tyler smiled.

A look of alarm suddenly bloomed on her face. "Where's Orr?"

Fresh anger welled up, but Tyler tamped it down. "Don't worry. We'll track him down."

Stacy closed her eyes and sobbed. "Carol. Carol's gone."

"Shh. Don't talk. Save your strength." Tyler was still in a state of disbelief. The first of the five stages of grief. A part of Tyler hated himself for being so analytical, even now.

Not that he lacked emotion. Every time he pictured Orr's face, pure hatred flowed through him. He didn't hate many people. Sometimes he hated himself, like now, when he'd failed so totally. But Orr had earned it, and Tyler swore he would track Orr down if it took him the rest of his life.

He completely understood the powerful need for vengeance. It was appropriate that he'd found it in Italy, so famous for its blood-soaked vendettas.

Grant came trotting back toward them with a cell phone triumphantly held in his hand.

"I got emergency services," he said. "An ambulance is on the way. I told them it was a heart attack so the police wouldn't come right away."

"Where'd you get the phone?"

"Some kid on the street. I saw him talking on it. He told me to buzz off until I offered to trade my Rolex for it. He spoke English, so he helped me with the operator."

He handed the phone to Tyler, who dialed Miles Benson's number, one of the few he had memorized. He prayed that Miles would answer the unfamiliar number.

He did, on the second ring.

"Miles Benson," he said in his curt tone.

"Miles, it's Tyler." He could hear the exhaustion in his own voice.

"Tyler? I've been trying to reach you for hours! Where the hell are you?"

"I'm in Naples with Grant. Stacy's badly injured, but we've got an ambulance coming. Miles, I think my father is dead."

"Dead? Jesus. Last time I heard, the general was just coming out of surgery at George Washington University Hospital. Doctors said he'd be in critical condition for a while, but they expected him to make a full recovery."

For the first time in hours, Tyler felt a surge of energy. "He's not dead? You're sure?"

"I know what I heard."

"What about Carol Benedict?"

"Scared, but she didn't have a scratch on her."

"Thank God!" Tyler said. He lowered the phone. "Stacy, it's all right. Carol's safe."

"Carol?" she said, her eyes flashing open. "She's okay?"

Tyler nodded, and this time Stacy wept tears of joy before her eyes closed again. He put the phone back to his ear.

"Miles, Orr is still alive. Did you find the nuclear material?"

"No," Miles said, "but the FBI confirmed that the site where we found your dad had unusual levels of radioactivity."

Damn. Sometimes he hated being right. But not often.

"Have you found anything else?"

"No, the investigation is just getting under way."

"Tell them to keep an eye out for a Giordano Orsini."

"Orsini? Who the hell is that?"

"I think it's Jordan Orr's birth name. Have the FBI flag him in case he tries to get back into the U.S. And he has an injured right eye."

"Will do, but they're pretty fixated on some Muslims for the explosion."

"What explosion?" Tyler heard sirens wailing, getting closer. "Never mind. You can tell me on the plane. Can you have the pilots fly the Gordian jet down here from Rome? We'll meet them at the Naples airport." Tyler and Grant had made the right decision leaving their passports in the plane. The last thing they needed was a hassle getting back into the U.S.

"Sure. I'll get on it." Miles hung up.

The sirens got the attention of the resident priest, who brought Tyler a shirt from the church's donation pile. A minute later, two EMTs carrying a stretcher came into the cloisters. Grant handled the priest, while Tyler dealt with the EMTs. They didn't speak much English, but they made it clear that they'd been expecting a heart attack victim, not somebody with a bleeding wound.

He eased Stacy onto the stretcher with the EMTs' help. She looked in bad shape, but still beautiful.

As they strapped Stacy down and rebandaged her, the motion woke her.

"What's happening?" she said.

"You're going to the hospital." He held her hand. "We can't come with you."

The police might get involved, and then there would be questions and delays. Tyler and Grant needed to get back to the U.S. and help stop whatever Orr had in mind.

"I wish I could go with you," Stacy said, her voice a thin reed. "You get him for me."

"We will."

"Tell my sister I love her."

"You'll tell her yourself."

"Kiss for luck?"

Tyler smiled. He leaned down and kissed her softly. Her lips burned with heat, but they welcomed his touch.

He pulled away and said, "You won't need luck. You'll be fine." Given her condition, he wasn't sure about that, but what else could he say?

"The luck isn't for me," she said. "It's for you."

She slipped into unconsciousness. Tyler and Grant followed her to the ambulance and stayed there until she was safely on her way.

Then, before the *polizia* arrived, they walked to the nearest busy street and hailed a cab. Within two hours, they were winging their way toward Washington, hoping they could find Orr before he detonated his nuclear weapon.

MONDAY

VENDETTA

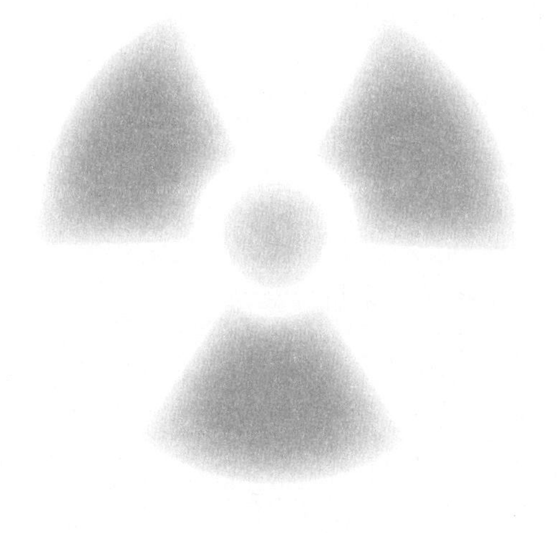

SIXTY-SIX

Twelve hours later, Tyler was in his father's ICU room getting his ribs wrapped by a nurse. He didn't know if they were broken, because he'd refused an X-ray. His father was still intubated and continued to float in and out of consciousness during his recovery. Even lying there unconscious, with tubes hanging out of him, General Sherman Locke looked powerful, as if he would wake up any moment, rip the sensors off, and take charge.

Tyler had slept fitfully on the plane ride home. He felt guilty about leaving Stacy behind, his father wasn't out of danger yet, and Orr still preyed on his mind. If Orr got away only to cause a catastrophe on American soil, Tyler would never forgive himself.

Just before the Gordian jet landed in D.C., he received an update from Aiden, who had been researching any info he could find on Orr's birth name. Aiden had discovered a Giordano Orsini from Connecticut who would be the same age as Jordan Orr. Orsini's parents had been killed in a car wreck when the boy was ten, and the short newspaper article intimated that the crash might have been a murder-suicide. At Tyler's request, Aiden was following up to see if there was more to the story, but it was really in the FBI's hands now.

When the nurse was finished, Tyler put his shirt back on. At least on the plane he and Grant had been able to get a fresh change of clothes, but they both still stank. The compression bandage eased the ache in Tyler's chest, but he'd turned down painkillers. Not only did most meds leave him nauseated, but he didn't want his senses dulled. He could stand the pain until he was sure they had Orr in custody, assuming the one-eyed wonder was stupid enough to try to get back into the country.

Before he had tried to get some rest on the flight, Tyler had a long talk with Miles about Sherman's escape from the warehouse and how he saved Carol Benedict and the two Muslim fall guys. The body found in the building's wreckage still hadn't been identified but was assumed to be one of Orr's accomplices. Tyler told Miles about Gaul in the hope that the FBI might be able to use the link to track down Orr.

Grant knocked on the door.

"Hey," he said. He glanced at Sherman's inert form. "How's he doing?"

"Still out."

"Well, if you have a minute, I've got two FBI agents here. I've told them what I know, but they want to talk to you."

"Sure. Will you keep an eye on my dad?"

"No problem."

Tyler left the room and found a man and a woman in pressed suits standing outside. Only FBI agents could look so fresh at 6 A.M.

Tyler held out his hand. "Tyler Locke."

"Dr. Locke," the man said, "I'm Special Agent Riegert, and this is my partner, Special Agent Immel. Is your father going to be okay?"

"We think so."

"Has he said anything?"

"He can't. He's got a tube down his throat. Where's Carol Benedict?"

"She's already on her way to Naples to see her sister."

Tyler was itching for news about Stacy's condition, but he hadn't been able to get an update from the hospital because he wasn't a relative.

Riegert flipped open a notepad. "Your friend Mr. Westfield told me quite a story. Care to give me your side?"

On the way back, Grant and Tyler had agreed to tell most of the tale but to leave out the parts that made them seem like criminals themselves, such as the incident in Munich and the heist at the Athens museum.

Tyler told the agents about the ferry puzzle, their investigation leading them to Gia Cavano, and the fight in the tunnels under Naples.

Despite the same story from both Grant and Tyler, Riegert and Immel were clearly skeptical.

"And you don't have this geolabe anymore?" Immel said.

Tyler shook his head. "It's underwater in the Midas chamber."

"And you don't have any visual record of this chamber?"

"We did, but Orr got away with it."

"You mean the man you're also calling Giordano Orsini?" Riegert asked.

"Yes. Any luck finding him?"

"We're looking into all possibilities right now, Dr. Locke."

"How could you think Orr isn't responsible for my father's abduction?" Tyler said. "Miles told me you found evidence of radioactive material at the warehouse fire, and you have the proof-of-life videos we sent."

Riegert put up his hands in a conciliatory gesture. "We are taking you seriously, Dr. Locke. Your credentials are beyond reproach. But you have to admit that your story does sound far-fetched. And, with two Muslim men involved, don't you think radical fundamentalists are the more likely culprits here?"

"They're innocent. I'm telling you, Orr is going to set off a radiological device somewhere in the U.S., and it might very well be today."

"But why?" Immel said. "Where? What's his plan?"

"I can think of half a dozen sites," Tyler said. "D.C., New York,

Chicago, Fort Knox, Philadelphia. Anything within a twelve-hour driving range."

"That's the entire eastern seaboard," Riegert said.

"That's why you need to have every immigration terminal flagging both his aliases."

"We're doing that."

"And what else?"

"We're not at liberty to say."

Tyler sighed. "I don't know what else I can do for you, then."

Grant appeared at the door. "Tyler, your father just woke up."

Grant stepped aside as Tyler rushed into the room and went to the bed. Sherman's eyes were open, but half-lidded. When he saw Tyler, he held his hand up.

Tyler thought he wanted reassurance, so he took it in his own hand.

"I'm here, Dad."

Sherman wriggled out of his grip. So much for sentimentality.

Then Tyler realized that he wasn't reaching out to his son. He was trying to sign.

His arms were weak, but he put them up long enough for Tyler to make out the two signs he was making.

At first Tyler thought his father was hallucinating, but Sherman repeated the sign. *Blue truck?*

Tyler turned to see Riegert and Immel standing in the doorway.

"Was there a truck at the warehouse?" he asked them.

Riegert narrowed his eyes. "How do you know that?"

"My father knows sign language. He just told me that the truck is blue."

Riegert got his notepad out again. "Anything else?"

"Dad, can you remember anything else about the truck?"

Sherman made a slight nod. He used his left hand to spell out letters.

W I L B I X.

"Wilbix?" Tyler said. Another nod.

Grant plugged the word into the search engine on his replacement smartphone.

"Top find is Wilbix Construction," he said.

"Dad, is it Wilbix Construction?" Another nod. Sherman patted Tyler's hand and fell unconscious again.

"Where is Wilbix based?" Tyler asked Grant.

"New York," Grant said. "Oh, man."

Riegert tried to see Grant's screen. "What?"

"Wilbix Construction is doing work at New York Downtown Hospital. That's less than a mile from Wall Street."

Immel already had her phone out. "This guy might be trying to detonate the bomb in lower Manhattan?" she asked.

"Possibly," Grant said. "Maybe this has something to do with his parents' deaths."

"How?" Riegert said.

"I don't know, but we need to get to New York," Tyler told them. "Grant and I can identify Orr."

"I'll see how fast we can get a plane," Immel said, looking at her phone contacts.

"That's okay," Tyler said. "I have my own."

SIXTY-SEVEN

After Orr found an all-night infirmary to bandage his eye, even getting an old-fashioned black eyepatch in the process, he indulged in hiring a charter flight back to the U.S. from the Rome airport with the last of his funds. His phone was underwater in the Midas chamber, so before his flight left he found an Internet terminal and e-mailed Crenshaw that he was on his way to Newark.

With Tyler, Stacy, Grant, and Cavano dead, the Midas chamber sealed up again, and the warehouse destroyed, there was almost no evidence left of Orr's true identity and his connection to the Midas Touch. Crenshaw was the final loose end to tie up, and Orr would take care of him after he exacted his vengeance on the smug investment-banking firms of Wall Street and all who profited from their greed.

Crenshaw picked him up at Newark Airport at seven in the morning in a taxi. The weather was bright and clear, with only a slight breeze. Without a word, they rode to a truck stop where the semi was parked.

When they got into the truck, Crenshaw looked at Orr's eye and said, "What happened to you?"

"Accident. Don't worry about it."

"Let's see the Midas Touch."

Orr reluctantly opened the pack and held up the container with Midas's desiccated hand inside.

"That's it? I was expecting rays to be shooting out of it or something."

Orr had to admit that it looked less than impressive.

"Believe me," he said, "it works."

"I *don't* believe you. You have proof?"

Orr gave him the camera, which Crenshaw hooked up to his laptop. He played back the video that Stacy had shot. Even on a tiny computer screen, the chamber was amazing.

Apart from saying "Wow!" a few times, Crenshaw was silent. When the video was over, he tapped a few keys on the keyboard and detached the camera. He removed the videotape and, before Orr could stop him, smashed it against the dashboard.

"What in God's name are you doing, you moron? We need that to show the auction bidders!"

"I know. And now we're full partners. I e-mailed it to myself. Don't think I didn't know you were going to kill me as soon as I armed the bomb. You've got the buyers, and I've got the video."

Orr peered at Crenshaw and then laughed. A full-out belly laugh. "I didn't think anyone was as devious as I was, Crenshaw. But I underestimated you. That doesn't happen often."

Crenshaw looked as if he didn't know what to make of Orr, but he seemed satisfied. He put the truck into gear.

They took the Lincoln Tunnel into Manhattan. Orr noted with irony the sign at the entrance, which said NO FLAMMABLES OR EXPLOSIVES.

"Which location are we using?" Orr asked. They had five possibilities for where to park the truck depending on conditions, all of them locations where a Wilbix truck wouldn't be out of place.

"Vesey Street, just east of Church." It was just a block from the PATH train station.

The plan was simple. Park the truck on the street, set the timer on the detonator for ten minutes—too short an interval for any tow truck to respond—and walk away. They'd be on their way out of the city before the semi exploded.

• • •

Using every trick he knew, Tyler had piloted the flight from D.C. to Teterboro Airport in New Jersey in just one hour. Riegert had called ahead and arranged for a helicopter to meet them at the airport so they could avoid the rush-hour traffic. Agent Immel brought a Geiger counter to help locate the bomb. Grant, of course, had insisted on coming along.

The four of them had landed at the downtown heliport on the East River at 8 A.M. The New York FBI office had arranged for a car to be waiting for them.

On the way, Riegert discovered that a man fitting Orr's description had gone through customs at Newark Airport an hour before under the name of Gerald Oren. The flag hadn't gone out fast enough to stop him at the airport, but Riegert showed Tyler a photo from the security cameras, and the eye patch made identification easy. It was Orr.

Aiden had come through with more info about Giordano Orsini's life. His father allegedly committed suicide because he'd been fired from his position as an investment banker and was up to his ears in debt with no prospect of finding another job. Orsini subsequently went into a never-ending string of foster homes and eventually fell off the map.

Tyler now understood why Orr was in Manhattan. Orr believed the ultimate revenge was to make himself rich while making the people he blamed for ruining his life suffer. The scope of his vendetta was staggering, requiring patience and planning that must have taken years, even decades. But Orr's scheme had a twisted sense of poetic justice. Tyler just couldn't comprehend the boundless reserves of hatred Orr would need to carry out his plan.

Riegert had taken the wheel and headed straight for New York Downtown Hospital. Given the time Orr had landed, he could already be in the city with the bomb. If Orr wanted to blend in, he'd head to the place where he'd expect to see other trucks from Wilbix. The FBI put out an all-points bulletin on the truck and asked Wilbix Construction to make sure all its vehicles were accounted for. But the search would take time, even with the FBI's enormous manpower.

Four police cars had already converged on the hospital site, so when they arrived an officer told them they'd checked every Wilbix truck in the lot. None of them was the model stolen from Clarence Gibson in Virginia.

They'd stood beside the unmarked car, the wind blowing bits of dust from the construction site over them.

"What now?" Riegert said. "He's not here."

"He's got to be in New York," Tyler said. "I know it. I know Orr. He'd want to complete his mission as soon as possible."

"You're sure he's coming to lower Manhattan?"

"He landed in Newark. The truck company is delivering material to New York construction sites. Wall Street and the Federal Reserve Bank are here. It's the only location that fits."

"We've got standing patrols both on Wall Street and around the Fed. Any suspicious truck will be stopped."

"Orr won't be that obvious. He'd want the gas cloud to cover as much of the downtown area as possible." Another tuft of wind tugged at Tyler's shirt. *The wind.*

"Grant, check the weather. Where's the wind coming from today?" It was hard to tell the general wind direction among the swirling air coming off the skyscrapers.

After a few pecks at his phone, Grant said, "From the west." The hospital was north of downtown.

"Orr won't be here," Tyler said. "He needs to be in a construction zone upwind of Wall Street."

As they piled into the car, Riegert asked where they were going. Tyler told him to head toward the World Trade Center complex.

• • •

After they got out of the tunnel, Crenshaw headed south on Ninth Avenue, which turned into Hudson Street. The morning traffic was heavy, but Crenshaw handled the truck with ease. It had been his idea to use the semi in the first place, because he'd gone to truck-driving school.

It was 8:30 by the time they reached the intersection at Church and Vesey. Crenshaw turned and came to a stop next to a sign that said NO STANDING ANYTIME.

On the right was a grassy cemetery directly behind St. Paul's Chapel. How appropriate, Orr thought.

On the left were a smoke shop, a camera store, and a delicatessen. One of the vacant buildings was under renovation. The sign said, "Coming soon! The Safe Cracker. A unique New York restaurant experience. Wine and dine inside an actual turn-of-the-century bank vault." A man was unloading supplies for the renovation from a truck that was double-parked in front of the restaurant. A brand-new bank was next to it, which had rendered the old bank obsolete.

Behind them was the vast construction site to build the new World Trade Center tower.

Orr smiled. The signs couldn't be more auspicious.

Crenshaw shut off the engine. Orr put Midas's hand back in his pack with the Archimedes Codex and the golden hand.

"We ready?" Crenshaw asked.

"Do it."

They both set their watch timers to ten minutes. The bomb itself had no displays of any kind.

Crenshaw entered the code. "Say 'money'!"

They clicked their watches, and the countdown began. In ten minutes, the bomb would go off. Even they couldn't stop it from exploding now.

Orr stepped down out of the truck. A car with government plates screeched to a stop in front of the cab.

"Shit!" Crenshaw hissed. "Cops!"

Orr's hand went to the .38 revolver Crenshaw had given him at the truck stop along with six extra rounds.

"Don't panic," Orr said. "Let me take care of this."

He put on his best smile and walked around the open door, but when he saw who was getting out of the back of the unmarked car, the smile shifted to a look of pure horror.

No. No!

It couldn't be, but there he was. It was Tyler Locke. Back from the dead.

How in the hell did Locke find him? The man simply did not give up.

For a split second, their eyes met, and even though Tyler was unarmed, Orr felt a rush of unfamiliar emotion. Fear.

"It's Orr!" Tyler shouted.

Orr raised his pistol to fire. Tyler dove back into the car before the bullets slammed into the opened car door, hitting a woman behind it. She clutched her shoulder and went down. Pedestrians screamed and ran in all directions.

Orr turned to get his pack and make a run for it, but Crenshaw seized it first and jumped out of the driver's door, shooting blindly as he went. Three shots came from the police car. Crenshaw cried out and went down.

The cemetery was too open for an escape. Orr ran to the rear of the trailer and around the back. He peered around and saw Crenshaw lying on the street, cradling his leg. The backpack with the Midas hand lay next to him.

Orr raced for the pack, but another officer came charging up to Crenshaw and kicked his gun away. He spotted Orr and yelled, "Freeze! FBI! Drop your weapon!"

Orr fired two shots at the agent, who dropped to the pavement.

Normally both his shots would have hit, but the lack of depth perception caused him to miss. With his damaged eye, he'd be at a severe disadvantage in a standing gun battle.

Orr abandoned the backpack and ran across the street into the deli, cursing Tyler Locke the whole way.

SIXTY-EIGHT

The lightning-fast gun battle had been a blur to Tyler. Agent Immel went down with a shoulder wound. It wasn't fatal, but she was out of action and stayed in the car to call for backup. Tyler circled around the truck to see Orr disappear into a deli.

He stooped to pick up the gun of Orr's injured confederate, ready to give chase, but Riegert stopped him.

"I'll get Orr!" He pointed at the man on the ground. "You make this guy tell you about the bomb." Tyler nodded and tucked the pistol into his waistband. Riegert ran for the deli next to the bank being renovated into a restaurant. Tyler wanted to chase down Orr, but disarming the bomb had to be his first priority.

"What's your name?" Grant said, nudging the man with his foot.

"Crenshaw," the man said with a grimace, still holding his leg. "Peter Crenshaw. We have to get out of here."

Tyler grabbed him by the collar. "Crenshaw, is the strontium bomb already set to detonate?"

Crenshaw looked surprised that Tyler would know about it.

"I don't know what you mean," Crenshaw said.

"The FBI found a lead hazmat suit at the warehouse you blew up. Half the building showed traces of radioactivity. That jog your memory?"

Crenshaw nodded slowly.

"Did you set it to go off?"

Crenshaw nodded again.

"When?"

Crenshaw held up his watch. It was counting down and just under the eight-minute mark. Even if the bomb squad were on-site now, that amount of time would be slicing it thin, but Tyler had no idea when they would get here. It would be up to him and Grant to secure the bomb.

Grant took the watch and put it on. "How do we disarm it?" he said, taking Crenshaw from Tyler and hauling him to his feet.

Crenshaw shook his head. "You can't. I designed it so that no one could disable it once it was armed."

"Where is it?" Tyler demanded.

"It's in the center of the trailer, but I'm telling you we have to go."

"Describe it. Now!"

Crenshaw hesitated until Grant increased the pressure of his grip. "Okay! Okay! It's two separate parts, unconnected but both synchronized to identical timers. The black box is the lead shield for the strontium, and it's packed with C4, so the shield gets blown apart one second before the main bomb explodes."

"How big is the main bomb?" Grant asked.

"Five hundred pounds, plus three hundred gallons of gas to incinerate the sawdust."

Holy God! Tyler thought. That was enough explosive to wipe out the entire block.

"How do we disarm it?" Grant said, shaking Crenshaw, who began to blubber.

"You can't. No one can. I designed it with a collapsible circuit. Please! We need to leave."

"I'll get the Geiger counter," Grant said, and dragged Crenshaw to the FBI vehicle so that Immel could keep an eye on him.

Tyler recognized Orr's backpack lying on the ground. He unzipped it and saw that it still held Midas's hand, the golden hand, and the Archimedes Codex. Tyler couldn't let Orr get the Touch back, so he pulled the pack over his shoulders.

Armed with the Geiger counter, Grant was first up the trailer's ladder, followed by Tyler. They trotted along the taut tarp stretched across the open trailer. Tyler sliced it open with his Leatherman. He and Grant pulled it back to reveal the pile of sawdust that filled the truck all the way up to the tarp. It had the consistency of mulch and supported their weight. Grant waved the Geiger counter over it until he found the strongest reading.

They dug, revealing a black metal box buried in the sawdust.

Tyler checked his watch. Seven minutes left.

"Which bomb do you want?" Grant asked. He was already on Tyler's wavelength. They had to separate the bombs, or they'd have a radioactive cloud over the entire downtown area.

"You're the better truck driver," Tyler said. "Find someplace empty."

Grant glared at him. "In Manhattan?"

"Just do your best. First, help me carry the strontium bomb. We'll take it off the back of the truck."

"And then what?"

Tyler remembered the new bank building and turned to look at it, but the bank renovation next to it caught his eye.

Wine and dine inside an actual turn-of-the-century bank vault.

"The old vault in the Safe Cracker restaurant," Tyler said. "If I can put the bomb in there and close the door, it should contain the blast." And he wouldn't have to destroy the new bank's vault in the process.

They heaved the black box up. Their combined strength was barely enough to lift the lead container. They got back onto the tarp and shuffled to the back of the truck, Tyler's ribs howling all the way.

After they put the box down, Grant dropped over the side to open the rear doors. Tyler looked over the edge to see sawdust pour out, forming a pile on the asphalt.

"Okay!" Grant shouted.

Tyler sliced through the tarp and fell through the tear with the lead box next to him, guiding it as he slid down the avalanche of sawdust.

Grant met him at the bottom with a handcart.

"Courtesy of the delivery truck across the street," he said.

They put the lead box on the cart.

"Go!" Tyler yelled as he dashed across the street with the cart.

By this time, four police cruisers had converged on the truck. Immel was directing them despite her injury. Running for the truck cab, Grant shouted at her.

"There's a bomb in this truck and it's about to go off! Where's the bomb squad?"

"Jesus," she said. "They're five minutes out."

"That's too long. I need a police escort now!"

"All right, where do you need to go?"

Grant consulted his cell phone. "Albany Street. We've got five minutes."

He started the truck and didn't wait for the police cars to get out of the way. He gunned the engine and smashed two of them aside. The other two cruisers roared off in front of him.

"Agent Immel!" Tyler yelled before he went through the door where the Safe Cracker was being renovated. "This is the radioactive part of the bomb. Keep everyone out of here."

"You got it." She pointed at the two remaining officers. "You at the front entrance. You take the back entrance. Get everyone out, and make sure no one else goes in."

As Tyler entered the old bank, he saw that the renovation was in its early stages. The floor had been stripped to the bare concrete, and the walls were prepped with white primer, ready for a coat of paint.

Many of the workers had already gone outside to see what the commotion was. One of the police officers ran past Tyler, herding the remaining workers out the back door at the far end of the building.

Tyler couldn't miss the vault on the right. The immense circular door was ten feet in diameter and two feet thick. The bronze still held its luster after a hundred years of service, and the mechanism controlling the six-inch-diameter locking bolts was visible behind a new Plexiglas shield. The door's massive weight would be more than enough to contain the blast of the bomb and shield the exterior from radioactive exposure.

He wheeled the handcart through the aperture and into a space far larger than he was anticipating. The twenty-foot-deep vault extended twenty-five feet in each direction to the right and left. Here the work was more complete. On the inside of the vault next to the door was a hostess stand. A bar extended half the length of the long wall where the safety-deposit boxes would have been, leaving enough room for twenty tables. On one end, lumber was piled up in anticipation for laying the hardwood floor.

Tyler pushed the handcart to a stop next to the stacked two-by-fours. A shame that the restaurant would never open now. No one would ever want to eat in a place that had been exposed to high-energy radiation.

Tyler heard the footsteps of someone outside the vault door coming toward him.

"You need to leave now!" Tyler yelled, thinking it was the police officer. He turned from the cart, and out of the shadows he saw the glint of a pistol aimed at his head.

Tyler ducked just as a gunshot blasted. The bullet whistled past his ear. He ran and dove behind the lumber, Orr's pack digging into his shoulder blades. He drew Crenshaw's pistol and looked around the side, but two more shots chewed bits out of the wood before he could see anything. He fired blindly around the corner and heard the thump of someone hitting the floor. He peeked out, but he didn't see a body. A voice confirmed his misses.

"It's simple, Tyler," Jordan Orr said. "Either you toss the Midas hand over to me or in four minutes we both die."

SIXTY-NINE

Orr must have come into the back of the old bank building and seen Tyler wheeling the bomb into the vault with the backpack on his shoulders. He was taking cover behind the other end of the bar. The lumber pile was large enough to shield Tyler, but they were in a stalemate. If Tyler made a break for the vault exit, Orr would cut him down.

Tyler was hoping the police had heard the shots, but nobody came running to his rescue. He shrugged off the backpack.

"It's over, Orr," he said. "I have the Midas Touch right here."

"That's why it *isn't* over," Orr said. "If you give it to me, I'll go."

"Where?" Tyler said. "Terrorism is a capital offense. The CIA will track you down wherever you go. You'll be a wanted man the rest of your life, Orsini."

Orr was silent at hearing the name.

"Did you know my father and Carol Benedict are alive, too?" Tyler asked.

He heard Orr rasp out "Crenshaw" like a curse word.

"I heard about your father, Orr," Tyler said. "I know that's why you're here. Your big plan is a failure. Why don't you give up?"

"For what?" Orr said. "To serve consecutive life terms in an eight-foot cell? Or get the death penalty?"

Tyler knew he was right. Orr now had nothing to lose, but Tyler had no intention of letting him get away with his crimes to live a life of luxury courtesy of King Midas. Not after seeing the appalling condition of his father this morning. Besides, even if he were thwarted this time, Orr wouldn't give up on his vendetta, and with millions of dollars at his disposal he would eventually exact his revenge.

"You failed every way you could, Orr. Grant and I found you. Crenshaw's in custody. Your men are dead, and your bomb won't irradiate Manhattan. You've left a trail of destruction behind you, and for what?"

"You didn't mention Stacy Benedict," Orr said with delight. "She didn't make it, did she? At least I got that right."

Orr's breezy taunt hit home. Tyler's stomach had been churning all morning because he hadn't yet heard from Italy whether Stacy had pulled through.

Something in Tyler snapped. With no time to think through his plan, he threw the backpack as hard as he could so that it landed behind the hostess stand.

"You want the Midas Touch so badly?" Tyler shouted. "There it is. Go get it."

Even though his destination was only a half mile away, Grant worried that he wasn't going to make it. Too many tight corners with this beast of a truck. It was already down to two minutes to go, and he was only turning onto Albany now.

Grant hadn't told the police why he wanted to get to Albany Street, but it was the only thing he could think of, and he didn't have time to listen to other opinions. If they'd known what he planned, they might not have paved a path for him.

He didn't know New York well, but he'd checked the map on his smartphone when he got the idea for where to dump the truck. The closest option had been Albany. The entire route was just eleven blocks.

Now he was four blocks away, and he could make out the blue water of his destination from his perch high in the truck cab.

He was going to dump the trailer in the Hudson River.

• • •

As Tyler had hoped, Orr couldn't resist the chance to get the Midas Touch back. Firing shots as he ran across the open space, Orr dove behind the hostess stand.

If Tyler went for the vault door now, he wouldn't get within five feet of it before Orr shot him. Orr thought he was safe behind the thick wood of the hostess stand knowing that Tyler's 9-mm bullets wouldn't penetrate, but he'd missed one crucial detail Tyler had noticed. The stand wasn't anchored to the floor, because the hardwood hadn't been installed yet.

When he heard Orr unzip the pack to make sure the Midas hand was there, Tyler launched himself at the heavy-duty handcart and shoved it with all his strength toward the stand.

As Tyler released the handcart, it fell backward onto its handles, but loaded with the lead box it had more than enough momentum to continue rocketing toward the stand.

Orr heard the scraping of the cart's handle and looked around the corner of the stand to fire, but the handcart smacked into the stand, knocking it backward into him. The pack went flying.

With Orr down but out of sight, Tyler made a run for it.

With less than a minute to go, Grant blasted down the street, the needle on the speedometer pushing fifty. He kept the pedal mashed to the floor. He needed as much velocity as he could get.

Albany was a narrow tree-lined street, and it dead-ended at a small circle. A courtyard separated the street from the Esplanade, a pedestrian path running along the river.

Grant blew through South End Avenue, the last intersection before the river. The street was free of cars from here on. He pulled on the truck's air horn, hoping the cops got the message to get out of the way.

Then he saw the courtyard bordering the circle. In addition to a few small trees there were more formidable obstacles: seven brick pillars spanning the width of the courtyard. The police cars could go no farther and had stopped directly in front of them.

There was just enough room separating the last pillar and the apartment building on the left, so Grant aimed the truck between them and opened the driver's door. The speedometer read thirty-five. He leaned on the horn again to scatter any pedestrians who might not be expecting an forty-ton semi to roar across the Esplanade.

Then he jumped.

Orr shook off his daze and heard Tyler's running footsteps. Still lying on the floor, he looked past the stand and saw that Tyler was through the vault door.

Orr screamed in frustration at being duped.

"No!"

He fired the pistol until it clicked on an empty chamber, but Tyler was already pushing the massive door closed.

Orr got to his feet, picked up the backpack, and ran to the door. He was pushing against it, trying to prevent Tyler from getting it closed all the way, when he saw the lead container near his feet. The bomb was no more than an arm's length away.

His eyes widened with terror when he realized that he'd lost track of the time. In disbelief he stared at his watch counting down.

Eight, seven, six . . .

Tyler strained against the door, but even though it was well oiled, moving its bulk took time.

He had heard Orr yell and then the sound of gunshots. Slowly, the door swung closed. When it was flush with the wall, Tyler spun the wheel until it hit its stops. Just as the lock fully engaged, he felt more than he heard the explosion through the door.

The interior of the vault was now bathed in intense radiation. It would stay sealed shut until a containment team arrived.

Tyler leaned against the door, but he didn't expect to hear any pounding from inside. He wondered how he would feel if he did. He decided not to find out and walked outside, turning his thoughts toward the fate of Stacy and Grant rather than toward a criminal who'd made their lives hell for one week.

Whatever happened in there, Orr got what he deserved.

Grant got plenty of practice cushioning his falls during his wrestling days, but landing on the dirt trim bordering the Esplanade at thirty-five miles an hour was an entirely different experience. His left knee smacked hard as he tumbled, barely missing the trunk of a tree and collecting about a thousand nicks and cuts along the way. He rolled more times than he could count as the truck catapulted into the Hudson with a tremendous splash. He came to rest on the concrete Esplanade in time to see the truck flip over and begin to sink.

Grant waved for the police officers to get back, then saw two startled joggers, a man and a woman, stop and go to the edge of the Esplanade to watch the truck disappear into the water. He stood, but could put little weight on his leg. He hobbled toward the joggers, yelling, "Get down!"

They turned and saw Grant's limping form and more police cars screeching to a stop behind him. They gawked in astonishment but didn't move.

The truck was now underwater. Grant had no time to explain. He used his bulk to crash into them and throw them to the ground. Just as they hit the pavement and Grant covered them with his body, an earsplitting boom erupted from the river.

A wave of water surged over the embankment and drenched them, and parts of the truck pinged on the ground as debris rained down around them.

It took ten seconds for the water to subside, and the three of them were soaked through. After the last bit of truck landed, Grant rolled off the joggers and sat up.

Both of them gaped at Grant, who smiled back.

"Sorry about that, folks," he said through gritted teeth. "Nice day for a run, eh?"

The lumber pile that had hidden Tyler provided the same protection for Orr when he instinctively dove behind it as the bomb went off.

Smoke permeated the room but didn't overwhelm it. Orr, deaf from the blast, rose and saw chunks of lead embedded in the wood.

Orr knew what that meant. The air he was inhaling was suffused with radioactive dust. Even if he got out immediately, radiation poisoning was a death sentence. He'd seen the pictures of radiation victims. An agonizing end.

He didn't want to go out that way. His life would soon be over, but at least he could end it himself, the way his father had. He raised the revolver to his head and pulled the trigger.

It clicked. He pulled the trigger again. Nothing. The cylinder was empty. He'd used all his rounds shooting at Tyler.

He dropped the gun and sagged to the floor. Orr opened the backpack, took out the container with the Midas hand, and wept bitter tears for all that had been taken from him.

Tyler was sitting in the back seat of Riegert's FBI vehicle when a police car pulled up and Grant got out. With a distinct limp, his clothes sodden and torn, and dozens of scratches and bruises on his face and arms, he shuffled over to the car and plopped down.

"You okay?" Tyler said.

"Feels like a torn ligament," Grant said, holding his knee.

"Nothing a little arthroscopic surgery won't take care of. How about you?"

"My side hurts like hell, but otherwise I'm fine. The bomb?"

"At the bottom of the Hudson. No one hurt. Except me, that is. And yours?"

"In the vault when it went off. The time lock won't let us open it for twelve hours."

"Did they catch Orr?"

Tyler looked back at the bank. "He's in the vault, too."

"Think he survived the blast?"

Tyler shrugged. He realized now that he just didn't care. "Either way, we'll get the whole story about his plan. Crenshaw's already talking, hoping to cut a deal."

"Any other news?" Grant asked gingerly.

Tyler knew that he meant Stacy. The last time they'd seen her, she was being wheeled away in critical condition. Tyler shook his head.

Ambulances had taken away the two cops Orr had injured getting into the vault, so they sat there in silence as they waited for another officer to arrive and take Grant to get his leg examined. After five minutes, Special Agent Riegert walked over, his phone in hand.

"You guys did good today," Riegert said. Grant and Tyler both nodded a simple acknowledgment.

Riegert held the phone out for Tyler. "Got a call for you."

"Who is it?" Tyler said, taking the phone.

"Carol Benedict from the hospital in Naples," Riegert said, his face impassive. "She has something to tell you."

EPILOGUE

Two months later

The blazing August sun roasted Tyler's skin and forced him to squint even through his mirrored sunglasses, but he wasn't complaining. After twelve hours in a cramped plane, he was happy to go for a hike in the hills.

Tyler put down the shovels he was carrying and paused to admire the crystal clear Mediterranean. Just a few miles west of Syracuse on the island of Sicily, he gazed at the port, trying to imagine Archimedes' famous death ray, which supposedly burned the Roman ships assaulting the city during the siege more than two thousand years ago.

"Amazing, isn't it?" Stacy beamed at the view. "I've always wanted to come here."

She looked better than ever, despite the injury she'd suffered in Naples. She wore a black tank top and shorts, and her blond hair had grown longer since then. Tyler liked the change.

He had feared the worst when he heard that Carol Benedict was calling with news, but she wanted to tell him that Stacy had come through the surgery and was asking about him as soon as she woke. Her recovery had been arduous, with weeks of rehab before she was back on her feet, but she soon lobbied to get back to work so that she could tell her story to her viewers. When she was at full strength, Tyler agreed to meet her in Syracuse to investigate Archimedes' final puzzle.

Stacy had picked him up from the airport when he arrived that morning, and they drove straight out to the dig site. The three guys who made up her camera crew trailed behind them, but they weren't filming yet. Stacy had already agreed to Tyler's one rule: he was not to appear on camera, and she would cut him out of the broadcast. The publicity from the show last time had resulted in his defusing a bomb on a ferry, and he didn't feel like tempting fate again.

"I bet you never thought this thing would be what brought you here," he said, pointing at the new geolabe in his hands.

Because Tyler still had the codex translation, he was able to rebuild the geolabe after he'd lost the original in the Midas chamber, and, with his experience building it the first time, the new one took only a month to construct. It was clear now that the geolabe and the Antikythera Mechanism were one and the same. The original reproduction had been missing some pieces because the meager remnants of the shipwreck artifact were incomplete. Tyler was generously donating the new geolabe to the Athens National Archaeological Museum to replace the replica that had been so callously stolen.

But before it went to the museum, it had one more use.

Tyler consulted the instructions he'd put on his smartphone and twisted the knobs on the geolabe. The dials turned and pointed in a new direction.

"This way," he said.

They headed toward Eurialo Castle, a fortress built by Dionysius the Elder and then modified by Archimedes. It was claimed that the castle had never been conquered, thanks to Archimedes' engineering skills, one of which was building a series of tunnels underneath the castle as a first line of defense against burrowing invaders.

"How's your father doing?" Stacy asked as they walked.

"As ornery as ever and completely healed. Miles still wants him to join Gordian, but I'm not so sure about that."

"I'm glad to hear things are back to normal," she said. "I'm sorry Grant couldn't be here."

"Don't be. He said he's had enough of tunnels for a while. Besides, he's eating up the challenge of designing a display case for the only radioactive museum pieces in the world." After some legal wrangling over ownership, it was decided that the Archimedes Codex and the golden hand would become part of a traveling exhibit that would go first to the British Museum. Grant, whose torn knee ligament was nearly healed, was working with Oswald Lumley and his staff on how to properly preserve it.

The codex had become irradiated along with Jordan Orr while it was sequestered inside the Manhattan vault until the time-lock release. By then, Orr had suffered a lethal radiation dose. The doctors called it the worst case they'd ever seen and documented the horrifying details for medical journals. Orr lasted five excruciating days before finally succumbing.

The Midas hand survived the explosion intact, but the extremophile microbes did not. Apparently, radiation was the only extreme they couldn't withstand. With Midas's body now underwater, the king's magical touch was gone forever.

But it was the codex that yielded a final secret, thanks to its being in Orr's pack when the radioactive bomb had gone off. The radiation had caused some previously invisible text to fluoresce under UV light. It was a final set of instructions left by Archimedes, seemingly scrawled and then erased by the scribe before it was overwritten.

The instructions indicated that Archimedes had hidden something in Eurialo Castle, in a specially constructed tunnel that he had reserved for his own use. The geolabe would lead them to it.

"I know you're a charming guy," Stacy said. "But how in the world did you persuade the Italian authorities to let us dig at one of their historical sites?"

Tyler smiled. "Well, the FBI recovered a video from Peter Crenshaw's e-mail system. Apparently, it's narrated by you and shows a chamber made entirely of gold somewhere under Naples."

"And they believed the video? The chamber was flooded with boiling acidic water. Nobody can dive into it to confirm its existence."

"Gordian happened to develop an undersea robot that can survive under those exact conditions."

Stacy stopped. "You proved to them that it exists?"

"Last week. The Italian Ministry of Cultural Heritage asked me to join them in making the announcement to the press, but I told them I had someone better."

"They want me?"

"If you're available next week."

She launched herself at Tyler and planted a big kiss on him. For a moment, he forgot all about why he was here.

Just as abruptly, Stacy pulled away, her eyes lit with anticipation. Tyler was suddenly aware of the camera crew staring at them.

"Come on," Stacy said. She lowered her voice so the crew couldn't hear. "Maybe we'll have even more to celebrate tonight. I have champagne chilling in my room. You're welcome to share it."

He didn't know if she meant the champagne or the room. Maybe both, if he was getting the signals right. Ancient puzzles were so much easier to decipher than women.

"One more thing," Tyler said. "They want you to talk in more detail about the writing on the chamber's pedestal."

"You mean about how Midas was originally from Naples?"

Tyler nodded. "The ministry seemed very interested in that part."

The pedestal had confirmed the once mythical story that Midas had been a traveler in what was now Turkey and arrived in the ancient country of Phrygia just in time for his father, Gordias, to be dubbed king. Years later, after his own uneventful reign, Midas was riding his horse in the wilds near his palace and came across a previously unknown volcanic spring. He decided to take a swim, but when he got out with the help of one of his courtiers, the man died almost instantly. He fell into the water and turned to gold.

Midas's ability became legend throughout the world, but he found it to be a curse. He could not even hold his beloved daughter again for fear of killing her.

The king of Persia had heard of the Midas Touch and wanted it for himself, so he set about to conquer the kingdom of Phrygia. Midas's army was no match for the Persians, so he fled with his court back to his home of Neapolis. During the journey, his daughter fell ill and died, contrary to the myth in which he accidentally killed her. Midas, having heard of a hot spring hidden under the city, thought it would be a suitable tomb befitting his status, because he could adorn it with gold and preserve his daughter for time immemorial. His last loyal subjects excavated the chamber and interred him there when he finally passed.

Now Tyler and Stacy had one final treasure to unearth, but Tyler couldn't imagine what else Archimedes might have hidden for them. This time, however, he was willing and happy to find out.

A local Sicilian archaeologist met them at the entrance to the tunnels that had already been excavated beneath Eurialo. She would be along to assist Tyler and Stacy and make sure they didn't disturb anything they found.

The geolabe guided them through the catacombs to a spot that was otherwise unremarkable. The earthen wall they were supposed to dig through looked like all the others.

"You're sure this is it?" Stacy said.

"Don't ask me," Tyler said, pointing at the geolabe. "Ask Archimedes."

While the crew filmed, they dug into the wall, the archaeologist helping as well. An hour into it, Tyler's shovel plunged into open air.

He shined a flashlight through the hole and saw some kind of chamber. Reinvigorated by the find, they widened the hole so that it was big enough for them to crawl through.

Tyler went first. As he crept into the hole, his heart pounded at the thought of what might be revealed about one of antiquity's greatest intellects. *What was Archimedes' reason for creating this hidden chamber?* When he was through the hole, Tyler stood and focused the light on a treasure as fabulous to him as Midas's gold chamber.

Fearing eventual defeat at the hands of the Romans, Archimedes must have created this room to secure his most valuable possessions. He'd been right to worry about his legacy. According to the Greek historian Plutarch, when Syracuse was captured a Roman soldier burst into Archimedes' study. Instead of surrendering, Archimedes defied the soldier and went back to his drawings. The soldier killed him, despite orders to capture the engineer alive.

The room before Tyler held dozens of mechanical devices more intricate and beautiful than he would have thought possible for an inventor of that period. One was a globe that showed the map of the known world at that time. Another device suspended the earth, the sun, and the planets so that they would rotate in their orbits. A third one could have easily been a counting machine, literally the world's first computer.

Agog at the genius on display, Tyler knew that Orr had been after the wrong treasure all along. The wealth of amazing mechanisms in this one room would alter everything that historians had assumed about the scope of knowledge in the ancient world.

Tyler stopped when he spotted a table holding an exact duplicate of the geolabe, an original version of the Antikythera Mechanism constructed by Archimedes himself. He approached it with reverence. The only difference between the one in his hands and the one on the shelf was the green patina on the ancient version.

Next to the device were documents laid out across the surface. One was clearly a map of Neapolis. Tyler recognized the island where Castel dell'Ovo now stood, as well as the Naples acropolis, the two landmarks that had led him to the well.

Beside the map were a series of drawings. Without touching them, Tyler inspected them more closely. They looked like sketches of statues. One of them was familiar, and then he realized what it was: the statue of Herakles from the east pediment of the Parthenon, drawn in incredible detail, which would be nearly unrecognizable to anyone who had seen the eroded and handless remnant in the British Museum. There were dozens and dozens of drawings, some of them long-distance views of the ancient temple, some of them close-ups.

"My God," Stacy said as she came through the entry hole and gawked at the wealth of drawings. "Do you realize what this will do for our understanding of ancient Greece? No one has ever found drawings of what the Parthenon looked like two thousand years ago."

"Archimedes must have drawn these pictures himself and then used them when he designed the geolabe."

The rest of the group entered the room, all agape at the treasure trove. While the archaeologist gesticulated wildly and spoke rapid-fire Italian, Stacy directed the camera crew as to how she wanted to document the once-in-a-lifetime discovery.

Tyler, who smiled as he recognized Stacy in her element, stepped back, happy to be out of the spotlight. It was time again for Archimedes to speak from the past and change history.

AFTERWORD

Exploring the history, settings, and technologies that I drew on for *The Vault* was almost as much fun as writing the book itself—sometimes even more fun when it meant racing down the autobahn at 150 miles per hour in the name of research. The world has a wealth of astonishing places to visit and mysteries to delve into, which made it difficult to choose just a few to include in the novel. It might surprise the reader to know how little I had to make up for this story.

Although the geolabe is fictional, its real-world cousins, the Antikythera Mechanism and its replica, are on display at the National Archaeological Museum in Athens. The display cases for them are just as I described, and a security camera in the room with the Antikythera Mechanism really was missing the day I visited. Although theories abound as to the function of the Antikythera Mechanism, the best guess is that it was used to predict the motion of the sun, the stars, and the planets. For more on the Antikythera Mechanism, I recommend the intriguing *Decoding the Heavens,* by Jo Marchant.

Who built the Antikythera Mechanism is also open to argument, but many archaeologists believe its design could have originated from antiquity's greatest scientist and engineer, Archimedes. His long-rumored treatise, *On Sphere-Making,* has eluded historians for more than two thousand years, but if it ever comes to light we may discover that Archimedes' genius was even greater than we imagined.

In fact, Archimedes' manuscript may still exist somewhere. As recently as 1998, a codex called the Archimedes Palimpsest was purchased at auction, the Greek writing hidden for hundreds of years under the text of a thirteenth-century prayer book. If you'd like to read more about that fascinating story and about Archimedes' puzzle, the Stomachion, I highly recommend *The Archimedes Codex,* by Reviel Netz and William Noel.

The Greeks invented steganography and did hide messages under the wax of writing tablets. Another real method of concealing communications was to shave a messenger bald, tattoo the message onto his head, and wait for the hair to grow back before sending him on his mission. Slow, yes, but it got the job done.

As of today, the British Museum in London and the New Acropolis Museum in Athens continue to spar over the fate of the Elgin Marbles.

I have yet to park my own car in a robotic parking garage, but the structures do exist in many European countries. They're starting to make their way into crowded downtown areas in the United States, so I may get to try one out someday.

If you ever want to eat in a real bank vault, there are several restaurants in New York City offering that unique experience.

Naples is a beautiful city, and it's hard to believe that a vast world of subterranean tunnels and caverns exists under the bustling metropolis. Every year more underground passageways are discovered, so I'm sure we'll continue to learn more about their Greek and Roman excavators. To get a feel for the dark and claustrophobic spaces, take a tour of the tunnels at Napoli Sotterranea, near Piazza San Gaetano, the next time you're in Naples.

The Camorra has been entrenched in the Naples area for more than a century, and women are starting to take over some of the crime families. For a sobering exploration of the Camorra, read *Gomorrah,* by Roberto Saviano.

The bizarre true tale of Louis Dethy's booby-trapped home needed no embellishment from me.

The strontium-90 nuclear fuel from radioisotope thermoelectric generators is a real threat to international security. Many of the devices have gone missing since the collapse of the Soviet Union, raising the specter of the radioactive material being used in dirty bombs. Security analysts around the world are already searching for them, and some were found when the thieves turned up with severe radiation sickness.

While the Midas Touch is a fantasy, distilling gold from water is not. Extremophiles, which are microbes called archaea, thrive around hot springs and black smokers on the ocean floor, and some species consume the heavy metal dissolved in the water before excreting it as a solid. No one has yet figured out how to profitably extract the tiny concentrations of dissolved gold from seawater, but billions of ounces of it are waiting for whoever can.

The legend of Midas is just that—a legend. But, as with most legends, there is some historical basis for the characters involved. Scholars do think that Midas was a king of Phrygia in modern-day Turkey, but to this day no one has found his birthplace or tomb. If and when someone does find his final resting place, I wouldn't be shocked to learn that a huge cache of gold was buried with Midas. I hear that guy was rich.

ACKNOWLEDGMENTS

I'm fortunate to know so many smart and capable people. Without them, this book wouldn't be in your hands.

My agent, Irene Goodman, is a dream. Every writer should have it so good. I couldn't navigate the publishing business without her.

My foreign-rights agents, Danny Baror and Heather Baror, are the best in the business and a blast to hang out with.

Sulay Hernandez, my wonderful editor at Touchstone, was incredibly patient in guiding the book from its crude early stages to a polished product. I'm lucky to work with one of the publishing industry's rising stars.

Stacy Creamer, David Falk, Shida Carr, Marcia Burch, and the entire team at Touchstone deserve a hearty round of applause for the amazing effort they've put into the novel.

Although I consulted with several people on this book, any errors in fact or detail, whether intentional or not, are mine alone.

David Phillips, professor of history of UCLA, is fluent in Greek and advised me on the nuances of the ancient language, including the translation in the prologue.

Jennifer Hesketh, a riding instructor at Wimbledon Village Stables, taught me the finer points of cantering on an English saddle.

Alessandro Fusaro, a guide at Napoli Sotterranea, gave me a fantastic tour of underground Naples, answering all my odd questions without blinking.

My good friend and trauma surgeon, Dr. Erik Van Eaton, spelled out the effects of concussions as well as many other medical issues.

I'd like to thank Susan Tunis for again focusing her sharp editorial skills on my work.

My brother, retired Lieutenant Colonel Martin Westerfield, is a former Air Force pilot who gave me the inside scoop about the U.S. military.

My sister, Dr. Elizabeth Morrison, curator of medieval manuscripts at the J. Paul Getty Museum, was a valuable resource for my countless questions about ancient codices, foreign languages, and museum operations. And, as a thriller fan, she's an expert at finding those pesky plot holes.

My father-in-law, the geologist Dr. Frank Moretti, continues to be one of my treasured early readers, giving me feedback that improved the book immensely.

Finally, it is impossible to overstate how much I cherish having such an understanding, supportive, and loving partner as my wife, Randi. She was intimately involved in the development of this story from beginning to end, and I want to thank her from the bottom of my heart.